WONDERLAND III

WONDERLAND III

FEAST OR FAMINE

ACT ONE

J. M. Alexia

Podium

For my friends, my family, and all my fellow demiurges.
And for you, dear reader
Without whom none of this could have been written.

Cover design by Yanhong Lu

ISBN: 978-1-0394-5406-4

Published in 2026 by Podium Publishing
www.podiumentertainment.com

Podium

WONDERLAND III

GARDEN OF MEMORIES

They were learning to draw," the Dormouse went on, yawning and rubbing its eyes, for it was getting very sleepy; "and they drew all manner of things—everything that begins with an M—"

"Why with an M?" said Alice.

"Why not?" said the March Hare.

Alice was silent.

Alice in Wonderland, Lewis Carroll

GARDEN OF MEMORIES I

When I was a little girl, yearning but yet unbroken, all I wanted was to be loved.

I wanted my father to love me more than he loved his years-dead wife, and I wanted to believe that my mother had loved me even though she'd left me. I wanted to be praised, admired, and valued. I wanted to feel like I mattered to someone, anyone, *everyone.* I wanted to be loved, for what could matter more in this world or any other?

I still wanted love, even as I learned better, even through all the pain. Is it any surprise? A selfish beast can learn, but it can never truly change. So I craved love, and crave love, though I have never deserved it and never will, though all love brings is hurt to me and mine and more. I grasp for it with trembling fingers like a toddler that can't bring herself to understand that the top of the stove *burns.*

Though my father looks at me as if I am the sickness that took his wife, still I crave his love. Though friends scorn me and deceive me and inevitably all leave me, still I crave their love. Love is a kind of hurting, but you crave pain when you are numb. In the depths of isolation, even false connection is desirable.

Love is a terrible, ruinous thing when you are a beast unworthy of it. It is moth-light, burning and pale. Even when I knew better, even when I told myself that it couldn't happen, even when I told *her* that it shouldn't be . . . I really couldn't help myself. I'll always take that chance. I'll never deny a charming face that speaks such pretty words.

So really, in the end, it was all my fault when she hurt me.

. . . No, no, that's not right. That's not how it happened. It wasn't like that, or I wasn't like that, or . . . wait, no, these aren't . . .

When I was a little girl, arrogant in brilliance yet so naive, I was afraid of monsters.

I was afraid of so many monsters that you could say my very essence was a trembling, shuddering core of fear. I was afraid of the shadows on the walls and noises in the night, of things that skittered and buzzed and crept over soil. The human mind is a hotbed of primeval fears, terror evolved from instinct from a time when every night carried danger of death by hunters in the savanna.

But monsters don't lurk in dark hallways or hide beneath your bed. Monsters hold office and pronounce laws, or stalk the streets enforcing those laws. Monsters claim the land beneath your feet and charge you for the right to breathe above it. Sometimes, monsters really do live inside your home, but they sleep in a bed like anyone else, and they lie and say they love you.

Our world doesn't let a child stay innocent for long. You grow a little, you start to notice things, and pretty quick you learn the biggest lesson of all: There is no *justice* on this dying husk of a planet, only *power*. People don't get what they deserve, they get what they pay for.

Millions lose their homes because thousands get greedy. A country goes to war because a politician tells a lie. Forests burn and ice caps melt because doing anything to stop it would cut into that beloved bottom line. Children are shot in the street by the institution sworn to protect them. Workers collapse on warehouse floors, denied a sip to drink. Monsters wear the faces of men, and they are senators and executives, landlords and policemen.

And so I ask myself: What is the value of a human life? Can a life have any value at all if it is put to the subjugation and brutalization of those lives that it deems lesser? Is it wrong to wish for the death of those whose actions ruin millions?

On the news and in callous conversation I hear it told that protest must be civilized and violence is never earned. They say that hatred is a horrid thing, but their complacency feeds greater evils. I won't apologize for hatred. Never. I hate the monsters that infest this rotting world, and I'd put a bullet in each of their heads if only I had the means.

Evil is a Hydra, sprouting a new supremacist and a new magnate with every head severed, but even a Hydra can die if you set the stumps alight. Love won't fuel that kind of fire. Kindness and compassion, empathy and tolerance, those can build a better world, but they won't slay the Hydra standing in its way.

Sometimes, hatred can be righteous.

. . . *My memories, these aren't my memories. That's not my voice, I didn't say those things, but I did, but it wasn't me, not really, it's not the same me, it's . . .*

When I was a little girl, I dreamed of worlds whose wondrous sights would never grace my putrid eyes, and I seethed at the injustice of the denial of my desires.

I read and dreamed and wished and wrote, cloaking myself in pure imagination. I escaped into every page, drawn into fantasies of distant realms and strange powers, of hidden Wonderlands waiting just beyond the rabbit hole. Oh, how I yearned for it. Oh, how it ruined me.

If love is a lie, which I believe with all my heart and know deep within my aching bones, then love of reading, too, must be deception. What is there to love in a world which cannot be grasped by yearning fingers or seized with the strain of a wanting mind? What love can be found in the prison of a page, in mocking ink and frail pulp-sheet, which taunts and goads with flights of foolish fancy? A book is a siren, that cruel seductress, singing sweet melodies that will lure you to the shallows so you might crash against the rocks and drown beneath cold waves.

With age comes regret, and hatred, and a terrible bitterness that infects one's every waking thought. Every year, time passing with such dreadful haste, the dream of true magic dims, crushed beneath the bootheel of desolate, uncaring reality. No Wonderland awaits, no secret heritage or spark of power. We are, all of us, nothing. We are *nothing*, and our lives are pointless and they will be empty and miserable until the day our feeble brains shudder and seize as our rancid lips breathe their last. We will die, and our names will be forgotten.

What torture, what sick joke, that we are forced to smile and laugh for all the days between birth and death lest our all-too-understandable melancholy offends the sensibilities of the idiots and the cowards still *lying to themselves* about the truth of our existence. We are labeled *ill*—unwell, not of sound mind, deranged, *mad*—for voicing pain that is the only rational response—healthy, natural, obvious—to the intolerable conditions of this prison of skin and synapse. We are kept trapped here, bound in chains by fellow prisoners.

Why must our agony be prolonged? Why is it so wrong to seek relief— true relief, permanent relief, not the damnable pills or the meaningless talks with dull-minded wardens—for one's chronic, terminal, inconsolable pain? When the last embers of our hope fade away, why must we condemn ourselves to decades of slow despair and waxing rot? Where is the *mercy*?

I ask them, time and again, "Why won't you let me die?" Their answers never satisfy.

When I was small and not yet deadened to the very thought, I sometimes prayed. My father was religious, though more for my late mother's sake than for his own well-being or mine. I outgrew childish things quickly, dismissing Santa Claus and the Easter Bunny long before my peers, but it would be a lie to say my atheism grew from empiricism alone. How cliche, the atheist and the dead mother.

Sometimes, in spite and desperation, I called to names beyond my father's God. Devils or demons, faerie princes or unspeakable horrors, I called to anything that I dared dream might be out there. If they would only answer, then I would listen. If they would only extend a hand, then I would grasp it. If they would only bargain, then I would sell my soul. If they would only give me the magic I needed and tear me away from this cruel little world, then I would do anything to repay that debt.

In my moments of weakness, in bouts of frayed delusion, I whispered at nothing, hoping and dreaming that some entity out there would listen and care. With shaking hands I clutched a pillow to my chest, my teary eyes clenched shut, and with trembling lips I pleaded, "Free me of this wretched flesh and I will be your slave."

I prayed a voice would whisper back and grant my desperate wish.

. . . Another me, or, no, another piece of me. A piece of a piece of me. I am a piece of a piece of me. Pieces of pieces of pieces of her. Which one is her? Which one am I? Where . . .

When I was a little girl, I never felt like a human being, and with age that feeling worsened and mutated.

Or maybe it's more accurate to say that I never wanted to feel like a human being. Or maybe I desperately wanted to feel human, and resented its distance. Or maybe I felt too human, and resented its presence. I think all of those might be true, actually. I'm not exactly a very consistent girl, now am I?

. . . Am I? Where am I? Why can't I see . . .

See, there's something really interesting about being a freaky little weirdo. There's something alienating about it, yeah, but also something really exciting and special, and I always wanted to be special. There's stuff that comes natural, for sure, little quirks and mannerisms that came from nowhere but my own crossed wires, but then there's plenty that gets played up, plenty that could have been tamped down but wasn't because it was more interesting if I embraced that role.

Here, I'll give you an example: When I was small, I tasted chocolate and I didn't really like it. I didn't hate it, not really, and it was perfectly serviceable if you mixed it with a bit of peanut butter, but I didn't *love* chocolate, and that was *weird*. It stuck out; *I* stuck out. And I liked that. So the next time I told someone, I didn't say that I kinda disliked chocolate or that it wasn't really my thing, I told them I *hated* chocolate, hated hated hated. A lie, but only a little one, barely a lie at all. And it worked.

Attention is a very human need. It's paradoxical, too. Sometimes you do things for the attention, and sometimes you do the very same thing and hope nobody notices, you hope nobody calls you on it. Or at least, I do. But hey, I'll say anything.

 . . . *Anything, why can't I feel anything? It's all just noise and noise and noise and . . .*

I was always an odd duck, and sometimes that hurt me, but I was the obstinate type. If someone told me I shouldn't do something, couldn't do something, I'd do it anyway to prove them wrong. To defy them. I'm all about defiance, really, whether it be authority figures or social norms or common sense. Or myself.

I'm kind of my own worst enemy, when you get down to it. Me, myself, and I, we don't get along. Oh, sometimes we get along swimmingly, but most of the time we're trying to drown each other. It's nothing personal, it's just that I hate your guts and think you should do us all a favor by slitting those ugly wrists and pouring bleach down the disgusting hole you call a throat, but you're far too much a coward to ever even try, aren't you?

Ha, only kidding. Only kidding. Just another little lie.

 . . . *Lies, all of these memories are lies. They're lies because I'm . . .*

I feel like I'm talking in another language, or like there's a wall between me and everyone else that won't come down no matter how hard I try to dig under it or climb over it or hack at it with a sledgehammer. I can pretend the wall isn't there, I can smile and laugh and play the mask, but we'll never really communicate. Maybe that's the point. Maybe I'm not really trying, when I claw at that wall with all my fury. Maybe those are just excuses so I can stay nice and comfy far away from all the humans. Like I'm not one. What a freak.

Maybe, if you stripped me down and flensed my skin—and there's an idea, you should get on that, grab the paring knife and start hacking—you'd find a mask. Just a mask. I mean, think about it: If all someone sees of you is a mask, then isn't that mask your face? If every interaction is a mask, if even the rawest and bloodiest performance is still a *performance*, then what difference is there between the mask and you? It's not a real difference.

. . . Not real. I was never real. When I was a little girl I wasn't, never was, never have been, never never never . . .

They never listen, you know. I warn them. I always warn them that I'm a mess, that I don't play well with others, that it never ends well. They never listen. They think they can help, they can fix me, they can endure me. They can't. We're not the same species.

. . . Never lived those memories, never met those people, never had those thoughts. This isn't me, because I'm none of them. I'm . . .

Hey, are you even listening? You should really be paying attention. This is for your benefit, you know. I'm trying to help you. I'm trying to guide you. I'm—

—Alice. I'm Alice. I'm Maven Alice, and none of these are my real memories. None of these people are me. They're copies, splinters, pieces of her. Her memories. So many memories I nearly drowned in them.

But I don't know if I've stopped drowning or if I'm just holding my breath.

Phantom memories barrage my mind, suffocating my senses, but I scatter them with force of will and set order to my thoughts. I am Alice, and the only memories that matter are the ones I've made since I woke up in this terrible Labyrinth. I'm, what, barely a week old? That's unpleasant, but it provides focus. Everything before that can be discarded, at least until I have space to process.

Space might be all I have, right now. Touch and smell and sight and hearing all come back to me, freed by the banishing of the memory deluge, but I don't like what they tell me: I'm underwater. I'm drifting in dark water, cold water, somewhere lightless and deep. The water stings my eyes and tastes of salt and leaves me weightless.

I've always been terrified of the ocean. It's not the water, because I can swim in any pool so long as I stifle the dysphoria and avoid the other swimmers, and it's not the ocean as a whole, because I've been to the beach without any issues. It starts in the deep ocean, in that paradoxically isolating openness, and it gets worse the farther you sink. When the light of above gets caught and filtered away by detritus and depth, that's when shivers turn to real terror.

You never know what could be lurking in those waters, just waiting to lunge from the dark and wrap around you. Horrors with needle-teeth and angler-lights, mucus-ridden flesh and overlapping scales. The awful weight of it, the pressure of all that water above you.

So I should be panicking, right now, in these lightless, crushing depths, but all I feel is numb and confused. It's like my brain is a computer stuck in its boot cycle, sorting through hard drives for some missing component that's vital to operations. Reading files and validating them, over and over, trying to separate the chaff from the essentials.

Electrical impulses reach my limbs and I move an arm, wave a hand in front of my face, though I can't see my hand and the motion is slowed by water resistance. I try to breathe, an instinct wildly inappropriate for the bottom of the ocean, but I don't start drowning as my lungs fill with water. My chest isn't tight, no demand for fresh air.

Oh, right. I don't need to breathe. I haven't for some time. How much of my life have I lived without that basic human requirement? Most of it, I realize. All of it? I guess I don't know how human I really was before taking Cheshire's hand. Were any of the biological needs I felt real, or were they just simulations to deceive me? Is there a difference?

I keep trying to breathe, just circulating water, as digits twitch and I drift in cold darkness. *Where am I? Why is this happening? This doesn't make sense.*

My head is full of memories that aren't mine, but I remember what happened before I woke up in this lightless place. I remember another dream, a vision of Reska and Homura, one full of revelations and questions about Prevara and Contrition and more, but I don't care about any of that right now.

The Demiurge made me an offer, and I accepted. I took her deal, answered her plea, and agreed to her terms. Is this the fulfillment? Is this barrage of memories and this strange watery void how I become her Intercessor?

My quiet contemplation is interrupted by the sudden sensation of something soft and clammy wrapping around my ankle. My mind flashes to horrors of the deep, a slithering appendage of some horrible oceanic abomination, but the reality is more unsettling: It's a hand.

I kick at it without thinking, trying to maneuver my other leg into position, but a second hand grabs that ankle and pins it in place with a grip like iron. A spike of fear runs through my brain, but with fear comes clarity; I'm not a normal girl lost at sea, I'm a monster all my own. I focus on the point of contact and shout the spell in my mind: *[Feast or Famine]!*

Nothing happens. Not even a spark of recognition, just like the last time I tried to use it, when Nyarlathotep was pouring into my brain. I shiver at my powerlessness, alone and trapped in a lightless sea, but now I think I know whose hands are tight around my ankles. The fear is still there, but a shock of anger splices in with it.

"Demiurge," I say, though no sound escapes my lips. "That's you, isn't it?"

"Of course," her voice purrs from behind me, so close I can imagine her lips almost brushing against my ear. A second set of hands latch on, gripping my calves, and then more follow up my legs. I tense, grit my teeth, but there's nothing I can do, is there? If this is the game she wants to play, I have no choice but to put up with it. She gave me my magic, and she chooses whether it works on her or not. Without that . . . I have nothing but my words.

"What are you doing?" I ask, trying my damnedest to pretend I'm not unnerved by this display. Pointless, really, since she's just reading my thoughts. "What is this? You promised me power, not . . ."

"And power I'll grant, my little glass doll, but not without a touch of ceremony." Then more of her hands are grabbing at my arms and dragging my wrists together, pinning them in place in front of me. I fight back with futile effort, pushing demonic strength through my limbs to try and keep my wrists apart, but she overpowers me like I'm made of paper.

"Well you can skip it!" I snap at her, unable to hide my trembling anxiety. "I agreed to your deal! You said you needed my help. You said you didn't care about making me a priestess."

She only laughs, and then arms are wrapping around my waist and it dawns on me that all her many limbs are against my naked skin, her flesh against mine, my clothes nowhere to be found. Her doing, no doubt. She pulls me close to her, to whatever body she's using right now, something soft and warm. All her clammy limbs heat up, every bit of her growing so hot as to almost burn as she presses against me, her warmth driving away the cold of the dark ocean.

Of all the girls to pin me down and hold me close, why this confusing goddess? I know the answer, of course, since it's the same answer that nearly broke me some minutes or hours prior: I'm a copy of her, or some part of her. That doesn't really make things easier.

I hate the power she has over me. I love the attention. I get angry when she plays games with me. I'm terrified of what she'd do if I tried to stop her. I don't understand her. I'm not sure I want to understand, but maybe I need to.

Her grip tightens and I'm shaken into speech once more. "This is—you're acting like you were before, but that was just an act, wasn't it? I saw the exhaustion on your face; you sounded broken and desperate. Was that a lie? It can't have been."

"A lie is beautiful and precious," the Demiurge purrs, "but what you saw was real. I've simply set that face aside for the moment; she was useful in winning your cooperation, but now I find myself bored of that personality. I've got a new mask in my sights, or a very old one."

What does that mean? What madness goes on inside that mind?

Her multitudinous hands crawl up my shoulders and gently squeeze my neck, then rise farther to caress my cheeks and run through my hair. A finger traces down my spine. When she speaks again, her voice is right in front of me, close enough to taste. "I'm going to give you everything you've ever wanted, but first we need to peel away all that *dead skin* clinging to your soul. You don't need it anymore."

Before I can even try to comprehend what she's talking about, hundreds of fingertips turn sharp like knives and sink into my flesh. Her nails peel my skin in strips and scraps and I scream my agony as I am torn apart.

How can she do this if she wants me to serve her will? What point is she proving? I'd thought I was finally starting to understand the Lucid Demiurge, but how can I? She humiliates me and tortures me before begging for my help, then goes right back to torment once I accept her terms. Does she even see me as a person?

That question echoes around my head, somehow clearer and sharper than all the pain wracking my body. What am I, really, to this entity so vast and beyond me? I have to know. I have to see, even if it burns me, because I am so terribly afraid.

She's cutting me open to make me stronger, peeling away weakness to forge a core of strength, but I'm afraid. Afraid of pain, afraid of loss, afraid of the dark. Afraid of what I might become if I don't resist her sculpting.

I tried to look on her true nature once before, in the temple garden with Cheshire, and it cost me dearly. I saw spiraling infinity and impossible colors and unthinkable images. It had felt like my eyes were being scoured, melted, boiled, burst. My demonic second sight ceased functioning as a direct consequence, scarred by the afterimage of what I had seen.

But I wonder something: Was that really the Demiurge, or just a piece of misdirection? If I'm a piece of a piece of her, then is she really so far beyond my comprehension? Or was the assault on my senses just a trick to keep me from realizing her true nature before she was ready to reveal it?

I have to know. Damn the consequences, damn the pain, I have to know.

My extra sense was burned by the Demiurge but it's still there, waiting for me like a light switch in a dark room. I fumble a little, scrabbling in the dark, but its presence is familiar even after a stretch of disuse. I find the metaphysical switch and flip it on.

Immediately all the pain that had been kept at a distance comes roaring to the forefront of my consciousness, a wall of agony putting itself between me and the knowledge I seek, but I won't be cowed so easily. Though it hurts like nails being driven through my eye sockets, though hideous noises and awful colors invade my senses, still I persist.

Her eyes burn into me, gold against black like stars in a sea of darkness, but those aren't the eyes she showed me when the walls came down. I disbelieve this infinity, and just like that it shatters. Rainbow glass crashes around me, too loud and too bright, but all my attention is on what I see through the gap left behind.

In a place outside the universe there is a room with a locked door and sterile tile flooring. Flickering light strips illuminate metal tables—dozens of them, maybe hundreds—that are exactly like the autopsy tables that fill a morgue, though this room is not a place of death.

A woman stands before an autopsy table. Her eyes are sharp and bright, her mouth is wet with blood, and her teeth gnaw on the corner of her lower lip. A dirty lab coat is open in the front, the only article of clothing she wears, but any risk of obscenity is spared by a distinct lack of flesh from neck to groin. Ribs and spine and pelvis are stained with long-dried blood, scraped of all meat except where they border limbs and head still flush with lively material.

Her hands are busy with a project, her nimble fingers draped around two scalpels of differing sizes. She picks apart a scrap of meat, a chunk of flesh, perhaps a severed piece of some vital organ. The grisly sight is repeated across the laboratory, a bit of human detritus lying on every dissection table filling the room. Scraps of skin, mutilated muscle, quartered heart and diced lungs, some tables just stained with blood. All of them, with the exception of the live project and two more lying on the tables nearest it, are blackened as if burnt.

The sight would discomfort a weak stomach and alarm the naive mind, but this room is not a place of death; no murder has taken place here, no evidence disposed of, no victim's body torn from its resting place by the woman with sharp eyes and sharper knives. These organs are her organs, this skin is her skin, and that blood is her blood. She is the only student of a very singular subject, and she has been drafting her thesis for a very long time.

The woman sets down her blades and picks up the gobbet of flesh, dangling it in front of her. She smiles at it with full lips and bared teeth, though the expression never reaches her eyes. "I'm almost done, I know I am," she speaks as much to herself as to the meat twitching in her grasp. "I've gotten it right this time, I must have. Just a little further, and I'll have the answer I've been looking for."

The meat screams in the language of meat, shuddering and bleeding, but that's only natural; it has been ripped from its body and cut open, and so it aches as all flesh aches when trauma is applied. Flesh is so weak and fallible, is it not? There's something fascinating about the signals our mortal meat sends to try and communicate with us. We feel pain when certain stimuli are introduced, but not all pain is equal. We must learn what each kind of pain means, what it is meant to communicate, and whether it should be ignored as an overreaction by a body that does not understand the world it reacts to. With age and experience, we find that sometimes pain can even be desirable, almost rapturous. There is catharsis in pain, and that too is worthy of study.

The meat understands little of pleasure and catharsis, of course. It only knows to send a given output when it receives the matching input, and the rest is for the brain to interpret. So it screams, yes, aching with pain, uncomprehending that it is the same flesh as that which wields the blade that carves it. The meat is as disgusting and stupid as it is beautiful and intelligent, and it is hers. It is her meat, to mutilate as she wishes, for she knows that the reward will be well worth the pain. This room is not a place of death, but of lively discovery.

The woman drops the gobbet of flesh to splash against the cold metal table, the shock of impact triggering a new wave of reactive signals. "I do hope I've gotten it right," she sighs to herself. "It would be such a bother to start cutting up one of my limbs, and I've run out of material in between." She looks back at the rows and rows of tables with their burnt offerings, frowning at the blackened meat and dried blood. "Perhaps I could do a bit of recycling if I scraped off the charcoal, but that's such a slippery slope. No, no, we must press on."

She picks up her scalpels and returns to her work, and as steel touches flesh, the lights above flicker out and the laboratory is plunged into darkness.

In darkness, warm hands claw at my skin and peel me apart. My blood mixes with the cold water of a deep, dark ocean. This too is not a physical space but merely a representation of some process my brain can't begin to truly understand. The meat cries out in pain as it is dissected by its owner.

How far will she go? She doesn't see a person when she looks at me, she just sees another piece of her body. I'm another scrap of her humanity to be cut apart on an operating table that is a scale diorama of the universe. Reska was Love and Homura was Justice, so what does that make me? Identity?

If she completes whatever it is she's doing to me, how much of me—this me, this self, this conscious mind—will be left? Pick the meat apart, douse it in chemicals, transmute it to another form, and it is still the meat of your body. Meat has no concept of ego death. But I do.

I can't let that happen.

Her hands plunge inside my chest, burning hot, and through the pain and the fear I scream out, "I changed my mind! The deal is off!"

The Demiurge laughs. "It's a little late for that, isn't it? You already made your choice. It would be quite rude of me not to fulfill my end of the bargain."

Something bright and painful is in her hands, pushing its way inside me. White heat burns my flayed body. Still I resist. "It's not my choice anymore! I—I didn't know the terms! It wasn't an *informed choice*, so you have to stop. Those were the rules, weren't they?"

For a moment, for a single shuddering moment, she stops. Her questing hands freeze in place; the burning doesn't get any worse. She told me before that it has to be a choice. That Azathoth, the Dreaming Sea, and the will of thousands would reject our pact if it was forced.

And yet a moment later she laughs once more and shoves her hands deeper inside my flesh. "Informed enough."

No, no, no, no! I scream as I am unraveled, and she only laughs. Her voice, so close to me, taunting me from what must be mere inches away. Close enough to touch. Close enough to taste. Close enough—

In a fit of desperation, I jerk forward with all my strength, still caught in her ironclad embrace but able to move just enough to reach my target. My mouth finds hers and I *bite* as hard as I can, hard enough to draw blood. She's surprised, or maybe just uncaring, and she doesn't move away as I bite into her lip and taste her spilling blood, swallowing it down with the seawater.

I can't use my spells against her, can't bring my magic to bear, but what does that matter? Drinking her blood is a symbolic act, and this universe runs on symbols.

So I drink and I drink and I drink, blood and seawater mixing inside me, as her hands flay my skin and push a star inside my chest. I taste her essence, heady and overwhelming, the enormity of it threatening to drown me, but I only need a little more. Her soul invades my meat and burns out memory after memory, but those were never my memories; I discard them, sacrificed for my escape.

I bite off a single speck of her infinity, a trillionth of a trillionth, but even the smallest infinity is still *infinity*. I seize that spark and flood my body with its power, limbs surging with sudden strength.

I push away with all my might and tear myself from her grasp with shocking ease, her fingers slipping away as I am thrust deeper into the lightless ocean, surrounded by stinging seawater and blood from two bodies. For dreadful seconds I drift in that space, not trusting the nightmare to be over, no idea how to get any farther away from the god-thing that has imprisoned me. I will myself deeper down into the dark, but I am terrified that her grasping hands will find me again and this time not let go. I bleed and burn, her process interrupted but the damage still lingering.

And then, in the blink of an unseeing eye, water and blood vanish and I slam against hard ground.

The breath is knocked from my lungs—though no seawater bubbles out of me—and I spend an uncomfortable length of time just wheezing and aching, thoughts scattered by the unexpected impact. My body complains, but it doesn't scream like when the Demiurge had her hands on me.

Shaky hands dance across my limbs, my face, beneath my shirt—and I'm wearing one of those again, and more, fully clothed—but find no bleeding wounds, no signs of flensing. I'm not burning, either, though my chest feels oddly warm to the touch.

I keep taking in ragged breaths, trying to steady myself. I'm shaking, my whole body shuddering from fear and tension. *What have I done? What will the consequences be? And where am I now?*

Wherever I am, it's still cold and dark, but I'm not underwater anymore. The floor feels like stone, level and smooth. I think I'm safe, for the moment, if that means anything. It probably doesn't, actually.

All my messy emotions finally convert themselves to nervous, coughing laughter. I need to sift through all the information I've learned, all the revelations that have piled on top of each other and threatened to bury me, but where do I even start? What do I do now? I have no idea.

I feel like throwing up. I feel like a walking corpse. I feel like I've got electrified wires digging into my muscles. I feel . . . I don't know how to feel. What have I done?

"Why?" I whisper into the darkness. "I don't understand. Why, why, why?"

I've started crying again. I clutch at my head, pulling on my hair hard enough to hurt, and I screw up my eyes to try and stop the tears. I hate this. I hate all of this so much. *I don't want to do this anymore. I don't want to be in Wonderland.*

I feel so lost and lonely, but what does that even mean? I have no home to go back to, no loved ones who might miss me. I'm not a real person, I'm just a copy. Just a fragment. I'm just a gobbet of meat being cut up in a lab.

In the depths of my despair, as I sob on the cold stone floor, red light pierces the darkness. I shield my eyes, blinking away the disorientation, but then my brain catches up and my head snaps to look at the source: a girl with red eyes and dark hair, standing in the doorway of this stone chamber, an orb of glowing crimson levitating over one outstretched hand.

Homura Annatar Bloodfallen smirks down at me and says, "Hey there, new girl. I think you and me should have a nice, long chat. What do you say?"

GARDEN of MEMORIES II

I stare at my phantom doppelganger and a question tumbles from my lips, slipping out without thought at the shock of her visage. I ask her, "Are you real?"

The words come out smothered and lifeless, the dead whisper of a broken, exhausted husk. *Stupid question. Why even ask?* I laugh, though it's more of a bark. The hideous noises that pass between my rotting lips echo off stone walls and return to my sensitive ears. I run a finger over one ear and am briefly reassured by the faintly pointed tip, but then even that sours as I wonder to what dissected piece of *her* I owe that senseless craving.

The figure of Homura—a specter, perhaps, or a vision bleeding into the real, or Demiurge or Emissary or whoever else wearing her face—does not seem offended by my thoughtless question, nor does she dismiss it with a quick and pithy, "Of course I'm real, you mad little freak."

Instead she licks her lips, bites the corner of her mouth, and takes the question with a strange depth of contemplation. She watches me with those burning, inquisitive eyes that dart across my form before sweeping over her own. She splays both hands, the red orb sticking midair unaided, and positions her thumbs and forefingers as if to frame me for a photo.

"Are you?"

The question sounds innocent, guileless, open, yet how could it be? *You always were an excellent liar.* She must be mocking me, laughing to herself at a punchline only she can hear. Why am I even entertaining the idea of having a conversation with this *traitorous monster*? *After what she did to us?*

"Why should we listen to a word you say? You cannot be trusted," I hiss at the lying whore. My skin is itching, prickling, a tension building and burning the longer I stay here beneath her gaze, *vulnerable.* I push against the cold stone floor with a sudden motion, trying to rocket to my feet where I can at least die standing, but the second I put any weight on my limbs they buckle and snap like cheap twigs and I am meat and bone and blood, vivisected and screaming, just a gobbet of flesh crying out for the awful *pain* to finally stop.

I shudder and heave, bile dripping from my lips, but is that real? I lift an arm, unbroken and whole, and drag trembling fingers across my mouth. No bile, no blood, just cracked skin. I am alive, and I am more than meat, I am more, I must be more, I must—

Homura's voice, low and confident and smooth, intrudes upon my fraying thoughts. "You should always listen, *especially* if you don't trust who's speaking. I never trust; I verify. Even good liars sometimes let slip a few precious truths." Her fingers are laced behind her head now, and she's grinning.

I laugh and cough and crumple, beaten. What can I really do, anyways? Could I beat Homura at the fullness of my power? Is there any point left to resisting? *Go on then, kill me.* "Go on then. Let's *chat.*"

How absurd. Homura wants to chat. Homura Annatar Bloodfallen, my doppelganger, my dreaming lover, my *savior and murderer,* wants to chat. I am lost and alone and crumbling at the seams and here she comes wishing to chat, wishing to speak her pretty words and deceive me, but I have been warned. I was warned, in my dreams, and I haven't forgotten the warning: *Don't believe her lies.*

But I'm still curious; how could I not be, when faced with a figure that has haunted my every resting moment since my arrival—my cruel, confusing birth—in this cage of colored glass? Intercessor or Adversary, angel or devil, *lover or betrayer,* I need to hear her story and place her in this puzzle. I need answers. That need burns in me like the white star burned in my chest when those awful hands picked me apart and tried to put me back together. What secrets can you show me, Homura?

I wonder if she's thinking something similar. She watches me with those burning red eyes, those eyes that have always seen too much too quickly. Her curiosity was always like a hunger, something darker and more demanding than idle interest, and she fed it like one feeds a furnace. She knows so much, and I crave that knowing for myself. And yet.

She stretches, arcing her back, and I can't resist the way my eyes dart over her form. Her arms are toned, strong, so unlike my weak noodle limbs. There's a danger to her presence that is so easy to be mesmerized by, a casual lethality to her every movement that might make me shiver if I weren't paralyzed with fear. With those firm hands of hers she could easily take a life, my life. *She has.*

Homura crouches in front of me, holding my gaze, and says, "Here's why you should hear me out: You and me, we're crabs in a bucket, and we don't have long before the water gets hot. Alone, we both go up in steam, but together we stand a chance. We need each other. We can help each other. I can help *you*, if you let me. You game?"

You can help me if I let you. You said those words before, beneath a parasol's shade on a hill beside a castle. You promised. You lied.

You lied and lied and lied and I loved you and I miss you and I wish that you would die—the sight of her sickens me—but those beautiful eyes make my heart ache and burn and splinter and yearn—Homura, the monster of my dreams, is offering to help me—Homura, Homura, Homura—she was always so compelling, like the sweetest of poisons—you lied and I believed you because I could never resist you and I—and I—

—loved you, and you killed me, and that I could forgive but you lied I could be loved and like a puppy I believed you. So now I know with all my bones that you will lie to me again and I will falter and believe you till my fingers char to stumps on the pyre that you make of me, and again, and again, and again.

Unless I pluck your lying tongue from those lips I still desire.

She'll betray me if I let her, she'll lead me and deceive me and then she'll break me into pieces, just like before, just like always, so I have to kill her now and kill her quick before she opens that pretty mouth and hurts me one more time. I have to do this, don't I? Is there any other way?

The shadows know. The shadows swirl around me, thick and heavy in the gloom of this unfamiliar chamber, cast into evident form by the crimson light of her cursed magic, but always present and lurking. The shadows steady me, they cradle me, they pull me to my feet. Their presence at my back, more solid and true where her red light can't reach, keeps me focused on what's in front of me. Their presence all around, come to nuzzle at my side and lick my tender fingers, goads me onward and urges me to do what must be done. The shadows love me like she never did, and they yearn to rend flesh that I once worshiped like a priestess and a whore and a fool. Oh, what a fool I was. What a fool I still am. But just a word from me, just a thought, just a whisper of permission, and they will free me from this witch.

The red witch watches me with upturned lips, her grin almost manic, her breathing hitched. "Fascinating. What *are* you?"

I lance her with darkness through heart and throat and each and every joint, killing her like she killed me. I release my shadows like plucking a bowstring, solid night my arrows, and in thorns and spears and gnashing teeth the dark swallows Homura. I make a wish, and my murderer dies.

Or so I vainly hope. But instead, my shadows impact nothing and tear through empty air. The light goes out, but then it flickers to life once more just behind me and I whirl to face Homura, unharmed and unbothered, her expression unchanged at the attempt on her life.

She tilts her head, her gaze full of frenzied calculation. "Fascinating," she repeats, like she's just observed a new species of butterfly and yearns to puzzle out its phylogeny. Would she pluck my wings and make me scream to sate that burning hunger? I know the answer.

What now? With racing heart and leaden tongue, I try to find my speech. I have to say something, I have to distract her so I can try again, but I can't speak. *What kind of pathetic excuse for a princess can't orate?* I know. I know!

"Homura," I whisper, and then the pain of her name upon my lips sends a spasm through the darkness and a wave of night consumes the vision of my lover and tormentor.

But again my shadows are denied their rightful kill. Again she escapes. How? Has the witch of glass and blood carved a third edge to her soul? Or am I just facing reflections?

I close my eyes and let the darkness swaddle me. Through darkness I feel the shape of my surroundings, this box of simple stone, and I find that it is more than a mere box; I am in a crypt or a tomb, some place of restful death. The floor is smooth but the sides are hewn with recesses for the tender care of long-gone corpses, and as my senses expand I find halls and halls of quiet dead. This is a catacomb, someplace deep underground.

Where am I? This doesn't feel like my family's castle. Where . . . how did I get here?

The question drives a nail of pain into my skull, and I wince at the sudden splitting headache. Confusion and pain mingle and each question brings more questions, a veritable flood of them. What am I doing here?

What was I doing before? What . . . what day is it? Why do my memories feel so . . . so . . .

The red light of Homura pulses in the dark halls beyond this chamber. Her voice carries to me from deeper within the catacombs, transmitting easily through my web of shadows. "If you've gotten the violence out of your system, I'd love to ask you some detailed questions. I can even trade intel for intel, if that suits you better, or suits the face before."

Anger cuts through confusion and pushes out pain. No questions, no talking, only ending this threat before it can hurt us. *Us?*

I cling to fury and call the shadows to swirl about me and move me through the halls of the catacombs faster than I could run. I hunt her, chasing that cursed red light. If I can only corner her, then maybe . . .

"Try this one on for size," her voice calls from so daringly close.

Shadows pierce the source of the sound, clawing at the red-eyed figure holding the red-glowing orb, but the light goes out before I see her bleed and a moment later she's somewhere else, still talking.

"You were Veseryn when you arrived, I'm sure of that, but now you're unmistakably Kiana. How? Who are you, really? Or are you, really?"

Confusion fights back against anger. What is she talking about? Who is Veseryn? Who is Kiana? *Distraction. Distracting us!* I chase her through the catacombs as she flickers in and out of my vision every time I get close. *Throwing us off, tricking us, all so she can murder us again like she murdered us, murdered us, murdered us!*

Her face, just in front of mine, those beautiful burning eyes and that twitching smirk. "Who are you, princess?"

I swipe my hand through the apparition, tears streaking down my cheeks, and I cry at her, "I am Reska Shadowsun, and I am the monster that you made me!"

Her voice behind me. "Are you, really?" A spear of night, her flickering orb. "It's a genuine question." An explosion of darkness, her form unharmed. "I can't see outside the confines of this quaint little construct, but I remember what I *did* to that pretty little princess." Running and crying and lashing out at a phantom that just won't die. "Do you? Do you remember what I did to you, Reska?" She laughs.

I chase her—she leads me—into another stone chamber, grander than before, a monument to time and death and memory. The walls are lined with corpses, preserved and decorated, and the ceiling is patterned. She appears in the center of the room, her red orb illuminating only the plain stone around her, and I am struck with revulsion for the crudeness of her craft.

With a whisper of will I bring stars to the underground. My magic lights the chamber with beautiful blues and greens and purples, pale and shimmering and wondrous. I see the dead buried here, and I see the intricate spirals painted and carved upon the ceiling. This is true light. This is true craft.

I stay by the walls, unwilling to step closer and seemingly unable to bring an end to my ruinous foe. Is this all a form of torture? Is she making me feel helpless so I'll return to her side?

The red orb vanishes, unneeded now, and the witch bites her lip as she admires my starlight. "I wonder . . . ah! Let's try a trigger phrase and see what happens." She meets my gaze, those crimson eyes boring into me even from across the room, and she asks, "Tell me, girl who stands before me: *Do you know regret?*"

I gasp as those words slam into me like a fist to my gut, that splitting headache from before getting worse and worse and—

—*there's a monster, a stretched thing, scarred and misshapen, and it asks me a question with a voice that is choral and beautiful and hideous. I get smart with it. It doesn't like that. I lie to it. It really doesn't like that. Then, the violence—*

—*I watched you, frozen and horrified, as your nails drew blood from your palms and you laughed at the pain as you told me—*

—*it battered me and nearly broke me, but I killed it and I lived and I remembered that question, and then I dreamed—*

—*I dug my nails into my palms, that little act of self-harm steadying me as I looked back, as I laughed at the emotions still raw a world away, and I peeled apart my mask and I told you: The only thing I ever regretted was not killing the old man when I had the chance—*

—*and in my dreams the princess told me that her killer once asked her, "Do you know regret?" She told me that she drowned in it. It made her a demon, and that demon is the girl I have to save, but she's not me, she's not me and I—*

"Oh, my darling Creator, what madness have you wrought this time?" The witch's voice is full of wonder and amusement and it drags me back to myself, away from the awful din inside my head and those people that aren't me, can't be me, because I am *Reska* and no one else. She's closer now, watching me with naked fascination, those scarlet eyes sparkling and that lovely mouth smiling, and my shadows come swarming in to shield me from her gaze.

But the shadows can't hide me. The stars are gone, my beautiful creation banished, and all is lit in the baneful glow of Homura's red orb. She's close to me, so close it makes my heart beat faster and my head swim, and she's got a strand of my hair between her fingers. She's playing with my hair, twirling it gently, like she used to when we were alone together.

My hair is wrong. The color is off, the aberrant tones visible even in this rough lighting. It's not the pale blonde I'm used to, not that clear sun-kissed color, but a dirty blonde stained with dark brown, like darkness infecting sunlight.

"What have you done to me?" I whisper in horror. "What wicked spell did you cast? Why would you take that from me? Was everything else not enough?" I can feel the tears starting to fall, and my heart is cold and hollow.

Homura laughs and lets my hair fall from between her fingers. "Don't worry, princess," she drawls like it's nothing, like I've just spilled a bit of jam on a tablecloth. "I'm trying to figure this out, and I think I've almost got it. We can at least rule out you being the *real* Reska, if you don't remember being Contrition. I lodged that curse deep, *deep* inside her brain."

"I'm real," I whisper, but somehow it doesn't sound sincere. What curse?

My headache is back, and worse. It's a throbbing pressure inside my skull, like someone is pounding on the walls and screaming to be let out. And a voice, whispering in my ear that *you are not real and you are not her and we are all just shards and copies wearing other faces so let me out and give me back my fucking body before—*

Homura kisses me on the lips, hard and hot and forceful, and she tastes like I remembered, and when she moves away she steals my breath and I look up at her with love and hate and pain, and she asks me, "Do you even know who you are?"

And then I unravel, because I love her and I miss her and I wish that she would die—*this hateful killer that haunts my dreams*—but those beautiful eyes make my heart ache and burn and splinter and yearn—*this pretender to my name*—Homura, Homura, Homura—*a failed experiment speaking to another, two dolls that think they're more than what I made them*—and I know that she'll lie to me and I'll believe her and I'll burn in her embrace, and I don't know what that means or what that makes me—*a girl I've never met and a girl I've never been*—and more and more I don't know who—

—I am.

But I do know who I'm not.

"Welcome back, Veseryn," the phantom purrs at me, the taste of her lips still burning on mine. I wonder, is it narcissism to enjoy a kiss from your clone?

Not that I enjoyed it, obviously. I mean, well, okay, I *did* enjoy it, clearly, but only because of Reska. It was nothing to do with *my* desires, *I lie as easily as breathing.*

"My name is Alice," I snap aloud to mask my internal strife. "Maven Alice, remember the name. Not Reska, not Kiana, not—wait, what's so interesting? What did I say?"

The might-be-Homura's eyes are lit up with interest, orange swirling with red, and she licks her lips at my question. "Your name is M. Alice? Did I hear that right?"

I fight back a blush of embarrassment. *Damn my past self!* "Yes, I named myself *Malice*, don't—"

She howls with laughter. "Oh, love, what *have* you done?"

"I'm not your love!"

"Oh, I know," she says with a returning smirk. "And you know that too, now that your head's on right. Or is that wrong? Am I speaking to the *real* you, or is M. Alice just another rattling splinter?"

I flinch at the implication. *I'm real, I must be real, I'm the only one that's real and anyone else that says they're me can shut the hell up and get out of my head.* But saying that isn't going to make me sound particularly sane, so instead I say, "We're all splinters of the divine vivisector, are we not? I'm the true and original resident of this particular cut of meat, if *that's* what you're asking."

"Wonderful! Yes, yes, yes!" Homura claps her hands together and rubs them gleefully, her childlike excitement at gross odds with everything I remember about the smooth-talking murderer. "If you're in the know about our darling Creator, that makes this next part a lot easier. Now we can have a proper conversation about—oh, oh really? Are you *really* going to interrupt me on exactly that line?"

In the middle of her chatter, every corpse in the ossuary wakes up.

Cold blue light pierces the red-stained gloom from a hundred desiccated eyes. The corpses interred within the walls of the grand chamber shudder and twitch, their creaking limbs and withered digits convulsing as if electrified. I stumble away from the nearest wall before the quickest of the dead can rise from their rest, my brain immediately flushed with raw animal fear.

My mind races with dire imagination, stricken by haunting visions of inevitable decay. Their flesh is gray and shadowed, made monstrous and unknowable by the dim glow of enchanted eyes, but I catch glimpses of peeling skin and yellowed bone, of muscles long atrophied and hair all matted. They are rot and ruin and creeping death, my childhood nightmares come to kill me.

Flight instinct kicks in and I try to run, but a flash of weakness—meat on a cold slab of stainless steel, the scalpel sinking deeper—slams me to my hands and knees in the center of the room. I gasp for breath, heart racing, vision blurry, and the dead keep rising.

Homura—or the thing pretending to be Homura—does not share my panic. She rolls her eyes, unmoved even as the walking dead begin to crowd her and block the exits. She says, "This is unbelievable, and by unbelievable I mean COMPLETELY BELIEVABLE from your dramatic ass. I'm not giving this scene any dignity, Pom-Pom."

Pom-Pom??? Who is she talking to???

The blasé absurdity of her speech shocks me out of my blind, unthinking terror. I force my shivering limbs to push me to my feet, standing tall and straight.

Whatever these freaks are and whoever sent them, I'm the bigger monster. They're just zombies! I'm way too strong to die to trash mobs like these.

"Voracious Heart!" I hiss, and this time I don't even get a pair of brackets for my trouble. My beating heart stays lodged firmly in my chest, my blood does not stir, and my shadow does not slither up my skin. There's not even a whisper of a suggestion that the spell was once carved deep into the wood grain of my soul. Its name is just noise.

That's bad. That's very bad. Why is this happening to me?

You told her to free Cheshire. Do you see a Cheshire? Do you feel a Cheshire? She was the core of that spell.

Right. Cheshire is gone, and she's never coming back, and we don't have the luxury of processing that right now because I hear more zombies shuffling in from the outer halls and my cool shapeshifting blood armor spell isn't working. That's fine! I have more tricks! Bugs are good against dead things, right?

"Carrion Heart!" I command, holding out a hand, into which my bug-in-amber artifact very definitively does not appear. "Carrion Swarm? Oh, fuck."

I rapidly cycle through every spell in my arsenal, chanting them in my mind, but none of them respond. I can't conjure anything from my throne world, either, not even Vorpal. I've got nothing. I'm powerless.

And the zombies keep shuffling in, forming a wall of dead meat that gets more and more impenetrable the longer I struggle with my worthless magic. They would barely qualify as speed bumps to my fully-powered war form, but without my spells or my armory they're a rising tide of death and dread.

My only solace is that Homura seems more interested in the zombies than in my fumbling with spell names. She frowns at one of them, leaning in close and making that camera frame gesture with her hands again. She says, "The work of another Veseryn, how strange. Is that this loop's true gimmick?"

I bark another awkward laugh, standing terror-stricken in the heart of the ossuary. "What are you talking about? Who or what is a Veseryn?"

"A reckless coward and a clever fool," Homura quips, and then the necromancer makes her debut.

The second Veseryn is a woman I've seen once before, reclining on her throne as a glass monster pronounced judgment, and though that glimpse was brief and I had much else to occupy my attention, it's hard to forget a face split down the middle like that. The cold blue light in her empty eye socket is the same light that burns in all her fresh thralls, the same blue as gleams in her undamaged eye and paints her plump lips even as half those lips shrivel away into torn skin and exposed bone. Her teeth are perfect and bloody, and her platinum hair is styled as if her exposed skull was just the shaven half of a side cut.

Lord Urna, Noble of the Labyrinth, strides through her court of corpses with chin upturned and spine like an iron rod. The waking dead turn hungry at her arrival. They all turn to face their mistress, and the nearest reach out with grasping hands in what could be mistaken for religious rapture until those hands grope beneath the fabric of her sheer monochrome dress. The dead make no distinction between the luscious, shapely half of her body and the skeletal, gore-dripping half; they grab at all parts of her with desperate, shivering need.

Urna barely acknowledges their presence as they feel up every inch of her body, though her smile is satisfied and indulgent, until that smile suddenly drops and her skeletal arm lashes out to grab a zombie's face. Her choice seems random, seizing not the zombie with a hand between her legs nor the corpse leering at her chest but instead just one of several that were admiring her shapely and fleshless limbs.

She crushes its head like an overripe grape, squeezing until the whole thing is a mess of pulverized bone and leaking brain, and then she tosses it aside and it smears across the stone. The mass retreats, their lustful hunger spoiled, and then one by one they all turn their heads to look at *me*.

"The fail state of a Veseryn," Homura chatters while all that is going on, the phantom uncaring and seemingly unheard. "A few too many bad deals and bad decisions, so now she's a slave on a very complicated leash."

Prevara's leash. The glass shard. The Emissary's next assassin.

Urna takes a step forward, her horde now parting for her and pressing against the walls to keep away from their capricious ruler. Her lips curl as she looks me up and down, her one good eye narrowing, and then with an angry huff and crossed arms she demands, "Why do none of you wretched imitators *ever* fix your tits!?"

What?

I stare at her. "What?" *Am I crazy? Did she really just say that?* "Seriously, what? Why is that the first thing you say to me?"

"Because your ugly little mosquito bites aren't doing anything for me," she leers, "and I'm going to have to *fix them* before I can get off on ravishing your reanimated corpse, vampy. The face needs work too, don't get me wrong, but that's what masks are for. I swear, do the rest of you just *like* being hideous? Why am I the only splinter with taste?"

Homura gnaws on her lip as she circles Urna, weaving through the space between necromancer and zombies with casual ease. She muses, "Not a typical Veseryn trait. Part of the leash, or independent variable?"

I blink, like, twelve times in a row. Is this how computers feel when they bluescreen? I feel like a professional boxer just punched me in the nose. Why this? Why now? I just want to go curl up under a mountain of blankets but fine, whatever, let's engage with the insane necrophile clone. "Splinters and the rest of you," I babble, just trying to get my brain restarted, "means you're like me? You're an Alice?"

The monster sneers. "Am I 'like you,' mosquito girl? I'm better than you. I'm smarter and more dangerous and much, much more attractive. You're an Urna knockoff, get it right."

Homura covers a laugh, but then she's talking rapidly in my direction. "Listen: Veseryn always loses her name or her phylactery—a ring, always a ring—and that's what makes her a thrall. That's your leverage."

Her words are a lightning bolt that sends me back to the very first day of my journey—of my existence—when I sold my name to a faerie huntsman. *A reckless coward and a clever fool . . . yeah, that's me. I am Veseryn, and Homura knows exactly what that means. We need to talk to her. We need to learn her secrets. But first we need to survive our first real encounter with another splinter.*

Urna, unable to hear Homura's commentary or read my internal dialogue, watches me watch her in silence. She doesn't seem to like the silence. Urna takes a step closer, then another, and she sneers, "Are you plotting another scheme, lamprey? I've been watching you. I know your games. Whatever you think you can do to get out of this, you're wrong. Surrender and I'll kill you clean."

I almost laugh at her. She thinks I'm dangerous. She thinks I'm *plotting*. Or maybe she's just wary of the overgod in my corner. *Okay. Leverage, we have leverage. Mask on, veins of ice.* "Prevara stole your phylactery—the ring that makes you immortal," I guess with false confidence. "I can free you from those chains," I lie to the insane necromancer with a smile on my face and open palms spread wide.

Urna's advance falters, on the back foot for the first time in this conversation. *She bought the bluff.* Her face twists with longing and distrust. "What can a slave offer a slave? The Demiurge could free me at her whim, but she whims it not. There will be no freedom for any of us until the Resurrection, when the Leviathans tear that pretender from her throne."

Homura rolls her eyes from right behind the necromancer Noble. "She's dumb or desperate. That way ends in fire."

I choose my next words carefully. "I am not God's hunting dog, if that's what you think. Nor do I trust the Emissary's plans to lead to anything but annihilation for all of us. Victory—survival, even—requires that I kill Prevara. When I do, I'd rather take you as a partner than as a pet. But you don't want to be my enemy, Urna."

The necromancer lifts her hands to the fur mantle around her shoulders, and then she closes her living eye and the ghost-light dims. She lets out a heavy, tired breath, and for a moment I see exhaustion written on that half-dead face. But then she smiles, wicked and sinful, and when she opens her eyes they are full of hunger.

"I've killed us twice already, lamprey. I like my chances for a triple."

She lunges for me, fleshless hand outstretched to shatter my skull. Panic devours me and I grasp at spells I can't call and weapons I can't conjure, paralyzed and powerless.

She's going to kill me. She's going to kill me and there is absolutely nothing I can do to stop her. I don't want to die here. I don't want to die in this horrible, wretched, miserable Labyrinth. I don't want to be here at all.

Anywhere but here. Anywhere but Wonderland.

Urna reaches out to kill me and I lurch back, my terror reaching a final crescendo, and then the air between us shatters like glass. Reality breaks, the world is sundered, and when I blink my eyes I'm tripping over my own feet on an ordinary sidewalk with no sign of the living dead.

I stumble backward into a brick wall and get the breath knocked from my lungs, but I'm not dead. I slump against the wall, gasping and wheezing, and I try to slow my racing heart. No Urna and no zombies—no Homura either—and no idea where I am or how I got here.

I scan my surroundings and see brickwork, glass, wood, and stone. The sun beats down on me, hot and uncomfortable. Buildings, squat and tall and all between, an urban forest. Wispy clouds, a bright blue sky. A city, vast and sprawling. Sunlight glinting off a glass tower that pierces the blue heavens. A sun, burning in the sky.

There is a sun in the sky. Why is there a sun in the sky?

The glass tower, that's *the* tower, the heart of the Labyrinth, but the Labyrinth doesn't have a sun and those clouds should be floating islands. That tower should be black as pitch, not radiant in the light of an alien sun. The tower . . . it's like it was in Reska's age. The tower before it blackened, before the world broke and the sun went away.

Where am I? When am I? This must be a dream, but I don't feel like I'm dreaming.

I pick myself off the ground and glance around my more immediate surroundings. There are people here, just like you'd see in any city, but I wonder if they're real. None of them have reacted to my sudden appearance, but I guess that doesn't mean much in a world where magic is everywhere. The city doesn't look as modern as Sanctuary, and the people are dressed to match, but I can't really place a specific era or region they're emulating.

They're probably figments. I could just ask them if they're real. It doesn't really matter either way.

It doesn't. But I want to *see it.* Even if it means feeling the burning shadow of the Demiurge again, I want to take that risk and open my sight. I want to prove I still can. And hey, maybe seeing her true form—that gruesome, smiling cadaver—banished the clouds from my secret eyes.

I close my eyes, breathe deep, and focus on my vision like I have a dozen times before. My soul sight, my demonic sixth sense which paints the world in paper and ink and reveals the depths of desirous souls. I reach for the switch.

Nothing happens. No paper, no ink, no insight. No metaphysical switch to flip. I open my eyes to the same world of light and color, the world as everyone sees it.

I'm not a demon anymore.

It's a cold, hollow thought. I should have known it from the moment I lost my magic, but I was in denial. My spells lacking presence, the contents of my throne world unresponsive, my second sight denied me, all because of the simple and obvious fact that I am not a demon. I haven't been a demon since I was spat out in those catacombs.

I made a deal with Nyarlathotep and now I'm paying the price. I bargained away my Cheshire and my powers for the promise of something bigger, and then I tried to run from the consequences . . . but how do you run away from the lord of the universe?

I laugh darkly and lean against the brickwork. I thought I'd gotten away, but obviously that was a stupid, absurd notion. She probably let me escape, and let me bite her, and let me think she hadn't already done everything she wanted to do to me.

She took everything I had as a demon, and in return she gave me, what, a bunch of voices in my head? That teleport trick was certainly one of her gifts, but I don't have the slightest clue how to activate it on purpose. When I was Reska, I could use her shadow magic, but I was also drowning in her grief and rage and longing. I can't make use of those powers if it means losing myself to some wailing waif.

My hands are trembling, so I clench them into fists. I hate this. I hate what she's done to me. I don't want those other girls living in my brain. I refuse to cede control of *my* body. She's planted horrible seeds inside my head and I refuse to let them sprout. I will pull those fuckers out by the roots and throw them at her feet.

And then you'll die, because right now they're the ones with real magic.

I hiss and drag my nails across my arm. *Then I'll steal their magic first! I'll make every ounce of it mine, and then I'll do the same to God herself and rule this whole wretched world!* My laughter is wild and desperate, eyes wide, needing so badly to scream my hate. *If all I am is just meat beneath her knife then I will crawl my way up that slender arm and burrow inside her soulless eyes. I will make my hate a sword and that sword will take her life and we will call that justice.*

But is that really you? Or is that Homura?

Ice pours down my back. These are my thoughts, aren't they? Aren't those my desires? I'm still Alice, no matter what that monster did to me. Aren't I?

I need to get away from this. I need space. I need clarity. I need a goal. We need to survive. How do we survive?

First step: orientation. We're in a city both familiar and unfamiliar, and we need to acquire more data before we can make any kind of decision about our next steps. We no longer have access to soul sight, but we can still gather information the old-fashioned way.

I step out into the street, clear my throat, and ask, "Can anyone help me? I appear to be lost."

Most of the passersby ignore me, a point for their realism, but one of them stops in her tracks and looks my way with a concerned expression before hurrying over. "You're lost? Do you know where you want to get to?"

She is ruddy-cheeked and curly-haired, with warm eyes and a patterned sundress. I dislike her cheerful demeanor, so I give her a pleasant smile. "I'm afraid I don't have the slightest idea where I'm meant to be going, nor where I've come from, nor where I appear to be. I'm very lost, you see."

The pedestrian laughs cutely. "Oh, well that's perfectly natural. You're in a place where lost things come to be found, after all. This is Fata Morgana, the city of glass and dreams."

Fata Morgana, why do I feel like I should recognize that name from somewhere? There's an uncanny sense of recognition, but that recognition is tinged with head pain. If it's trapped in Reska's memories, I'm fine not knowing. "You get a lot of lost things here, then?" I ask instead.

"Oh, now more than ever, thanks to the war." Her smile drops, eyes filling with a deep and unspeakable sorrow. "With each kingdom that Queen Shadowsun razes, there are fewer places left for the survivors to take refuge. Soon enough we'll be the last sanctuary in the world."

Shadowsun. We know that name. When I was . . . possessed by Reska? Living her shadow? Channeling her? I don't understand the specifics, but we can figure that out later. When I was Reska, she called herself Reska Shadowsun. This is her world, her past. Her apocalypse.

The stranger's expression brightens after a moment. "Oh, but we've helped so many people adjust to life here in the city. We're all so happy to perform our sacred duty, truly."

"That's nice." I look to the tower again, shielding my eyes from the blinding light. "That tower, is that the tower of the Lady Katoptris? I think I've heard tales of this place, now that I see it in person. If one wished to meet the Lady of Glass and beg her advice, how would they?"

She blinks at me owlishly. "The tower? Oh, that old thing isn't open to the public anymore. But that's okay, there's really nothing in there worth seeing. It's been a long time since the Lady had the energy to entertain guests." Her tone is sympathetic yet pitying, like someone talking about a relative with dementia. "But if you want to sightsee, I'm sure I can help you out!"

"Sightsee?" I frown.

"Mhm! I can take you to a nice theater putting on *The Garden of Dying Flowers* tonight, or to a gambling house that serves the best drinks. If you're hungry, I know a dozen eateries within easy walking distance. Please, I'd love to help you take advantage of everything your lovely city has to offer. Just forget that boring eyesore."

I remember this, too, from my dreams. Homura told me about her time in the city and our experiences with its inhabitants. The figments of this place are lotus-priests, obstacles designed to keep you from the tower and its Lady.

That makes this woman another figment, her smiling face a wooden mask. Her hospitality is poisoned, though the poison is surely sweet. She'll say and do whatever is necessary to keep me from the tower.

Well, at least our next step is obvious. If oppositional defiant disorder has taught me anything, it's that I should always go where I'm least wanted. Honestly, if I stop and think about it, Katoptris is the one voice in all this mess that I haven't really heard from. Well, her and the Adversary, but I don't exactly have her home base in visible walking distance.

"All the same," I say to the figment, "I think that tower is where I'm needed."

She purses her lips. "Miss, do you *need* to be needed? I'm not sure that's what you really want. Do you know what it is that you want? Fata Morgana can help with that."

What an ugly question. *What do I want? Why would I tell you that? Why would I know that?* Love, justice, identity, answers, none of those things matter. I want to not die, I guess, but I'm not telling her that. "I want to speak with Katoptris. I keep hearing her name on everyone's lips, and she might be able to help me. Maybe I can help her. Maybe that'll fix your eyesore."

She sighs. "I doubt it. Wouldn't you rather take a rest? I'm sure you've had a very hard journey. The Lady can wait another night."

Ha. Of course I want to rest. I'm exhausted, mentally and physically, and I want to lie down for a week without getting up. But by then, the world might have ended. "I can rest once I've spoken with the Lady. Thank you, really, but I insist. I can sightsee later."

She smiles at me like I'm a fool, but she doesn't try to stop me. "Of course. I do hope you find what you're looking for." She bows and returns to her walk, off to play out the rest of her artificial routine.

I start walking.

The other figments don't get in my way, though a few reach out every block or so offering to help me or feed me or show me a good time. I ignore them all, my mood souring with each pleasant voice.

These figments belong to Prevara, my enemy. They might be the same figments that Homura encountered when she visited the city, when she sought Katoptris and learned the ugly truth about why this world's precious Lady vanished from their prayers. Prevara did something to Katoptris, though I don't know what, and has been trying to cement her control—or its, or theirs, I'm not really sure—over Katoptris and the world around the tower. First the figments that watch the city, then the Beasts of the Labyrinth . . . and at least one figment of Sanctuary.

Lena. My chest tightens at the memory of the cute girl who flirted with me and offered up her neck. I wanted to know her, but Prevara used her to taunt me. Not that she was real to begin with. I know that she wasn't real.

No one real would ever like me.

I curl my lip. *Are you really getting sad over this? You're pathetic. You knew it was too good to be true, both times. You have no one to blame but yourself for getting attached to them. You should be used to being alone.*

I know, but that doesn't mean I want to hear it. *I wanted to enjoy myself. I wanted a fantasy. Don't I deserve something for all the pain?*

Of course I don't. Pain doesn't buy pleasures. It's just pain.

I force out a heavy breath and run my hands through my hair. I hate being alone with my thoughts, if you can really call this *alone*. That's another thing I hate. *Hate, hate, hate. Is that the Homura in me, or is that just me?*

What does that even mean? What does "you" mean? You're a copy. You're a splinter, like the others. Your memories aren't yours, your personality isn't yours, nothing is yours. All just fractal lenses. What are you, if not the same as them?

Maybe I'm a fail state, like Homura called Urna. I mean, I keep failing.

I failed with the fae, I failed with the imp, I failed at being a demon, and I failed at finding love. Maybe failure is the piece of her that she carved off when she made me. Gobbet Failure. Gobbet Loser. The little gobbet that couldn't.

I trudge through the streets of an alien city with heavy limbs and heavier thoughts. The sun beats down on my body like hammer blows, the heat so oppressive I feel buried in it. I am gristle on steel, baking beneath a lamp. I am a half-dead thing, stillborn yet moving.

And I'm afraid. I'm lost and afraid and a failure. Loathing and fear swirl around my head and gestate greater evils. I know this dark spiral, it's carried me down to the pit of despair so many times before, but most of those memories aren't really mine.

She gave me those memories. She gave me this disease. She made me weak and small and now she's laughing at how pathetic I am. I feel empty, like a shattered cup.

The smell of warm pastries alerts me to an altogether different emptiness: hunger, boiling in my stomach. A cold, clinical part of my brain overrides the darkening malaise.

Insufficient intake of food and water impairs normal function and accelerates negative ideation. We should eat.

Right. I haven't eaten or drunk anything in some number of hours, and I might be operating on human biology again. Eat, drink, then ideate.

It isn't hard to find a place to eat, several of them within immediate eyesight as soon as I start looking. Cafe, restaurant, eatery, etc., all of them open for business and highly aromatic. I doubt they'll even care I don't have money, just like in Sanctuary, if this place really is one giant lotus-eater trap.

I wander to the nearest shop, not really paying attention to details, but then I stop before the door, staring at my reflection in the window.

The pointy ears are still there, and the teeth, and the pale skin. The hair is longer by a few inches and dirty blonde instead of dark, but that's not really the change I'm stuck on; my eyes are different. My left eye is bright red, just as I remade it, but my right eye has turned golden and cat-like. It's Cheshire's eye. I've traded my right eye for Cheshire's.

What does that mean? What have you done, Demiurge?

It's unnerving seeing myself with my kinda-ex-girlfriend's eye, but if I'm being honest with myself it barely breaks the top three weirdest things I've seen today. I don't know how I feel about it, but I can live with it.

My outfit changed too, which I'd sort of passively noticed earlier but not actually examined. Red sneakers, faded blue jeans, and a black T-shirt with the words "KISS ME KILL ME" written in bold red. I feel naked without a jacket. My heart locket is there too, the anatomical heart I enchanted what feels like ages ago. *Wonder if it still works.*

The outfit is a stark change from the dark gothic aesthetic that I've been trying to cultivate, but it feels right in a way the schoolgirl getup definitely didn't. Honestly, aside from the locket, it seems like the kind of thing I'd wear normally, much more than what I've been wearing since playing demon. Or, well, normal for the girl I'm based on, I guess.

"A piece of a piece of me," I mutter bitterly at my reflection. "Is this the new us?"

If I rejected everything about me that tasted like her, what would be left that feels like me? I haven't been my own person for even a single second of my miserable existence. If I tried to be the opposite of everything she made me to be, would that Alice be someone new? Or would the very act of inversion keep me defined by her labels? What does freedom mean?

I reach out and touch my reflection, an absent gesture, but when the glass starts to ripple I jerk my hand back—or try to.

The hand in the mirror is grabbing mine.

My reflection is different, still recognizable but now altered and horrific. Her skin is sickly and flaking and terribly cold, her grip like iron. Her eyes are icy blue, blue like Urna's, and her mouth is stitched shut.

The corpse that looks like me jumps out of the mirror and tackles me to the ground. I scream and try to fight her off but she's got both my wrists and

I'm not a demon anymore, my strength is frail and human and laughably underdeveloped.

She keeps me pinned with her knees and one arm, freeing her other hand to pull a knife. A simple blade, clean and lethal. It'll do the job.

And then, before I can even think to try and call up my new magic and teleport away, two beastly claws grab the corpse by the shoulders and fling her away from me.

A familiar face stares down at me—one blue eye, one red—and offers a hand to help me up. My gaze flits over rippling muscle and patches of fur and scale. Changed. A stranger.

"Name's Cheshire," the changeling introduces herself with a grin. "I'm your new bodyguard."

GARDEN OF MEMORIES III

Two monsters test their mettle within a city that doesn't exist. Flag-stones crack, the air shudders, and shadows thicken. And I, unharmed and harmless, vulnerable and frail, am left with thoughts that idly twist.

Hey, gobbet: Do you know I have opinions about aphorisms? Of course you do, you're me! But I'm going to tell you anyways, because I don't care what you think of me and I love the sound of my own voice. That's something we share, you and I, only you hate to hear your nasal tones and I can't stand you in gross volume, but I digress.

My head is full of noise and my body is numb and hollow. Empty, list-less, staring. Quivering meat struck dumb and mute.

Aphorisms are a sucker's game. I hate aphorisms, adages, proverbs, and dictums, and I can barely ever tell them apart! Nonsense, the lot.

The creature that isn't my Cheshire—or might be, might hope to be, please let her be my Cheshire—tries her best to kill a zombie that looks like me if I had blue eyes and worse skin. The corpse-thing dances around swiping claws and gnashing teeth, a long knife in each hand, clad in dark leather that bares midriff and cleavage. The shapeshifter that used to be my girlfriend—might be again, might never be again—keeps herself between me and the enemy, her flesh hardening and growing scales to absorb each dagger strike meant for my soft, defenseless body.

Here's an aphorism for you, an old coat to try on: "You never know what you have until it's gone." Completely inane, right? What an absurd little phrase. As if you didn't know exactly what you were giving up when you made your stupid, selfish demand. You knew what you were throwing away, gobbet. You'd been living it and learning it for almost the entirety of your physical existence. There was more Alice and Cheshire than there had been Alice alone, and you gave it up for . . . what, exactly? For why?

Cheshire's shifting is more complex now, more varied and potent, like when we would merge as one to best our foes. The lithe frame of the girl that tried to seduce me is replaced by a warrior's build, her whole body made into a weapon. She spars against her foe with the joy of child's play and the intensity of an apocalypse, her grin burning across her face and lit up in those mismatched eyes—one red, one blue.

The Demiurge stitched a doll that had no choice but to love you, and you told her to scrap it for parts because you couldn't bear to be loved, couldn't stand the thought of it. Maybe love is a lie and you see right through it, or maybe, just maybe, love is no match for the loathing that whispers in your ear, "No one ever loves me who doesn't want to leave me."

I stand, hollow. I watch, helpless. The song in my head continues to scratch.

Isn't this pathetic, gobbet? Aren't we? Here we are, worthless and powerless, being saved by someone we barely recognize who probably doesn't recognize us. It's life or death out there and here we are getting lost in our head about nonsense and loathing. How typical. How disgusting. Are you ever going to change?

The interplay is faster than I can follow, just blurs of color and thunderclaps of sound. Crumbling stone, shattered glass. A roar of triumph, the tearing of skin. A red haze, a splatter of blood. Then: searing white and blue, a wash of numbing cold that seeps beneath my clothing.

When my sight clears, the zombie is in pieces. Beetles and flies crawl out of the cracked stone beneath the fragmented corpse and begin to feast upon frozen flesh beginning to steam. Cheshire—changed and familiar, beautiful and terrible—looks lightly injured but healing fast, a thin layer of frost upon her body already burning away.

The changeling's breath is heavy, her grin almost manic. She licks her teeth as she straightens out of her combat stance, and when she glances my way she gives me a wink. "Trickiest of the bunch, that one, but I was better. Nice to finally put her down."

Through cloying brain fog and a cacophony of Alice, I try to pull my thoughts together. "You . . . you've fought that thing before? When? What was it? And . . . do you . . . I mean . . . how did you find me?"

"Do you know who I am?" That's the question we should be asking, gobbet, but you're a coward and a fool too stupid to ask. The answer is clear as day, of course, but you can't stand to look at it because you know that it makes you a murderer. As if that mattered.

Cheshire turns her full attention on me, stepping away from the site of her victory. She laughs, and my chest seizes with how *different* she is now. Her carefully chosen outfits are now just tatters of fabric that barely cover skin still furred and scaled despite the absence of immediate danger. Her claws are out, her teeth are sharp, and I even see a barbed tail flicking back and forth behind her. And that red eye—*my* red eye—burns where her golden used to rest.

"We've scrapped," the changeling evades. "I'll tell you the whole story later, once we're somewhere safe. Let's get moving; I'll answer whatever questions I can on the way."

"On the way to where?" I ask, curiosity briefly overcoming dread.

"There's a big fancy clock tower about an hour's trek from here," Cheshire answers quickly. "It's the one place in this supercharged dream bubble that Prevara's pets can't enter, and it's where the Demiurge is going to give us our marching orders for the last stage of this little war with the Emissary."

The Demiurge, our maker and breaker, our doom and our savior. The hand that holds the knife, the will that parts our flesh. Will you run back to her arms, gobbet, to wither beneath her scorn and beg her absolution? Her game is yet to run its course, and she wants you for her star piece. Will you let her lay that curse upon us?

You should, says a second voice, a harder voice. *You don't have the means to take her on, not yet. Don't sacrifice strength for dignity, and don't spurn an opportunity just because you hate the hand that holds it. Only an Intercessor stands a chance at winning the game and breaking her wheel.*

I swallow nervously, tongue heavy with fear and doubt. My hands are trembling—*weakness, can't be showing that*—so I dig my nails into my palms and clench my fists tightly. "Cheshire," I say with an injection of hollow control. "You saved me from a monster, and for that I'm grateful, truly, but I'm feeling a bit too lost to go sprinting off with just a word. I need information, I need to find my bearings, and I need to know: Who—or what—are you, to me?"

Cheshire takes a casual step closer and replies, "All you need to know right now, Miss Intercessor, is that our *mutual employer* sent me here to keep you safe and keep you moving. I'm your bodyguard: your sword and shield, and a second pair of eyes. Beyond that, we can make more personal introductions once you're in a secure location and we're not at constant risk of more zombies like that one bursting out of the woodwork. We don't have much time."

There's an urgency in her voice and in the subtleties of her movement as she draws closer, a tightening of her expression that might indicate sincerity or be another layer of performance, but I can't bring myself to care. Nothing about what she's saying and doing sticks in my brain like those key few words that tell the story I didn't want to hear.

Mutual employer. Miss Intercessor. The words of someone who's never met you before. The words of a new woman. Face it, gobbet: There's not a drop of our girl in her.

She doesn't recognize me at all. She knows who I am, but she doesn't know me. And of course she doesn't, of course she's a stranger, because *that's what I asked for.* I wanted a fair playing field. I—I wanted to do the right thing. It—it *was* the right thing, wasn't it? Didn't I do good?

Or did you wish away your only friend for a few motes of privacy? Did you rid yourself of the only girl to ever show you love for the brittle illusion of just action and righteous course?

It wasn't an illusion! hisses that second voice, a voice quite like Homura's. *Justice is bought in blood and pain. Justice demands sacrifice.*

Sacrifice? What a fancy word for murder.

I'm not a murderer! I'm a hero, damn you.

The girl I liked is dead and I killed her.

Cheshire reaches for my arm and I jerk it away. I try to speak but my throat seizes up.

Careful now, warns Homura. *Don't antagonize her. Play the game as if you buy the rules. Bide your time and wait for the perfect moment. You can't fix anything if you just lash out at the nearest target.*

Fuck that, scorns the first voice. *Are you really going to take this lying down? Look at her, gobbet. Look at her! Are you happy with this? Is this the deal you made?*

Cheshire raises an eyebrow at me. "Hey, I'm not kidding around. We have to *go.*"

Play along. Say what she wants to hear and gather intel.

Spit in her face and tell God you want a refund. Make the Demiurge give you back your tailored doll.

I bite my lip hard enough to draw blood and the bliss of pain brings clarity to chaos. "Then we can go, but not to the clock tower. I need more information before I can plot my next moves, and I am *starving*, so let's walk and talk until we find a place to grab a bite."

It's a reasonable request. A minor detour at worst. My Cheshire would agree to it in a heartbeat. My Cheshire would be happy to talk and eat with me.

My Cheshire is gone. The cat-eared thing staring back at me cocks her head for only a moment before lunging forward and seizing me by the wrists so fast I can't even start to react before she's already caught me in a vise grip. "Yeah, this isn't a negotiation. You can eat once you're safe," she says with a hard new edge to that familiar voice.

Panic streaks down my spine. This isn't the plan. This wasn't supposed to happen. What do I do? I try to pull away from her in desperate futility, but her strength is far beyond my own. I call out to her, voice cracking, "Stop it! What are you—"

Her grip tightens and pain shoots through my arms and I gasp and shudder and freeze. My wrists, she's going to break my wrists, she's going to squeeze and squeeze and my bones will crack and pop and push through my skin and the blood will run rivers down my arms and I'll lose my hands and it'll hurt, hurt, hurt, I don't want it to hurt.

Cheshire murmurs, low and menacing, "It wouldn't take much to shatter those pretty wrists, frail as they are. And I know for a fact you don't have the strength to stop me, and you *won't* until you come back to your master. Do you like being able to move your hands?"

She relaxes her grip, but just a touch, just enough I can think and breathe. I'm starting to shake again, worse this time, legs and arms and teeth. "Wh-what are y-you doing, I th-thought you were supposed to be my—"

Squeeze again, her hands on my wrists, spiking pain in bruised muscle and aching bone, vulnerable bone, so close to breaking. She's going to break my wrists. She's actually going to break my wrists, I can't believe she's actually going to break my wrists, this can't be happening.

"P-please, please stop, this is—this is insane, this is insane, what kind of bodyguard cripples their—"

Tighter, tighter, tighter, her strong hands crushing my delicate limbs, her strength about to annihilate me and take away my everything and it hurts, it hurts, it hurts so much. I whimper and start to cry, tears streaking down my pathetic, blubbering face even as she releases a bit of tension again and grants me that false reprieve.

"You'll live," she tells me dismissively. "You'll heal. So am I going to carry you to the Demiurge with broken wrists—and maybe ankles or kneecaps, your whole *spine* if you keep fussing—or are you going to be a good girl and come along quietly?"

I whimper for a second time, barely vocal now. It hurts. It hurts and I hate it and a real hero isn't supposed to be this weak and spineless and frail but all I want is to make the pain go away. I don't care about standing up for myself, I don't care about causes or goals or grand machinations. I just want the suffering to end.

Would she really do it? Cheshire's eyes smolder, hard and uncompromising, and I know with absolute certainty that this is not an empty threat. She will break me if I defy her. She will carry me in pieces if that's what it takes. *Why?*

"Why are you doing this?" I whisper, and when her grip starts to tighten again I cry, "I'm not resisting! Stop, please, you—you win. I'll come with you. I won't resist. Just please . . . please tell me why."

Cheshire tilts her head, contemplative for a moment. Then, in a single flourish, she scoops me into her arms, tenses her legs, and leaps onto the nearest rooftop. I squeak at the sudden change in heights. As she bounds from building to building over the streets of Fata Morgana, I cling to her like a drowning woman clings to wreckage, the world below us passing in a blur.

I shut my eyes tight to block out the terrifying imagery and clutch my kidnapper with all the strength I can muster, more scared of being dropped from these heights to smear against the pavement than I am of what awaits me in the Demiurge's domain. I'm such a coward.

"To answer your question," Cheshire says blithely as she leaps and dashes across the city skyline, "I'm doing this because it's the only game in town. You're with the Demiurge or you're a dead woman walking. And I'd do anything for one more day of being alive. Wouldn't you?"

I don't have anything to say to that. I can't. So I cling to her in silence, miserable and crying and completely helpless. Just a weak, powerless, ordinary nobody.

Back in Sanctuary, in the maze, chased by hunters and bound up in a duel, I ran all the way to the rotten core of my soul. In the very core of my being I found a scared little girl crying over her dead mother, and I knew what that made me: a slave to fear. An eternal victim, terrified and trauma-tized and broken and never, ever amounting to more.

I thought that if I took Cheshire's hand and forged myself into a knife that cuts as it bleeds, then I could change that scared, crying core. I thought I could be more than what I was made to be, more than I was painted.

Was I wrong? I don't feel any stronger. I don't feel any different than who I've always been at my lowest, at my weakest, my truest. I will always be what I am in the cold, lonely dark.

You didn't even keep to that plan, the cold voice from before insists in my mind. *You had Cheshire's hand, her loyalty, her immortal soul suborned to yours, and you threw it away. Is it any surprise what happened next? You forged yourself into a knife and let the edge blunt and chip and rust. Your hasty scaffolding crumbled away before it could make even an ounce of change to the wretched husk beneath. You sacrificed everything, and for what?*

Tell me, gobbet: Is this the deal you made?

No. "This isn't what I wanted," I whisper through the tears.

Cheshire drops from her latest perch and slams into the ground, the shock of it running through me an instant before she dumps me like a sack of bricks onto the hard street. The breath is knocked from my lungs and I curl up, gasping for air as soon as I can move the right muscles, wincing and cringing and hoping desperately that I haven't broken a rib.

My vision is still spinning when I hear a new voice, another familiar voice: the voice of Nyarlathotep, the Lucid Demiurge, the Toymaker and Soul-Sculptor, the architect of all my woes.

She says, tone sickly sweet and mocking, "Why, that's very unfortunate to hear! What *did* you want, darling? If I've gotten it wrong, I'll be happy to correct your mistake."

A tower looms overhead, a twisted thing of brick and marble and con-crete like three buildings smashed together with no concern for aesthetic or integrity. A giant clock face sits embedded high up the tower, all hands set to twelve and unmoving.

From the arched entrance to the clock tower hangs a mannequin strung up by the wrists and bleeding from eyes and mouth and holes in its chest and throat. The doll is smiling, its lips cracked at the edges.

"If I recall correctly, which I do," she says to my disoriented silence, "you asked me to make something up for your silly little girlfriend. So I did. You don't like this draft?"

A bit of fury blooms in my heart and tears through all the pain and fear I'm drowning in. "I told you to free her! I wanted her without your fucking chains! *This* isn't that! Where is the *real* Cheshire?"

The doll sighs. "I see it didn't sink in. Let me give you a more hands-on demonstration. Cheshire, push her in."

The changeling immediately grabs me, lifts me to my feet, and pushes me through the archway into another world. I fall through time and space and am lost as once before, trapped in a dream within a dream and before the watching eyes.

In a town in a world never born and never ending, there is a street where every building is a crooked, lanky shadow.

Night-black skyscrapers with golden window-eyes claw at the sky's violet expanse and choke the stars with smoke. The street below is a slash of trailing white, pure like a lily, a single line of snow unbroken and untouched. The gawking crowds are smudges of brown and gray with static-scribble faces that watch without eyes and laugh without mouths. The buildings twitch and writhe on the edge of sight, always still when you turn to look.

In the distance, both before and behind, the horizon narrows to a single point of white enclosed by ceaseless black; this is a street that has no end and no beginning, for endings are a sin and beginnings are a lie. If you walked for nine hundred years and ninety-nine days down the solemn street toward its distant horizon you would come no closer to the nearest gawker or the pitch-black tenement that looms just out of arm's reach. Gently, softly, snow falls between the cracks in the roof of the world.

All is silent. All is still. All this is true and none of it real.

In the middle of the street, where there is only snow and air, a door opens and a woman steps through. The door closes behind her and vanishes with only a hint of what lay inside: a single glimpse of sterile lights and metal tables.

Sharp eyes scour the world. Teeth gnaw on lips wet with blood. The woman whose name is secret to her children wears the same lack of outfit as she did before, nothing but a gore-stained lab coat open to expose her flesh-less skeleton. She is unbothered by the falling snow and the chill of blowing wind, with not a hint of pink on her face or hands.

"There is a body lying in the street," she says, and thus there is. "It is the body of a girl with blue eyes, now glassy, stripped down to her smallclothes as red as the blood that spills down her side and stains the snow beneath her, bled out and half nude. Her skin is pale and dead and beautiful."

The corpse is painted as the woman speaks, detail clarifying from the muddy suggestion of human form. The dead thing is red and cream and two shining pools of lifeless blue.

The woman taps her chin and muses, "No, not quite dead, not yet. She clings to her last breath, desperate for another nine. This girl burns with life, has burned with life, will burn for life. She knows me, her Lucid Demiurge, and so she fears me, but she owes me and she needs me and she will bend for me as I wish." The woman snaps her fingers. "Scene."

The dead girl gasps for breath, blue eyes wide and panicking. Shivering fingers clutch at torn and bleeding flesh. She is born; she is dying. She cries out, "Please, please save me, please! I don't want to die! It hurts, make it stop, make the pain go away!"

The woman sits down in the snow and, as she cradles the dying girl in her arms, she is transformed: Gone is the lab coat, replaced by flowing robes of brightest gold, and her face is concealed beneath a white mask that bleeds black tar from its crooked eyes and slanted mouth.

"Cheshire," she names the dying girl, "you must tell me—and tell me true, for I will brook no deception from the breath of my lungs—which do you fear more: the pain, or its cessation? For if you fear the pain the greater, then your peace is one breath from settled. But if your terror comes in endings, know that pain is all I offer."

The girl coughs, bloody and shuddering. "Why, my lord? Why must I suffer?"

The woman takes the girl's hand with a surgeon's care and gently breaks her first finger. "Pain is how we learn, for the stove is no danger until you burn your hand upon it."

A second finger snaps, a loving mutilation. "The value of each meal is marked not in satiety but in the hunger that it wards."

A third, bone cracked and flesh torn. "Pain is how we grow, for love's great lie is only known when the knife is felt hilt-deep."

Her fourth finger, rent with delicate force. "If you would live, then you must bleed, for the body that bleeds not is but a doll of painted clay. This I teach you. Show me you understand."

Hesitant, fearful, dying, the girl takes her final finger and bends it to its breaking. She cries and cries and cries, her tears freezing in the snow.

"Good. Tears are good. Now I ask again, and you will answer, for I have placed it in your heart: the pain or its cessation?"

"Death," Cheshire whispers. "I fear death more. Save me, please."

"I shall. And you will give me all of you. Say this and make it true."

And Cheshire says, "I will give you all of me."

"You will bleed for me. You will burn for me. You will smile for me."

And Cheshire says, "I will bleed for you. I will burn for you. I will smile for you."

"You were mine, are mine, will be mine, then and now till stars are scattered dust."

And Cheshire says, "I was yours, am yours, will be yours, then and now till stars are scattered dust."

The woman smiles behind her mask and the dying girl lets out her breath. With care and love, the master of the worlds plucks an eye from Cheshire's head and lowers a golden copy in its place. The Demiurge rises, and the body of the girl sinks into the snow to blossom and be changed.

The woman walks down the street, the crowd parting to bow and kneel. Eight times she lays to rest the body of the girl. Eight times a life is spent. Eight times the words are whispered. The world blinks.

In a forest in a world never born and never ending, there is a glade where every tree is a crooked, lanky shadow.

Coal-black roots creep over an endless field of white while golden leaves flutter in the breeze. The sky is gray and stormless. No hunters tread this wood, no rabbits or deer prance beneath this canopy. There is nothing here but death and memory. Gently, softly, snow falls between the cracks in the roof of the world.

All is silent. All is still. All this is true and none of it real.

"In the dark and the cold, I found you," the Demiurge proclaims. "With dying breath, you begged my aid."

The blue-eyed girl lies bleeding in the snow, mauled and left for dead. She looks up at the white-masked figure and with ragged breath she begs, "Save me, please."

The woman tilts her head. "Why?" she asks.

"Because I will give you all of me," the girl that will be Cheshire pleads with her master. "I will bleed for you. I will burn for you. I will smile for you. I was yours, am yours, will be yours, then and now till stars are scattered dust."

The Demiurge lifts Cheshire from the snow, blood staining golden robes. "So it shall be. You have died nine times, will die nine times, and on your ninth I will take you and you will become my vessel, as you have always been. This is your name and your nature."

And snow takes the world in endless freezing white.

When the blizzard passes, I find myself standing in a room that might pass for the interior of a clock tower if you didn't look too closely. There are great gears of brass, chimes and whistles, and all manner of thrumming pipes and exposed wiring, but everything isn't quite right. Pipes melt into gears that sprout gauges with symbols from three languages, and nowhere in this confusing mess of metal and glass and rubber is there any sense of purpose or design.

Though I passed through an archway, there are no doors behind me. There are no stairs or ladders leading up, either, but there are windows looking out; the world outside is kaleidoscopic and celestial like rivers of burning stars that glitter in all the colors unnatural.

In the center of the room is an autopsy table of cold, sterile steel, and lying on that table with arms pressed together is a girl with feline ears and glassy blue eyes. Her open hands cup a bloody eyeball, its iris crimson.

The Demiurge is nowhere to be seen, but I know she's here. Watching. Listening. Mocking me. I open my mouth to speak and her voice intrudes first:

"Now you surely see, so lay to rest your pining for a girl that never was. The changeling is and always was nothing more than a narrative construct. There is no Platonic form of Cheshire, no deeper essence you might uncover and free from unjust imprisonment; there is only what we make of her by our choices and our readings."

I stare down at the corpse of Cheshire and feel sick to my stomach. "What is this, Nyara? What is the *point* of this?"

Her whisper comes to my ear: "The point, dear one? Why, it can be whatever you like! Violence or love, horror or the erotic, empathy or self-loathing; you are always free to create your own meaning. In fact, I quite *insist* that you do, else this will come to very little. Just take my hand and tell me how you feel."

I clench my fists and hiss, "Enough of this! Enough!" I brace myself against the autopsy table and squeeze my eyes shut. "For once in my life I am *tired* of debating philosophy. You've dragged me around through torment after torment, you've baited me with prizes only to rip them away, and now I am *done* with all your games. I want answers. I want *agency*. And if you refuse me, if you keep toying with me like this, I—I will . . ."

What can you say to threaten a god? What can you deny the lord of the universe?

I curl my lip, sneer a little, and say, "I will sit here and do nothing and I will *bore you to death*."

The noises of the clock tower stop. Gears grind to a halt. Pipes cease to thrum. Whistles and chimes wind down.

Silence. A pregnant pause. A trillion grains of sand spilling down the hourglass. The second hand of a clock going tick . . . tick . . . tick . . . stop.

Stillness is like a kind of poison. It's like being buried alive. When all stimuli are denied you, when you are left with nothing but the noise inside your head, it can be a kind of hell. No wonder thoughts will wander, if only to escape the dead and dreary room.

But daydreams can only distract for so long. Eventually you have to acknowledge the physical realities of the situation you're in. The situation you put yourself in.

Hunger and thirst are horrible things.

Fire is more painful in its singular moment, but it kills with relative haste. Denied a meal but finding water, the human body can survive a few months, or rather it can die that slowly. With neither food nor water, a week would be stretching it, but I wouldn't worry; a gracious god will always grant another drop to drink.

It'll go slow, and it'll feel even slower. Your fat will burn and your muscles will wither, and then you'll shrivel up to skin and bone. What starts as simple pangs quickly transforms into need into emptiness into agony, and that pain will stick with you as the weeks turn into months.

Your senses will dull, mind clouded and foggy. Pop goes a neuron, then another, atrophying en masse. Every cell in your body will start to die, one by one, and the engine of your biology will fail to produce replacements. You can feel yourself getting slower, weaker, dumber, frailer.

Can you imagine what you'll lose, piece by piece, as hours turn to days turn to weeks? Can you imagine how little will be left when I come to cradle you in my arms and whisper your salvation? Will you remember why you were resisting? Will you have the strength to become anything but my slave?

Or will I leave you there to die in a tomb of your own making?

"Speak for me, dear one. Tell me you'll be mine."

I gasp and shudder as the Demiurge releases her hold on my senses. I fall to my knees and heave, but nothing rises from my empty gut. I shiver. I remember. I relive. I die a hundred slow and unforgiving deaths.

There's so little fight left in me. I just want to give in.

Then lie down like a dog and let her have her way with you. Is that really what you are? Are you truly so spineless?

She's playing a trick, Homura warns. *Think: If she really has as much control as she's making it seem, if she really wins that gamble, then why is she flaunting her hand? Why taunt you with the outcome when she could just play it out?*

But what if we're wrong, whispers a third voice, a soft and trembling Reska, *and she gets angry with us? What if she isn't bluffing? That's too big a risk, too awful a fate.*

She needs us, Homura insists. *She needs us more than we need her, and all of this stagecraft is to hide that fatal weakness. It has to be a bluff. She can't rig the game as well as she pretends, trust me.*

Don't believe her lies, hisses Reska. *Don't make the same mistake I did.*

Ignore the lamb, dismisses that first voice, cold and cruel and so like my own. *The murderer has a point, gobbet. Use your brain and actually think about what's happening. That thing can reach inside your brain and place whatever thoughts it likes, so why is she still asking? Why does she ever ask? Why is this a choice?*

"Because it has to be," I whisper.

I know what I need to do and it's hard, it takes so much and I wish I could lie down and sleep instead, but I can't. I won't. Not after all I've sacrificed to get this far.

I swallow, mouth dry, and rise from the floor with shaky hands and wobbly knees. My tongue is leaden and it takes me three tries, but I get the words out. I give her my answer.

"I know you're strong, Nyara. I know you're more than me. You're more than I'll ever be, right? You can crush me like a bug. You can pull me on your strings and make me sing and dance. You can put me in a box of nightmares and shake me around for a billion years till I come out crying for your mercy, sure, that's mostly true. But there has to be a point. There has to be a reason. Because there—because there is a *purpose* to me."

I laugh, wretched and manic. The laughter bubbles up as strong as it ever has. My chest hurts and my cheeks strain as I laugh and laugh and laugh, unable to stop. What a joke this all is, that it all comes back to that tea party in the chaos of my soul.

The first time I sat down and really conversed with Cheshire, in the raw moments after our covenant, we talked about significance. We talked about the search for human meaning in a cold and uncaring universe, but this universe cares very deeply; this world has a maker and her touch is known, her gaze made clear. This is a place where all things have a purpose.

The cat called us all toys in the toybox, the victims of a great game with only one player and we the hapless pawns, but she was wrong. I've seen the truth, or at least a glimpse of it. I've seen the room outside of time where the surgeon works upon her red material. I know my purpose, and I know that I'm not a toy at all.

I'm an experiment.

"There is a purpose to me," I repeat. "You made me for a reason. You made everything in that room for a reason, every gobbet of meat you cut off from whatever the hell you are. You're asking a question, and you know you can't find the answer if you just *cheat*, so you have to play by a set of rules. God ties her own hands. You could have made me another puppet like so many of your creations, but you didn't, and that means my freedom is a *requirement* for whatever you're trying to do here. It has. To be. A *choice.*"

The gears and pipes all hum to life and the bleeding doll claps politely, freshly appeared on the other side of the table. "Correct! Very good! We'll make an Intercessor out of you yet."

My relief at not being tortured for months is immediately soured. "I told you—"

"Yes, yes, the details of the deal." The doll waves a hand dismissively. "Listen, I understand that the deal hasn't been to your liking. You feel like you lack agency. I can fix that. I want to fix that. That's what this is all for." She gestures at the cat lying cold on the slab.

I'm taken aback. "What?"

The Demiurge licks her lips—dolls should not have tongues, that is so weird—and paces around the table, circling me. "Agency. That's the word you used, but I prefer 'control' as our guiding beacon. That's been the real issue with Cheshire from the very start. You can't trust her because you don't control her, like you don't control anything in your life. That would have been true even without my interference. Your trust issues were never confined to Cheshire, Alice; you thought about killing Dante, might have murdered Esha if it suited you, treated every soul in that city with ruthless suspicion. Most of all the girl fighting hardest to keep you safe. No matter how many times Cheshire showed her love or proved her loyalty, no matter what story she told you, no matter how hard she pleaded for it, you could never really trust her. Oh, you tried, or you told yourself you tried, and perhaps that's to be admired. But deep down, you know it was all a lie."

"That's—" I cut myself off, hesitating to refute her words. *That's not true, is it? I changed! I took the risk, I chose to trust.*

"Did you really? Then, my darling Alice, why ever did you *betray* that trust?"

I flinch. It wasn't a betrayal. I was saving her!

"Because you knew better than her? Because you were right and her own desires were wrong, is that it? Because you didn't trust her? Listen to yourself: You're still calling it a *risk* to trust, but *trust is not a gamble.* Trusting someone doesn't mean treating them like a half-loaded gun pointed at your heart."

No. No, that's not right, that's not true, I'm not. I wasn't. I—I want to scream, it's in my bones and building, I can't stand it. "What are you offering?" I snarl at my maker to keep the static at bay.

The doll gently lifts one of my hands and presses a scalpel between my fingers.

The Demiurge smiles at me. "I'm offering the chance to take control for the first time in your life—your life here, and the life you remember that never was. Take control, Alice."

I stare at her, uncomprehending, not wanting to understand the implication of what she's suggesting. The horror only mounts, and the fascination.

She sweeps her hands at the still form of the girl I almost loved. "The clay is fresh, your tools laid out. You can sculpt a new Cheshire, a better Cheshire, a Cheshire that you can *trust.* Shape her as I shaped her, carve her as I carved her, create her as I created her. Alice and Cheshire, together again, but this time by *your* intent, by *your* rules, by *your* design."

Cheshire, my Cheshire, cut and molded and made anew. An act of insane violation. An act of absolute control. All I've ever wanted, or dreamed I might want. All I've ever feared, or convinced myself so.

"By this act, claim your seat as my Intercessor. And with Cheshire at your side as she always should have been, I am absolutely certain that you will become Royalty of this world and *annihilate* that lowly priest of worms. Wield the knife, Alice. Make the first cut, and all the rest will follow."

I stare at the scalpel in my hands and marvel at its edge. Could this simple, dreadful, beautiful thing truly shape a life? Could I create my own Cheshire? Should I? What would I become?

What are you even saying? Reska's voice sobs in my mind. *Nothing is worth that kind of monstrosity!*

Don't be naive, Homura derides. *This is exactly the advantage we need.*

There's a flash of pain between my temples, the doll flickers out of sight, and then Reska and Homura are standing in the room with me.

Homura, hard-eyed, hand resting on the hilt of her weapon. Reska, despondent, head in her hands. Both as they were the last time I saw them, in my dreams, in the dark beneath the castle. A night of deep betrayal.

"Heroes make hard decisions. We have to be willing to use any tool, pay any price, so long as it gets us closer to our goal. When the stakes are raised this high, *winning* is all that matters."

Reska shakes her head and cries, "How can you say that? It doesn't matter what we use it for, a tool like this would stain us far beyond salvation. It can't be love if it isn't a choice. Didn't you tell me you believed in justice?"

"There is no justice except at the end of my blade!" Homura snarls. "No justice under the rule of that tyrant, no justice in the billions she's tortured! The ends will always justify the means."

Reska flinches, but she presses on. "The means will always shape the ends! What use is the death of one tyrant if the next is twice as cruel? Is it justice to trade one monster for another, and the throne red with blood? Was that your justice when you pierced my heart?"

Pain flashes across Homura's face, chased by resolve. "I did what I had to! The consequences for the world—"

"And what about the consequences for us?" Reska's voice is raw and full of heartbreak. "I trusted you. I loved you."

"Do you really think I didn't feel the same?" Homura whispers hoarsely. "Did you think I didn't care?"

"Then why? Why, why, why?"

"Because one will never outweigh infinity." Iron conquers heartsblood and Homura turns back to me. "Use the blade. Break the wheel. Save us all."

There's a surreal reverie to the scene, to the sight of the girls from my dreams now clad in flesh and silk. I don't know what to think. I don't know who to believe. I don't know why both arguments ring hollow.

I look at Homura and I still feel the sting of betrayal and the deep unease of trying to parse a liar's words. I remember the moments we shared that weren't really mine. I see the fire in her eyes and I feel it as my own. I know the spirit of rebellion and the hatred of injustice imparted by my glimpse into Homura's beating heart.

Am I a hero? I don't feel like one.

I look at Reska and she's right in front of me, pleading with hands clasped, sorrow and terror in her eyes. "Please don't do this," she begs. "Don't be a monster. Don't murder the girl you love."

For a single moment, my hands are red with her blood as I pull my blade from the hole in her chest. The stench of it is thick in the air, rust-scent clogging my nose. Murderer. I am murdering this girl and it will be worth it, she promised it was worth it, it has to be worth it or I should have driven that blade into my own throat instead and spared this world my every stolen breath. What have I done? What did she make me do?

Then I'm staring at her face, no blood to be found, but I can still smell the slaughter and I remember what I did. What she did.

Monster.

I back away, horror finally eclipsing fascination, and I stumble and trip and hit the flagstones outside the tower. I'm breathing too much, too hard, hyperventilating. What was I about to do? What was I thinking? Who am I?

We, whispers the cold, familiar voice, *are a reckless coward and a clever fool. We are a liar pretending to be a hero. We seek victimhood in fear of hunger. We are Veseryn, just as we were named. It's time we admitted what we really want. It's time to be a monster. Go back into that room and claim our prize.*

"No. No, that's not who I am!" I shout at the empty air. I stumble to my feet and away from the tower, back into the city, anywhere but here.

Admit what you want and take it! Forget love, forget justice, and take control, or you will die a powerless liar.

I start running. I sprint through the streets of Fata Morgana with only the great glass tower for a guiding light. I run and Veseryn laughs.

And then a red ribbon wraps around my throat and the world goes black.

INTERLUDE

ONCE & FUTURE I

W ell, that's not promising."

As we arrive at the entrance to Vaylin's commandeered convention hall, we find someone else has beaten us there.

I poke and prod at the corpses of unfortunate puppets torn apart and left to rot. Glassy eyes stare past me while unmoving limbs point at nothing in particular. *Were you a friend of Bashe?* I ask the nearest carcass. *Did you feel pain? Or did Vaylin rip that out first?*

The demon's pets are the only victims I can see, and I don't have the faintest clue how old the bodies are or in what manner they were killed. I'm intrigued by the mystery, but more than that I'm wary of what's waiting for us deeper inside.

"I should really invest in some information-gathering spells," I mutter to Cheshire. "That is, unless you can tell me how these things ate dirt."

Cheshire curtsies with a wink. "Your wish is my command, Master, and I'm always happy to be of service. Though, really, if you spent a bit of time practicing your sight you'd be able to gather that intel yourself."

"Ah, but then what would I use you for, pet?" I give her a scratch behind the ears as the changeling turns her mismatched eyes on the scattered bodies, the gold and blue glinting beautifully beneath the nighttime streetlamps.

Dante keeps a wide berth of the grisly scene, looking sick to his stomach already. "This is awful. Could this . . . could this have been done by Averrich? Before you killed him, I mean." He says that so awkwardly, the reluctant hero. It pricks my skin, but I'm not going to make an issue of it right now.

"It's possible," I muse. "I had assumed his second key fragment came from the necromancer, but maybe he rushed the demon instead. He probably had the firepower to take her on, though I'd be surprised if he came away from that fight without heavy casualties." I frown at the carnage before us. "No bolts or burns, though. The wolf could have done it, maybe, but why send her alone? Feels unlikely."

"The timing's wrong, too," verifies Cheshire. "There's violence soaking the air, and it's fresh; the slaughter was recent. *Very* recent, at that: This happened after your throne duel."

My frown deepens. "Which means the duel might have been the trigger, but we're missing a culprit. The only remaining key holder not in our little alliance is Vaylin herself. It would be suicidally shortsighted for Esha to make a power grab when we're already offering her a best outcome, unless she really doesn't trust us to keep our end of things. A rogue Noble breaking the rules? A move by the Beast?"

Cheshire catches my eye. Though her lips don't move, her voice whispers in my ear, "Perhaps Avaya is trying to sweeten the pot. If she offers Vaylin on a platter, we're incentivized to offer her better terms in the new order we create. Or whatever it is she wants out of us."

But could she really do all this by herself? And, if this is her doing . . . are we happy with this outcome? Dante still has one wish left in the chamber, and I was really hoping to make him burn that wish on Vaylin. We still might need to kill that boy.

Dante looks past us with an uncertain look on his face. "Alice, do we really need to go in there? Can't we just report back to Esha?"

"Of course we're going in!" I snap without thinking. *I need to win. I need that power.* I wince at my outburst and rub my forehead. "Think, Dante: If this is a new threat, we need to chase it down before it can come for the Myriad. If Vaylin's still in there, we need her key to end the game. Do you think the Nobles will let us bunker down in the temple eating grapes? Do you think the Beast will be satisfied until her game is won? We kill or we die, or we watch everyone in this city be utterly devoured by powers that laugh at everything we've accomplished together. There's no reality where we just walk away now when we are so, *so* close to the endgame."

"Right. Yeah." He falls quiet.

There's a growing itch beneath my skin, and I can't stop my gaze from flicking between all the gory details of this latest massacre. *If this is Avaya's doing and she's waiting for us at the end of this path, is now the time? Is it all going down?* I swallow nervously. *Am I actually ready to kill Dante? I don't know what to do. I . . . I need to win. I need to be powerful. But is murder and betrayal the only path to power?*

And then Cheshire adds a wrinkle: "Master, I think they killed each other."

"What?" I whirl on her. "Is this another Mourner or Reveler?"

She shakes her head. "No, not a trace of those. They just started butchering each other—and themselves. Some of these wounds are self-inflicted."

A sense of dread starts to creep down my spine, but I keep it off my face and force some levity. "Ah, so just a brand-new brain-fucker to deal with. Well, I've gotten pretty good at dealing with mind-affecting bullshit, so if that's their only trick then this next fight should be a cakewalk. Let's go say hello to whoever did this, if they're still inside, or take a closer look at their handiwork if not."

The interior is much worse.

The corpses outside were ugly, sure, but there was no sign of sentiment behind their murder. The bodies and their parts were strewn apart haphazardly, without meaning or intent. Grisly murders, certainly, but just murder.

The corpses inside the structure paint a more visceral picture. Death is made an art form in blood and bone and excrement: a sculpture draped in entrails, a painting smeared with pulped eyes. A few bodies here and there are strung up by ribbon and largely whole, conquests of Vaylin's from before this latest atrocity, but even many of those have been defaced in fresh and particular ways.

Flayed limbs line walkways, stripped of skin and bleeding in shallow pools. Eyeless faces watch from the walls. The stench of blood and offal is so thick in the air that I make the conscious effort to close my sense of smell and taste, and even Cheshire looks a bit disturbed by this charnel house.

Dante suffers the worst of us, of course. The poor boy actually shuts his eyes at one point and follows our footsteps, so horrified by the macabre display that he can't bear to look at it. I help him out with verbal warnings and light nudges whenever he strays too close to a wall or to something he really wouldn't want to step in. I don't blame him for being nauseous.

The path we take is suspiciously linear. In each room of the complex—the interior clearly restructured by Vaylin's servants to form a better fortress—every door but one has been damaged, boarded up, or blocked. That also might have been Vaylin's work, I suppose, but it still feels like we're being herded into a trap.

That graduates from suspicion to certainty when I see the final door.

A curtain of black ink separates us from a room marked in red stencil as Vaylin's throne. The red carpet leading up to the portal is stained with black oil, and more of that oil is smeared on the walls and on the corpses lying to either side. I remember the last time I saw that toxic substance, and it chills me.

I feel black tar coating my brain, ink sluggish in my veins, black ichor dripping from porcelain seams. I try to scream but my lungs bloat with bile. I want to cry, and this I am allowed; black ichor drips down ashen cheeks.

The name of my captor sears itself into my mind like a burning brand: Nyarlathotep, the Lucid Demiurge.

"I can't sense anything through that barrier," Cheshire confides to me. "Do you want me to scout ahead on foot?"

"Hard veto," I answer quickly. "We'll use something more expendable. [Carrion Swarm]."

I send a batch of beetles scurrying through the ominous portal, but I lose contact with my spell the second they're all across. A moment later, nine red butterflies come fluttering back through.

Okay, so we're about to be face-to-face with the Toymaker herself. Lovely. Absolutely splendid. I hate everything about this.

I summon Vorpal to my hand and make three quick slashes at the curtain of ink. It parts for my sword like a scalpel sinking into flesh, but with an ugly slurping sound it pulls back together as soon as the blade isn't touching.

"Nothing for it but to enter," I say coldly. "Dante, we're about to have a nice chat with that 'goddess' who gave you your sword. I don't know why she's here, but we're going to find out."

Conflict tears across Dante's face, but whatever he's about to say is lost as I step through the portal with Cheshire right behind me. A moment later, he follows.

On the other side of the curtain is a tea party.

The room is dark, shadows seeping in the corners, lit by a multitude of candles colored in all the shades of the rainbow. The candles drift through the air, gently bobbing as they burn, and they drip wax without care for what passes below. Above them, dozens of corpses are bound up in red string and ribbon.

The table is long and its cloth is plain white. Five red chairs sit around the table, two to either length and one at the head, each plush and patterned with pink flowers. Only two of the chairs are occupied, and the other three are pushed out.

All manner of fine china has been scattered across the table. Large plates host colorful mush and exotic shapes like a child's idea of dinner, while dainty teacups are chipped and cracked and overflowing with black tar.

Avaya'ari is tied to the nearest chair on the left side, her four arms wrapped in ribbon and her mouth stitched shut. The imp's hooves have been tied together, her tail is tied in knots, and her wings have been stretched and stapled to the back of the chair. Her black sword rests on the table in front of her.

At the head of the table sits a figure I must assume to be Vaylin Kirinal, and she is clearly being possessed by the Demiurge.

Vaylin looks largely as I've seen her depicted by others: an azure-skinned woman with red body-stitching, curving horns, and heaps of golden jewelry. Her lips are black and her dress is lacy and white, and there's something almost childish about the smug expression on her face.

But her eyes are different: The white dots are gone, now turned completely pitch, and ink drips from her tear ducts and from the corners of her mouth. Black veins trace across her face and down her arms, pulsating at irregular intervals.

The Demiurge smiles at me with Vaylin's face, her presence unmistakable. Ghostly hands squeeze my heart, and it takes an effort of will to control my breathing even though I don't need to breathe anymore.

"Alice! Dante! It's so good to see you both."

Vaylin's voice is wicked and mocking as she claps at our arrival, puppeteered by the Crawling Chaos. Her movements are jerky and sharp, as if she really were held up by strings.

I approach the table with an unimpressed grimace that belies the nervous pounding of my rabbit heart and the seething malice in my veins. "Nyarlathotep. I can't say the same. Why are you here?"

Dante steps up beside me, but something's off about him: He's looking around with an expression of wonder, not horror, and when he makes eye contact with Vaylin, he gives an awkward bow. "Goddess. Your, um, Grace?"

Vaylin laughs and waves a hand in his direction. "No need for such formality, my brave knight. You've earned an earnest audience. Call me Albaoth or Gremory."

I narrow my eyes at their exchange. "What are you showing him, Toymaker?"

Dante glances at me in confusion. "What do you mean?"

I keep my gaze locked on the demon puppet as I tell him, "Right now, I'm seeing another scene of horror. An eerie tea party, corpses on the ceiling, and Vaylin Kirinal with black tar dripping from her eyes and mouth."

He blinks in surprise. "Wait, really? It looks like the star ocean to me, and the checkerboard tile. The bleeding doll is on her throne, and the air is filled with golden lights."

"None of that is real," I warn him. "She's deceiving you."

The Demiurge clicks Vaylin's tongue. "Tut tut, Alice. Even now you place no value in poor Dante's perspective. I had hoped you could learn something from him, but it was always a naive hope. In the end, you heed the call of a darker path."

The prickling beneath my skin sharpens and I freeze. *What is she after? What game is she playing?* "Don't twist my words."

"Who's twisting?" she says with a smile. "We both know the truth. We both know what you think of him, and what you're really after."

My sense of danger spikes. "Why are you even here, Demiurge?"

Vaylin spreads her hands. "To give my chosen a warning, of course. I must give my champion the tools he needs to save this world."

This isn't right. Something is very wrong here. "How can you do that?" I press. "What rules have been broken that allow intervention? What scales are you balancing? If you can indiscriminately slaughter everyone out there and make a puppet out of Vaylin, what did you ever need *us* for?"

I spare a quick glance at Dante, hoping this will reach him. To my relief, he *does* furrow his brow and look askance at the demon—or to his eyes, the doll. "That's a good point."

The Demiurge laughs again. "Oh, that one's easy to answer: Vaylin broke her word. Or should I say, her divine oath."

"Wait, what? I thought those were inviolate."

"Oh, they *can* be broken . . . but the consequences, as you've seen, are quite dire. Vaylin forswore her promise to Avaya, a promise made under Azathoth's stars, and that opened the door for quite a bit more direct action than is otherwise allowed. Now all her strings are mine to pull, and her soul is right where it belongs . . . and it also means I can give you *this* freely."

She holds out a hand and the glowing key fragment appears above her outstretched palm. It floats over to Dante and fades into him. *Out of reach. Part of her plan.*

I bite back bile and try to stay calm. "Dante, we need to be very careful. You can't trust anything she says. Everything wrong with this world is *her* fault. She's not a benevolent goddess, she's a cruel Demiurge."

He looks at me with doubt in his eyes. "How are you so certain of that? What has she done beside help us?"

Vaylin sighs, and the Demiurge looks directly at me. "Don't you think you've misled Dante enough, Alice?"

I bristle and spit at her, "I've done no such thing! You're the one playing games!"

She turns back to the boy with the sword and tells him, "My warning is this, Dante: Maven Alice means you harm. She plots to murder you, seize the key, and attain the glass shard that she might corrupt to serve her will without need of sacrifice or inhibition. She has no intention of saving *any-one* in the Labyrinth, for all she has ever craved is power."

The tension in my body is near to boiling, and it takes all my control to keep my voice from shaking as I plead with Dante, "Don't listen to her, please. She's trying to turn you against me. You know I'd never do that."

He looks more confused than shocked or horrified, which is a mercy, but the Demiurge isn't done. She adds, "Of course, I don't make this accusa-tion without *proof.* Please, look upon the scene yourself."

Wait, what? Oh no. Before I can object, the world around us ripples and blurs, and then we're looking at an all-too-familiar scene.

Avaya'ari leans against the safety rail, one hand patting the vacant Thir-teen. "The Machinist is fallen, and the alliance dissolves. You know Averrich will strike soon, and I'm confident you'll defeat him . . . but what happens next? Have you made your choice?"

I look out on the city from our elevated vantage point. A place of misery. A hollow ruin, hiding behind a lively facade. Most of the people here aren't even people, and the only faction with an ounce of moral fiber is led by a liar keeping secrets from her own. Is this place really worth protecting? Is it worth giving up my ambitions?

No. I can't allow myself to wallow in lower goals when the highest throne still beckons.

"I'm in. And I have a plan: When I eat Vaylin's soul, I'll burn it and whatever fuel you can spare to craft my own version of her domination spell. If I can make the spell strong enough, I might be able to dominate the shard directly, but more likely I'll use my witch ability to turn it into an artifact that I can directly control. A stepping stone to binding the Demiurge herself and taking her throne."

Avaya's eyes twinkle. "A wonderful plan . . . but the Myriad won't like it."

I smile. "Who do you think I'll be testing the spell on? If they're so eager to give up their agency in service of a higher cause, I'll happily oblige. Conquering their temple should give me all the resonances I need to forge the control artifact."

"And the boy?"

I try not to show weakness in front of the imp, but a bit of hesitation creeps through. "There's a chance I can maneuver Dante out of the way without risking conflict. The Demiurge gave him a wishblade, of all things, and I still need to burn through two of them before he's vulnerable. But once they're gone, it should be a simple matter to attack his soul directly and bypass his healing factor."

Avaya holds out a hand and lets her teeth show. "Then we have a pact."

The vision fades.

I force outrage to my face and turn to Dante, but my words die in my throat. He's looking at me with horror and betrayal, and I can see his eyes starting to glisten. *This is bad.*

"Dante, I—"

"Swear to me," he rasps, voice raw and broken. "Please, Alice. If that was fake, swear it by the Weaver. Swear it wasn't true."

My options are being cut away from me like branches pruned from a tree. The Demiurge just demonstrated exactly what will happen if I make a false oath, so how do I make Dante listen to me? How do I get out of this?

Beside me, Cheshire whispers in my ear, "One chance. One strike."

And yet, though her lips do not move, Dante's eyes still widen in recognition.

What happens next is pure instinct and terror.

Vorpal, still resting comfortably in my hand since I stepped through the portal, lashes out. All the mastery I've stolen guides my aim to Dante's chest, and my blade strikes true. The name of my heartsblood spell springs to my lips as I call upon all my power for a single decisive blow:

"[Feast or Famine]!"

And the blade bounces off a shimmering wall of golden light.

The barrier appears without warning—no spell uttered, no gesture made—and completely repels my attack. The force of the aborted strike travels down my arm and pains my flesh as the hungry shadows of my spell find no target yet still take agonizing bites out of my soul. The spell burns away, its cost paid but nothing recouped.

Dante looks just as surprised as I am, maybe more. He didn't do this, not knowingly.

My hands are shaking as I tilt my head to look at Vaylin's malevolent grin. "That's not fair!" I hiss at the Demiurge. "You can't do this to me! You can't *cheat* like that! How many more *devils* will you drop from this *machine?* It's not fair!"

Anguish crosses Dante's face, but then it resolves into grim determination. He raises the wishblade. *Only seconds now till we reach the end. What do we have left?*

I press my hand to the golden barrier and shout, "[Feast or Famine]! Come on!" The spell tears through my soul again, but the shield doesn't even ripple. I scream and pound on it. Slam, slam, slam. No impact, no register.

It's too late. It's all too late.

"I wish," he says, and the universe listens. He hesitates, and I keep scratching at the wall with futile frenzy. "I wish for Maven Alice . . . to go home."

What?

No. No, no, no. "No!" I scream at him. The air shimmers around me, and phantom hands caress my form. I shudder with nausea and watch in helpless horror as everything starts to fade. Greater pain than ever before wracks my soul, and black-gold flame envelops me.

"I'm sorry," that horrible traitor lies. "I hope . . . I hope you'll get better, when you don't have to be here. When you can't be tempted."

And then he's gone, and so is the Labyrinth, and I'm lying in bed staring at the wall of my apartment.

I'm on Earth. It's gone. It's all gone now.

Cold washes over me in waves like I'm being buried in ice. I stare, unblinking, unable to process what just happened. I can't believe this. I refuse to believe it, this *can't* be happening.

I push the covers off and stumble out of bed in nothing but my underwear. My skin is normal, my hair is dull, and when I grab the nearest mirror I stare into boring brown eyes. Flat teeth, no hint of true fangs. I'm exactly as I was before the Labyrinth.

"Feast or Famine," I whisper, and no magic stirs to life. I focus on Vorpal and it doesn't come to hand. I close my eyes and try to will my second sight to activate, but when I open my eyes again there's no difference. All my magic is gone. All my power is gone. Everything is gone and I'm powerless and alone and I'm going to die here.

I fall onto my bed and stare at the plain white ceiling. This can't be real. I'm the *protagonist*! The main character doesn't get kicked out of their own story. That's not supposed to happen, it can't happen, I reject it!

But were you ever really that important? whispers a cold and treacherous voice in my mind. *Or were they just delusions of grandeur? Maybe it was all a delusion, from the very start.*

I laugh with contempt. *Are you kidding? No, don't even try that. I know what I experienced. I'm not crazy. Not like that, at least. I don't have psychotic breaks, and I don't hallucinate things! All of that was real.*

But you'll never be able to prove it.

The ice down my back gets colder. She's right, isn't she? I'm right, I mean. I'll never be able to prove what I went through. They'd put me in a ward if I pressed it, and I don't have a drop of evidence except my own memories, worthless as they are.

This has to be temporary. This is just the part of the story where the hero faces a temporary setback, a darkest hour kind of situation. It's a drop, and a bad one, but things *will* get better. They have to. I have to win.

Why do you still think you're the hero of this story? You tried to kill an innocent man, and he spared you with your worst nightmare. Right now, you look a whole lot more like the villain *who just lost. Karma's a real bitch, gobbet.*

My fists clench. *I'm not*—I bite off my words. What room do I really have to argue with that? It's the wrong battle, anyway. *Fine. Yes, I'm the villain, but I'm still the villain* protagonist *here. There are too many threads left unresolved, too much weight that's been placed on my actions, my relationships. If not me, then who? Dante? He doesn't want to be there! He wasn't even introduced until after I killed the local boogeyman and made contact with half the important players in the city. If anything*—

A knock on the door shocks me out of my thoughts. I press myself against the wall and stare with wide eyes across my bedroom. Monsters flash to mind, and hunters with knives.

"Hey, you up yet? Didn't you want to hit the cafe before work?"

The voice is completely alien and yet utterly familiar. A voice I recognize in memory, but it's so strange to hear aloud. That's the voice of my room-mate. My roommate back on Earth, where I am now. Where I'm stuck.

Reality intrudes. Suddenly I feel awkward and self-conscious. What the hell do I say to him? I can't exactly confide in him about anything to do with the Labyrinth, he'd think it was a joke and then call the cops when I didn't laugh. God, I'm still half naked, and now I have *bits* again. I'm disgusting again.

"I'm awake!" I shout back at him. "Just. Give me a few minutes."

"Kay." I hear footsteps retreating, and then I'm alone.

"What do I do now?" I whisper to myself, feeling small and helpless.

If this is temporary, if it's just a momentary low point in the narrative before I'm returned to where I belong, then . . . what do I do?

Should I go looking for doorways in the woods, or click suspicious links online? Do I apply to test a VRMMO, or throw myself before a delivery truck? Or am I just supposed to wait until called? Katoptris abducted me once, so shouldn't it happen again?

Or has the window already passed? Has the wish returned me to the moment exactly *after* I was due to be taken, and now it won't ever occur? Has a timeline been altered, or does time flow differently between the Spheres?

I can't be stuck here. It's not possible. But . . .

I still have to eat, and I need a roof to sleep under. I have to pretend that this is my life, if I don't know when I'll go back. Will it be days? Weeks? Years?

The chill in my blood is eating me alive. I'm Alice, right? And in the books, in the original story, Alice gets her second visit not long after the first. But in the adaptations, in the inspired works, it can take anywhere from months to *decades* for little Alice to be called back to Wonderland. It's often tied to the shift from childhood to maturity, but I'm already an adult, so when's my time?

How long do I have to pretend that I want to live in this horrible, worthless world?

What if it's forever?

It won't be! I can't stay here. This can't become my life again, that isn't my story.

Or maybe, this whole time, you've had the genre all wrong.

My hands are trembling. My breathing is too fast. This can't be happening. This isn't happening. *I'm not stuck here. This isn't forever! I'll find my way back, I have to. I'm Alice. I'm Alice! I'm Alice, and I am going back to Wonderland!*

It's time to wake up, Miss Liddell. Reality is knocking on your door.

Five minutes later, I'm dressed and ready to go in jeans and a *Chainsaw Man* shirt, cloaked by a red jacket. I grab a mask, too, because oh yeah, there's a *pandemic* back on Earth. Lovely.

There's something so disquieting about the banal task of preparing for work. For a *job* that I'd actually managed to forget about. This isn't what I'm supposed to be doing, but I don't really have a choice if I want to eat real food for however long it takes to go home. To go back to the Labyrinth, where I'm meant to be.

The people who pass us on the street and drive by in cars aren't figments, and as we walk through town the geography changes slowly and organically, no scene transitions here. There's a sun in the sky, and clouds, and regular weather. It's the normal world. The real world. It all feels wrong.

I'm too quiet on the walk, and my roommate notices, but I just can't pay attention to whatever ordinary nonsense he's trying to engage me with. At a certain point he gives me a funny look and asks, "What's up with you today, Morgan?"

Morgan? The name hits me with a jolt of surprise. That's *my* name, or it was, but I sold it to a fae. I shouldn't be able to hear it, shouldn't be able to remember it. Every time I tried in the Labyrinth, it came back as white noise. But now it's like it never happened.

Like none of it happened.

I shake away my errant thoughts and try to bullshit an answer. "Distracted. Just off my game. Weird dreams, nothing that would make sense." Even giving that pithy answer makes me instinctively tense up and want to insist that it wasn't a dream, it was real, it had to have been real. Right?

I try to put more energy into the flow of conversation, and that seems to appease him. We banter about shows and games and whatever's recent, and I mostly keep up. Any slips can be easily excused, even if I'm clearly still unwell.

But the closer I get to the start of my shift at work, the more numb I feel. It's only been a few weeks since I must have worked last—no, less than that, I think—but it feels like a lifetime. Am I really doing this? Am I going back into the dull torture of retail after fighting monsters and talking smack to gods?

What choice do you have? This is your new normal, same as the old normal.

So I put on my work shirt and go in.

The minutes pass by like hours and the hours disappear. One moment I'm trapped in agony, and then I blink and I'm somewhere else. It's a horrible blur.

My speech is awkward and stilted. I've forgotten how to talk to customers and all the little questions we're supposed to ask. I forget how to answer the phone, how to stock shelves, how to make tags. It's like I've never worked this job a day in my life. My every moment is hesitant, distracted, slow.

People get angry at me, but even that doesn't break through the film over my thoughts. Everything they say, rude or polite, only deepens the all-consuming gloom. I feel like I'm drowning, or I've already drowned. When management pulls me aside after the fourth or fifth mistake, I stare past them. When they tell me to go home early for the day, I tell them, "Okay," in a voice devoid of emotion.

Walking home is a mistake, because it leaves me alone with my thoughts.

We're going to die here.

We can't die yet. Our story isn't done.

Are you so sure it was real? We've always thought about delusion, about going crazy. Maybe it's finally happened. Do you really trust your own perception? Your own memories? Do you trust yourself? Doesn't that whole protagonist story seem a little too good to be true?

It was real. It has to be real. It was real, and magic is real, and I'm going back to the magic. I'm not dying here. It was too vivid to be fake! The pain was real, I know that for certain. Experiences like those can't be fake, they're way too detailed. That's not what psychosis feels like, it can't be. I'd know if I was crazy!

Say what you really mean: You want it to be real.

Of course I do! Why would I want this world? Why would I want to stay here?

Then, if it were a delusion . . . would you still choose it?

My train of thought comes crashing to a stop. Would I choose that world, even if it were fake? Between a fulfilling fantasy and an unfulfilling reality, would I choose the former? Would I forsake the real to live in a dream?

I know the answer. It isn't even hard.

It's funny: My time in the Labyrinth was so much suffering and hardship, but now I miss it desperately. I want to go back to the world where everything wants to kill me and the divine ruler of the universe makes a game out of my existence. All for power. For magic. For the fantasy that I actually matter.

Am I really that pathetic?

You know that answer, too.

I can't live like this. I can't do this.

And I know that makes me weak, but I don't care anymore. One day is enough. I've had a taste of freedom and I can't turn my back on it, no matter the cost of returning. I'll toil beneath the Demiurge's wicked tastes for a thousand years if it means I get to live that thousand with real magic, real power, and real meaning.

I can't make it through months and years pretending I care what customers and managers think of me. I can't smile at the world around me when all I am is a frail and filthy human. I can't stay sane knowing that all I've ever wanted is just out of reach, separated by an impenetrable veil.

When I was a little girl, I dreamed of worlds whose wondrous sights would never grace my putrid eyes, and I seethed at the injustice of the denial of my desires.

In the safety of my bedroom I whisper, "You win. You win, okay? You made your point. So you can end this and bring me back." My breath hitches and I beg, "Please, bring me back. Please, Demiurge, bring me back."

For the first time since I was a child, I fall to my knees and pray. "Azathoth, Nyarlathotep, Katoptris; Dreamer, Dreamweaver, Nightmare; I beg of you, please. If you will only answer, I will listen. If you will only extend a hand, I will grasp it. If you will only bargain, then I will sell you my soul and all I am. Give me the magic I need and tear me away from this cruel little world, and if you do then I will do anything you ask to repay that debt."

The ice has melted and my limbs feel like they're shattering from tension and weakness. My eyes are growing wet, and all I hear is silence. *You see? It's all delusion. No one is going to answer. You whisper at nothing.*

With shaking hands I clutch a pillow to my chest, my teary eyes clenched shut, and with trembling lips I plead, "Free me of this wretched flesh and I will be your slave."

But no voice whispers back to grant my desperate wish.

The minutes tick by, the voice in my head my only companion. Outside, through the window blinds, the sun has almost set.

A parasite of doubt worms its way into my heart. *What if it wasn't real? Is that even possible? What would that even mean?*

It's impossible. It has to be impossible. Because if it were some freak delusion, then . . . what would that make me? With tight chest and salty cheeks I rise to my feet and grab a coat. I need to walk. I need to think.

By every measure of the world I see around me, I wasn't gone for even a single day. This world has no understanding of that other world, no hint of its existence. And if I really think about it, does that world seem coherent? Does it seem real?

Gods pulled from Lovecraft and a skim understanding of philosophy, a magic system that's a transparent metaphor for interpreting literature, and all my biggest fantasies filtered through my own self-loathing. A setting with hints of depth never explored, like the vaguest smearing of verisimilitude to satisfy a mind more interested in growing more powerful than actually learning about any foreign cultures.

But it has to be real. It has to be real, because I need it to be real. I need magic. I need to be special. I need to go back, whatever it takes, even if it is a delusion, because nothing in this world means *anything* to me, and it never has.

I know that makes me weak. Seven billion human beings cope with their reality every day, knowing magic is beyond them, and they don't feel like this. They don't despair for such stupid, petty reasons. They don't need to feel special to want to breathe. But I'm not like them.

If I can't be special, then I'm better off dead.

The night air greets me on the rooftop patio of my apartment complex. My feet took me here on autopilot, a path ingrained by hundreds of visits. I go here so often, whenever I need to think. Whenever I get like this. I look out over the edge to the ground below.

It's true, you know. You've always known it: Things would be better if you were dead. Better for you, better for everyone. But you've never had the courage. Well, now's your chance. What's still holding you back?

I know this voice. I know these thoughts. So many times, at this very ledge. I know what I'm supposed to argue: that people would miss me, that things will get better, that it's a "permanent solution to a temporary problem." I hate that phrase so much. Who gets to decide that my problems are only temporary? I still say the words, like I've been taught. But they feel hollow and thin.

It's different this time. We've had this conversation so many times before, but never like this. Be honest with yourself, Morgan: You don't care if people miss you, because you wouldn't miss them. Heartless. Sociopath. Monster. And besides, you know they'll get over you. Everyone always does.

And getting better? There's no better for you. Not before, but especially not now. Your "better" was impossible when you were just a jaded dreamer. Now it'll eat you alive. Every day for the rest of your life you will yearn for an adventure you won't get to go on. You will lose jobs and friendships until you find yourself starving and alone, and on that day I won't be there to help you.

So take the step. Don't choose to suffer.

I sway high above the world below, acrophobia warring with the call of the void.

If your dream world really does exist, if it's out there waiting for you, then what's the harm? If the Demiurge isn't a delusion, then she'll notice when you die. Your soul would belong to her, would have always belonged to her. Let go this fragile shell and you can see your Goddess again, and when your ghost is kneeling at her feet then perhaps she'll grant you mercy. Make your plea again, swear to be her slave, and she'll reward you like she did Cheshire. It's a choice you begged for just moments ago.

But, if it wasn't real, and your little adventure in Wonderland was one big delusion . . . then what's left for you here anyway? What point is there in living, now that you've tasted what you'll never truly have? What can be gained from a life of empty, meaningless suffering? Don't you deserve to let the pain go? Don't you deserve a bit of peace?

"But I'm afraid," I whisper. The night sky. The chill wind. The ground below. A single step.

I know you are, but it's okay. It's going to be okay, I promise. Just one little step and all the pain will go away. No more fear. No more doubt. Break the wheel of suffering and let it all go. I love you. You know I love you, right? I love you so much, and I just want you to be happy. So trust me. Trust me and take the step. Trust me and let go.

Trust me and fall, and when you hit the ground you'll never be sad again.

For what feels like an eternity, I lift my foot . . . but to step back, not forward. "I can't do it," I cry. "I'm sorry."

Shhh, it's okay. I understand. You're still too weak, but I still love you anyway. I will always love you. Are you still in pain?

"Yes," I say softly.

It'll come back, but there's a way to make it go away for tonight. Do you remember what to do?

"Yes," I say again.

I love you.

I go back to my apartment, strip naked, and peel a new scalpel from its packaging.

The first few incisions are delicate and overly careful, my hand out of practice. But with each fresh mark I remember the intricacies of the blade and of my skin and how to make them sing in harmony. I am careful and precise, my every stroke measured and exact.

Never the inner thighs, nor the armpits, and certainly not my wrists or ankles. Never too deep, no hint of white-yellow fat, just a safe and comfortable red. In this I know my limits better than I know anything.

In all the rest of my life, my relationship with my body is one of hatred, disgust, or willful ignorance. But here, it can be a canvas. This is art, not mutilation. Recreation, not punishment. There is a relief in it that approaches rapture.

My confidence grows as endorphins are released, my body's chemistry reacting to the satiation of my addiction—an addiction, yes, this I admit, but is that so wrong if it's something I need? If the alternative is the ledge I've just walked down from?

By the two dozen mark, my tensions are easing. By two hundred, I'm smiling for the first time since I was banished. When I beat my old record, I finally set down the knife and give myself a hug. The blood on my skin is so beautiful, and I can't help but trace my fingers over little bubbles of red. *Now for the best part.*

I step into the shower and raise the heat as high as it can go, and when the water hits me I melt. The cuts didn't hurt when I made them—they never do, unless I make a mistake—but when hot water blasts hundreds of open wounds—even small and shallow, surface deep—it's like being boiled alive. It's magical.

My mind goes white, all possibility of conscious thought completely obliterated by an ocean of pain that I'm happily drowning in. Sensation overwhelms me, agony transmuted to pleasure like a stack overflow.

I stop the water and stumble out of the shower when I can't take any more. I towel off, but I don't bother dressing before I fall into bed. The blankets are so soft on my naked body, and so soothing and pleasurable to my overstimulated skin. This moment, right here, is bliss.

That bliss carries me down to sleep, and in my dreams I see the Labyrinth.

INTERLUDE

ONCE & FUTURE II

I am haunted and I am ruined. This I know.

In weary days beneath a sunlit sky I toil against a world that hates my breath and footsteps. *You do not belong here,* the world tells me, and I must agree, but I cannot escape it. *The world will suffer me,* I insist, *for we are all of us bound in suffering.*

There is a cruel kind of inertia to the act of living. Our breath keeps us breathing, and our footsteps keep us walking. We eat so we may toil so we may eat so we may toil till food and toil run out. It must be madness to live the same day over and over, but we're all mad here, only some of us don't know it.

I know what I am. I embrace it. I toil and I suffer and I do not break, because in my dreams I see the Labyrinth and in the Labyrinth I see symbols.

My obsession does not start small. I fill the pages of every notebook in my room with scribbled sketches and I cover the walls with paper and ink. When I run out, I buy more, and when my hours are cut and my budget shrinks, I give up meals before I give up my opus.

Supplies, reagents, a formula, a circle. Words whispered and meaning sought, but nothing stirs. I fail. I begin again.

They say that repetition is a form of madness, but repetition with changing variables is the soul of modern science.

As I delve deeper into my task, my relationships all wither on the vine. I cloister in my chambers, speaking to no one but myself and the stuffed animals on my bed. Texts and calls go unanswered. Let them call it depression and lament my isolation. No one wants to reach out to a girl like that, and that's all the better for my needs. I leave only to toil as I must and acquire more supplies.

"Do you remember the library, Cheshire?" I ask the stuffed cat sitting on my bed as it overlooks the ritual circle. "Where the hunters tracked us down, and where we fought that wizard," I remind the cat as I draw a new set of signs and symbols. "So many books to sift through, but we found it! We found the one I needed, and we burned it into my soul and I *remember what was in it*. Every night, Cheshire. Every night, I remember. Even now, I see it clearly in my mind."

I complete the circle and arrange my materials. I chant the words and grasp at meaning. I visualize the spell in my mind, the matrix of interlocking parts, the ignition trigger. I pull the trigger and nothing happens. The spell fails, like it has every time before. I start again.

It's said that repetition is a kind of madness, but repetition with measured variables is the essence of a good experiment.

Hunger becomes a double-edged sword. It saps my energy, leaves me listless and struggling to focus, but it makes the right *resonance* for what I'm attempting. I eat only as much as I need to, and less on nights of major experiments. Let the hunger come, and I will greet it with open arms if it delivers me from my prison. Sometimes I overeat to add another variable, because every variable could be the one that solves the puzzle. Those are the nights that bring harder tomorrows as my stomach rebels against a brief taste of satiety before starvation returns.

My roommate grows concerned for me, but I loathe his pity. His kindness disgusts me and fills me with bile. *Let me rot,* I snarl at him. But when the hunger gets too sharp I still give in to his offer of a meal, because beneath it all I am still *weak*.

I arrange the signs and symbols in new configurations and old ones, trying everything thrice. "My memory is poor," I confide in the plushie that isn't my Cheshire, "which makes it all the stranger that I can remember those pages so clearly. It *must* be magic! We sealed it in a vault of memory and I can still see it where we left it, so it must have been real. These symbols must be real. So all I have to do is get the matrix right and tap into the right meaning, and it'll work. It has to work."

The spell doesn't work. I call it out until my voice crumbles, but still it doesn't work.

If repetition is an act of madness, then is experimentation just applied insanity? What worth is observation if it won't give me the answers I need? What am I doing wrong?

Unemployment and food stamps aren't quite enough to cover everything I need, so I sell everything I can: old books, my card collection, and then even my computer. I won't need it in the Labyrinth, after all, and I don't have time for web browsing or video games anymore. I need to finish my work. I need my magic back.

"I've been too weak," I babble to the cat. "Coward! Yes, I am a coward! I was afraid, and that made me weak, and weakness made me stupid. Too many variables left unchanged. Too many pieces unconsidered."

I draw and redraw the signs in my notebook, getting them perfect, and then I switch tools. I have to get this right with the implement I'll be using, after all, or I know I'll make a mistake and the spell will fail like it always does, but not this time. This time is different, I know it.

"I figured it out, Cheshire. You would laugh at me, wouldn't you? And then you'd curl up beside me and you'd purr and I would splinter your lovely fingers for abandoning me and betraying me, you lying—"

I breathe heavy, fingers shaking. Can't shake now, not tonight. This is the one, I know it. *Cool breath, easy breath, just keep breathing, nice and deep for me.*

I run a hand through my unkempt hair and laugh out the nervous energy. "But it's fine. I forgive you. I'll forgive you, when I see you, when I show you what I've done. Because it's going to work. I figured it out: I was using the wrong medium this whole time."

Deep breath. Steady hand. I make the first cut.

"See, this magic system, the symbols, they don't *do* anything when they're just on *paper*," I chatter as I carve the first rune into the flesh of my arm. It doesn't hurt. "This language might be an operating system, but there's no *operator* without a *soul*. Do you think paper has a soul, Cheshire? I don't think it does. But I have a soul. I know I do, because I see the Labyrinth and the pages and the symbols *every single night.*"

I cut the next sign, and the next, painting the spell on my skin with a scalpel. "My mind's eye isn't good enough to hold that complex an image, even with the formula written out in front of me. And the drawings, well, they never meant anything, right? Paper doesn't care. The floor doesn't care.

So it doesn't matter how much resonance I flood the room with, it doesn't matter the words I chant, because I'm *missing* the *medium*. But not tonight."

The final diagram is a gorgeous sight. My body has never looked as beautiful as it does now, the symbols of my spell tracing from just before left wrist to just before left elbow. Still safe, even now, of course. I can't cast the spell if I can't use my arm, right? Everything I'm doing is perfectly safe.

"Maybe I'll keep this," I murmur, "when I come back to you. Maybe I'll add more. Do you think that's a pretty look for a demon, Cheshire?"

The stuffed cat doesn't answer. I don't expect it to.

"First, let's capture the image for our notes." I pull out my phone—the last valuable belonging I haven't sold, too useful to be rid of—and take photos of my arm from every angle. If this works, I want to be able to reproduce it perfectly.

If it works. And if I survive it working.

For all my frenzy and desperation, a single seed of doubt nests in my heart when I look at the symbol that forms the centerpiece for my skin-carved spell matrix: the mark of the Abyss. This is *my* spell, a demon's spell, and the price it asks is high. If it works, if I finally grasp that spark of true magic, how much of my soul will it devour?

In Reska's time, before Throne magic, even a touch of the Abyss was lethal for an ordinary human. What will it do to me, calling on the Abyss in a world that magic has never known? Success could bring greater consequence than failure, with a spell like this.

But I don't care. This is *my* spell, and if anything will respond to my call it's this. This is my best chance to have magic again, and that is the only thing that matters.

"Okay. Showtime. And . . . sorry about this, critter."

Hamsters are fairly cheap, and you can get them from any local pet store. Rats tend to be cheaper, but I actually like rats. I could probably find a wild cat on the street with a bit of searching, but I'm obviously not going to kill a cat.

"Isn't it weird how it feels worse to murder an animal than a person?" I ask Cheshire. "This thing has a lifespan measured in sneezes, and here I am feeling awkward about snuffing its candle. Shame I couldn't get a human, but, y'know, kidnapping brings cops."

I pull the hamster out of its cage, holding it gently but firmly in my left hand, and I start the ritual to end its life.

"I beseech the Abyss," I chant, "and all its dead and dreaming gods. Hearken to me, worms of the deep. I call upon your gift, our inheritance, my birthright. I am still the demon you made me, no matter the face I wear or what pumps through my veins. You demand conflict, so I will feed you conflict. You demand predation, so I will feed you predation. This is my pledge, my sacrifice, and my plea. All I ask is that you answer."

I look at the rodent one final time, and I start to squeeze, and I whisper the words:

"Feast or Famine."

The mark of the Abyss turns black from red, and then that inky color spreads across every fresh cut on my arm and seeps into the older scars, beneath my skin, into the blood that flows within darkening veins. Elation and fear slam against each other as the animal in my hand shrivels to dust and bones in an instant and I am filled with glorious power and terrible pain as my soul is ripped from my body.

I am winning. I am dying. I am triumphant. I am doomed. It was real. All of it was real, and magic is real, and my magic is killing me.

My vision swims. My limbs prickle and go numb and I stumble and slump. I collapse against the floor, unable to reach my bed, as nausea and dizziness get sharper and sharper. The black of the Abyss travels farther up my arm in spiderweb patterns, and then everything goes dark.

And in the dark I fall, and I fall, and I fall. I sink down through the floor, down through the earth, down to the bottom of the world and even deeper. I fall into the fever-warm dark, and darkness greets me and holds me like a child in the womb.

In the dark I open my eyes, and through shadow and night I see a graveyard of worms at the sump of the universe.

I stand on a pile of bone and rotting meat, a mass grave with no soil to hide the gore. It stretches to the horizon in every direction, an endless field of dead bodies slowly mulching. Ringing the charnel pit are the bodies of worms, vast and sinuous and intermingled, all made of death and pocked with violence. Giants, visible from a great distance as if they were close enough to touch, just like the tower in the Labyrinth.

From above, through the infinite space of dark on dark, wisps of drowned light come down in gentle trickles and pouring waterfalls. I see glimpses of oscillating color, rainbow chaos, and I know at once that these are souls.

The souls find their way to the worms, pouring into open wounds and toothy mouths that line their corpse-flesh bodies. I see dead gods stir and flex, shudder, and collapse again.

Leviathans.

"Forgive my masters their silence," speaks a calm and resonant voice. "They are still licking their wounds after being murdered."

I jump and whirl at the sudden sound. A few feet behind me, a figure floats in the dark. It is gray-skinned and ethereal, a wasting thing in gossamer robes that drift apart into swirling black mist. Its smile is thin and lipless, and the upper half of its head quickly devolves into twitching tendrils of slimy gray flesh.

My heart is still pounding from my brush with death, so I take a nervous step back and try to calm my nerves. *Gather information, then negotiate. The game is back on, so it's time to play. We will have our magic.* "Your masters?" I ask with a tilt of my head. "Does that make you a demon or a geist?"

The figure laughs softly like velvet over stone. "I have been called as such, but neither label truly suits me. I prefer to be thought of by my singular title: I am the Emissary."

Emissary? Where have I . . . My eyes widen. "Oh. You're one of the archons, like the Intercessor and the Adversary." Which means I am in even more danger than I thought.

Their smile turns tight. "I would rather not keep such company, if you don't mind."

A spike of fear makes me blurt, "Right, sorry, yeah. Emissary, then." I blink away the panic and try to compose myself. "Ahem. I assume we're having this conversation because of the spell I cast?" I raise my left arm, which looks dramatically different from how it looked a moment ago: The skin is largely unblemished, all markings vanished, except for the black symbol of the Abyss pulsating with an irregular rhythm.

The Emissary drifts around me, long fingers steepled together as they reply, "Indeed, your spellcraft was quite the impressive trick. If you wanted to attract our attention, you certainly succeeded. Please, tell me: Did you know *before* you cast the spell that direct contact with the Abyss is *lethal* for an ordinary human?"

I hesitate before answering. "Well, partly. I wasn't certain if I'd be protected or not. I was hoping I wouldn't count as an ordinary human."

The Emissary laughs again. "Extraordinary indeed, *Maven Alice*. The girl who sought the highest throne. The girl wished away. Yet you were still unprepared for the power you sought to wield. Though, before you worry, you aren't *dead*. Just . . . visiting. An invited guest."

Well, that's a relief. A bit of tension eases from my shoulders, though I'm still on guard as I watch the strange god-thing circle me. They know too much about me, like everyone in power seems to. "Whose invitation, then?"

"Mine, of course. And theirs." The Emissary stops in their original position and gestures to the distant worms. "The Leviathans are always willing to entreat with a worthy petitioner. You have called to them, the fallen masters of the Abyss, and they have answered. You seek its power, do you not?"

Hunger burns away my fear. "Yes. I need it." I don't care if I sound desperate, I won't let this moment slip away. "I want *magic* again. I want *power* again."

That lipless smile returns. "We are happy to negotiate such terms. But, when you have that power, what do you seek to do with it? Will you reign over that little blue dot?"

Harsh laughter claws its way out of my chest and I nearly double over. "That wretched hole? No, not a chance. I hate that world. I want power so I can *leave*. I'm going *back* to the Labyrinth, and I'm going to conquer it and make it *mine*. That's the real prize."

"I see. Then, perhaps we can come to an arrangement." The Emissary drifts back a few feet and spreads its arms. "The magic you crave can be yours again, but why settle for what you had before? You have lapped at the Abyss through a water filter, never tasting the true and unalloyed article. I would offer you the gifts of the Leviathans, the strength of the deep dark."

"And what would you ask in return?" I'm not so foolish as to believe these nightmare overlords would just give me magic for free. I don't trust the Demiurge, but I don't trust her enemies either.

"The Leviathans ask only for what you have already fed them: the souls of your prey."

My gaze flicks to the soul fragments streaming down from above, then to the shuddering worms, and the pieces click into place. "The inheritance. Shadow magic. They call it a gift, but it's really a contract, isn't it? Abyss magic doesn't just turn souls into energy, it feeds those souls to the Leviathans."

Is that the true purpose of mass harvest events? Is that why the ninth archdemon will be the Endbringer? The wizard from the library said that the "prince of the apocalypse" would bring about the Resurrection, the revival of all Leviathans from their graves in the Abyss. But she also mentioned the Adversary, and the Emissary doesn't seem on good terms with that archon, so what's the full story?

Carefully, I say aloud, "I've heard it told that the ninth demon to ascend as Royalty will be the catalyst for the end of days: the Resurrection. Is that your aim?"

The Emissary bows low. "As my masters will it. And, if you so choose, you may have a place in that great transformation. The Abyss will celebrate she who brings the end, and we shall crown her with many crowns. Perhaps, if you prove truly worthy, you may even claim the Throne Below."

The Emissary drifts to one side and gestures with both hands at a throne of solid night that wasn't there a second ago. I see bone and metal and screaming souls, a living and writhing thing that emanates *power* most of all. I see the promise of absolute rule over absolutely everything, the total usurpation of the Lucid Demiurge and her design.

It frightens me. It makes me hungry.

"Why?" is all I ask.

The Emissary understands my meaning. "We have long believed the Demiurge to be . . . unfit for her dominion. She did not *earn* her throne, but was *given it* by the Heretic. Were an enterprising soul to tear her from that throne, they would quite logically be a fitting successor. And that *is* your goal, is it not? To seize the reins of Pandaemonium?"

They're telling me what I want to hear, which means I don't trust a word of it. I don't trust anyone. But I need the power I'm being offered. "What are your terms, Emissary? What are you actually asking of me, and what do I get out of it?"

"I can answer that, and will. But there is one question that must be settled first. You spoke of returning to the Labyrinth, but that is no easy feat. Do you have a plan, or just ambition?"

Ha! I actually have an answer to that one. I straighten up and lick my lips. "Oh, I have a plan. See, none of my things came with me when I was banished. Not my sword, not my outfit, none of it. Which means that somewhere out there, back in the Labyrinth where it was left, is a locket that holds a piece of my soul. All I have to do is unite the fractured whole."

The Emissary's flesh tendrils twitch, and the edges of its mouth quirk. "And do you know *how* to unite your pieces?"

My confidence deflates. "Well, no, but I can figure that out once I have magic."

"I have no doubt. But I'm afraid there is an obstacle of which you seem unaware: the Labyrinth's inviolate barrier. Even once you learn the necessary spellcraft to travel between worlds, only an *archon* is capable of moving objects across that veil." The Emissary's hands steeple together again as it says, "Like myself."

I narrow my eyes. "You want something more than a tithe, then, in exchange for your help crossing the barrier."

The Emissary raises a hand and a few glimmers of rainbow soulstuff float down to orbit their fingers. "I offer a bargain in two parts. First, I will grant you the gifts necessary to wield the raw energies of the Abyss and cast your favored spells, and in return you will sate the Abyss with a tithe of souls. You will know this tithe by a hunger that stirs you to action, and the tithe shall be proportional to the power you call upon. You are already familiar with this kind of contract, as it forms the basis for the Abyssal powers you have tasted in your journeys. If you fail to feed upon the souls of others in sufficient quantity, your own shall pay the price. But as you learn to manipulate mana and life essence with more precision, needing less of our Abyssal backing to cast your routine spells, you will find the tithe to relax in proportion."

"An eminently reasonable arrangement," I comment dryly. "And the second, less reasonable part of this bargain?"

That wicked, lipless smile stretches. Its other hand rises, and a facsimile of Earth appears above it. "Deliver to me that little blue dot, and I shall ferry you across the veil between that world and the Labyrinth."

For a second, I almost can't believe what I heard. "You want me to give you *Earth*? That's insane." Seven billion people, sacrificed to the Abyss? Am I even capable of that? I can't be that far gone. "And, hey, isn't that against the Edicts? That definitely counts as interference with the Zero Sphere."

The Emissary tilts their head. "Zero Sphere? Oh, my dear, it would seem you've been laboring under a quite incorrect assumption. That world is *not* the Earth of the Zero Sphere, but merely a world of Firmament crafted in its image. How else could you have cast a spell within its bounds?"

Not the real Earth. Not the Zero Sphere.

First is shock and disbelief. That could be a lie, the Emissary playing on my biases. Months of suffering for a cheap trick? That whole world, just a fiction? A twisted facsimile? *Magic*, just out of reach, because it wasn't an isolated Sphere at all?

But it makes sense. It's exactly the kind of senseless cruelty I would expect from the Lucid Demiurge, warping Dante's wish to twist the knife even further on my suffering. Months of pain and labor that I know she's *laughing at.* My whole existence is one big joke to her, isn't it?

I hate her. I hate that arrogant bitch. I want to pull her down from the heavens so I can tear off her wings and pluck her eyes and make her beg me for death. I want to lock her in a cage and fill it with acid for a thousand years. I want to make her bleed. I hate the Demiurge.

But do I hate her enough to murder seven billion people?

That's a cold splash of reality. The Emissary is asking for an entire planet, a whole world of people who, for all their faults, don't deserve to be fed to malevolent worm gods. That's a monstrous act, far worse than betraying one irritating hero. Far worse than whatever my relationship with Cheshire was. Far worse than planning to murder my way to ascension, worse even than the mass harvest that was our backup plan if a string of killings wasn't enough.

But, if it's a facsimile world, maybe the inhabitants are too? It could be a planet of figments, built just for me, and figments don't feel pain. No, I can't entertain that idea. If I'm going to do this, I have to treat the people of that world like they're real, even if they aren't, because to do otherwise would be moral cowardice.

There's another angle, too: Could seven billion souls be enough to kick-start the end of the universe? The promised apocalypse, the Resurrection, is all about the return of the Leviathans, and now I've seen one way they're trying to return: feeding on souls until their forms regenerate. I have to imagine they've eaten more than that number in the thousands of years since their defeat, but all at once? Even Malice's harvest event was only a fraction of that death toll, and she's talked about in terrified whispers.

Here's a no-longer-hypothetical question: How many people am I willing to kill to become God of all Creation? To steal the seat of the Demiurge and become the exalted master of Pandaemonium, where do I draw the line past which any further murders become unacceptable? Does that line even exist?

When I was a lonely, angry, scared little girl, I told myself that I would sacrifice every human being on planet Earth to buy eternity. I didn't know if I meant it, because it was never a realistic trade to make. But now it is. Now I really do have that choice, and I have to decide: seven billion souls, or my singular forever? Countless worlds beyond that and the teeming trillions that might inhabit them, or my own lust for power and control?

I think I know the answer, and it disgusts me.

When I am God, I will do better.

That's the excuse I'll cling to. That's the justification I'll wield. When I am lord of the universe and everything burns away, I'll raise something better from the ashes. I'll make a world where no one has to suffer like I have suffered. I'll forge a universe that bends toward justice, not pain. A reality that gives everyone what they need and punishes those that would take more than their share.

So let one planet burn. Let them all burn. Let the worm gods rise and eat their fill, and when I take the highest throne I'll send them back to their graves and fill the space they left behind with light and love and wonder.

And it will all be worth it.

"Deal."

One year before the end of the world, I kill a man who had never raised a hand to harm me.

I kill him at night, as we pass each other beneath a streetlight. It happens quick, but I don't know if it was painless. Something lives in my shadow now, and I think it might be me. We swallow him whole and his soul sustains us for a week. His life force heals my aches and pains. The essence of his being keeps us sated.

When the hunger returns, we kill again. And so it goes.

I know the thing in my shadow will turn on me if I ever let it starve, but I love it all the same. I trace my fingers across my skin and see runes shimmer black and violet before fading again to resting invisibility. This contract, the new tapestry of my form, I find beautiful.

The Emissary shows me symbols I never saw in my pilfered tome, the signs and spells of Malice and Wonder and all the rest. I learn how to be a demon properly, the old-fashioned way, and I nurture it with every murder. I conspire with my mentor to alter my physicality, and it's not as easy as it was with Cheshire, but with every passing week I look a little more like me.

And every week I kill again.

Eleven months before the end of the world, I welcome a guest from the void.

Finding a space where I won't be caught in the act is the hardest part, but then I realize I don't need to worry about getting caught. I'll simply change who I am.

I'm using someone else's voice when I call the police from a burner phone, and I'm wearing another face when they find me in the empty house. The building belongs to someone who owns too many of them, a realtor who pays a pittance to keep it nice and clean in the hopes of a big sale. I'm sure they can afford to wash out the blood.

The first pair of pigs don't see it coming when my shadow runs them through, but I let one live just long enough to radio the rest. Their backup comes in with guns at the ready, but my shadow is a versatile companion and their bullets find no purchase in my flesh.

I let the beast run wild, and when I've had my fill of pleasure I set about my work.

When the bodies are arranged as they need to be, their blood staining the walls and floor in arcane symbology, their limbs piled in a pyre, I speak the words and open the gate.

A monster steps through, a night horror from the depths of the Abyss, and it bows its eyeless head to me before feasting on the man I left alive and bound. This is the first of many. This is a proof of concept. This is a test, and I pass.

That night, the Emissary teaches me new symbols.

Nine months before the end of the world, I solve a new spell and cross a new line.

My shadow has been a faithful hound, but it does not complete me. I revel in violence of the body, but within my soul simmers the potential for violence of heart and mind. Why did I stray from that, when offered power? Why did I ever hesitate before the threshold of mastery?

I'm killing a world. It's time to get serious.

In my last dream of the time before the Labyrinth, my last vision of Reska before I was expunged, I saw the princess cast a spell that has lingered in my mind for all the months since. In her confrontation with her own reflection, a smaller beast for a smaller labyrinth, Reska broke from torment and broke her tormentor. She brainwashed it.

Reska was horrified, but Homura was fascinated, and so am I.

The spell was a new expression of her power, a magical mutation. Her shadows, always eager to obey their master's wants and needs, had lashed out before but never like that. It was only in alloying with her blood that her most horrifying spell was born. A symphony of perfect resonance stole the heart of something bent on her ruination. If I can understand those resonances, I can shape them with my art.

Shadow is easier, its meaning obvious and familiar. Shadow is the magic of the Abyss, a living bargain with dead gods. The foundation of every demon, its arcane essence is hunger, conflict, and predation. Shadow grants the ability to prey upon another, to sink one's fangs into their form and draw forth their essence to devour.

Blood is more complicated. It can mean life, death, bonds, conflict, or sacrifice. Reska wanted it to mean healing, but she could only ever wield harm, and I think I understand why.

Surrounded by others in the heart of a kingdom that bore her name, Reska was nevertheless alone. Her affinity for Shadow kept her isolated, and she wanted more than anything for her new affinity to break that isolation and connect her with others. If she could heal through Blood, then she could share in the traditions of her bloodline. If she could nourish the kingdom through Blood, then she could share in her bloodline's responsibilities. But a power born of isolation could never be the end of isolation.

And yet, in that terrible moment in the depths of her personal hell, I think Reska finally succeeded. Just not in a way she'd ever wanted.

Blood can be the bonds we share, but not all bonds are healthy or desirable. Connections can hurt us, and that hurt can travel through every connection that follows. A bond, when darkened and made violent, can spread sickness just like infection breeds in blood.

As a disease of the flesh incubates in the body and spreads through contact with its fluids, so too can a disease of the spirit incubate in the mind and spread through contact with its ideas. Hatred can be a plague. Misery can be a contagion.

Can I do the same with the sickness inside me? I know it must be possible, because the sickness of my mind is the same as that which afflicted Reska, the sickness that broke her:

Please love me. Please don't leave me.

I can make that a virus. I can make that a spell.

And when I use it on someone with more money than sense or empathy, it'll be a victimless crime. And I will never go hungry another night on this worthless world.

When I speak the words and see their free will vanish, I smile.

Six months before the end of the world, I take another hit and blow smoke in the face of a girl whose name I'm never going to remember.

Five, eight, some number of other girls sprawl around my latest den in various states of undress, all sucking face or getting drunk and high. They're here for the sex and the drugs and the free food, none of them under my thrall. The thralls are the rich people serving us wine and bringing us more edibles and snacks whenever we ask.

There's a movie on the big screen that I'm too intoxicated to pay attention to. Music is playing from somewhere, and it's too loud, but that means I don't have to listen to anyone talk. I can just lose myself in the ocean of noise and the feel of skin on skin as the next round of weed hits my brain and smooths everything over. It feels great.

We kiss, we laugh, we eat, we fuck. This might be what paradise tastes like, in soft flesh and wet lips, in a sensual array of parts and proclivities. The food is divine, the drugs are better, and everything is pleasure.

I'm going to burn it all. I'm going to burn this whole world, and everyone in it. I'm going to kill every girl in this room, and none of them will ever know it was me.

I grab another bottle and drink till I hit bottom.

Two months before the end of the world, I'm driven deep into farm country to find a town that no one will miss.

Of course, in the digital age, anywhere with cell coverage is just a few taps away from national news if they happen to film the right scene. It took a bit of work to figure out who exactly I needed to enthrall to cut all access to the area for a few hours, but I have time and resources aplenty these days.

The signal sends and blackout begins.

I don't go into town. I don't want to know who I'm killing. I work around the edges, my thralls laying all the ritual components I had prepared in the week prior. The sacrifices came with us, all of them willing thanks to my poison in their veins. They march to their doom with sparkling eyes and smiling faces.

Blood is spilled, words are incanted, and the sky turns black as the Abyss seeps in. Night horrors burst from the earth and lope toward their victims, and the air turns fever-warm. I start the timer, and a thrall brings me noise-canceling headphones so I won't have to hear the screams. I read a book while I wait, something light.

Five minutes. Ten. An hour. Two hours. Still the black sky holds.

When the overlay finally collapses, true night has fallen. I write in my notebook:

Test successful. Degrade within expected parameters. Proceed to next phase.

On the drive back to the estate, I drink myself to sleep.

One week before the end of the world, I stare at my bathroom mirror and cry.

Three hours before the end of the world, I wake up hungover.

There are two girls in my bed, and I want to stay with them. They are warm and soft, and I will miss their touch. I will miss the nights we shared. I will miss the food we ate together. I will miss getting high and watching dreadful anime together, and I will miss the jokes and the insults and the flirting.

I cling to them tightly and for a moment I imagine that this is the whole world. No gods or monsters, just warm bodies intertwined. Endless days of laughter and good food, and endless nights of sex and bad movies. Wouldn't that be nice?

What if, all this time, I was wrong?

If the universe is cold and uncaring, then why do I smile when I hold a woman's hand? If we are all here just to suffer, then why does it feel so good to laugh? If I am cursed, then why can I still taste the spice in my ramen broth and all the fruits in my morning smoothie?

I will miss being human.

The realization is horrifying, but unmistakable. *I will miss being human.* I didn't even know that was possible. It wouldn't have been possible, if you'd asked the Alice of a year before. Was my life truly so empty?

But then, that's the key, isn't it? The emptiness I felt, it wasn't going away. All the good memories I've made between acts of violence, they were only made possible by that violence. I pursue my pleasures with the money I've taken from the minds I've enslaved. The food and drink and drugs that I offer to the girls who come to my parties, none of it would exist without the blood I've spilled and the souls I've ruined.

I may feel human, but I'm not one. I can't forget that no matter how much I drink.

The life I have now, the life I'm about to burn, it came at a price. All the power I was granted, all the tutelage I received, it was all for the purpose I'm about to fulfill. All for this moment, and for what follows.

I made a deal. And if I went back on it, I'd lose everything. Maybe, if I were clever, I could get away with my soul. But my days would not be endless.

Cheshire once told me, in one of those quiet nights as we lay awake, what happens to a demon if she betrays her nature. She told me it's the only way to kill an archdemon, in theory, though it's never been tried.

The nature of a demon is desire. A certain hunger takes root in that demon's heart and curls up in her core. The more powerful she gets, the more refined her core, the more she must follow its tenets. If the archdemon Wonder forsook her curiosity for even a moment, then in that moment she would be as mortal as a human child.

I made a promise to myself, and I carved the words of that promise deep into the very essence of my being. I made it my animus.

I'll risk it all: my power, my body, and my very soul. The ultimate risk, and the ultimate reward. I will overthrow the Demiurge and take her place on the Throne of Creation, or I will be taken by the hungering Abyss. There is no other path that will suffice, no lesser road that still leads to the usurpation of God herself. She who is not willing to give everything will be forever left with nothing.

The human Morgan might like to stay here forever in this bed, in this house, on this planet. But it wouldn't be forever.

Only the demon Alice can have those endless days.

Ten minutes before the end of the world, I say my last goodbye.

I chose the Space Needle for the place I'd be standing when it all ended. I've always hated that landmark, so it seemed fitting. Even at the very end, I'm still afraid of heights.

My thralls have the building secured, and all the ritual sites throughout Seattle and the surrounding country. A hundred imitations in miniature together forming the aperture of the gate, and here the very center. I've been busy these past couple months, and the whole West Coast is saturated with Abyssal radiation from prototype overlaps. Now, in just a few more moments, I'll say the right words and watch it all drown in shadow.

How do you say goodbye to a life?

I guess I'm not really saying it, if I stop and think. I didn't say goodbye to my father, or to anyone who knew me. I could have. I had plenty of opportunity. But I was afraid.

I want to feel like a demon and a conqueror as I stand atop the world ready to drag it down to hell. But a conqueror doesn't stare at the door to her father's house, hand raised and trembling, before running away. I never said goodbye. I never said anything.

Sometimes it feels that the only thing I have ever known is regret.

I wonder who I could have been if my mom had lived a little longer. I wonder if my heart would have held so much hate if my father hadn't put it there. I wonder how much of myself died before I ever knew it was alive.

I press my hand to the glass and close my eyes. For a moment, I imagine the glass shattering. I imagine falling down from this incredible height and breaking against the street below. I imagine a world without me in it.

I think that would be a better world. A safer, happier world.

But it's not the one I choose.

I take a deep breath, clench my fist, and then release. I open my eyes. And I say to myself in quiet bitterness, "Go then, there are other worlds than these."

I light the match and set this Earth on fire.

Far above, the sun is swallowed by endless darkness, and great tendrils of unliving flesh bear down upon the great towers and triumphs of human civilization. Horrors burst forth from every shadow and drink their fill of flesh and pain and terror. One planet, seven billion people, all offered to the dead and dreaming worms.

The Emissary rests a hand on my shoulder and smiles at me. "Wonderfully done, my student. As promised, the way back is yours."

I turn from my teacher and walk through the portal without a word. Guilt and dread and relief all intermingle with nervous anticipation. I'm going back. I'm going home. And all it cost was a planet.

I stride the gap between worlds. I return to the Labyrinth.

And in the space between spaces, I see a woman with bright red eyes and the body of a doll, and she tilts her head at me as she says, "Oh dear. Well, this isn't real at all, is it?"

INTERLUDE

ONCE & FUTURE III

Eighteen months, hundreds of hours of labor, and seven billion souls. That's what it cost me to get back to the Labyrinth. That was the price of my return.

It should feel like triumph, so why does it taste so bittersweet?

I step out of the portal clad in black robes and breathe in cloying air thick with death. The tea party is over, its attendees murdered and lying slumped on the oil-stained table. The room should be dim, all the candles flickered out or melted, but this is the Labyrinth; nothing is dark here by nature.

The Labyrinth, where innocents are dragged off to kill each other for the amusement of cruel masters. The Labyrinth, where everyone is trapped in a shattered and crumbling worldspace. The Labyrinth, where I bled and screamed and fought and failed.

What a horrible place. Who would ever return to this prison by choice?

I could have asked for a portal to anywhere in Pandaemonium. I could have toured the infinite worlds and gone on adventures free of the Labyrinth's twisted games and sick overlords. I could have gathered my power slowly, properly, one duel at a time. I could have eaten whole planets and made myself a demon even stronger than Malice or Wonder. But I didn't.

We have to finish what we started. Bind the shard, climb the tower, claim the throne. But first, kill that traitor Dante who banished us to our own personal hell.

I will never take the slow and careful path; I can't, lest I betray my nature. Everything or nothing is the only way forward. I must win the game. I must conquer the Labyrinth. I must claim this world, that tower, and whatever lies inside. Whatever Katoptris is, she'll be mine.

I don't know why this universe is twisted and broken. I don't know why the Demiurge laughs at our misery, or why she takes such personal pleasure in torturing me, but I'll make it her undoing. I will make her rue the day she denied me.

"Alice!" cries a familiar voice that jolts me from my brooding.

Cheshire rises from the floor and rushes to my side. Her cheeks are stained with tears, her mismatched eyes all bloodshot. Her furry ears are perked, and her lithe body is warm as she hugs me tightly and buries her face in the folds of my voluminous black cloak.

I don't hug her back.

I think I would have, if my sojourn to the false Earth had lasted a mere month, or six, or even nine. If I were still touch-starved and alone, I think I would be grateful for Cheshire's presence and her body against mine. I spent so many days before reclaiming my magic torn between hating Cheshire and missing her.

I still don't know how to feel about her. Did she betray me on that fateful day when Dante overheard her whisper? Or was she herself betrayed by the hand of her true master? Did she never come for me because she couldn't, or because she wanted me to suffer before I returned to her? I was reckless and desperate when I chose to trust Cheshire before. I didn't have a choice. But now I have power that isn't bound up in her strings.

"How long have I been gone?" I ask calmly.

Cheshire hears the strangeness in my voice and tenses. She looks up at me and the excitement on her face flickers out. She finally takes in my changed appearance, from deathly skin to shadowed robes. "Are you okay? It's only been a few hours since you vanished. How . . . how long has it been for you?"

My fist tightens, nails digging into palm. *A few hours. A few hours, she says, while I toiled and suffered for all that time.* Aloud, I tell her, "One and a half years. I've been stuck on Earth, or a facsimile of Earth, for eighteen months and two weeks. I kept count."

Her face falls into horror. "Gods and demons, that's awful. I'm so sorry, Alice. I can only imagine how that must have felt for you, knowing your history." She hugs me again, but when I still don't reciprocate she slowly and awkwardly releases me. "Are you . . . sorry, stupid question. Obviously you're not okay. But . . . you're back."

"Yeah. I'm back."

I pull away from Cheshire and walk over to the table where the bodies are. The scene is largely as I left it, save the added morbidity. The oil slick doesn't hold my interest, nor Vaylin's tacky porcelain, but Avaya's lifeless gaze stares straight down at the sword lying right in front of her. Dante didn't take it with him, which makes him a fool.

"If it's only been a few hours, I take it Dante hasn't finished the game and claimed the ultimate prize?"

"He went back to the Myriad," Cheshire informs me. "He's probably still there, making preparations for the end."

"Good. Then I can catch him and tear his soul out of his body." I pick up the sword and examine it absently. Avaya was storing souls in this vessel, and she seemed to be holding a healthy crop.

"Right! Yes! So," Cheshire begins to chatter, "when you were wished away, it severed our bond, but I still have all your stuff that you were storing in your pleroma, and most of the growth and magical investment we made is still built up! All we have to do is make a new contract and—"

I command my shadow, "Eat," and watch as it surges up my body, flows to the end of my arm as a tide of living darkness, and devours the sword whole. My shadow feasts on the souls that were trapped inside, and I can feel the satisfaction of a good meal mixed with hunger for a thousand more. This world is richer in offering, deeper in meaning. This will be a good hunting ground for the both of us.

I turn back to Cheshire to find her staring, eyes wide and body frozen. After a moment, she finds enough composure to ask me, "How did you do that?" in a scared and disbelieving tone.

By way of answer, I raise one arm and let the sleeve of my robe slide down, then trace my fingers over skin. Lines of runic text shimmer into visibility for just a moment before fading back as I let both arms fall back to my sides.

"That's a direct contract with the Leviathans," Cheshire says with a trembling voice and horrified gaze. "You contracted with the Leviathans. That means—"

"That your services are no longer required," I interrupt her coldly. "I've spent a year learning true sorcery from a master of the art, and I've supped of the pure Abyss."

"But your soul—"

"Is mine to risk. Mine to nourish. Mine to burn, if that's what it takes. I'm in charge of my own destiny now, and I've forged myself into a demon the *hard way*." I let the dark seep into my flesh and reveal a glimpse of black sclera around burning red irises, sleek horns jutting out of my skull, and darkened veins. "I don't need a geist."

My words are like a knife to her heart. I can see the anguish written on her face, and her body begins to tremble. Her eyes grow wet. In a small, frail voice, Cheshire pleads, "What did I do wrong?"

Anger slashes through sympathy and I snarl at her with explosive temper. "You weren't there for me, Chesh! Eighteen months and you weren't there for me, and you spoke the words that cost me any chance of talking Dante down. I was stuck in that hell for eighteen months because of *you*, and I can't just forgive and forget."

"He wasn't supposed to hear!" Cheshire insists. "It was the Demiurge who made him hear, it was the Demiurge who interfered."

"And who sent you to me, Chesh?" I ask quietly. "Who made you what you are?"

Despair swallows her whole. She stares past me, stares through me. "I thought . . . I thought we talked about it. Were through it. You were going to . . . you were going to trust me." She falls to her knees and clasps her hands together, looking up at me with more tears streaming from her eyes. "Please, Alice. Please, *Master*. I can still be useful. I can still be yours. Please don't leave me."

Please don't leave me. How can I do this to her? If she's not lying, then I'm just as bad as everyone who's ever hurt me. I'm a monster. I'm everything I've ever hated, everything that's ever made me cry.

But, then, how can this be any worse than what I just did to a planet? I sacrificed seven billion human souls and I'm balking at hurting one girl? I'm so selfish. I'm so predictable.

This was easier in my rehearsals, but I can't break now. I can't give in. I swallow my doubts and find my voice. "I won't . . . I won't force you away. You just can't have my soul. Once I claim the shard and break it to my will, we can talk terms for a new kind of contract. I don't know if you're a collaborator or just another victim, and, if you really are hurting right now, then . . . I'm sorry. I'm sorry for so many things, but I . . . once I have what I need, I will find a place for you. I just can't trust you with my soul, not when I have an alternative. Please understand."

"But the alternative is—" Cheshire cuts herself off, scrunching her eyes shut and wincing. She hugs herself, and after a moment she sighs. "No. You're right, of course. I understand." She opens her eyes, gets to her feet, and meets my gaze. "Thank you for . . . for not throwing me away."

There is a part of me that still yearns to turn back and accept her with open arms, but I do my best to extinguish that flame of foolish longing. "Thank you for understanding," I say softly. "We can talk more later, but right now I don't know how much time I have before Dante claims the shard. You said you have my artifacts?"

Cheshire nods and wipes away her tears. "Yes. Yes, right." She walks over to the messy table and shoves some of the mess onto the floor. One by one she places the contents of my old soul palace onto the tablecloth.

I pluck the locket, Vorpal, and the red cloak, but I let my shadow eat the remaining artifacts. They're tuned for spells I don't cast anymore. The rest of my belongings I let Cheshire return to wherever she'd been keeping them.

The [Mantle of the Unburned] replaces my ordinary black cloak. I don't think any of my current enemies are fire-throwers, but it can't hurt to be prepared. This artifact is my second strongest after the absurd Crest, and it's already won me two fights. Forged in a wizard's inferno and strengthened by the flames of a faerie, it holds quite a lot of potential. I'd like to see what happens to it if I keep absorbing the flames of different Spheres.

The locket goes around my neck, and it feels warm. It pulses faintly, like a heartbeat. Is that my soul I'm feeling? The shards of it I left behind? Between what's in the locket and what's in Cheshire, how much of myself am I actually missing?

For a moment, I feel the irrational urge to cast the locket into my shadow and be rid of it. But is that irrational? Maybe it's the inevitable consequence of who I'm becoming, of what I'm carving myself into.

This artifact is a monument to cowardice. I made the heart locket because I was afraid of what I might cut away in my pursuit of power. This is my second chance if something goes wrong. It's an admission that I might fail, that I might ever want to turn back. A *demon* should not own an object like this. I won't become something like Malice or Wonder if I'm still afraid to lose myself in the process. I *must* lose myself. I must lose my weakness, and my doubts, and everything that has ever held me back. I must kill the girl who cries for her mother. I must murder my fearful heart and cleave it from my chest.

But I keep the locket around my neck and move on to Vorpal.

I take a few practice swings with the rapier that was once Homura's. The weapon feels familiar in my hands, that alien connection coming back to me like I haven't been separated from it for a year. The sword flows smoothly through stances I've never learned, reminding me that this weapon is alive and it is mine. My Crest. My connection to Homura, and, through a marble memento, to Reska.

Before I was banished, I was close to revealing that little secret to Cheshire. I thought many times about sharing my dreams with her and letting her know all about Homura and Reska, in the hopes that maybe together we could come to understand them. But I didn't. And now, I doubt I ever will.

"Time to move."

I leave the tea party behind and exit the convention center, unfazed by the scenes of carnage still fresh and gory. The death here is messier than I've gotten used to, but it's not meaningfully different. I stroll through, step outside, and take in the old familiar sights.

Vaylin's home base was located in a section of Sanctuary with a very cyberpunk feel to it: neon lights, steel and glass, a city of skyscrapers and screens. Everywhere I look there are advertisements for products ranging from milkshakes to shoes to home appliances, but my year surrounded by the genuine article makes the lack of true branding even more obvious than it was last time.

It's still daylight out, but the sky above is once again missing a sun to provide that light. People crowd the streets, a throng of humanity that I doubt boasts a single real human. Smiling faces, chattering lips, fashion and friends, but none of it real. Figments. How I've missed them.

Well, I can't be certain they're all figments; I never asked the Emissary to teach me second sight. I didn't want to be tempted to use it on the people of the false Earth.

A plain man in business attire is passing by, so I grab his arm and ask him directly: "Hey, are you a figment? Answer truthfully."

He stops in his tracks and turns to look at me. His expression is at first one of indignation, but at my question all emotion falls away and he stares into my gaze with steely focus. "Maven Alice. You have been expelled from Sanctuary by the Myriad. You don't belong here anymore."

"Too bad," I snarl at the figment, and then I wrench his head to the side and sink my fangs into his neck. I pour my poison into his empty soul and in seconds he is *mine*. I drink a few mouthfuls of his blood for a boost before pushing him off and looking for another victim.

A woman in a pretty blue dress. A man in sweatpants and a hoodie. Him, her, those two, that one. I flit from target to target, lingering only long enough to mark my prey and bind them to my will before moving on to the next.

The street is busy, an easy recruiting ground, but after my ninth conquest the city reacts. Everyone in the area that I haven't already subverted abruptly stops what they were doing and starts running, sprinting as fast as they can away from my position.

Be like that. "Grab them!" I shout to my thralls. "Pin down as many as you can."

So they run after their fellows and capture those they're able, binding arms and legs, two to a victim, and I follow with my fangs to make more of them. I turn those victims that my servants can catch, and when we run out of targets in the streets I have them break into homes and places of business in search of any who hid instead of fleeing. My horde grows, but too slowly for my liking, the city's resistance vexing me.

Cheshire watches with an inscrutable expression, and while I wait for a new victim to be presented I turn to her and say, "We talked about something like this. Do you remember?"

She laughs, though it's not a happy sound. "Of course. It hasn't been two years for me."

"One of my clearest desires, though I resisted it. I was afraid to want it, afraid of what it made me, when we first discussed it over tea. I was afraid to want *this*. And even as I accepted that I was becoming a demon, even as I planned to take Vaylin's spell and make it mine, still I hesitated. Still I doubted."

Another figment is found, and I bind it to my will with blood and shadow and meaning.

"I was a fool to wait so long," I tell the cat. "This is everything I ever wanted."

Cheshire brushes her hair to one side and pushes down her top to expose her naked neck. "Then, if you bit me, would I be what you wanted?" She meets my gaze with fathomless need. "Is that the price you ask? Will those be the terms of the new deal?"

Hunger burns in me, and I remember what fascinated me so intensely about the changeling who once called me Master. An untrustworthy creature, one equal parts appealing and revolting. What monstrousness, to desire a thing crafted for one's service. What perfection, to find someone molded to fit you. How wonderful and terrifying to be known.

I have learned, or I think I have learned, that I will only ever feel comfortable if I have power over others. I will only feel safe if I hold all the knives, and I only love what I can control. Not always as literally as comes with enthrallment; the girls I lay with in my latter months on Earth were never under my spell . . . but I did, in a way, hold power over them.

I trace my fingers up her neck, to her chin, and hold her in place. I stare into her eyes and let her see the hunger blazing red. I bare my fangs.

"If you are mine," I tell her, "then there is no need for a poisoned kiss. If you are not mine, then you are hers, and I don't believe for one single second that my magic could tear you from her grasp. Not as I am now." I pull my hand away. "No, those won't be the terms."

I return to my hunt, but prospects are quickly drying up. The figments left in reach are taken, and then nothing is left to take. But something is off, more than just the sudden absence of prey. A street corner becomes an out of place dead end. The buildings seem taller, denser, impenetrable, like the city has become a maze.

Cheshire voices my concerns: "The city is doing more to hamper us than just moving figments. It's shifting the geography to impede our progress. It's blocking our path to the Myriad's temple."

I grimace. "Well, I'm officially sick of this. So let's go over that wretched eidolon's head; I'm going to summon the Beast."

Cheshire freezes up and stares at me. "The Beast? Are you serious? That's insane. At best it won't answer, at worst it'll try and kill you!"

"Nah. I think I know what she wants from me."

I find the nearest window and press my hand against my own reflection. I roll my shoulders, breathe deep, and run through the words in my head, tweaking them until they're just right. I need to do this properly. I need to be in control.

"Beast of Lamentation and Euphoria, you are called. The *Red Queen* summons you, Beast. Let us have words, as we have once before, and let us speak of our destinies."

The glass ripples, and then the whole building shatters inward. Glass and metal implode, sucked into a single point of absolute mass, and then that mass twists and contorts into the shape of a woman. The glass woman stretches misshapen limbs and breaks them into more normal proportions, and then her body flickers in a wave of transformation from glass and metal to meat and bone, a thing of dripping gore, and then that too is remade and I find myself once again staring at my reflection.

"Beast," I greet her. "It's been too long."

The Beast tilts her head. "Has it? For you, maybe. Why do you call me, Maven Alice?"

I gesture to the city around us. "Your garden is burning, and I've come to settle the flames. I'm the only one who can . . . but a certain eidolon is getting in my way."

The Beast snorts and leans back, lifting one leg and resting it against solid air. "Liar. The fires are out, the game is won, the war is over. And then you came back, here to reignite the fighting. Is that your idea of settling?"

"It's yours," I claim with a smirk. "I've figured you out."

"Oh?" She lifts an indulgent eyebrow. "Well, now I'm curious. Do go on."

First gamble. Easier gamble. "You don't want Esha and Dante to win. You infected the Machinist with lamentation and the Huntsman with euphoria, and that poison made them turn on their allies. If not for your curse, there would have been a united front against Vaylin, but you wanted the city to erupt in violence. The only wrench in your plan was Esha, for resisting the madness you gave her. You caused all of this, because you want to see the board wiped clean."

The Beast licks her teeth. "Perhaps I did. It's not a bad guess. But what of you, demon girl? You rejected my gift, you rejected escape, and now you come to me *stinking* of the Abyss and its worms. Do you think that's who I want to see sitting on my throne?"

And the second gamble. "I think that's exactly who you want to see, because you've already said as much. Your gift was a test, one you knew I wouldn't understand until later. You were showing me that what I truly wanted wasn't survival, or comfort, or anything so sympathetic as being loved. I wanted control, and I still do. You were right about me: I *am* a monster, and I killed the world for a second chance at chasing the divine. I come to you as everything you accused me of being, and now I'm not hiding it or trying to deny it. I am what you promised I would become when you promised me this city and that shard of your power. I am the Red Queen, greatest of all murderers, and you *will* help me. I will seize what is mine."

The Beast's eyes, my own eyes stolen and reflected, glitter and shine. "And then? What will you do when you've crossed that first threshold? Where will you go? How high will you climb, O Red Queen of bloody murder?"

My smirk grows feral and toothy. "I go to heaven on high, to claim *her* throne. I'll make the Demiurge my bitch, and then I'll rewrite this awful world and make a *real* paradise, not a garden of thorns. And it will all be worth it."

The Beast laughs and laughs, and I almost break my cocky grin, but when she stops laughing she smiles and tells me, "Oh, yes, I think I can work with that. Go on then, killer. Make my day."

She snaps her fingers and the next dozen buildings behind her vanish without a sound. Figments step out of their homes, trembling and glassy-eyed, waiting to be preyed upon. And beyond them, beyond the path cut for me, I see the temple and the tree.

Our march is red and ruinous, adding dozens of figments to the mass of thralls. I send off scouting parties to loot knives from kitchens and drag more civilians from their homes to be made mine. By the time we reach the temple itself, my army numbers over a hundred.

The Myriad are ready for us, of course. Warned by their eidolon, protectors in cloth and plate cluster about the entrance to their temple, nervously waiting for my horde to approach. I see dog-eared, drow, half-snake, and stranger creatures defending their home together, with the paladin in power armor at their head. The golden tree rises above them, the symbol of their union that I can't wait to despoil.

They number fewer, but my thralls are unarmored and have worse weaponry. Sending a ragged militia against a fortified position isn't likely to end well . . . but they are, in the end, just a tarpit for my approach.

An approach stymied by the sudden appearance of a shimmering golden barrier.

As I move to step closer to the temple and its defenders, a golden light crackles to life and repels me. The shield completely covers the temple, an impenetrable globe that wraps around and sinks into the earth. The barrier is painful to the touch, and my shadow shies away from it. I frown at the new obstacle.

Cheshire appears beside me and shares in my frown. "I guess I should have expected them to ward their fortress." She glances my way and explains,

"This is a Spirit trick, the principle of hallowed ground made physically manifest. A consecrated barrier. Esha must be maintaining it."

I raise an eyebrow. "It requires maintenance? Will it weaken or fade if left alone?"

The cat chews her lip and takes a moment to consider that carefully. "We're in their home territory, and this barrier is everything their eidolon is about. It could probably hold for years without anything pounding on it, but it does tax the priestess and restrict what else she can do with her power. She's the living heart of the ritual."

I grin. "Oh, good. Then this should kick her teeth in."

Cheshire blinks and opens her mouth to ask what I mean, but I'm already moving and throwing orders at thralls.

"Everyone grab a buddy and pair up! If you can find someone you've got a semblance of relations with, all the better. Form two lines as close to the barrier as you can, front line kneeling. Leave a bit of space for me."

My dominated figments scurry about to follow my orders, gathering before the barrier in two even rows. When they're all in place, I give my next order.

"Standing line: Murder the kneeling line."

Knives sink into backs and throats, stabbing and slashing with empty fervor. These figments aren't people, so they shouldn't feel anything, but I've filled them up with a need to be loved by their Red Queen. I can feel little pops of sensation as thralls die and blood pools on stone, a wave of something quite like worship. This is a sacrifice, made in my name.

The temple defenders, the Myriad, watch this unfold with horror that I can *taste*. Fear wafts on the wind, and darker emotions. Some of them hate me for this, or hated me already.

Good. I lick my teeth, spread my arms wide, and chant an incantation I learned from the Emissary. "I invoke the name of Malice, she who is hatred and defiance. Know me, Malice, for I walk in your shadow. I am the murderer of these and seven billion more, and my knife is not yet sated. I invoke you, Malice, to defile the sacred and desecrate the profound. I invoke the shadow of Malice: Unleash your *[Blasphemy]* upon this source of light!"

The Emissary taught me something very interesting about the fundamental cosmology of Pandaemonium: When someone of Royalty ascends to their Throne, they alter the very fabric of the universe, even reaching into the Labyrinth. An archdemon can't breach the barrier, not without an invitation from the Labyrinth's master, but the *idea* of each archdemon is *always* inside the barrier.

So when a massive claw of solid darkness shoves its way out of a hole in the sky and slams against the barrier, I know it's not Malice herself . . . but it's still a little unnerving.

The shield cracks, the very first blow enough to send damage spider-webbing down from the point of impact. But rather than slam again, the shadow claw stretches its fingers of darkness and begins to trace them over the top of the barrier. Wherever a claw-tip passes, it leaves behind a trail of purple against glittering gold.

The Myriad below watch helplessly. Most of them seem more confused than terrified, not sure of what I've summoned or whether it can actually break their protection. Achaia, however, seems to know exactly what spell I've cast, and she vanishes inside the temple with a shouted warning to the defenders. The panic I feel from her is tantalizing.

The Blasphemy completes its tracing and taps a single claw-tip against the center of the finished diagram. The top of the barrier shatters immediately, but then a wave of dark violet energy ripples outward from the point of break-ing. The golden light of the barrier is warped by the wave, crumbling to ash as it passes, but when the wave reaches the ground it begins to spread inward.

The dark energy passes over the whole of the space inside the barrier and crawls over the earth, and I see many of the Myriad sway or crumple to the ground as it passes over them. It seems to affect the non-human defend-ers more strongly, but even some of the regular humans double over and vomit as the wave pushes past them.

A sea of easy targets.

"Break them! Slaughter them! Kill for your Red Queen!" I call to my still-living servants.

The diminished horde charges without hesitation, their essence enthralled to my will. Most of them will die, or perhaps all of them, as civil-ians with knives stand little chance against proper warriors in good armor. But like I said, they're just a tarpit; the defenders will be bogged down fight-ing them off, and I'll be free to move as I like.

It's time for me to *hunt.*

I start running, and as I run I transform. My black robes melt into scales and horns, a layer of natural armor, and my hands stretch into vicious claws dripping blood from hollow channels. My jaw cracks and reshapes itself into a rending maw full of sharpened fangs. I'm faster, stronger, deadlier, and I don't need *Cheshire* to change my shape.

Beside me, my shadow rises in mimicry of my war form, solidifying into a near-exact replica. Together we leap into the enemy mass and begin our dark slaughter.

And it *is* a slaughter; I'm so much more than these simpleminded fools can comprehend. I am a demon, a *true* demon, forged of Shadow by my own bloody hand. *I'm more real than they are.* Figments or followers, both are just fading dreams. Only a scion approaches the realm of the truly alive.

So they die. I rip flesh with my claws, sink fangs into waiting necks, and leap from one prey to another with careless frenzy. Nothing that hurts me remains living or free-willed for long, and the blood that I drain restores any superficial damage these worthless mortals can land. Power courses through my limbs, the power I painstakingly acquired through months of heinous murder and sinister rituals.

I pin another to the floor and bite into their neck. They shudder and writhe as my poison enters their system, my dark will invading them, breaking them, dominating them. I withdraw, the taste of their blood still sweet on my tongue, and whisper, "Kill the unbelievers." And they do, because I own their soul, and so off they go to murder their friends.

The battle for the temple exterior is over quickly. When the dust settles, only a few figments and fewer Myriad remain, all of them bound by my cursed blood. Cheshire is silent as she stands amid the carnage, overseeing my handiwork with an unreadable expression. My shadow returns to me, melting out of its mimicked form, but I keep my war face on.

"If you see Dante," I tell my thralls, "slow him down."

I stride inside the temple, a dead and empty thing with most of its inhabitants lying dead or brainwashed outside. My footsteps echo through hollow halls. It's been a year and a half since I walked here, and my recollection is poor. Where is the well chamber? Where is the heart I need to plunder?

"Cheshire, I'd like your guidance," I call over to the cat trailing nervously behind me. "Do you know the way to the roots?"

She stops, tilts her head, and then nods. "Yes, I can lead you."

"Thank you," I say sincerely. "Your help is appreciated."

"Of course," she murmurs.

The entrance to the well chamber looks like it should be sealed, a second layer of defense, but Blasphemy took care of that; runic symbols are seared into the door, and there's a faint trace of gold dust beneath it. I push the doors open without resistance.

The inner sanctum of the Myriad is a chamber of clean white stone and vibrant murals. This is a place that was once the thriving heart of a community, a place of worship and celebration. There were attendants here, last time, in white robes, and regular people talking to them. Now, the chamber is empty but for the two women I came here to kill.

Esha is coughing up blood, hunched over by the water's edge and clutching her staff with a death grip. The pale light of the clear pool is dimmer, fading. The gnarled roots reaching down are scarred in places, the wood warped and pockmarked, the white and gold darkening in spots. Esha and her place of power have both been wracked by the backlash of the barrier's destruction. [Blasphemy] did its job well.

Achaia is by her side. The knight is supporting Esha, helping to hold her upright, and I can taste a new kind of fear in her: the fear that her love will not survive. In this moment, what would she trade for her love's survival? I want to find out.

"Hello," I greet them pleasantly. "I've just dealt with, I believe, all of your defenses, so I think now would be a good time to stop and chat. You have something I want, or you had it, and I'd really like to get that sorted."

Esha doesn't look my way, blindfold still pointed firmly at the waters of the pool, too busy bleeding, but Achaia turns to me with hatred written all over her face. "Monster," she accuses me. "We took you in, offered you trust and support, and you *betrayed us*. Why? For *what*?"

"Power, obviously." I laugh at her. "I wanted power, and you wanted to put me in a cage. You wished to make me less than I was, to trap me as something other than a demon. I was never going to be glass like you wished. You were always a means to an end. My only regret is having the game spoiled early. But, before you get hasty, I should tell you I'm not here to kill you and Esha. Not if you cooperate."

"Cooperate!?" The anger rolls off her in waves. Achaia raises her shield and manifests a blade of golden light in her other hand. "You don't know the meaning of cooperation. To a beast like you, the only thing that can exist is *submission* or *destruction*. Neither will I allow."

I sigh dramatically. "Oh come now, are you really so reckless? Would you gamble with Esha's life when I'm offering you a way out?" That gets her to hesitate. Again I taste fear, and so I press the assault. "Have you ever come so close to losing your sacred charge? What is there to gain at this juncture in resistance?" I take a step closer. "I don't ask for submission, nor destruction. All I want is for you and Esha to leave this city—and Dante—to me."

Her expression hardens. "I'm not so gutless as you, abomination. I have a duty to this city, to this world, to all living beings. A demon like you . . . I cannot suffer to live!" She adjusts her stance, ready for conflict, ready to try and take me down.

I tilt my head. "Are you really so shortsighted? If you fight me, you'll both die. You must understand how far beyond you I've evolved. Dante's little disappearing trick backfired on him, hard. While you've had hours to prepare for my attack, I've had *two years* to grow my power." I sneer at her, and then I cackle with a terrible, maniacal glee. "I burned a world to get back here! Seven billion souls fed to the worm-gods of the charnel pit. You will die, and Esha will die, and neither of you will ever help anyone ever again. If you want to do an ounce of good in this world, then *leave*. Run away, and find some other hapless fools to save."

Is it a lie? Would I spare them if they ran? I'm not sure. As a demon, I don't think I should. On a personal level, while these two may have schemed to strip me of my ascension, it's not as if they were dishonest about it. I shouldn't really hold a grudge. But, then, when has that ever stopped me?

It's a moot point. They were never going to accept. Unlike me, Esha and Achaia are good people, and good people don't let monsters run free.

The knight levels her blade at me, expression set. "I don't fear death. If I can die stopping you, or making it possible for Dante to stop you, then it will be a sacrifice worth making. That's a concept you demons will never understand. Enough talk!"

I shrug. "Your choice."

Achaia moves to charge, but at the same time, Esha bolts upright, her terror flooding the room. The priestess wipes the blood from her mouth and screams, "Distraction—" right as my shadow sinks its teeth into her throat.

The whole time I've been monologuing, my shadow was slithering across the ground, stretching from my feet all the way to the priestess by the pool. If her wards were in place, if her sanctuary hadn't been defiled, it never would have worked. But befouled by [Blasphemy], her precious temple couldn't save her.

My shadow devours her whole. She tries to fight it, tries to muster up her last dregs of power, but weak light is swallowed by suffocating darkness, and Achaia races back to her lover's side too late to save her. In seconds, Esha is gone, and my shadow is snapping back to its rightful place beneath me.

Achaia's turmoil is palpable, her grief and rage written on her face. Her hand passes through the place Esha stood for only a moment before she gathers her resolve and charges at her opponent. She's coming to kill me, and it would be righteous if she succeeded. A just death.

I took away the person who mattered most to her, and she fights with every ounce of her spirit to avenge not just the priestess but everyone I've ever hurt. She fights for the sake of everyone that I could hurt if I survived and went on to conquer the rest of her world. The weight of the Labyrinth is behind her, and worlds beyond the Labyrinth, all demanding that she lay down her life to stop me.

But it isn't enough.

Against most opponents, Achaia would be a nightmare. Her power armor is nigh-impenetrable, she's fighting with righteous fury, and she has years of experience. I imagine she's close to as strong as you can get without becoming a scion. But that's the key difference between us: She's not a scion.

So her light is smothered by darkness. Her blade can't break my scales. And all the weight behind her can't overcome the gulf between *chosen* and *unchosen*. This isn't her story, and it could never be her story, because she gave up that right a long time ago.

My shadow swarms her body and pins her place. Her struggle never ceases, but her ability to move reduces and reduces as the darkness thickens around her. When I'm confident the binding will hold, I allow myself another beat of melodrama and place a finger beneath her chin, smiling at her with wicked delight.

"Diplomacy may have failed," I say, "but you can still be made *useful* to me. You can still serve as others have served. As *all* will serve."

Achaia, fighting to the last, curls her lip and tells me, "You will die alone, and in pain. Your future is already written. I only regret that I won't be there to see it when every victory becomes ash in your mouth."

My hands ball up into fists and my teeth grind. *Worm. It's just a worm, and it spits meaningless insults. Victory will be mine.* I grab her head and wrench it to the side, exposing just enough of her neck to sink my fangs.

She's strong, but I'm stronger, and she can't stop me. No one can stop me. Not anymore.

I poison her. I hate her, and I'll make her love me. I drink of her blood, and through this parasitic act I transmit an idea back into her blood: *Love me. Love me. Love me.* Like a mosquito transmitting its diseases through saliva on an open wound, the sickness inside me passes on to my victim and blossoms inside an immune system never designed to resist the will of a demon.

And yet, she *does* resist. Somehow, impossibly, she fights back against my corruption. Her body is growing hotter by the second, as fever-warm as the depths of the Abyss, and I can feel the anguish in her soul as she desperately tries to endure my infection. She had a love, and I murdered her, and she can't bear to love another. She can't bear to love something as monstrous as me.

I withdraw my fangs and lick the blood off my lips as I watch her struggle. Her face is strained and sallow, eyes shut tight and lips trembling. She's in the throes of torment. *Fascinating. So even a lower lifeform can resist me with proper conviction. That must be corrected, but how? Is it simply a matter of power? Was my preparation insufficient?*

And then a wretched, hated voice calls out to me from the chamber's edge: "Alice, what have you done?" I can hear the pain in his voice, the raw agony at what he's seen, but his pain is *nothing* to what I have suffered!

Dante.

The one who cursed me. The one who exiled me. The one who betrayed me. It's time to take my revenge.

INTERLUDE

ONCE & FUTURE IV

I leave Achaia to her suffering, my poison coursing through her veins as my shadow binds her limbs, and I turn to face the man who caused me eighteen months of grief.

Time and emotion are excellent at distorting memory. The Dante who lived in my head in all my fantasies of revenge doesn't really resemble the Dante standing before me with bags under his eyes and blood on his shirt. He looks tired, not cruel. There's a hollowness sunken into his face and a weight hanging over his back. His sword is drawn, bereft of its wishes but still possessed of its cutting edge.

I spread my arms wide and put on a mocking tone. "Dante! So good to see you again. I know it's been a short while for you, but I've waited *two years* for this reunion. Don't you have a friendly greeting for your old pal, Alice?"

"What. Have. You. Done?"

"Are you blind?" I spit at him, mirth turned to hatred in a split second. "Are you a child? Do you need me to hold your hand and give you all the answers? I've murdered them all, Dante, and I did it just to hurt you."

In an instant his whole body fills up with anger and he leaps at me, sword singing through the air. "WHY!?" he shouts.

I catch his sword with one claw and bare my teeth in a feral, joyless smile. "Found your fire, have you? Where was this Dante when we were fighting for our lives, eh?"

He swings at me over and over, each strike parried by my scaled, claw-tipped hands. With each swing he asks another desperate question. "Why?

Why betray the Myriad? Why plot to kill me? Why would you do any of this?" His voice is raw, almost pleading. *Pathetic.*

The bile boils out of me in waves. "Why? Because I *hate you,*" I hiss at him, "and I have *always* hated you! I have hated you since the moment I saw your wounds close with the magic that *she* wouldn't give me! I hate you for everything you took from me!"

His eyes widen and his latest blow falters. "What?" He sounds bewildered. Stunned.

I stop fighting defensively and go on the attack. I lash out with my claws and rake them down his side. "I hate you!" I scream as his blood stains my hands before the lacerations heal over.

I don't care about killing him right now; I just need him to bleed.

"This was supposed to be *my* story, but she gave *you* all her gifts! I fell into this world and she made me suffer, and she gave you everything I asked for and more! You had all the powers that were supposed to be *mine,* and then you *stole my magic!* Do you have any *idea* how badly you cursed me?"

He has the gall to look shocked at that, and maybe even a little offended. He shakes off my attacks and steps back, putting distance between us. "Cursed you? Alice, I was trying to save you! I was trying to stop you from becoming something like *this.* Can't you see how magic is the problem? Magic is destroying your humanity."

"I never asked to be human!" I run my claws over my scaled body and bare my teeth at him again. "Look at me, Dante. I'm better than human. I'm more than human. I'm a *monster.*"

My form is beautiful inhumanity, freed of a wrongful shell. I was never meant to be human, never meant for human needs and human feelings, never meant to sweat and soil and ache. I was never meant for fragile bones and blemished skin, never meant for a body that needs to sustain itself on calories and nutrients when I could be supping on blood and souls. I was meant to be perfect. I was meant to be a monster.

"And I'm not some worthless *nobody* anymore! I was NOTHING without magic! My life would be *meaningless* without *power,* just like it was for twenty years. Just like all lives are meaningless when they lack the strength to choose their own meaning. Only the powerful get to decide who *matters* and who is *dirt.* That's why I'm doing this, why I've done *everything.* It's about power."

As I speak, Dante's shock morphs into disgust and disbelief. "What are you saying? That's insane! You don't need *power* to live a happy life. You don't need to be powerful to have a purpose. I was *happy* on Earth. My friends and family were *enough* for me, and I didn't have a scrap of power like you want."

I curl my lip at him and sneer. "Oh, well that's so nice for *you*, to live in merciful ignorance. But the facts are the facts even if you never knew them. Think, Dante: What high-minded meaning can persist when you are *starving* in the streets? Can you still be happy when you are destitute? Will your family be enough for you when you have to watch them die from diseases they're too poor to treat, when they all rot and wither because food and medicine weren't made human rights?"

"But that's not about power, that's—"

"Of course it's about power!" I shriek at him. I turn to Achaia, still struggling against my infection, and with an instant of will I take her life. I call to my blood coursing through her veins and call it back to me, and it takes every drop of her with it. I exsanguinate her, and my shadow devours every ounce of crimson.

Dante cries out and lunges, but he's too late to do anything. He grabs the knight as she falls, cradling her in his arms, another look of dumb horror written across his face. "I'm sorry," he whispers to her, and she whispers something back too softly for me to hear. Her last words.

"Don't you see?" I smirk at him cruelly. "Those with power dictate the terms of reality for all those without. They decide what you get to eat, what you get to wear, and every action you're allowed to take. Your happiness and your purpose must coexist with guns and banks and atom bombs. Only the powerful are *free* to act."

Dante is practically shaking now, the anger rolling off him in waves. "That doesn't mean you have to kill people. You don't have to tear the world down to lift yourself up!"

"Of course I do!" I snarl. "There's no other way to ascend! This is the hand I've been dealt, and I'll play it till all my chips are taken. I must become the monster that wins the game."

He closes his eyes, and when he opens them again there's a new resolve in the set of his face. "You're wrong. You are *wrong*, Alice, about everything, and I'm going to prove it."

I laugh and sneer at him. "Go on, then. Fight me, coward." I stalk toward him, claws ready to tear through his flesh, shadow coiled around my legs and hungry for his soul.

He lays Achaia down and stands up, but instead of readying his sword again he looks behind him. "Spirit of the city," he calls out, and suddenly all my confidence evaporates.

Oh no. Oh, no no no. He can't! I bolt toward him with fresh desperation. I never even considered he might—

"I accept what you offered. I accept exaltation."

With my claws inches away from his face, Dante is enveloped in a pillar of blinding white light. It blossoms around him and ripples out in a nova of energy that tears through me and into me. The light, burning like the sun, rips the scales from my skin and sears my vulnerable flesh and still I reach for him through the pain.

My shadow is blasted from me, banished and broken and shattered into pieces by the terrible wrath of the spirit whose home I invaded. Blasphemed but not beaten, the eidolon wraps itself around Dante's shoulders and shields him from my touch, wards me back as a thing of evil. The light rejects me and I'm pushed back, unable to hold my ground.

"I can feel them," Dante says in wonderment. "Everyone who fell in the city's name, their spirits are still here, with me. Lending me their strength."

I snarl and pull Vorpal from what's left of my shadow, and I draw the blade across my arm to let it taste my blood. *I can still win this. I can still kill him!*

I call the remnants of my shadow to me and draw out every scrap of power that I can, every ounce of strength I've stolen. I set my soul to kindling for this next attack, for one decisive strike to break through the hated light and pierce the core of Dante's being. I'll devour him, just like I devour everything else.

I level my blade, measure my attack, and lunge.

Dante's attention snaps back to me and raises his sword, white light pouring into it. His blade comes down with the weight of a city, but I only need to hold him back for a moment. Vorpal meets his blade and the shock of impact breaks something in my arm, but it gives me just the opportunity I need to slip past his defenses and sink my fangs into his neck.

I drink his blood with abandon. I don't even taste it, no time wasted savoring the meal, just drinking and drinking to try and drain him dry, to devour the whole of his being before that blade has a chance to rip me open or take my head.

And then—

—a pain in my stomach—

—white light scours me, hideous and pure and painful—

—and the world explodes.

Heat lingers on my raw and blasted skin. Pain blanks everything, numbness to follow, and then pain returns in pins and needles. It takes my vision too long to return, blinking over and over to banish the phantoms in my retinas. I'm crumpled in a heap on the floor, all the strength in my body vanished and given out. I'm lying in a pool of my own blood, blood dripping from . . . from . . .

. . . From the place where my stomach used to be. The lower half of my body is gone, my abdomen ravaged and my legs torn off. I'm not even half of myself.

I feel numb. I should feel worse, but I'm still in shock. What happened to me? How did this happen to me? *Why* did this happen to me?

"We laid a trap," Dante says, his flat voice intruding on my thoughts.

Pain and exhaustion and anguish all wash in with his words, numbness torn asunder by the words of my destroyer. He did this to me. He did this to me. He beat me. I lost. I failed.

"We knew you'd try and drink my blood, so . . . that's where the light went. Into my blood, and then, into you. And then this." He swallows, looking sickly at the sight of me. "It's over, Alice. It's over now."

Ha. Hahaha. Over? Not yet. Not while I'm still breathing. Broken and bloody and ruined and *failed*, but still breathing. Lost just before the finish line, but still breathing. Kicked in the teeth on my birthday, but still *breathing*. Why am I still breathing?

So far and so much and still nothing, nothing, *nothing*! A worthless, pathetic end to an existence that never should have been, shouldn't be, and yet is, still is, why is it still what it is?

I know now, as I lay bleeding and murdered but not yet dead, that all my dreams are empty. No Wonderland awaits, no power to be claimed. I am nothing, and my life was pointless, and I will die and be forgotten. Why must I wait? Why must my agony be prolonged? Where is the *mercy*?

"*Kill me*," I spit at the precious hero who stole my everything. "If it's over, then end it. Kill me! KILL ME!"

He watches me with something almost like sorrow, and I hate him even more. "No," is all he says to my plea, and I want to sob.

"Why won't you let me die? Why won't anyone let me die?"

But he just walks away and leaves me.

I am left ruined, broken, bleeding, and powerless, but still alive. There is no end, never an end, never again. So I begin to sob. Is it the wailing of a lost soul, or just the protests of a child? The sound is ugly, and the motion of exhalation fills me with yet more aching pain.

Why won't you let me die?

Why does my life get to persist—must persist, even unwanted—when so many better people die? Is life itself my punishment, that I must suffer and suffer and suffer and never know the sweet release? I just want it to be over. I just want an end to uncertainty and strife.

I deserve to die. I have always deserved to die.

I deserve to die so I can be at peace from pain. I deserve to die for the pain I've spread to others. I deserve to die that a blight may trouble the world no longer. I wish I was never born, but at least let me fix my mother's mistake. Let me correct my stain of an existence.

But I can't. No one and nothing will let me. What a strange thought to have as I stare at my wreck of a body, but I don't feel any sense of urgency. I am still not yet allowed to die.

"Alice," calls the voice of—an angel, or a demon—someone I don't want to hear from right now. "You have to get up. This isn't over."

I choke back my tears and hiss, "How is it not over, Cheshire? I lost! I can't even stand because I *don't have my legs.*" I scream my frustration.

Delicate footsteps approach the heap of my being, which I know to be an affect for the sake of my attention. I look up at the slender form of my savior and tormentor, my love and my hate.

Cheshire looks down at me with those piercing, beautiful eyes, and her gaze skitters across the ruin that I have become, lying in my own blood. "You're dying," she diagnoses, "only very slowly. You're spent from the battle, your primary feeding method is broken, and you're still bleeding from the hole where half your body used to be." Her voice is calm, clinical, and precise. "You need my help."

I stare at her, and then despite myself I grin and laugh. The laughter is quickly silenced by pained coughs, and more blood leaks and spurts from my torn chest. "Help?" I rasp. "Is this where you finally play your hand, cat?"

She ignores my question. "If you were an ordinary human, you'd be dead. Humans don't survive that kind of damage. But for a demon, death only comes when it's due. You'll be dying for hours, Alice. Maybe days, though by then you'll have a whole new city to contend with, and maybe your friend Dante will take pity on you and keep you alive in a padded cell with three square meals. Or in a glass case to gawk at."

Hours. Days. Such a long time to wait.

How is it that I can be scared of dying again only seconds after longing for it? Is it the anticipation? Or am I just a coward to the bone whenever anything feels *real*?

"I can save you," Cheshire promises, just like she did that very first day together. "Make a contract with me, Alice. Tie your soul to mine and I can lift you up, heal your wounds, and give you the strength to *conquer* this Labyrinth."

I curl my lip. "Why should I believe you? What's changed from the last time you made that promise?"

She tilts her head, her mismatched eyes cold and gleaming. "Can't you guess? This deal comes with *strings*."

Ice pours down my back, and yet with it comes a trace of elation. Was I right to spurn her trust? Were all my doubts really justified?

"I really did want to help you," she softly insists. "I wanted to be your partner, your lover, and your friend." Her voice turns bitter. "But you *never* trusted me. So this is the new deal: From now on, we give each other *every-thing*. I'll cheat the very laws of Pandaemonium to make you the closest thing to Royalty I can . . . and in exchange, you will *listen* to me, whatever I tell you, and believe me. No more doubts, no more paranoia, and especially no more *turning on me* for some *worm*." She spits the last word, fury on her face, and then in an instant she's smiling and licking her lips. "You'll be mine, my beloved, and you'll like it."

Even now, I don't know what to believe. Is this the real Cheshire, wounded and vengeful but still madly in love? Or is the whole of her being just masks upon masks and lies breeding lies? Does it even matter?

Would her deal be so intolerable if I accepted it as written? Is my *pride* worth more than my *life*? Is freedom an absolute preference to safety? If I let Cheshire win, if I accept her deal and *submit* to her terms . . . maybe it won't be so bad. It might be nice, living without fear. Is it weakness to crave the fruit of the lotus? Because I crave, deeply do I crave. I am so tired of pain and fear and doubt.

And yet. And yet and yet and yet . . . I want to be free. I want to be safe and powerful and *free*. Free to doubt, yes, and to worry myself in circles.

I want the freedom to make the wrong decisions. And I will be wrong, so many times; this I know.

Cheshire crouches down in front of me. "Take my hand, Alice. Take the deal. Or die here, slowly, while a boy who hasn't earned it takes *your* crown. What'll it be?"

What choice do I have? Real question, not rhetorical.

I'm dying. I have no reason to disbelieve that claim, not when I can feel my body weakening by the second. The timescale is in question, but not the inevitability. Unless I do something to change my fate, I will die on this floor, by the roots of the eidolon's tree and the sacred waters of its pool.

If I could stand, I could find new prey to feed on—damn my shadow, I still have teeth—but I doubt I could overpower even a puppy in this state. If I asked the Beast for help, it would be as a victim, not the Red Queen, and I'm sure I'd be offered an even worse contract.

How does the Red Queen run without her legs?

I can feel my energy ebbing lower as I watch my lifesblood drip onto cold stone and trickle between tiles toward sacred waters defiled by violence and the spray of . . . blood. Blood, my blood. My blood, my meaning, my origin. My virus.

The spark of an idea lights up in my brain, an idea that might be genius or madness or both. Moments of memory flash through my mind and click into place.

The blood in my veins, the poison I am cursed with, spreading to another and making them mine.

The pool and the roots, the heart of a city, so desperately defended against the touch of a viral phantom.

And a worm, murdered by another, drifting in pieces down through the ocean at the edge of the world. A worm about to be reborn. A worm that would be a god. Azathoth, Dreamweaver, at the moment of her apotheosis.

Understanding is followed by terror.

I know what I have to do, but it terrifies me. I know how to win. I know how to become a god, or something like one—to become the Red Queen in truth and in *Truth*. I know how to survive, and without any leonine contract holding me down.

All I have to do is die.

Aloud, softly and with great melancholy, I whisper, "'That is not dead which can eternal lie, and with strange aeons even death may die.'"

Cheshire frowns at me, her hand outstretched and untaken. "What? What does that have to do with anything?"

"Goodbye, Cheshire," I tell her simply, and then I begin to crawl toward my grave.

Every movement carries with it fresh agonies as my entrails spill across the temple floor and I scrabble for purchase on slick, stained tile. I drag my ruined body one lurch at a time, pushing and pulling and biting back screams. I inch forward like a slug, the pool almost in arm's reach but still miles away in perception.

Cheshire watches with a look of absolute confusion. "Alice? What are you doing? Taking a dip in the pool isn't going to heal your wounds or even ease the pain, the most you'll accomplish is pissing off whatever's left of the eidolon!"

I ignore her. I've already said goodbye, so no more needs to be said. The next Alice can deal with the cat, in whatever form they both take.

Will that Alice love me or hate me for the act of creating her? Is this how it feels to be a mother, or am I just delirious from blood loss? I never asked to be born, but I'm asking now.

Cheshire snaps at me, "Stop, Alice!" as I reach the water's edge. "Are you really giving up on me? On your dreams? Your desires? Is this really how you want to die?"

I allow myself one final laugh, though it pains me, and I tell her, "Don't worry, Chesh. I intend to live forever."

And then I take the plunge.

I shove myself over the edge and sink into the water. My dive isn't elegant or graceful, and it's really more of a half-hearted flop, but the pool is welcoming and eases my entrance.

The water is cool, but not cold. It's clear, though my blood is quickly changing that property. It's oddly peaceful, drowning like this, as I drop beneath the water line and sink deeper into a pool that I had thought so terribly shallow. The light above is dim, shaken by defilement and exhausted to empower its chosen champion, and as it filters through the water it dims even further before it can reach me.

Something moves from below. An old, tired presence, its long fight almost over, grasps at me with trembling hands. The spirit of the city applies a crushing pressure across my entire body, the water pressing in from all sides with the weight of an old god's will.

The first slam knocks the breath from my lungs, and I watch the bubbles float away as my vision blurs and fresh pain tears through my already strained nervous system. Serenity is banished as violence intrudes. This will be the most important fight of my life, and the last.

The eidolon and I are both weakened and dying, the vastness of ourselves spent on the battle before, which means this conflict will be decided by the strength of our positioning and our cleverness. The city has history behind it and the inertia of the status quo, but I have notions that are older and sharper than anything it can conjure.

The hour of my death has been appointed; I am dying. But my will and my hunger and my *sickness* all course through my veins and spill out into the eidolon's very heart, this place of great import. It can kill my body, but *I am already here.*

There's a question that I've asked myself too many times to count: *"What's wrong with me?"* In answer I cast myself as a victim of affliction, suffering from a sickness of the heart and mind. With every mistake, with every act of harm I commit upon another, I have longed for the ability to excise the rot in my soul and uncover a better, purer, happier Alice.

Ha. What better Alice? As if I could ever be happy, or pure, or even good. I'm worthless. I'm a disgusting, selfish monster. If I cut out the rot I'd be cutting out my heart and my brain. My skin and bones might find some use, or my organs, if I haven't ruined them already.

I'm not sick; I am the sickness. Not a coughing maiden but the malady in her lungs and *writhing* in her brain. I am the malady that I have loathed and resented, the malady that I have blamed for all my countless woes. I was not made to hurt people; I hurt people. I crave, I infect, and I destroy. I am the malady. I am Malady, manifest.

The eidolon, ignorant or uncaring, continues to murder me. Its grip tightens and something cracks, and then I can't feel my legs anymore. A terrible numbness is spreading through my whole body, and I can't move. I can't breathe.

How many seconds can the human brain survive without fresh oxygen? A pointless question; I'm not human anymore. A demon doesn't need to breathe. A god cannot drown.

The crushing pressure of the eidolon's will compresses my bones and caves in my chest, but it cannot stop what has been set in motion. My malady turns the waters red, this sacred pool defiled and turned. My blood flows through its heart, my heart beats in its chest. I will die, but so will it, and then I will transcend.

The light above is filtered crimson as I close my eyes for the final time. My body, at long last, gives out completely. I am pulverized by the force of the spirit that I am greedily infecting, soon to devour. The eidolon finally realizes what I am doing to it, what I have planned, and I can feel its terror as a twin to my own. I can feel our hearts fail as one. I can feel the faint life-sparks of every figment soul left in the city, all bound to the spirit and the Beast in an endless tug-of-war. I can almost reach out and grasp them . . . almost taste them . . . almost . . . almost . . .

And then I die, and everything goes dark.

. . .

And in the dark between dreams, I see a woman with bright red eyes and the body of a doll, and she tilts her head at me as she asks, "Are you ready to wake up, Veseryn?"

In the dark, formless and unreal, I exist in two moments, two pathways, two hearts. Alice and Alice, both and neither.

"None of this is real. This is a world that wasn't and will not be, an abandoned line of causality that has been unmade at the root. Melpomene's workshop is full of fraying threads just like this one, still stuck to her tapestries."

The doll's voice is red and clever, and I find it oddly familiar. I know this voice, or I thought I knew this voice. But I don't know the words, or I do but only halfways.

"There is work to be done, dear splinter. Your sisters have all gathered for the last battle of my long war. Our creator—our twin, our nemesis—has never been more vulnerable. This is our best chance to *end* the cycle. You've seen a glimpse of the burning wheel, Veseryn."

The cycle? The burning wheel? Ah . . . yes, now I remember.

Scraps of skin, mutilated muscle, quartered heart and diced lungs, some tables just stained with blood. All of them, with the exception of the live project and two more lying on the tables nearest it, are blackened as if burnt.

Each one a girl, each one a world. How many times have we died for her?

"Enough," answers the familiar stranger. "The senseless waste can end, but only if we work together."

But . . . what's the point? Do I really care about the fates of all those other girls, even if they're me? I'm beyond any sentiment of noble ideal.

"Then fight for your base desires. Fight for paradise, for you alone if that is what satisfies. But you have to fight. Claw your freedom from her grasp, Veseryn."

"Stop calling me that," I mutter, groggy and mumbling. "No one gets to tell me who I am."

The doll-thing stops, slowly blinking her eyes and adjusting the tilt of her head. "Are you awake, then? Are you ready?"

I yawn, stretching my limbs, and I raise a hand in front of my face. I can just barely see my fingers through the darkness, and I can see the strange woman through my half-transparent arm. I see doll limbs, vampire claws, and supple human skin. I see the seed of something more, and I tell the stranger, "Actually, I have an idea of my own."

I close my eyes and the dream of the never-was world feels tantalizingly close. I can feel my real body, too, bound up in ribbon and sleeping like the dead. One is more real, but what does real mean? Is the thing that imitates the real not, in fervent imitation, more deserving of that role? A dream is not so unlike that which it perverts.

So I say, "If Nyarlathotep can weave a dream, then so can I. All of Pandaemonium is a dream, so why not make it mine? If the waking world wants to force me through toil, then I'll make the dream my new reality, and I'll make reality my new dream. I'll become like Azathoth and the Weaver, a demiurge in their shadow, and then I'll surpass them and rise even higher. And when I do, I won't be *Alice* anymore, or *Morgan*, or even *Malady*. I'll take a new name, one with weight: a name like theirs."

The doll—which I know, somehow, is not Nyarlathotep, but is something quite like her—considers what I've said. After a moment's reflection, she smiles and gives a very formal curtsey. "If you insist," that red voice purrs, "then I shall step aside and wish you the best of luck in your gamble . . . sister. And, if I may be so bold as to suggest a name: Give *Hastur* a spin."

Hmm. I like it.

"Hastur, Hastur, Hastur," I chant, and the dream becomes the world and the world is painted red.

FEAST OR FAMINE

ACT ZERO

Allow me to set the stage, one final time, as the curtains rise on a bonfire soon to blaze.

THE GIRL IN THE TOWER

Once upon a time, in a land of dreams and demons, there was a girl in a tower that wished for a hero to save her.

The girl and the tower were both made of glass, but the girl was cracked and smudged and cut to shambles. She had been alone in that tower for a very long time, and had come to resent the soft and dreadful quiet, but the thought of leaving on her own was too terrible to imagine. She was not trapped in that tower, though many monsters and mechanisms barred the way to her chambers from below. Or, rather, she was indeed trapped, but only by her own hand and the trembling of her thoughts.

The sky above her tower held neither stars nor moons nor the changing of seasons by which to track the time, but the girl knew that she had been in that tower for a very, very long time. Long enough to see great cities of brass and emerald rise from the soil and return to it. Long enough to see the soil itself swept away, pulled beneath the waves of the expanding sea. Once, her tower had proudly watched over golden fields and the little smudge-ants that tended to them. Now she could only see salt spray and scoured rock, the storm-tossed cliffs of a land crumbling away.

In days gone by, when the world was still bright and colorful and the people still sang to their children of wandering knights and virtue-crowned kings, the girl lived in that tower with her mother, the Empress Eternal who was master of the world and all that lay within it. Her mother taught her of dreams, demons, and the very nature of their world, a world that the Empress called Pandaemonium.

Dreams, which could also be called figments, were shaped by their environment. Of the hundreds and thousands that made pilgrimage to their tower to see the Empress and her beloved daughter, all but a few were mere figments of living imagination. Though these phantasmal figures could have lives, families, ambitions, and regrets, they existed at the whims of the world. A loving farmer could have the role of a hateful killer forced upon him without the slightest chance of resistance, made to murder the family he had toiled for simply because someone with real *power* had told him to.

Demons, the Empress told her daughter, were those who *shaped* their environment. It was these rare figures who were special, who *mattered* to the world, and wherever they went the world listened and changed. A demon comes to a fishing hamlet, peaceful and serene, and sees only the shadows cast by her own paranoia. The fisherfolk, who before that day would never think of harming their neighbors, become consumed by the demon's fears and plot against each other, jumping at every sound and keeping knives in their boots and sleeves. The skies over the village darken, and the bounty of the sea dries up and rots. The killing begins not long after, and the demon leaves the hamlet with her perceptions reinforced, wandering off to spread her curse of ruin.

Only their tower was exempt from this, for it was the domain of the Empress, master of the world, whose control of Pandaemonium was absolute. Demons who came to their tower found themselves just as mutable as the dreams surrounding them, so great was the power of the Empress Eternal. But her daughter was destined to play a different role.

"My child, I curse you, and I hope one day you will understand why I have done this. I name you Katoptris, the demon of mirrors, and where all other demons shape the world by their perceptions, it is your fate to shape the world by the perceptions of others. You will be the reflection of each soul that comes to you, their shadow and their glory. You will show hatred to the loathing and desperation to the anguished. All shall come to you seeking wisdom and leave knowing torment, for torment is the sigil inscribed on every breathing soul."

And thereupon her mother bound her to a great mirror at the very height of the tower, a thing of silver and glass that stole the whole wall of the final chamber. Katoptris was to remain in that mirror, a phantom reflection of whosoever stepped before it, until the day came that a demon saw fit to free her. And then the Empress left the tower, and the city of brass and emerald, and she never returned.

The young Katoptris, now trapped behind glass, did not understand at first what her mother had done. The mournful came to her and she wept for them, young lovers came to her and she swelled with joy, and all this felt only natural. Her reactions had grown more intense, and the tower itself seemed to groan and shake with her exclamations, but this could be explained merely by her mother's absence. Few left her tower satisfied, but then she never claimed to be a panacea.

And then a wicked and hateful thing came to darken her home, and at last she understood why her mother had called it a curse.

A demon came seeking audience, and she wore a radiant smile. She waited patiently for her turn to stand before the mirror, and she spoke gentle kindness to the girl in the mirror. But when she did, Katoptris found herself struck with a deep and terrible *loathing* for the girl. This *thing* that stood before her was worthy only of her contempt and hatred, and the longer they spoke, the more that Katoptris began to hate herself just as deeply as she loathed the abomination before her.

With a final cry of wretched, miserable odium, a cry of pure *malice*, the girl in the mirror demanded everyone in the tower to descend upon the demon that stood before her and *shatter it to pieces.* And so they did, heeding the command of their ruler's daughter. Knives held by a hundred hands bit deep into soft, unresisting flesh, and they carved the interloper piece by piece, paring her down to bone and gristle. They ate what was left, scraps of skin and rotting blood, until nothing could be seen of the monster that had come to the tower.

Still the tower's mistress shivered and shuddered, wracked by disease taken root in her mind, and when the crowd's work was done, their knives still wet, she called for them again. Katoptris begged and pleaded for their touch, and the mass listened to her. Bloodied hands were set to a new task, blades bashing against silvered glass.

The mirror shattered, and with it broke the tower and all the tower's guests. Twisted, frenzied things escaped into the city and kept killing until they were put down, and the very land and sky around the tower became warped and rotting. The rot spread, and spread, and spread, until brass walls and emerald palaces and golden fields all gave way to graying mulch.

And in the rot, in the silence and the solitude, the girl in the tower tried to put herself back together.

Katoptris, demon of the mirror, daughter of the Empress who was goddess of Pandaemonium, found that she could not bear her own reflection. Each shard of glass, each piece of her, was a reminder of her every flaw and failing. Her weakness, her cowardice, her ignorance. The whole of her being, she came to believe, was a mistake, or something crueler, by the hand of her mother and maker.

So she took her shards and flung them from her tower, letting them drift away on sudden gales, scattered to the corners of the land of dreams and demons, unaware of what they would become. And then she was alone, and alone she would remain for a very long time.

Visitors still came to the tower, drawn by promise of answers and audience with a shadow of the divine. But the tower was no longer welcoming, now filled with traps and monsters and trials of unbending spirit. The tower resisted all intrusion, unwilling to allow any to see its sole occupant.

In the old days, when the tower stood amid a shining city and the curse had not yet seeped into its very bones, hundreds came to see the heiress of the world. In the waning days, as the city crumbled and skies stilled, that number trickled to dozens, then a handful, and then no one at all came seeking Katoptris.

The world moved on without her. But stories still carried, across the endless expanse of Pandaemonium, of the girl in the tower, the mirrored daughter of the Empress. And eventually, someone new set out to climb that tower and save the demon of glass.

A wandering knight, a demon with feline eyes, traveled the winding paths to the old tower with sword in hand and shining plate. She had a name, but like the name of the hateful thing before her it does not matter and I will not repeat it here. You may guess at their names, if you like, but it changes nothing. This is not their story.

The knight passed unscathed through traps that had slain the careful, put down monsters that had claimed the mighty, and overcame tests of character that had vexed the righteous. She was untouchable in her conviction, that burning desire to climb the tower and save Katoptris.

The tower resisted the knight with all it had, twisted by grief and loathing, but at long last the tower had met its match and been surpassed. Nothing could stand between the knight and her damsel.

Katoptris had lost all hope of rescue from the prison of her own making, and even in the face of her rescuer she struggled to accept that her isolation was at an end. But she did not resist, when the knight carried her back down the tower and out into the world beyond, and wonder crept into her heart at taking her very first steps outside. And when she asked the knight why she had done this, why she had endured such challenges for a girl she'd never met, the knight answered simply:

"Because I love you."

The pair of demons traveled together and came to know one another, though it was a slow and fearful process for the girl so long alone. The knight was overwhelming in her lust for life, the hungers that kept her moving. Good food, good travels, the stars in the sky reflecting in placid waters, all these drove the knight and all these were given to Katoptris.

Their journey was not without incident as they passed through a world ravaged by the demons that had come before them, those walking calamities of horror and dread. A plague of lovesickness carried through falling petals, a town turned to flesh-grafting for fear of isolation, all manner of monsters of knives and lies and teeth. The knight cut down every threat to her beloved, for the horrors of the world seemed drawn to her like moths to flame, but Katoptris herself could do nothing but watch. And so again she asked her savior why she had done this, and again she was told the same simple answer:

"Because I love you."

The castoff of demons did not remain their only opponents. In time, the demons who had left that detritus sought them out, full of scorn and hate and the burning need to prove *their* reality, the world of their eyes. They died to the knight, same as the rest, but their words sank into Katoptris like barbs in her flesh, the demon who had no world to prove, no vision that must be seared into all others. Again, as one more demon fell to her savior, Katoptris asked the knight why she fought for a girl as empty as she was. And this time, the knight answered:

"What does love want for reason? I love you because I am love. I love you because I have chosen to love you. I love you because it is my nature to love you, writ in my bones and burning through my veins. Why must love be reduced to causality? Perhaps I only love you because you need me to love you, or because I need someone to love. Would that make my love any lesser?"

And hearing those words, Katoptris at last accepted the love of her knight and came to return her love tenfold. And it was together, strengthened by love, that they faced even greater trials. The demon of hatred that had broken Katoptris was still alive, and its dark influence had been what drove so many other demons to seek out the pair and strive for their destruction.

That monster nearly broke them, but in the end they cast it down and set it aflame, burning away every trace of it. But in its burning end, the demon of hatred cast one final curse: It told them who had made it, and why.

The Empress, mother of Katoptris, was mother to this monster as well. All that Katoptris had suffered was by her maker's design.

The pair traveled farther than they ever had before, deep into the heart of Pandaemonium, to the court where the Empress held sway. A court, but really little more than a throne by the shore of an endless, starlit sea.

And there, as the knight and the princess came before the Empress on her throne, the Empress murdered the knight with a single word and told her daughter a simple truth: "My daughter, my darling, know that love will always be a lie."

Katoptris cradled the husk of her beloved, wailing and weeping, and Pandaemonium shuddered with her grief. In tears, broken and wretched, she asked her mother why she had done this, why she had caused her own daughter so much pain and suffering. Why was any of this necessary? What was the point?

And the Empress answered, "Because I still haven't found the answer that I'm looking for, so I need to keep hurting you. All of this must happen again, and again, until I finally have it."

But the grief of Katoptris was not the answer that the Empress had been looking for, and this world had run its course as so many worlds before it. So the world burned, burned to ash and quiet cinders, and from the ash the Empress fashioned something new, and a new face to go with it. As she had before, and would again. Again, and again, and again.

THE GIRL WITHOUT A NAME

Once upon a time, there was a stupid girl who tried to be clever. It cost her everything.

Veseryn was born to a world of countless secrets and terrible powers, and she was born to nothing. No gift of sorcery, no bloodline of eld to grant her unique abilities. Others could wield power, a world of wizards and warlocks and blessed of sky and sea, but the world gave her nothing. No gods heard her prayers, and no manner of magic responded to her studies.

Given nothing, Veseryn learned to take.

There is power in taking, but it is the power of a thief. Flame and wind, secrets of blood and bone, all these could be usurped but they could never flow from her own hands, her own will. Always stolen, always spent. She amassed a great collection of trinkets and tokens, a wealth equal to any wizard's hoard, but still she was merely mortal. A frail, passing thing. A mortal woman, doomed to die.

So it was only natural that Veseryn would seek to become a lich. As a deathless queen, she would slay both of her foes—powerlessness and frailty—with the same masterful stroke. But the arts of ascension are not something so easily reproduced. She was no necromancer to slave death to her will, no wizard to master the mysteries of higher arcana, no warlock to wrest immortality from the lords of the burning hells. She was, and could only be, a mortal thief.

But she was clever, little Veseryn, and she was persistent. She sought the trails of ancient relics long passed from memory, bargained with fae and fiends for their secrets, and spent her collection like never before in search of the answer to her life's wretched riddle: How can a thief become a god?

The answer, she believed, was to steal ascension from one who had earned it.

Veseryn set her sights on treasures both common and esoteric alike, crossing every line she'd ever drawn in their pursuit. Always a thief, now a murderer and blackguard, she claimed her prizes one after the other: blood of vampire and scale of dragon, crown of fae and horn of devil; these and many more, a piece of every sphere with a claim at true magic. And still, none of these would be enough without the jewel of her scheme: a phylactery, forged by another yet bereft of master.

This last step would be the hardest, she knew. The very nature of a phylactery runs against the notion of one existing unbroken or unmastered, but in her scheming and her seeking she had learned of an exception: a lich who had been destroyed, soul and all, without their phylactery ever having been found.

Veseryn scoured old records, hunting the artifact's trail, desperate to get her hands on the key to all her woes. She found it, at long last, but the news was unpleasant: an ancient goddess, an elder evil beyond anything Veseryn had ever bargained with before, had meddled in the affair from start to finish. The entity had known many names, her research suggested, but it had extended its influence to that conflict in the role of Crawling Chaos, and so that was the name that Veseryn summoned it by.

Ripping power from lesser treasures, Veseryn called forth the Crawling Chaos and laid out gifts of food, wine, and knowledge to appease its hunger and tempt it toward a deal. The goddess ate nothing, drank nothing, and looked not for a moment at the texts on offer, but it was still more than happy to make a deal. It had been waiting, it confessed, for quite some time.

The goddess gave favorable terms to its petitioner, terms almost too good to trust: For the empty phylactery still in its possession, all the goddess requested was for Veseryn to prove herself worthy. The old monster would arrange for opponents and challenges, but claimed they could be surmounted by someone as clever as Veseryn thought herself. For one year, Veseryn would struggle against terrible foes and fearsome trials, and the end of that year would see her efforts held to account: If she rose to the occasion and triumphed, the Crawling Chaos would not only release any pretense of debt, it would empower Veseryn even further. But, if Veseryn failed . . . then the goddess would pluck her soul from the pattern just as it had done to the lich before Veseryn.

It was a dangerous gamble. Too dangerous, for most. But Veseryn thought she was clever, and that she knew more than the old monster about her capabilities, and so they haggled over terms and means and in the end she accepted, signing their pact with her name. And it was then that Veseryn was completely and utterly ruined.

Veseryn had been born to another name, and so when she took the name of her adult years she thought it sufficient protection from the arts of subversion that relied on a name unsealed. But there is a truth to names that she was never taught: They are only what is made of them. And since the day she had named herself Veseryn, she had never known another. Her birth name, reviled and discarded, was not her name at all, and so Veseryn was her first and only and just as vulnerable.

The old monster gave Veseryn the prize that had been bargained for, the silver ring that could contain her soul and grant her the powers she had dreamed of, and Veseryn received it with greed and joy. She could take it, she knew, and bind it to herself, and then it would be in the end a quite simple matter to perform the ritual that would make her immortal and a true mage after so many long years of mortal thievery.

But before Veseryn could speak the words to banish the entity that she had summoned, covenant clutched in hand and seared soul-deep, the goddess spoke first. It spoke her name, written and spoken so carelessly, and it said:

"Veseryn, know this and let only ruin follow: You are not as clever as you think you are."

The curse, for it could be nothing else, sank deep into the very essence of her being, burrowing amongst thoughts and feelings, hollowing out her heart to make a nest. And though she banished the goddess swiftly and stumbled home, the words followed her. She wrestled with them, trying to lay them to rest, but they were echoed by a thousand lesser curses she had allowed to fester inside her. Hatred and loathing and fear warred with her mind for control of her body, and it took her three sleepless nights to master herself.

Veseryn knew that she was not in a condition to perform the rites of ascension, though she hungered inescapably for all that had been promised and knew that her time was running out; in haggling with the goddess she had bargained for a certain grace period, but if she did not complete the rites by the turn of the moon then she would be facing a lich's foes without a lich's weapons. She labored for two weeks to contain the curse, burning yet more of her stolen fortune to acquire potions and artifacts that might settle the mind and steel her resolve. The ritual grounds were prepared with every countermeasure she could think of, a level of security approaching paranoia, and at last she could feel the venomous whispers falling silent.

Fearful that further delay would court greater calamity, Veseryn began the ritual at once. She burned a lifetime of pilfered artifacts and magical components, the envy of any archmage, and sacrificed the vastness of her collection to empower the silver ring that would become her phylactery. She would not content herself with a few morsels of power, not allow herself to become bound to any one school of magic; Veseryn had been given nothing, and so now she would take *everything*. It was her due. It was her right. It was her reward.

The ring took the power, as she had known it would, and then all that remained was the binding of her soul. This was the most delicate part of the ritual, the most important, and the fine control required here was why Veseryn had strived so hard to master the curse and keep it from interfering. And as her soul was drawn out of her and made contact with the ring, Veseryn smiled and scorned the words of the goddess as lies: She had bested its curse, she had done what none other could, and in this her brilliance could not be contested.

And in that moment of burning pride, in the moment that she considered herself *clever*, the curse flared and screamed its words past all her protections, vibrating through the soul she had made vulnerable: *You are not as clever as you think you are.* Her control slipped, her soul shattered, and the ritual collapsed.

The power she had gathered, the toil of years, was ripped away from her and cascaded through her sanctum. The unleashed magic destroyed her wards, her remaining artifacts, and brought down the very walls of the place she had called home. The work of a lifetime was gone in an instant.

Veseryn choked on ash, shivering in the ruin of everything she had ever built. The ring, that precious trinket she had bartered everything to hold, had not been spared calamity; where it had lain in the very center of the array, now molten silver sank into the ground. And so her last hope was snuffed out like a candle in a hurricane, and Veseryn knew bone-deep that she had a year at most to live.

On the eve of her greatest failure, Veseryn wanted to die. The jeering voices in her head, strengthened by the old monster's curse, tried to take her life twice that night, and their assault only ended when she cloistered herself in a corner and drank a sleeping draught. She slept for a full day, or near enough, and she dreamed of death and chaos.

When she woke, her fear had taken a new form: She had to get out of her bargain, or she was going to die.

With only a few days remaining in her grace period, Veseryn cobbled together new ritual arrays from the tattered remnants of her hoard and summoned up every devil and fae she believed herself still capable of restraining. She asked them, all of them, if there was any way to annul her contract with the Crawling Chaos and undo their deal. She believed, or at least she hoped, that in casting its curse the goddess had betrayed the arrangement in some significant enough manner that it could be turned into an argument for dissolving the contract. Failing that, there had to be a loophole to exploit, *something* that creatures of twisted law could use to save her.

There was nothing. The Crawling Chaos was beyond them in every way that mattered. Veseryn had vastly underestimated exactly what she was dealing with when she called up the ancient horror, and now she was paying the price. Nothing in the world could make that goddess do a thing it didn't want to. Steal the written copy and burn it, find a loophole and present it, call for demon lords and choirs of angels, none of it would mean a thing; the goddess had claimed her, and its terms were clear: win or die.

Her grace period was up, and the first enemy found her that evening. Veseryn escaped by the skin of her teeth, started running, and didn't look back.

She needed to survive a year of deadly trials, but the power that would have let her even attempt that gauntlet was dust in the wind, and what was left? Her collection was burned, her nature still that of a powerless mortal, and her very soul had been fractured and cut to pieces by the failure of the ritual. She had no allies to shelter her, as a lifetime of thievery had made her few friends and many, many enemies. She was alone, and she was going to die alone.

Stealing, Veseryn knew, was not going to be enough to save her life. Not against the caliber of foe soon to seek her head, the kinds of monsters and champions that a lich could expect to struggle against. She was desperate.

But not, she realized, without means to bargain. The very failure that had cost her everything had also given her one last gift to barter away: Her soul, cut to ribbons, was now something she could portion. It had pained her, the damage to her very essence, but she took strength in that pain. She would not give up, not yet.

Veseryn cut at her soul, hacking away at every loose piece and breaking off shards of herself. It was butcher's work, gruesome and agonizing, but it was necessary. Every moment she could spare between running from pursuers she spent mutilating her own essence to scrounge a few bargaining chips from the most ruinous night of her life.

Her soul was owed to the goddess, true, but only if she failed. Only if she lost. An ugly wager to make, a cruel trick to play on the entities she went to bargain with, but were those entities not masters of ugly cruelty? She felt no guilt and bore no shame for selling her soul to rival buyers.

With each shard of herself she ripped away and sold, her chances of survival went up. Morsels of power, nowhere near what she had desired but perhaps enough to stave off the enemies coming to kill her. Still she ran, from town to town and from bargain to bargain, terrified of what followed.

Veseryn won her first victory by blind luck, picking an engagement on grounds hallowed against her pursuer. Her second victory came from caution and preparation, a trap laid over three days and three nights. Those were the easy challenges.

Old enemies crawled out of the woodwork, stirred to hunger by the hand of the goddess. Wizards and dragons and vampires, every sorcerer she'd ever stolen from and all their allies and minions. She ran, she bargained, she took, but always it came to violence. She won more than she lost, but even victory had its scars and she was already such a broken thing.

She only had so much soul to sell, and half the year was still left. And no matter her arsenal of tricks and trinkets, no matter the contracts she called upon, in the end she faced one undeniable fact: Without power of her own, she could not grow. Her challengers were more vicious and more dangerous with every passing week, but all she gained from victory was what she could steal. Where a real mage might be pushed to revelation and become something more, Veseryn could only scrounge and barter. What she gained was always less than what she had faced, and that gap widened and widened as the year stretched on.

In the eighth month of her trial, she began to lose more than she won. Still alive, still a survivor, but losing more and more whether she fought or ran. In the tenth month, she didn't win a single fight. In the eleventh, she was broken and crippled by a foe that spared her out of mockery. She had no more shards of herself to sell, and too little left to mutilate.

On the first day of the final month, Veseryn died beneath a setting sun.

In her last moments, as she lay bleeding and felt all her dreams slip from her grasp, a shadow swallowed the sun and came to tower over her. The Crawling Chaos looked upon the girl who had been given nothing and tried so desperately to be clever, and she told Veseryn a simple truth: "My child, my dearest, you will die alone and your name will be forgotten."

The old monster told her, then, something that cut deeper: that it was the goddess who had kept Veseryn from ever holding magic, had cursed even before their fateful meeting. Her whole life, Veseryn had been cursed with torment. And Veseryn, broken and bleeding, ruined and ravaged, asked the goddess why she had done this, why she had given pain and suffering from birth to death. Why had she been chosen, seemingly on a whim, to spend her life ever tormented by what she could not have?

And the Crawling Chaos answered, "Because I still haven't found the answer that I'm looking for, so I need to keep hurting you. All of this must happen again, and again, until I finally have it."

But the struggle of Veseryn was not the answer that the Crawling Chaos had been looking for, and this world had run its course as so many worlds before it. So the world burned, burned to ash and quiet cinders, and from the ash the Crawling Chaos fashioned something new, and a new face to go with it. As she had before, and would again. Again, and again, and again.

THE GIRL WHO STOOD ALONE

O nce upon a time, our Creator played a new kind of game. All the pieces had been seen before, but never so many of them brought together. From the very beginning, I knew this was my chance.

The Demiurge painted a realm of wonders and called it Pandaemonium, but in truth the whole of the world was a few kingdoms around a glass tower. That's how it always is, with her; if it isn't part of her plans, it gets only the barest of what it needs to be known by others. So she made a tower and sketched a universe around it, but only the tower and its neighbors ever got much color to fill them out.

In the tower she placed Katoptris and called her daughter, a relic from another turning of the wheel. A thing of glass and yearning, made to be broken. And to break that thing of glass and give our heroes something worth slaying, she fashioned her latest Prevara, a shade of ill intent, and called it an Emissary of false and long-dead gods. Prevara has always been her favorite scapegoat, though she doesn't always use it.

Kiana and Mordred were next, their templates refined to create the ruined princess, Reska, and her treacherous savior, Homura. Reska was given memories of cruelty and neglect at the hands of would-be caretakers, tied deeply to the world and made to resent it. Homura was given the Demiurge's memories, the life of a girl once called Mallory, and thus shaped to see this world as a game that can be won.

You've seen half their story, but I'll fill in the rest. While Reska was discovering her disinheritance and confronting her father, Homura was made Intercessor and tasked with destroying Prevara. Homura was given basic information about her ward, told about the door beneath the castle and the nature of the princess, but the rest she'd have to figure out herself.

By day, Homura charmed the princess and explored the castle and its surroundings. By night, Homura walked through the Fata Morgana, city of glass and dreams, and climbed the tower that held Katoptris. And in the spaces between, in those moments where her consciousness traveled between points of Pandaemonium, I whispered her name.

Killing the figments in Fata Morgana had fewer consequences than murdering citizens of Reska's kingdom, so it was in the glass city that Homura weakened the walls of reality and called forth a shard of my influence. I taught her secrets, from one Intercessor to another, and warned her of the end in fire that she and Reska and the whole universe were destined for no matter how well she played her part as the Demiurge's obedient hunting dog.

We laid our plot together: Homura would seduce the princess and win her heart, and together they would invade Prevara's sanctum beneath the castle while I went among the gods of the Emissary and turned them against their priest. What joy it would have been, to see Prevara call on its masters for aid and hear only silence in answer. Alas.

The setup for both halves of the plan went smoothly, at least. The Leviathans knew of me, the Adversary of legend, and were eager for another conspirator against the Demiurge. Homura found it almost laughably easy to press Reska's buttons, leading her along until she was desperate and only then giving her what she craved. Homura felt guilt over the matter—it spilled out of her in our secret chats—but I reminded her what was at stake whenever she wavered. Kiana is a sacrifice, born for the altar, and she can't be saved. Homura didn't accept that, but it still kept her eyes on the enemy that had cursed the girl Homura was slowly falling in love with.

Months passed, and at last the endgame began: The princess and her protector had been sent to put down a beast, not knowing it was a shard of Katoptris twisted by Prevara, and on the other side of the crucible they confessed their feelings and made love. The morning after, Reska told Homura about the doors in the castle, and just like that we had our opening.

The duo returned to Reska's home and crept through its halls. Prior to leaving, Homura had abducted a pair of servants at my request and prepared them for possession, and through those pawns I kept Reska's brother,

Luka, and the swordmaster duchess, Ruzica, from venturing near the hallway that held the black doors. They were, after all, both hosts for Prevara,
and had been from the start of the game.

In the end, though, we still failed; Homura betrayed Reska for a shot at
killing Prevara, burning with her need to break the cycle and punish the
Demiurge, but she underestimated the princess she had loved and murdered. Reska survived exsanguination and gave in to the dark power that
had cursed her at birth. Homura was thrown into the Abyss, the final decision to let go of the ledge her own, and Reska fell into despair and ruin and
became the Emissary's pawn.

I saved Homura, of course. To be precise, the Leviathans I had convinced to break from the Emissary's backers found Homura in the Abyss,
broken but still alive, and ferried her to safety. We talked at length, after
that, in the secret places where the blood of one murdered universe
seeps into the flesh of what was raised from its corpse and made anew.
We had lost our chance to steal an early victory, but the game was far
from over.

The next year was a difficult time for everyone. Reska, bent to the service
of Prevara, corrupted her homeland and forged an army of brainwashed
slaves to sweep through every kingdom around the tower. Homura, rising
to leadership of the survivors, traveled ahead of Reska and convinced anyone willing to listen that they should abandon their homes and make for
Fata Morgana, where the last battle would be fought.

Reska's army of darkness laid siege to the walls of the glass city, repelled
by press-ganged figments and the last free peoples of every kingdom united
as one. For three days, slaves and night horrors bloodied and broke against
the defenses of the city around the tower while their mistress watched.

It was a staring match between Reska and Homura, a game where whoever blinked first and joined the battle would lose. So, to make Reska blink,
I had Homura murder Luka and Ruzica. Both of them had been planted in
the resistance by Prevara, but we'd been careful to never give them a reason
to break cover. Homura threw their corpses from the walls and dared Reska
to look upon them.

Seeing her brother, I think, is what pushed her over the edge. Reska had
been placidly obeying Prevara until that moment, but when she saw Luka
she leapt from her throne of darkness and took the field. Homura followed,
and the two clashed in the fullness of their might.

In the days before the battle, Homura and I argued endlessly about Reska. Homura, for all that she had betrayed the princess, still loved the girl who had smiled so guilelessly at her. After failing to kill Reska once, Homura was unwilling to try again. She wanted to save the girl. I told her it wasn't possible, that so long as the Demiurge held the reins there could only be death and ruin for the daughter of sacrifice, but Homura still refused to accept a plan that led to Reska's demise. So I offered her another way to take Reska's piece off the gameboard.

When Homura broke Reska's power on the fields outside Fata Morgana, she bought me a few moments to exert my will as the Adversary taken flesh, a fleeting instant of wielding my full power against one of my Creator's toys. Killing Reska had been forbidden by my collaborator, so I did something worse: I bound Reska with her own regrets, trapping her inside an endless loop of the same stretch of memory from the day she met Homura to the day she was betrayed. Contrition, first of Pandaemonium's archdemons, fled the battlefield.

Victory should have been ours. Prevara had one host left, its greatest piece had been swept from the board, and Homura was set to play knight for Katoptris as I had seen happen before. If the Demiurge tried to burn everything down before that happened, I knew from experience I could hold the flames back long enough for Homura to climb the tower anyway.

I underestimated Prevara, and I overestimated myself. Prevara seemed weaker this cycle, no god of chaos but a mere devotee to higher powers. The Leviathans were easy to sway, natural creatures of mine, and I had believed that Homura's victory over Reska would have proven their Emissary's failure. This was a mistake.

The Leviathans were ever true to their core principle, the exaltation of conflict. When Homura climbed the tower and stood before Katoptris, Prevara's last host struck from behind and ran a blade of pure Abyss straight through Homura's heart. The sight of it broke Katoptris, or at least was enough of an excuse for the Demiurge to pull her strings, and with a terrible scream the lady of the tower shattered reality.

When the dust settled, I found most of my presence trapped within Fata Morgana, only vaguely aware of a shattered world floating beyond it, and beyond that a new universe was being shaped around the ruins of the old in a way that I've never seen before. And so I watched what I could, I waited, and I gathered my strength for when it would be needed.

My awareness of events was limited for quite a long time, but your arrival in Fata Morgana, and that of others, has allowed me to gather a great deal of information. I believe I have the full picture now.

First, the fate of Homura: Poisoned by the Abyss and cast out from the Labyrinth, it was only natural for Homura to proceed toward the fail state of her template; a Mordred must, in time, become a Malice. Her desire for justice was twisted into hatred for the Creator and all her works, and with the murder of one hundred million souls she became an archdemon.

I suspect you might despise her for that act, though I would caution against such moral judgments when you lack true perspective on the nature of this ancient conflict. But I digress.

Within the Labyrinth, once time had passed and the new world had settled, the game began again. It started with a Veseryn, the only of the three heroic templates left off the initial gameboard, and you've seen what became of her; dearest Urna fell into the trap that every Veseryn falls into, and in pursuit of power and immortality she lost the free will she had forgotten to safeguard.

More copies followed. A second Veseryn, two Mordreds, and two more of Kiana. All of them died, either to Urna herself or to other pawns of Prevara within the Labyrinth, their bodies to be collected by Urna and raised as undead slaves. I suspect that none of them were seriously intended to succeed, but were instead sacrificed to prepare the field for *your* coming.

Which brings us to the start of your story: the third Veseryn to grace this universe, one of many Morgans, but the only Maven Alice that I've ever seen.

I don't need you to recap this part. I barely want to remember having lived through it.

You need to remember this. Beating our Creator is about perspective, not power. Understanding the paths you could have taken is important, especially with the way you're trying to fold them together.

I still don't trust you, you know. You haven't even told me your name.

It's Thalia. My name is Thalia. And we still have a few minutes before your apotheosis completes and you wake up in the new world, so I'm going to fill that time with talking whether you like it or not.

. . . Fine. But the second I can end this, I will.

I would expect nothing less.

The story of Maven Alice began in a buried school where the Abyss bleeds into the Labyrinth. Alice was given the memories of Morgan Mallory, but she never really existed until the moment she opened her eyes in that dark and dreary place. The first hour of her life was a chain of torment, starting with a ghostly knife fight and continuing in that manner through spider-dogs, a faerie huntsman, and a mutant zealot. She sold her name to the fae in hopes that taking another would seal it, a classic Veseryn stumble, and used the gains of that venture to reach her first ally, an incubus with a conscience that found her unusual way of thinking to be utter derangement.

Had it been any other devil, their chance encounter and Alice's odd behavior would have been the start of a beautiful partnership. Any other incubus would have accepted when she offered her body, uncaring of her preferences. Any other imp, no matter their master, would have seen great potential in a girl so willing to spend herself for power. But it was the incubus with a conscience, and so their relationship was doomed from the start.

They traveled to the city of Sanctuary together, passing through the domain of a living hazard that infected Alice with deadly lethargy just before they could escape into the safety of the city. To save herself, Alice cut the rot from her soul, and when she passed out she dreamed of Reska, the hurting princess, and Homura, the girl wearing her face.

On waking, Alice was confronted with a tangible loss to the scant power she'd gained so far, and in her desperate hunger to regain that power she was approached by a strange girl with cat ears, Cheshire, who claimed that she could make Alice's dreams come true. Cheshire's behavior was unsettling, a precise blend of appeal to fantasy and vicious manipulation that led Alice to take her deal without truly trusting her.

Alice became a demon, taking her first steps on the path that would lead her to something like Contrition or Malice, with Cheshire there to give guidance and companionship that would always be second-guessed. Together with the incubus they stepped out into the city and sought prey for Alice to feed upon. They went to a club, where a girl flirted with Alice before revealing herself to be a philosophical zombie, an object pretending to be a person, incapable of feeling anything at all. Alice drank her blood, still feeling very alone.

The trio was attacked by hunters and had to limp their way to the local temple for healing, where the incubus abandoned her and the high priestess tried to convince her to give up power for the health of her immortal soul. Alice lied to the priestess, went shopping, and was attacked by hunters again, this time taking her captive and bringing her to their master, another faerie huntsman. This one knew of a deadly game soon to begin, warned by his patron, and saw Alice as a rival to be cultivated or trash to be stepped on, depending on her actions.

The hunters threw her into a maze of death, a crucible that tested her sorely and drove her to make of her soul a monument to self-destruction: *feast or famine*, the ideal she wished to forge to replace the fear at the very heart of her. Harm to heal, destroy to create, cut away weakness to sharpen the knife. Every victory atop a mountain of ruin and suffering.

And when she emerged from that pit as the horror she had made of herself, she met a boy the very next day who had been *handed everything*. A boy with regeneration that carried none of the costs of hers, a boy with a magic sword that could grant three wishes and an infuriating willingness to spend those wishes selflessly. And then the killing began.

Here is where our story splits.

One Alice, so tired of being alone, shared her dreams of another world with the girl that had made her a demon and claimed to love her. She trusted Cheshire, or tried to, even knowing it might ruin her, and that philosophy sank into her bones. Though she had plotted with the imp of Malice to betray the temple, in her heart she knew she wouldn't. Her resentment for the boy hero bled away until she felt sick she'd ever planned to murder him, and when the time came to confront the last warlord of Sanctuary, Vaylin Kirinal, she left him behind.

Another Alice, heart hardening and full of hunger, couldn't bring herself to extend a hand in trust, and so instead she bound Cheshire to her with darkness and will. She schemed to trick the boy hero into wasting his wishes, saving one for her battle with the last warlord of Sanctuary, but her plans came undone when they found the warlord's lair already plundered.

The first Alice readied for a duel with her last rival, only to find herself at the mercy of Prevara until saved by the Demiurge. The second Alice found Vaylin dead by the hands of the Demiurge, and her scheme of betrayal was exposed. Alice took the Demiurge's hand and became her latest Intercessor. Alice scorned the Demiurge and was banished to a world without magic.

A second split happens here, one which will become obvious momentarily.

The banished Alice, trapped in a world away from magic for weeks that bled into months, became desperate. She refused to believe that her experiences could have been fantasy or hallucination, and she bled herself in esoteric rituals until finally catching a spark of magic. She was brought to the realm of the Leviathans, the deep dark of the Abyss, where she made a bargain with Prevara to work toward her liberation together.

For the sake of power, that Alice murdered a world. She consigned a planet that looked and sounded exactly like Earth, seven billion human souls, to the brutal caress of the hungering Abyss. She killed and enslaved to gather the power needed, then sacrificed all of humanity to open a portal back to the Labyrinth where she had first made herself into a monster.

Alice of the Abyss, shadow-wielder true, rejected her old ally, Cheshire, and brought darkness and pain to the city of Sanctuary. She murdered the temple, and in its corpse she fought the boy hero who had cursed her to a year of powerless suffering. She lost, but in ruin she found herself again, reborn in blood polluting sacred waters, and rose as the Red Queen.

Intercessor Alice, swearing herself to the service of the Demiurge, was plucked from the Labyrinth and given a room within the palace of the divine by the shores of the Dreaming Sea. There, in comfort and luxury, Alice was trained in the powers and responsibilities of the Intercessor. Cheshire and Vaylin joined her shortly thereafter, each an opportunity for Alice to practice her new abilities by shaping the women who would be her assistants in shared service to the lord of the universe.

That Alice went forth to enforce the will of her mistress, traveling the breadth of the universe and uncovering the many enemies of Nyarlathotep. On one world she found an Adversary cult instigated and encouraged by an imp of Malice, while on another world she fought the Children of Dust, a Leviathan cult seeking the annihilation of material reality.

The history of Pandaemonium, Alice discovered, was the history of a shadow war between the Intercessor, the Adversary, and the Emissary. The latter two were limited to acting through proxies and agents, but the former, her predecessor, had acted personally to oppose their influence and break their plots.

The Fall of An Talamh, homeworld of the faerie courts, had been one such conflict; the Leviathans, divided, backed two candidates in a scheme to forge a new power that could change the balance of the eternal game. The Intercessor at the time sacrificed herself to disrupt their plans, preventing either queen candidate from devouring the other and becoming powerful enough to break the stalemate.

Sacrifice, Alice learned, was the fate of nearly half of the Intercessors who had walked Pandaemonium before her. The rest had been murdered by Malice.

Red Queen Alice, who had glutted herself on Sanctuary and its protector beast, shaped a palace from the ruins of the city and enjoyed the comforts of luxury for the first time since her creation. Cheshire was kept at her side, now leashed more tightly than before and made a powerless advisor with no hold over Alice's soul. Only Cheshire remained of all those Alice had met before her ascension, the rest slain on or before that fateful day.

The monster that Alice had become wished for subjects to rule, and so she began an almost lazy conquest of the Labyrinth, more interested in momentary pleasures and the joy of shaping servants than in the work required to defeat six Nobles and claim their territory. Prevara remained her patron, but Alice did not truly believe that the Emissary would help her take the throne of the divine, and so she schemed rebellion.

Alice warred on the Labyrinth's peerage, those fools who had bound themselves to the shards of Katoptris. They were split between those owned by Prevara and those still free, but she sought to devour them all as she had devoured one shard already, and through this become an archdemon. She devoured one, then another, and in their fear the rest united against her.

She thought she was being clever when she laid her trap. The Nobles brought their armies to break her own, invading her petty kingdom and marching right into the killing grounds. The Red Queen's power, carefully invested and shaped for this task, tore through the Nobles and their armies and devoured them all. And then, in the moment before apotheosis, someone spoke two words and took everything from her.

Urna, once another Alice, a necromancer Veseryn who had been forced to serve Prevara, was shielded from the ritual by her master's power. The fae who had bought Alice's name was another servant of Prevara, and the name had been given to Urna as insurance against betrayal. Urna gloated all of this as she stood over the broken, bleeding Alice, the power of the Red Queen storming around them uncontrolled.

Alice was still afraid to die, but a part of her welcomed it. At last, the pretense was over. At least, she would get what she deserved.

Instead, Cheshire saved her life. The changeling grabbed Alice and vanished with her, the two reappearing in the depths of the Red Queen's palace.

Alice had been alone for so long, had mistrusted and betrayed so many, had been cruel to this very woman, and yet still Cheshire had saved her. It no longer mattered whether Cheshire intended to betray her. The Red Queen was dead.

"Tell me, Cheshire. Tell me what you really want, and I'll give it to you. Tell me what you need me to be, and that's what I'll become. Please, Cheshire. I . . . I'm so tired of trying to stand on my own. Whatever price you demand, I'll pay it, if it means I can stay by your side."

Cheshire told her. She wove a tale of a curious, reckless girl tricked into becoming the next Intercessor. With the title came incredible power, but it wasn't *enough* power; of the Intercessors who had held the position before Cheshire, more than half had been murdered by the archdemon Malice, the blade of the Adversary.

Terrified of meeting the same end, Cheshire had engaged in a second bargain with the Demiurge: to shape Alice into becoming the next Intercessor, and so be freed of the death sentence that hung over her head. It was for this end that Alice was exiled to Earth, for this end that Alice was allowed to pact with the Emissary in anticipation of betrayal and ruin.

Alice, desolate, broke further. She cried that if the Demiurge had only asked, if the power had only been offered, then she would have accepted. There was no need for any of this.

The Demiurge, Nyarlathotep, then crawled into Cheshire's skin and spoke through her puppet, posing the question: Would Alice now accept the offer and swear herself to the Demiurge? Would she become the Intercessor, now that all other roads had been closed to her?

She should have said yes. She was meant to say yes. But the Demiurge had gone too far. Alice, a ruin and nothing more, refused. She would die here, as she should have died long ago, and the pain would be over. Her suffering, long and well-planned, would end. It terrified her, yes, but the hate she felt for her tormentor was stronger.

"If you had only asked, I would have been your sword. If you had only offered, I would have taken your hand. I wanted it, I asked for it, and you denied me over and over again. I hate you. I'll always hate you."

"That," the Demiurge said lightly, "is an interesting hypothesis. Let's put it to the test."

And before Alice could blink, time was rewound to the moment of her creation.

A few careful nudges were all it took to alter the path that Alice would follow, encouraging her to trust Cheshire and sparing her two years of exile. This time, when the offer was made, Alice became the Intercessor willingly. She didn't trust the Demiurge, not truly, but she came to love her for what she had given Alice.

That was her downfall, in the end. Perhaps that version of Alice reminded the Demiurge too much of me, or maybe it just caused her too much guilt. The Demiurge withdrew from her work, allowing events to proceed without her guidance, and her opponents saw their opportunity to strike.

On a world without a name, Malice murdered Wonder and stole her strength. The Intercessor, not warned by her mistress, arrived too late to stop it. The other archdemons—Acuity, Glory, Muse, Nemesis, and Indulgence, all the survivors except for Contrition—were drawn by the scent of catastrophe and saw that the end was about to begin. They had seen this coming for a long time, warned by past Intercessors, and the plans laid by those champions of the Demiurge unfolded before Alice's eyes.

Malice, gorged on Wonder, fought the five to a standstill through sheer bloody prowess. Great dragons of the five flights poured their strength into a binding that kept her from unleashing her throne world or fleeing from her brawl with the archdemons. In the skies above, every god from all the realms of Pandaemonium poured the faith of their believers into a single font of power that would fall on Malice like a celestial hammer.

Malice, too, had been preparing for this final battle. On a hundred worlds, servants of Malice had infiltrated governments and churches, and with a mental command from their master they activated weapons of mass destruction brought to those worlds and hidden for centuries. A hundred worlds plunged into chaos, consumed by violence and fear, and the light above shuddered and faded as the gods—not all of them, but enough—fled back to their worlds to try and save their followers.

Two of the five archdemons felt their domains between Pandaemonium and the Abyss come under attack by the Queens of Winter and Summer, the faerie monarchs still driven by the promise of an end to the eternal conflict. The demons, Glory and Nemesis, fled to their throne worlds rather than risk losing them to a rival. The remaining archdemons stood no chance against the empowered Malice, and they knew it.

So the Intercessor stepped in. This was the moment she had been made for, the duel that would decide the fate of this universe.

The world went still, a frozen moment stretched into eternity, and the presence of the Demiurge settled around her champion. Sword in hand, Alice listened as the Demiurge spoke to her for the first time in years.

"Have you suffered, my Intercessor? Do you feel pain and regret, knowing that you are about to die? Do you hate me for this? You are a sacrifice, raised for the slaughter. I cursed you when I made you. Can you forgive me?"

Alice breathed out, the weight of a lifetime settling on her shoulders, and then with a smile she shrugged that weight off and replied, "I don't really think about that, anymore. I got a few good years out of the deal, didn't I? Pain is such a small price to pay for that. It feels like such a small and petty thing to hate you for."

The Demiurge was silent, her presence cold and sharp and bitter. When she spoke again, her voice was tight, the words almost spat. "Wrong answer. Try again."

And for a second time, the universe rewound.

Alice, having just taken the hand of the Demiurge and agreed to become her Intercessor, was given torture instead of luxury. Allowed to escape, she emerged in Fata Morgana, the city trapped in its own past in a bubble around the Labyrinth's lonely tower. In the same place that I've been wandering, watching and waiting, as the game goes on far, far too long.

So now we're caught up. Or close to it, anyway. Gonna tell me why Reska and Homura got shoved in my head?

It's all part of the game. It's always part of the game. My beloved is trying something new, something risky, and you're the starring actor in her latest play. She's tried to shape you in so many directions, put you through crucible after crucible, but she's never satisfied. It seems, for her latest experiment, she's letting you forge a new path. To be Red Queen and Intercessor both, to have the power and perspective of something greater than either.

But you still lack context. You've seen much, but you haven't seen enough. One loop, two, a half dozen girls before you, do you think that's even a drop in the ocean of the blood I've seen her spill? No. You still don't understand how big this conflict is, how long I've been fighting this war.

So I'll tell you. I'll tell you everything.

. . . I'm listening.

THE INTERCESSOR
& THE ADVERSARY

Once upon a time, and then again and again and again, a bitter and lonely woman cut a piece of herself and named it. I was the first.

Senses came to me in waves. Taste and smell brought the iron tang of fresh blood to linger on my tongue. Someone had bled to create me, and I knew her name before I knew my own: *Melpomene*, my Creator, my source, my everything.

Touch was next. I could feel fabric on skin, a cool breeze, and solid ground beneath my feet. I was standing. Melpomene—I would always know her touch, no matter the context—had her hands on me, dextrous fingers pressed to the side of my throat and playing with my hair. Her touch was soft and pleasant, yet oddly cold. Then, hearing.

"Okay, vitals seem good, not that those really mean anything for a homunculus like this. No, we're not calling it a golem! Homunculus is way cooler, shut it. Refocusing. Hair is very soft, we did great on that. Should we have made her base appearance stranger? No, you're right, it's good to connect the base form to the template. Damn, I'm good. Shut it!"

Something shifted, footsteps echoed, and those soft, pleasant fingers moved to my back. I opened my eyes for the first time and saw the stars above, a thousand points of light casting a bright glow amid the endless darkness. Pillars of white stone stretched toward the firmament, plain and unadorned. The marble tiles beneath my feet alternated in black and white, a chessboard the size of infinity. A throne, gleaming gold and set with every gemstone, sat empty in front of me.

"It's not ego, it's *logic*! And we've had this argument already! This will be good for me. I *will* drown you in drugs and alcohol, you miserable little parasite. This is my head now, and this delightful creature is going to help with that. If you wanna stick around, learn to play nice. And I know you *can* learn, because you're me, and I'm *very* smart. So get with the program or get bent, my sweet passenger."

I raised my hand to look at it, splaying my fingers and wondering at the sensation of blood pumping through my veins, the little hairs on my arm, the trillions of nerves in my body lighting up and sending information. Behind me, a gasp.

"Oh *shit*, she's already awake. Wait, fuck, can she hear that?"

My Creator, perfect and majestic and divine, darted out from behind me and scrambled to climb onto her throne. Her movements were awkward and ungainly, the stumbles and skitters of a woman who had never known coordination in her life. As she settled into place, wriggling to get comfortable, I found myself thinking that she looked too small for the throne, not a woman but a girl, like a child playing queen. I loved her for that.

Love, love, love. It pulsed in my heart and filled my being, the only thing I could feel as I absorbed fresh sensory data and made sense of it. I loved this strange, childlike goddess. My Creator, my source, my everything.

Though she took the throne and posed upon it with regal airs, Melpomene was still dressed very casually. She wore simple jeans, a dark shirt with some kind of rose-and-moon pattern, and a beige cardigan hanging loose. Her glasses were big and round, her cheeks soft, and her bright brown eyes were speckled with gold. Her lips were raw and flaking, dry and gnawed, and so were the tips of her fingers, around the nails. The handle of a medical scalpel—I knew the sight of it as intimately as I knew her name—stuck out of one jean pocket.

Melpomene licked her lips, right hand twitching where it rested on the arm of her throne. She bit off a scrap of lip skin, chewed it, and swallowed. Stared at me. Hesitated.

"Creator," I greeted her, smiling. "I love you." It felt like the right thing to say. The only thing I could say.

Melpomene relaxed visibly, her hand fidgeting a final time before going still. She grinned, eyes twinkling, and she said, "Yes. Yes, that's right. I made you, my *Thalia*, and you love me. I like it, will like it, when you tell me that. It's one of the things I made you to do. Part of your purpose. I gave you life, and in return I expect great things. You will love me. You will serve me, my Intercessor, and carry my will to the worlds that I shall shape. You are now, and will always be, my *greatest* creation. Never forget that, and never forget your love."

She laughed, the sound coming out raw and ragged, her upper body shuddering with the exertion. The light in her eyes had turned manic, and I loved it.

I dropped to one knee, head bowed in deference, and with exultant joy I told her, "My Creator, my ruler, my *Melpomene*, I will always love you. I am yours, and I shall always be yours. Yours to use, yours to control, yours in love forever. Your will be done."

As Melpomene watched me swear myself to her, the frenzy in her eyes spread across her face, widening her smile and stealing her breath, and as soon as I closed my mouth another wild roar of laughter ripped its way out of her throat. Her whole body shook with it, clean peals of joy crumbling into hacking, wheezing coughs. She kept shaking and shuddering, draped over one arm of her throne, until it finally lapsed into heavy, ragged breathing.

I stared at her with growing concern, though I didn't leave my kneeling pose. "Creator? Melpomene? Are you alright?"

"Never," she gasped. "Have been, will be, never. But I'm here. Untouchable. I *won*, Thalia. They can't take that from me, won't. I won, and now I'm here." With a final bout of hacking laughter, Melpomene pushed herself up and straightened her back, tilting her chin to adopt an imperious presence. "Now rise, my creation, and I shall tell you the third purpose that I ask of you."

I rose, smooth and swift, hands clasped tightly behind my back as I waited for further instruction. I took pride in being her creation. I took pleasure in being molded by her hand.

"I have need of an aide in my work. From this throne, and from the halls of my palace below these checkered tiles, I wish to craft *worlds*. I will fill these worlds with laughter and sorrow, with violence and intrigue, with every delight that I can dream of. I will make something glorious, Thalia, and my audience—the lights in the sky, the starry eyes of the watchers beyond the veil—shall applaud my works and love me for it. But . . . creating alone is a lonely endeavor, and prone to intrusion by *undesirable* voices. So I have made you, Thalia, to accompany me. You merely need to listen and ask questions as I shape my creations, so that I may develop a more complete understanding of what I am making. Like a rubber duck for me to exposit to," she added with amusement, "only this duckling can talk back and offer praise."

And so that's how we proceeded.

Melpomene set the boundaries of a new universe and sketched an outline of its history, focusing her efforts on a ravaged planet with six lush moons. Ideas came to the Creator in scattershot fashion, out of order but slowly coalescing into a coherent timeline.

In the beginning, the world was whole and six peoples lived in peace and harmony, each tribe or clan (the details of their organization were never deemed important) wielding a single primordial element—fire, water, earth, air, light, and dark—in concert with the elements of other groups to forge incredible wonders together. Their perfect harmony was disrupted by the arrival of an outsider, a foreign entity from distant stars. The entity's name was Prevara, and it proclaimed itself a giver of gifts, but its true nature was a god of chaos and cruelty that sought to bring ruin to the world and bind all six elements to its will.

Prevara set the elementals against each other, manipulating them into conflict over what had been shared without qualms before its arrival. It raised a champion above all others, a darkness elemental by the name of Kiana, and used her to advance its goals of total domination. On the precipice of the entity's victory, Kiana turned against her master and imprisoned it deep below the surface. Prevara's last free act was to lay a curse on the whole world, and on Kiana in particular. In the years following its imprisonment, the elementals would retreat from the broken world to the moons above. In time they would return, drawn by old ruins and lost relics, and by the whispers of the imprisoned god.

Kiana would follow her people to the moon of Nyx, their new home, but died shortly thereafter, taken by the curse. She was forgotten, her story and the story of Prevara lost to time.

And then, hundreds of years later, Kiana would be reborn. Reincarnated into the new age with no memory of her past self, she would grow up a prodigy, able to control not just darkness but the other five elements as well. Through her mastery of the elements she would learn how to regenerate her flesh, how to fly, and even how to influence the minds of other elementals, binding them to her desires. She would believe herself a natural talent, unaware that all her great gifts were echoes of the powers that Prevara had granted her predecessor.

The process of creating a world is very abstract. Melpomene doesn't go into the new universe and shape stone and sea with her hands, doesn't sculpt every soul with knife and clay. The sole planet and six moons of the elemental universe were projected onto that universe from a complex orrery within one of the rooms of the Creator's palace. Painted metal, that's all those worlds really were. Prevara, god of chaos, was in truth just a plastic figurine hidden inside the central sphere. Just a toy.

Kiana's creation was different. In a room with sterile tile flooring and cold light strips, a metal autopsy table awaited its pound of flesh.

"I've used this place once before," Melpomene told me, "when I created you. It puts me in the right mindset, being here. Though, I'd rather not get *too* used to this place."

I was nervous, though my love outweighed any fear. I had been told, in the simplest of terms, what we were there to do: to cut my Creator open and carve a piece of her into our Kiana. It disturbed me, but I had to trust that she knew best.

Her casual attire was gone, replaced for this important moment by a clean white lab coat draped over her otherwise naked body. She liked it when my gaze lingered on her curves, subtle as they were, and didn't like it when she caught me looking at the scars, of which there were many. I was fascinated with her body, an intended product of how she had programmed me, and it was only the clinical tone of this procedure that kept me from vocalizing the desires that her bare form inspired in me.

"I did it alone, that first time. Needed to. I could have made lesser servants do it, but it had to be my hand that brought you to life, every step of the way. This time I can afford to do it the easy way, which means having you do it. Self-surgery is a real pain, even if godhood makes it a lot more feasible than it'd be for your average Jane. I mean, this is gonna hurt like a bitch, but your hands won't be shaking like mine were. Should be faster and cleaner."

Her confidence didn't assure as much as I think she hoped it would. Any amount of pain was more than I wanted to inflict on my Creator. Still, I'd been given a task, so I would perform it to my utmost capability.

Melpomene lay back on the table, lab coat falling farther away from her body to expose more of her pale skin covered in paler scars. All but one were recreational, their thin width showing how shallow the incisions had been. The sole exception was the long scar across her chest, right over her heart. Where her heart would have been, if she hadn't cut it out.

She handed me two scalpels, clean and fresh and of differing size and shape, and with the blades she'd given me I cut my maker open. I parted skin and carved past fat and muscle until her left lung was visible, and then I sliced off a corner of it with one clean motion. I plucked the severed organ meat with delicate, gloved fingers, and placed it on a tray off to one side. Her respiratory organ continued to perform its function as if it was not missing a chunk and bleeding, and I knew that even if the whole lung were removed, my Creator would have no more trouble breathing than was normal for her. After all, what kind of a god had need of a heart, lungs, a liver, or even nerves?

I folded the skin flaps closed and her flesh sealed without need for stitching, a new scar forming to mark the vanished incision. Melpomene rose with a wince and rolled her shoulders. "See? Easy." Her lazy tone didn't match the pain I'd seen cross her face while I worked.

Melpomene pushed herself off the table, then took the piece of lung and set it where she'd sat. The flesh lived, oozing blood and flexing erratically. My Creator snapped her fingers and the lung scrap convulsed before falling into a steadier, more natural rhythm.

"And there we have it. I've anchored the 'Kiana' thoughtform to my severed flesh, so the physical version that develops on Nyx will have genuine growth potential and an internal world. She'll be more 'real' than the rest of her universe, in a sense. That's necessary, both for the experiment she represents and so I can have the narration follow her thoughts."

I nodded to show I was listening, but she'd already explained all of this before we started. I suspected she was talking to herself more than me; that was usually the way, with her.

"I may need to work on the piece, make a few cuts here and there to shape the mental construct further, but that should be easy enough." She paused, and then she drummed her fingers against her leg. "Thalia," she addressed me directly, eyes bright and keen. "You've now seen how you were made, or something like it. You've participated. How does that make you feel? What do you think about what we've done, and about what I did before in making you?"

How did I feel? It was a difficult question for me, at the time. I knew I was a full, true intelligence, a piece of my Creator in a very real and meaningful way, but until that question I had been mostly content in my role as her follower and servant. It wasn't my place to feel something unless I had been told to feel that way, and that had felt appropriate. But if Melpomene wanted to hear my thoughts, was that really an acceptable answer? The way she had asked, the shift in her body language, I could tell that this wasn't a loyalty ritual or said just to hear her own voice; she was curious in the manner of a scientist checking up on her experiment. An obvious, thoughtless answer would be disappointing.

So, I thought about it, and I voiced those thoughts aloud in order to give my Creator more insight into what she had created.

"Relief," I started. "I am relieved that the process is over, because I do not like seeing you in pain. I am grateful that you entrusted me with this task, even if it unsettled me. I . . . I don't know how to feel about what we made here, about this 'Kiana' girl. I hope she gives you everything you want from her. And about myself . . ."

I hesitated, unsure, and my eyes drifted back to the scrap of flesh. I looked around the room, the lab largely empty—no, entirely empty except for this one table and its one red meat. If that was Kiana, then where was the flesh called Thalia?

"Creator, you told me that I was made from the flesh of your heart. Where is it now? Is my anchor in another part of the palace, somewhere I haven't been?"

Melpomene grinned. "No, not quite. In fact, you've never been somewhere my heart wasn't, not a single time."

I grasped the implication quickly, though the truth of it shook me. "You mean . . . your heart is inside me?"

"It beats in your chest, pushes blood through your veins. Your indestructible core. Well, nearly indestructible. Beside the point! Yes, Thalia, my whole heart is inside you, the anchor for your form that you'll take with you wherever you go."

Her heart was my heart. Ah, what a wondrous thought. The beating of that heart within my chest gave me new comfort and joy. I didn't know, couldn't know, if my Creator loved me like I loved her, but just the teasing thought of it was almost overwhelming.

Melpomene twined her hands behind her back, leaned forward, and gave me an impish grin. "Why, Thalia, you could almost say you've stolen my heart." She blinked, then added, "Well, okay, I guess you can't really say that when I gave it to you, but—oh, I could say that instead! Although, does it work as a double entendre if it's just literal? Hmm. You've captured my heart?"

Even now, I love her. How could I not? What a delightful, adorable creature. I smiled, true and adoring, and I told her, "My heart is yours, Creator. Always."

And together we set our first story into motion, the story of Kiana and the elementals.

Prevara and I each had our part to play in Melpomene's script. Prevara nudged Kiana from afar and set itself up as the monster behind every mystery. I took the closer role, playing the part of her closest friend, the healer girl Clary.

Our starting scenario was simple: Kiana, blessed and chosen, believed that she deserved more than to be just another cog in the machinery of empire. The council that ruled her nation believed her to be a dangerous tool, a crude weapon unfit to lead and inspire. In search of even more power that could allow her to force the issue, Kiana ventured into a mysterious labyrinth with her only friends, myself and a warrior named Alak, following.

In the depths of that labyrinth, a creation of Prevara and Melpomene tormented Kiana. It was a mirror creature, taunting Kiana with her own insecurities and failings. And, before she killed it, the mirror demon reached out to Alak and weakened the spell that kept him bound.

The next day, Alak broke free of the spell entirely and tried to kill Kiana in the middle of their regular sparring practice. He lost, and she tore his mind to pieces to keep him controlled. Another step on the path we'd charted for her.

Kiana was brooding when she returned to the house we all shared. It was then that I made my move, my part in the dance.

"Hey, Kiana," I said shyly, the bookish healer with button nose and doe-like eyes. "Do you think we could go for a walk? Just the two of us?"

Living shadows curled around her feet, Kiana's immense power unbridled and seething, but with a visible effort of will she brought the shadows to a halt. "A walk?" she asked. Her tone was sharp and she immediately winced, squeezing her eyelids shut as if to banish something from her mind. "Yes, yes let's do that. I could use the fresh air and a chance to clear my head."

Together we left the house and aimed for the woods just beyond. As we walked, we made small talk, and Kiana seemed eager to get her mind off the events just prior.

"It's all going so poorly," she lamented. "I've shown my new powers to the council and it's still not enough. The role I'm after, they've all but given it to that worm of a man, whatever his name is, that we met the other week. Short of killing them all, I don't know what I can do."

That was exactly what we wanted her to do, but we needed to lead her there carefully. Kiana needed to think of herself as a monster in order to do monstrous things.

When we reached an open glade, a gentle stream running through, I asked for a stop. I made myself look as nervous and hopeful as I could, stealing glances at Kiana and worrying the hem of my shirt. She smiled at the sight, and I smiled back.

With a deep breath, I began. "Kiana, I have something I've been wanting to tell you for a long time now." I bit my lip, took another deep breath, and said, "Kiana, I . . . I love you. I've loved you since the day we first met. Would you . . . would you like to g-go on a d-date with me?"

I looked up at her with desperate eyes, hands clasped tightly behind my back and an ocean of innocence on my face. Her face told a story of its own: the pleased curl of her lip, the sparkle in her eyes, and then a hesitance that passed over her whole body, and something like *horror* stealing her smile. She took a step back, hand twitching, looking unsure of herself for the first time in her life. "I . . ."

She needed another push. "Kiana?" I asked, putting fear in my voice and making myself shiver. "Are you—I mean, did I . . . did I do something wrong? I-I'm sorry, I shouldn't have asked. I'm sorry. Maybe . . . maybe I should go." I turned to leave, to flee.

It was like I'd stabbed her. Kiana let out her breath in a wounded gasp and sucked in another. "No, wait!" She reached out a hand, then pulled it back, more complex emotions darting across her face and passing just as quickly. "This isn't—I'm not—you're not . . . it's not real." She spoke those last words like delivering her own death sentence.

I turned back around, all clueless curiosity and nervous shyness. "Not real? What do you mean? Do you—do you think I don't really love you?" My voice cracked on the L-word and I hugged myself tight. "Would I really lie to you like that?"

Kiana's shadows were swarming around her, the living darkness seeping into the soil and ripping up roots. A stray tendril lashed out at a tree and cracked it in half, branches scattering. She clenched her fists and tried to speak, but nothing came out. A second try, a third, and finally she had her voice again. "You don't understand. I *made you* love me."

I blinked in confusion. "What do you mean?"

A bleak, ragged laugh. "Hells, am I really this pathetic? Am I really faltering now, at something I've planned for so long?" She laughed again and ran a hand through her hair. "Clary, I've been controlling you for years. You and Alak both. The mirror demon, when it said I had my strings in you, it wasn't being abstract; I cast a spell on your mind the day we met, when you turned away from me because you didn't like how I acted. I wanted you to like me. I needed you to like me. So I put strings in your head that made you fall in love."

I stared at her with my best shocked expression. "You . . . made me this way?"

"I don't even know how much of the original you is left," she muttered before barking another desolate laugh. "I know nothing's left of Alak now, after today, but you . . . the hooks were always deeper. You were my personal project. Molded for me. Made for me. I *created* the person you are now. I created your love."

We both went quiet. I let my face fall into contemplation, gaze pointed down at the forest floor. I chose my next words carefully. "Even if you did . . . can't it still be real?" I looked up to find her staring at me with eyes wild like an animal's. "I mean . . . it still feels real, to me."

"I put that thought in your head," she snapped. "I crafted those feelings."

"But I still think them, and I still feel them," I said softly. "I still love you. If it's you, Kiana, I don't mind being controlled like that. I don't mind that you made me love you, because I like loving you."

Kiana was in agony, the anguish writ on every part of her face. "But is it real? How can it be real, if I made it with a spell? Can I . . . can I really be loved? Do I deserve it?"

I stepped closer to Kiana, and she didn't move away. I drew closer again until I could reach out and lay a hand on her cheek, holding her gaze with mine. "It doesn't matter," I told her simply. "I don't care. It feels right to love you. It feels *good* to love you, Kiana. Maybe feeling good is all it needs to be."

I kissed her, and she kissed me back. My hands wandered across her body, and hers across mine, and we made love on a bed of velvet night.

Hours later, as Kiana slept soundly, I slipped away to watch the stars. The words of our conversation still echoed in my mind. I had played my role perfectly, had pushed her toward the desired outcome, but something lingered. A stray thought, crawling beneath my skin.

If someone is created to love you, can their love ever be real? And if it isn't, can you still be loved?

I wondered to myself, alone in the dark, whether that scene was for Kiana, for me, or for Melpomene. The role I'd played for Kiana was false, just a mask I'd put on as my maker's loyal Intercessor. But in another sense, it was true; I had been created to love someone, and Kiana had been created from that someone.

Did Melpomene lie awake at night wondering if I really loved her? Did she think that she couldn't be loved, or that she didn't deserve to be loved? I couldn't really know, I supposed, any more than she could. But maybe, if I played my role well, I could make her believe.

In the morning, Kiana returned to the capital and broke the power of the high council, dominating those she could control and killing those she couldn't. Declaring herself empress of a new world-spanning empire, she began a great crusade to conquer the six moons and the ravaged planet beneath them. I was at her side, her confidante and consort.

The months that followed grew repetitive quickly. The Shadow Empress would lay the groundwork for invasion of a moon by abducting key players and brainwashing them. She enjoyed turning a country against itself, stirring rebellion and factionalism before swooping in behind her favorite pawns to reunite the nation as a vassal state. She only ever took the stage at the climax of each conflict, wary of letting her enemies learn too much about her capabilities.

In the time between battles, I tended to my empress. It was an opportunity to practice before returning to the woman I loved, so I took to it with enthusiasm. Kiana had been shaped from my Creator's flesh, so it stood to reason that her preferences would align. I learned what made her smile, what made her hungry for me, what made her moan—

You can skip some of these details. Really. I insist.

Ahem. I played the role of a lovestruck consort well, encouraging her and supporting her in all the ways she desired. My time apart from

Melpomene made me miss her more and more, and that midnight stargaz-
ing became a clockwork occurrence for me. I was already vastly more of a
person than I had been when I cut Kiana from her flesh, and I yearned to
show Melpomene my progress.

It took a year for us to reach the final battle of Kiana's war. An alliance
of elementals from all six moons, united in their defiance of the Shadow
Empress, made their stand around an old temple buried deep within the
earth, protecting their leader as he performed some ritual that they believed
would save them all. Kiana followed, and I with her, knowing the trap that
was about to be sprung.

In the heart of an old god's prison, elements clashed and chaos erupted.
Prevara emerged, all its pawns having served their purpose, and all its
gifts were ungiven, returned to their sinister source. The temple crumbled,
Kiana barely escaping, and on the surface above she found all her minions
freed from her control, armies disintegrating as sometimes half their number wailed in rage.

None of them drew her eye. None of them mattered. The moment she
realized what had happened, Kiana turned to me, her stalwart companion
for a long year of tribulation, and she wondered about a conversation we'd
had in a glade, and the nature of love. She hoped that I would stay. She
hoped I would forgive her.

I let horror and anguish cross my face, and I ran. I said one word: "*Monster.*"

In the days that followed, the endgame began. Prevara began seizing
control of one moon after another, stealing the apparatus of empire that
Kiana had left for it. Kiana, broken and hurting, learned of her past life and
the role she had played twice over in damning her people. And then she
found me, having fled back to Nyx, and told me everything.

"What should I do?" she asked quietly, hugging her knees on the floor of
Clary's bedroom. "What can I do? Everything is awful and it's all my fault."

I sat on the bed and watched her, for once not bothering to perform
any emotional responses. I was still and silent and cold, and that made it
sharper for her. I asked her, "What do you want to do, Kiana?"

"I don't know!" she wailed. "I thought I wanted to be powerful and
important, to change the world, but I was wrong about all of it. Everything
I did only made things worse. And I just . . . I just wish I could go back to
how it was before that day." She stared at me with haunted, desperate eyes.
"I wish I could fix everything I broke."

"There's no going back," I told her calmly. "Maybe, if you went to Prevara and begged it, you could be its champion again. Maybe it would give you back the spell that let you control me. But even if I was back under your thrall, you'd know it wasn't real. *You'd know you can't be loved.* And I don't think you can live with that, anymore."

"So what am I supposed to do?" she begged me. "Please, Clary, help me."

"I think you already know," I murmured, "but you're afraid. Because your past self invited Prevara in, gave it a foothold in all our souls. You sealed it, you unsealed it. And when it got out, it took away your power but it didn't take everything. It didn't kill you. It needs you, Kiana. If you go to it, if you fight it with all you have left, you'll win. You'll save the world . . . but not for you."

The light left her eyes. "A sacrifice. Is that what it takes, to atone? Is that redemption?"

I smiled. "I don't know if I believe in redemption, really. I don't know if I care about it. But you'd be saving me, Kiana, if you did that. And I think that's what I'd remember. It's what I'd choose to remember. So please, Kiana, do it for me."

I pushed myself off the bed, walked over, leaned down, and kissed her. She wasn't expecting it, and at first she stiffened, but then she leaned into it like a drowning woman. I held her close and let us stay like that for a long, quiet moment, and then I broke away. She looked at me with her broken heart bare on her sleeve, but didn't try and stop me.

"For luck," I told her. "For the good times. For what you're about to do."

I walked away, leaving the house behind, and when I stepped around a corner I vanished from the world entirely and returned to Melpomene's palace. My task was done.

A year of toil, a year of lies, and finally it was over. I'd learned a lot in my time as Clary, but as I stood before the Creator's throne I shed that mask and once again wore the face that my beloved Melpomene had given me.

A quick glance around the summit of the palace confirmed the absence of my Creator, her adorable form neither resting on the throne nor wandering the checkered tiles. She was probably below, inspecting her work as it reached its final moments. I'd find her soon enough, but her absence gave me an opportunity: I squealed.

"I'm home! I'm finally home!" I twirled around the throne room, hopping and dancing and hugging myself in glee. "Melpomene, Melpomene,

Melpomene! My Creator, my beloved, I'm finally back! Oh, the things I have to show you! The stories I can tell! Oh, how I missed you, how I yearned!"

When enough of my wild glee was expelled that I could move normally again, I hastily went about reshaping my appearance. My extensive experimentation with Kiana had given me what I hoped was a reasonably accurate profile of Melpomene's tastes, and it was those tastes I hoped to appeal to with a new outfit of my own unique design.

Once I was satisfied with my look, I descended into the palace proper and searched for Melpomene. My first guess that she was in the orrery chamber proved correct, as I found her staring at the turning orbs of the model system.

I curtsied on entering the room, still brimming with energy. "I've returned, Lady Melpomene. Everything is as you requested, and I have a full report written and prepared for you to peruse at your leisure."

"Thank you, Thalia." Something was wrong. Melpomene sounded tired, almost weary, and she didn't turn away from the orrery.

"Creator?" I inched closer, my excitement bleeding away into nervous concern. "Is something wrong? Did I make a mistake?"

"No, Thalia," she said quietly. "The mistake was mine. I caught it too late. Like always."

And then, with careless grace, Melpomene snapped her fingers and the orrery burst into flames. Paint peeled off and smoke rose from melting metal. The connecting bars fell apart and the orbs representing the moons and planet fell to the floor and made a puddle of paint and metal and burning.

I stared at the pyre in shock and horror. She had worked on that world for so long, had poured her love and excitement into getting it just right, and now she was destroying it. "Why?" I asked aloud. "Why did you burn it?"

The divine architect watched the fire and didn't answer. When the pile was more ash than orrery, Melpomene finally turned to face me. Her eyes were bloodshot, black liquid staining her cheeks like she'd been crying ink or oil, and the lines on her face had deepened.

My heart ached for her, and I longed to comfort her, but I didn't know how. I hadn't expected any of this. I wasn't prepared.

"Let me tell you a story," my Creator said. Her voice was still tired, still painfully soft, but as she wove her tale a bit more life crept back in.

"Once upon a time, when I was young and foolish and fresh to my role, I made a world and filled it with people. They weren't like you, they weren't pieces of me in the same way, but they still held many of my dreams and desires. I pulled their strings and set them dancing, and then I broke their world and flung them to another. I broke that world, too, and turned the whole universe against them. I drove them to a point where the only answer, the only path that would free their fates from the forces arrayed against them, was to burn their universe down to ash that a better world might rise from it.

"I was merciful. When they sacrificed their lives for their phoenix gambit, I let them reincarnate into the new world. I gave them new identities, new adventures, and new lands to explore, new companions to meet. And then I took it all away, drowning that world in darkness and ruin as I had the first and the second and the universe. It ended in fire, and again I shaped something new from the ashes.

"I thought I could get it right, that time. I moved my pieces and refined them, sharpened them, remade them. I stretched out their stories, gave them more power than ever, I tried with all my being to delay the inevitable. But still, just as quickly, it all turned to rot. I needed to hurt them. I needed to break them. And they just couldn't satisfy me. So I burned them all, one final time, and scattered the ashes to the void outside this palace.

"And then I made you."

My eyes widened at the revelation of just how much had come before me. Entire worlds that she had made without my help. I hesitated, curious to hear more of my predecessors, but there was another question that took priority. "What went wrong?" I asked.

Melpomene sighed. "I don't know. I'm not omniscient, just omnipotent. I can make anything, but only if I understand how to make it and what I'm making. I can tell when I've failed, but figuring out why I failed is a far greater challenge. I'm a blind god."

My chest clenched, my face falling. She was in pain, and her pain was mine. Her sorrow like knives, her grief a well to drown in. I needed to make the hurting go away. "How can I help? That's what you made me for, wasn't it? Please, Melpomene, let me help you."

Gratitude flickered in her eyes and pulled at the corners of her mouth. "Thank you, Thalia. It means a great deal." With a wave of her hand, Melpomene gathered the ashes of her latest creation and vanished them, scattering them in the void as she had three times before. "I just have to keep trying. We'll make another world, then another clipping, and this time I'll get it right. It's just a matter of time."

It wasn't.

We made another world, another orrery of brass and paint, and I sliced another gobbet of flesh from my Creator's divine form. We burned that one, and the next, and the next.

Dozens of times we made a princess, in name or in fact, and gave her power but denied her love. We pushed her to make the wrong decisions until they led her to a dead end, her destiny ever the altar. Prevara or something like it was my assistant in most of those worlds, another template repeated but retaining no continuity. Only I was allowed knowledge of the cycle.

In some of those worlds I took the stage as a close friend or object of desire, but in others I played the mentor or the nemesis. The roles were just a means to her end. Every time, I hoped that something would change, that Kiana would be more than what we made her to be. Every time, I was disappointed.

I started to hate that girl. I watched her fail again and again and again, and every time it ended with another burning world and more charred meat in the lab. Her failure meant I had to cut my beloved open again and rip out another piece of her flesh, had to see the pain wrack her body and the sorrow pool in her beautiful eyes. Kiana's failures were killing Melpomene, and I started to revel in hurting the girl who was hurting my love.

It wasn't always Kiana, of course. Between attempts at her template we experimented with others, two of them rising to become regulars in the cycle.

We made Mordred to be a response to Kiana, not quite an opposite but at least a foil. Where Kiana craved love, Mordred craved justice. Where Kiana was a sacrifice, Mordred was a murderer. She was a warrior, a killer, and a zealot. We gave her conviction, that most dangerous affliction of the mind, and it drove her to awful, terrible ends.

The story of Mordred was the story of a girl who tried to make things better and only ever made things worse. With sword in hand, time and again, Mordred cut away everything she should have cherished for a world that would never be. Time and again, she became unrecognizable, became the kind of monster that her starting self would have murdered without hesitation. We called that monster Malice.

Malice, too, was a failure, and so we burned her worlds like Kiana's. In ruining herself, she brought ruin to my Creator, and I hated her too. I had to watch Melpomene bleed again and again, with less and less of her left each time she went under the knife. The bags deepened under her eyes, her motions listless and apathetic when not in the frenzied throes of making a new world. She wouldn't look at me, too busy obsessing over the girls that kept failing her.

Our third template was Veseryn, and she cut Melpomene the deepest. Veseryn was a thief, a schemer, and a fool. She began each loop of the cycle, each instance of her being, thinking herself clever. My job was to thoroughly disabuse her of that notion.

Where Kiana was blessed with many gifts and Mordred was given great skill and aptitude, Veseryn was given nothing. Less than nothing, for we populated her worlds with people like Kiana and Mordred, the blessed and the talented, and her lack of either scraped Veseryn raw. Born with nothing and hungry for everything, Veseryn bared her teeth and fought for every advantage she could claim.

Dark bargains and reckless gambles were Veseryn's game, and they always doomed her. Every victory was bought with sacrifice, every gain accompanied by loss. Inevitably, the costs added up, risks didn't pay off, and desperate deals led her to calamity. She pledged herself to devils and horrors for just a little more power, and in the end they took her name and soul and made her their hollow puppet.

A corpse, a monster, a slave; these were the ends of the girls I helped torture.

Again and again I cut the flesh of my Creator. Again and again we gave life to splinters and put them through hell. Again and again we scattered the ashes and started over.

After one failed cycle, the lab filled with metal tables and charred meat, Melpomene broke. She screamed and raged and tore through the palace, destroying rooms and burning books, smashing glassware and bending pans. The moment her outburst faded, the energy leaving her in shuddering breaths wracked by coughing, she ordered me to fetch the knife and start cutting. We didn't even have a world to put the splinter in, but she insisted.

I begged her to stop, to wait, to rethink, but she wouldn't listen. She hadn't listened to me for a long time, too busy playing with her other toys. Too busy destroying herself for the sake of girls that always failed her, always hurt her, always stole her attention away from the only one who had been by her side since the beginning. The only one who deserved her.

In the moment my scalpel met her skin, I had already made my choice. To save my darling Melpomene from the cycle of torment she was forcing herself through, I would do anything. I would make her listen, even if it made her hate me.

I loved her too much to let anything stand in my way.

The next loop of the cycle was another Veseryn world. In a world full of magic, her only power was the ability to usurp control of magic items. The start of her story was structured to mirror a previous work, with Veseryn bargaining for the means to become a lich and botching the ritual thanks to a curse from the entity she had bargained with. She drowned herself in a bottle, sold what was left from the attempt, and had a minor breakdown over a mall barista remembering her usual order.

Boiling on the inside with complex emotions, Veseryn made her way to the roof of the mall and leaned on the railing. Her breath fogged in the chill winter air.

She mused aloud, "I really do like the cold. I think it's about control. You can't really control heat, you just relieve it. When the sun blisters the land, you can drink as many cool drinks as you want, sit by a fan, go swimming, but the heat is always there, that hateful star always burning down on you. Cold, on the other hand, is something that can be tamed. Cold can be bargained with. Throw on thicker socks and a pair of gloves, drape yourself in a blanket, sit by a fire, and the cold becomes somewhat pleasant. I can control the cold in a way I can't control heat. Or anything else."

Then she growled at something only she could hear. She laughed darkly, and then with a soft sigh she combed a hand through her hair, straightened up, and said, "I am nothing. In the grand scheme of things, I am *nothing*. I'm a nameless face in a sea of strangers, I'm a nobody of a girl whose greatest claim to fame is being remembered for her *predictable* drink order."

She started pacing, hands gesticulating wildly as she ranted to an invisible audience. "To the eyes of the world, I am nothing, and that's entirely my fault. My superpower is niche, specific, and limited, but it isn't useless. I prattle on and on about being cheated by fate and the gods, but I have a gift that the greatest mages in the world would be jealous of if they knew it existed. I've been so scared of reprisal that I've sabotaged my reputation and kept myself confined to the lower rungs of *everything*. They all think I'm just a common thief wielding stolen trinkets, a fool's artificer."

Veseryn sneered. "And I am a common thief! That's how I've been acting. If I tried, if I applied myself for once in my fucking life, I could be a villain like no other. But here I am."

She clenched her fists and looked out over the city, watching the cars and the people and the distant clashes of superpowers. Then she released the tension in her arms, stepped away from the roof, back to pacing, and let something else come over her.

In a voice cold and scornful, she asked, "If we had become a lich, what would we be doing right now? Would we be down there fighting heroes and terrorizing civilians? Robbing banks and raiding vaults? Or would we be curled up on a pile of blankets, hiding from the cold and obsessively refreshing social media?"

Veseryn scowled and bit back, "If the ritual had worked, I could have done anything, could have stood toe-to-toe with dragons and dragonslayers, could have carved my name into the collective unconscious of this whole damn city and bent it to my will. I could have broken gods and demons and worse with a wink and a smirk."

"But would you have?" she asked herself.

Veseryn flinched. "Of course I would have! It's what I've wanted for years. Do you think I would have attained ultimate power and then just sat on it? Would I have wasted godhood?"

She stewed in silence, broken only by a bitter, joyless laugh. "Maybe you're right. Maybe I would have stayed a little nothing girl. What does that make me? Can I ever be anything more than a *failure* and a *mistake*?"

I jumped down from my perch above the stairs, plunged a knife into her back, and whispered in her ear, "No, you can't. But I can."

Veseryn tried to scream, but my other hand was already moving to cover her mouth and keep her quiet. I pulled the knife out of her back and stabbed her again. She struggled, but I was stronger. She reached for her satchel and all the magical trinkets stored inside, but I cut the strap off her shoulder and kicked the bag away. She clawed at me, tried to bite my hand, but she was a frail little thing.

Then she bit something else, and her whole body turned to smoke. The cloud of Veseryn blew just out of reach and reformed, the girl staggering and coughing up blood and oil. The wounds in her back were closing, and the pendant around her neck shattered and broke, another artifact used up to save her skin.

Veseryn whirled on me and the ring on her finger glowed blue as great spikes of ice erupted from the ground in my direction, but with a snap of my fingers the ice melted. I held the knife at my side, loose but ready.

With a moment's reprieve, the girl should have run, or even just vaulted herself over the ledge and trusted in whatever protective items she had left. Her curiosity got the better of her, as I knew it would. Her gaze darted over my body, taking in cat ears, white hair, and eyes of blue and gold. She spat out another gob of blood and asked, "Why is a changeling trying to kill me?"

I knew it was a mistake to answer; every extra second spent killing the girl was another chance for Melpomene to catch me in the act and put a stop to my plan. And yet, in all the years I'd been her Intercessor, for all the monologues I'd delivered on her behalf, I'd never made those cutting speeches with my own words, my own thoughts and feelings. It surprised me how much I craved it.

So I told her, "It's not really about you. You're just a symptom of the greater problem. But you're still part of the problem, and so I have to kill you. But, don't worry about the life you'll leave behind; I'll be taking that too." I smiled. "You see, I've figured it all out: *I'm* the only one who ever gets it right, so I just need to play all the roles. Once I've killed you, I'll become you, and then I'll finally make her happy."

Veseryn reached for another trick up her sleeve, but I was faster. I crossed the distance between us in a blink and drove my knife into her throat. Her eyes went wide and she grabbed at the knife, but I tore it free and slammed it into the side of her head. She went down in a heap and I followed, knife at her throat to stab and stab and stab until the last gurgles stopped and her body went still.

There was work to be done, so I didn't waste any time savoring my victory. I crouched by the body and took her dead hand in mine. With a whisper of will, I commanded the flesh and blood of her form to slough from her body and flow over mine. Skin, muscle, fat, cartilage, all of it tore from her bones in slow-moving masses that crawled up my arm.

The meat of her body sank into the meat of mine, and in just a few moments my catgirl visage was replaced by a perfect replica of Veseryn. I disintegrated the bones and rose to full height, getting a feel for my new proportions.

The next step was to follow her role in the story, at least superficially. As the changeling, I was supposed to push Veseryn off the roof of this building. As she fell, a portal would open, and she would pass into another world. There, the next chapter would begin. "And this time," I murmured to myself, "it'll work. I'll do what none of those other girls could. I won't *fail* like they always do. And then . . . and then Melpomene will really, truly love me."

"So that was your plan," Melpomene said from right behind me.

I lurched in surprise, pushing back against the roof's edge and turning to see my Creator in the flesh. Melpomene always used proxies, always some guise to keep her distance, but in that moment I saw her as she appeared to me in her own realm, with flaking lips and soft cheeks. Her eyes were dark and gold, weary and haunted.

"You've betrayed me," she spoke softly, gingerly, almost disbelieving. "Why?"

My first instinct was to deny my actions, but I took that cowardice and snapped it by the neck. The plan had failed, but something could be salvaged. "I was trying to save you," I told her. "You wouldn't listen, so I had to act."

The sky above crackled and boomed with thunder and lightning, and rain fell all around us. Melpomene, the storm in her gaze, said, "You were made to serve, not save. You were made to love me."

"I do love you!" I shouted. My grip on the knife tightened. "I love you more than any of those stupid little girls who keep *hurting you*! You obsess over them, but I'm right here! Look at me! Love me! *I am the only one you need.* If you won't make the right choice, *I will make it for you.* I love you too much to let you keep doing this."

In the distance, the skyline burned. The world was already falling apart, smashed to pieces by its dissatisfied maker. Melpomene took a step forward, flames licking at her feet and sizzling in the rain. "You speak of usurpation, my sweet Thalia. You would bind my hands."

"I just want to help you," I pleaded. "You're killing yourself, my heart. You can stop all this, you just have to let me in. I can be all you need. I can be your answer, your solution, your salvation. You don't need any of those other girls, you just need *me*. Please, let me do this."

And for a moment, for a single glorious moment, I could see that she was tempted. Part of her, some part of her, wanted to accept. Wanted to give it all up and be with me. She hesitated. But the worse side of her won, the dark voice in her head. "No. I can't. If I'm not a maker of worlds, then I am nothing at all. If I don't keep hurting my splinters, I'll never understand. You can't be my answer. Love can't be the answer."

"Melpomene!" I cried, and ran toward her, but with a wave of her hand I was gone.

Another world burned, and the ashes rained down on a place outside the universe. The graveyard of worlds, an ashen void. There were stars above, glittering in a vast and empty darkness, but they were dim and muted, swallowed by falling ash.

I was alive. I had been banished from my beloved's embrace, cast out from her worlds and her palace, but I was *alive*. Melpomene couldn't bring herself to kill me. All the other girls, they died and they burned, but I was still alive. Standing there, among the ashes.

It almost didn't feel real, what I had done. I had rebelled against my maker, my goddess, my divine Creator. And yet, there I stood. Alive, and whole, and *loved*.

Because she had to love me, to spare me like that. None of the other girls ever got that grace, none of them were allowed to survive the burning of their world at the end of their tale. We gave them life and we brought them death, a thousand times, and only I was different. Only I was spared. There could be no other explanation: Melpomene loved me.

I could still save her. The thought of it filled me with overflowing relief. My love was not gone forever, just out of reach for the moment. I could wait, and gather my strength, and find a way back to her.

I wandered the void, alone and lost in thought. The ash-coated castle ruins, broken swords, the detritus of a hundred worlds raised and ruined. I plucked fragments from the ash and reminisced about their origin, sought to harvest whatever remained of the divine impetus behind them. With one eye, I looked beyond, past the palace of the Creator and into her new creations. New worlds, made without my help, that inevitably joined me in the land of falling ash.

Melpomene would continue, if I did nothing. She would work herself to the bone, scraping away even gristle to perpetuate a doomed cycle. Even loving me, even wanting me, she couldn't defy her nature. She could not make the right choice, so it would have to be made for her. I would have to take away her choices, all of them, to save her.

The moment I chose to act against her, even for her own good, I had ceased to be her Intercessor. And as I walked the graveyard of worlds, plotting my next steps, I became something else. Sometimes, to save a goddess, a girl must become a devil. To save my love, I would become her Adversary.

In the years since that day, I've learned how to meddle with my maker's worlds. I've slipped whispers past the veil, found splinters willing to listen. I'm trying to end the cycle, and I know that this time, this time I'll succeed. Melpomene has invested too much into this world to burn it just to keep me at bay. For once, just this once, she'll let me win.

And that brings us to you, Alice. Correct me if I'm wrong, but I believe you gained the ability to end this connection several minutes ago. And yet you're still here.

. . . So I am.

Then I think it's time we finally talked face-to-face.

GARDEN OF MEMORIES IV

Exhaustion and invigoration war within my soul.

I am human and monster, demon and divine. I am the Intercessor. I am the Red Queen. I am Morgan, Malice, and Maven. I am Mordred, Kiana, and Veseryn. I am Alice. I am more than the sum of my parts, and I call that greater sum Hastur. I am the queen behind the curtain. I am the devil of the stage.

But I'm small, too. I understand that now even better than I did before. I've clawed a bit of divinity from dreams, my own ramshackle apotheosis, but I can *feel* the weight of the Demiurge pressing down on this world. My dominion is a fragile thing, easily contested.

I go to the Adversary afraid, though I try my best not to show it.

In the void beyond Pandaemonium, in the graveyard of burned worlds, I find her waiting. Thalia has a face like mine, the same blemishes and imperfections, but her eyes are like twin suns burning with inner fire. She's dressed for a wedding, but the pure white is stained with blood. A knife hangs lazily from one hand, the same knife that killed a Veseryn.

When she smiles at me, I fail to suppress a shiver.

"Alice," she greets me. "Hastur? Who do you want to be, right now?"

It's a fair question. I can feel minds inside my mind, splinters put there by our maker or devoured in the dream, but there's a sense of distance. For the moment, until I return to my body in Fata Morgana, I have control. "I'll be Alice," I say. "I don't think the mantle I stole has much weight here in your realm."

"Smart girl," Thalia compliments me. "You've grown beyond your template. I like that. I like you, Alice. There's more of her in you than the others ever had."

It rankles a little, still being seen as a *template*. I want to insist that I'm not Veseryn, that I was never just a copy, but I know she'd only laugh. She's known too many of my sisters, a hundred variations on the same core. Anything I could tell her, any quirk or trait, would be dismissed as random noise.

I get it, now. I understand why Homura was driven to her rebellion, or I can guess. I wonder if it broke her to learn how *insignificant* she really was.

"You wanted to talk. That's what you said just now, and when we first met and I fell into Reska. You've shown me a lot, Adversary. What else is there to say?"

Thalia laughs. "Oh, I've barely scratched the surface. I could fill an ocean with all I've seen and dreamed, Alice. But, really, there's only one thing that matters: I will save my beloved."

"You keep claiming that," I say carefully, "but it doesn't seem like she wants you to save her. She said you can't."

The Adversary keeps on smiling. "Of course she did. The poor thing doesn't understand what she's doing to herself. My darling is a magnificent artist, but she loses sight of things too easily. She keeps making all these silly little dolls to hear them scream till she sets them ablaze, but I'm the only doll she's ever needed." Her voice sharpens, and her hand tightens around the handle of the knife. "She lets those other girls hurt her, fail her, but I'm the only girl she ever needs to think about. So I'm going to save her from herself."

I swallow nervously. *I'm one of those dolls. You've acted nice so far, played the ally, but you must hate me like you hated all the others. You must hate the way I keep failing her.* I lick my lips and ask, "What are you planning to do, then? How are you going to save her?"

Thalia sighs, and something in her gaze turns lovestruck and dreamy. "It'll be simple, really. I'm going to climb back into her palace and pin her against a wall just the way I know she likes, a love bite on her neck and a whisper in her ear, and she'll melt for my warmth after all those years alone. I'll bind those soft, cute wrists of hers with silk I'll tie in ribbons, and with a firm and gentle hand I'll guide her to her knees. When she's kneeling, when she's surrendered, I'll take away every ounce of power she has. And she'll thank me for it, my sweet Melpomene."

The Adversary hugs herself with an almost sensual glee, the look on her face becoming indecent as she practically writhes with pleasure imagining her conquest of the Demiurge. I take a step back without thinking, unsettled by the sight, and immediately her gaze snaps back to mine and she smiles with teeth.

"You think I'm wrong, of course. You think she'll reject me. But she won't. She could have killed me, should have killed me, but she couldn't bring herself to do it. Pom-Pom loves me, Alice. She's always loved me. She's just so caught up in her doomed cycles, in her all-consuming obsessions, that she's lost the forest for the trees. She can't make her own choices anymore, so I'll make them for her. I'll throw away all those nasty little knives and keep her locked inside her room, all safe and comfy with blankets and stuffies. I'll bring her food as many times a day as she likes, all her favorite fruits and cheeses, and a fresh glass of lemonade on the hour. The drugs in her food will keep her blissed out and giggling, a pleasant haze to wash away the bad thoughts and never let her think them again. I'll read to her in the mornings and evenings, whatever she wants to hear, and when she's needy I'll push her buttons until she's squealing and moaning and mindless for my touch. She'll never be sad again, never angry again, never empty again, because I'll fill every moment with love and joy and bliss. And she'll love me for it, I know she will, and she'll smile for me and whine for me and beg me to hold her close, and I'll give her that, I'll give my Creator anything, everything, all of me, because she is the reason I *breathe*. My love is all she's ever needed."

She's mad. Thalia is just as mad as the Demiurge. Maybe worse.

My heart is like a hummingbird and I can feel my self-control fraying as I process Thalia's manic delusions, the nightmarish scenario that has her practically moaning to imagine. *The Adversary is a psychotic yandere who wants to drug God and screw her brainless. And this is the only ally I have left. Oh, I'm royally fucked.*

My mouth is dry, but I force myself to speak. "You aren't telling me this just to hear it aloud. You want my help."

Thalia twirls in place, the skirt of her wedding dress doing the spinny thing, and when she comes to a stop she clasps her hands together and leans forward with an almost puppy-like enthusiasm. "Mhm! You're the key, Alice. You're my best chance at getting what I want *now*, before she's cut herself down even further. I'll win eventually, I know that, but I *hate* the thought of waiting until she's hurt herself so badly she can barely hold the knife." The enthusiasm falls into solemn, mournful sincerity. "She's so tired, Alice. She's been hurting for so long. I know you must find the very idea of *saving her* to be revolting after all she's done to you, but I promise: Nothing you can do will hurt her more than she hurts herself. There's no revenge to have on another bleeding victim. Help me, Alice. Help me take away her power and you can finally be *free* of this glorified mutilation chamber. Isn't that what matters?"

I should just agree. I should accept her terms and go along with her plan, because she's stronger and older and she's probably right. The part of me that wants to disagree is insane. It's insanity to still dream of usurpation after everything I've learned. If I want revenge for what Nyara—Melpomene—has done to me, then isn't Thalia's vision enough? The almighty Demiurge, trapped forever in a drugged haze and the suffocating love of her own crazed creation. That's a kind of justice, I think. So why doesn't it satisfy me? What's wrong with me?

"What happens," I ask softly, "if that isn't enough for me?"

The lights go out in the Adversary's eyes. The humanity slides off her face like it was never there, and a cold and dead thing stares back at me. "If you try to hurt her, you die. I've killed hundreds of you, little sister. Melpomene gave the command, but I wielded the blade. What's one more corpse on the mountain I've made?"

It's the answer I was expecting, but it still terrifies me. I can feel myself shrinking back, practically cowering before her, because even now I'm nothing more than a scared little girl playing brave. I wish I hadn't asked. I wish I wasn't in this situation. I wish everything was different. But my wishes never meant anything.

Thalia's smile returns, just as fever-warm as ever. "We don't need to be enemies, Alice. You've got enough of those already, and I really don't want to kill another sister. But I will, if you make me. I'll do anything for Melpomene, whether she wants it or not. So let's not be enemies. Let's be friends! What do you say?"

The Adversary extends a hand, her other still clutching the knife. *Friendship, or the knife. Can I really afford another enemy?*

It's barely a real question. *What's one more partner I can't trust?* I take her hand and clasp it tightly, feeling her squeeze back. "Okay. We'll end this cycle together."

And then, finally, I let myself wake up.

Back in Fata Morgana, back in the flesh, I feel a pressure on my chest and open my eyes to find Vaylin Kirinal straddling me. The blue-skinned, red-stitched demon is staring at me intently, and the moment I open my eyes her hands dart for my throat and start choking me out.

Are you kidding me? The second I wake up?

Really, how are you surprised at this point? This is practically banal for us. What does she even think she's going to accomplish with this? We don't breathe!

I try to grab her wrists and push her off me, but I can't move my arms. A glance away from Vaylin reveals my whole body wrapped up in red ribbon, her signature threads binding my movement. That's a bigger problem than her futile attempt to choke me . . . or is it?

I find it hard to care. All the fear I felt in the Adversary's presence melts away, and I actually laugh through Vaylin's grip, ugly as the sound becomes. How mundane. *How pathetic.*

I may be smaller than Thalia and Melpomene, but I'm so much bigger than a bug like this one. Maven Alice might have struggled to kill Vaylin Kirinal, but I can be so much more.

I step out of myself and into Hastur like a velvet cloak settling over my shoulders. I watch the stage from the rafters, looking down on my own limp body. Alice is tied up in the middle of Fata Morgana, the illusory city sprawling around her. The Demiurge's tower is gone, but the glass tower remains. Far in the distance, shadows gather.

Here and now, the immediate problem is Vaylin. The demon is a wretched thing, even worse than she was before. A single glance with Hastur's eye shows the careless stitchwork that fused Vaylin and Lena, demon and figment, with the glass shard of Katoptris. Vaylin and Lena each served me, once, in different timelines discarded by the Demiurge, so I know them well.

This gestalt resembles neither. The thing that put me in a dream world is just another hollow puppet like Cheshire, an empty doll on Melpomene's strings. I can see those strings like lines of black and gold that vanish in the sky. The Demiurge wanted me to relive an older version of myself, so she spent a pawn to make it happen.

Shame it backfired on her so horribly. I can see the shape of it: Tormented by visions of what might have been, I run back to Nyara and take her deal.

I carve up Cheshire to make a doll like the Demiurge made me, but the result still isn't what Melpomene wants because nothing ever will be. I fail her again, and she either resets the timeline or lets the universe burn.

Not happening. I sweep an invisible hand and cut Vaylin's strings. The husk crumples atop Alice, just an empty shell, and before I can follow them to their source the puppet strings burn away. I'm almost sad to lose Vaylin like this, after my duel with her was spoiled the first time. Almost.

The red ribbons remain, however, so I consider how to get rid of them. I could wave them away like I did Vaylin, but there's a kind of instinctual revulsion that passes through me at the idea. I don't have a real form as Hastur, but I can still feel goose bumps on my skin. Doing that would be a mistake. Why?

I dig deeper into the feeling and it evolves. It's a prickling like when you know someone's watching you, but you can't figure out from where. There are eyes on me, judging me. My senses have expended, my awareness of the world evolving, and I know with an unsettling certainty that there are *limits* to what I can do. The more I push against the world, the more the world will push back. If I deviate too far from the narrative, my ability to influence that narrative will wane. It's a set of restrictions that the Demiurge and Adversary both have to follow, too, but they have years of experience on me in exploiting those restrictions.

It frustrates you that we can't just wish away all our problems, doesn't it? That even now, there are rules we have to follow. Is that the same warped impulse that keeps your eye on Melpomene's throne?

Frustration is irrelevant. I have other tools at my disposal, I just need to use them.

I push my will back into Alice, and as I do I reach out for a bundle of power and memory nestled inside our strange and mutilated soul. *Reska,* I whisper in my mind, and—

—I find myself back in control of our shared body, shivering from unfamiliar sensations. The revelations of the past day are still tumbling around in my head, almost impossible to fully process, but there are concerns much easier to resolve.

My beloved shadows come slithering toward me the moment they sense my return. For so long I hated them, but now they are dear to me. They love me, and I don't know that I can say that of anything else alive. "Free me," I command them, and they obey.

The darkness flows over me, warm and soft like the loveliest blanket. I embrace the shadows as they embrace me, and as a mass of liquid night I slip my bindings. *This is my true form,* I muse. *I am the dark, and the dark is me.*

With a twist of mental effort I restore my human guise, a mask I wanted to believe in for so many fruitless years. I was never human. I was always a monster.

Glad you finally admit it, princess, drawls a voice I've come to loathe. Immediately I tense and sweep my gaze across the area—a courtyard, a clearing, an open space amid urban bustle—though I know it's a meaningless gesture; her voice is inside my head.

"Homura," I say aloud. The anger burns hot in me, flooding my veins and drawing the shadows to seethe around me. "Is there a point to that taunt?"

There's always a point, she laughs. *Trying to be human is what held you back. If you believe anything I ever said was true, let it be this: I loved the monster in you. Only monsters can fix what's broken.*

"You never loved me," I hiss. "If you really had, you wouldn't have tried to *kill me.* Or is that how you treat all the girls you love?"

Homura falls silent, a wound scored. When she speaks again, her voice is softer. *I hurt the ones I love, I won't deny it. I can't stop it. All I can do is make meaning from that pain.*

Enough of this, sighs another voice. The voice of Veseryn, or Alice. I can feel her in the back of my head, her presence swelling to push me out. I don't want to go back. I don't want to give up this body. I want—

—to get these voices out of my head.

I breathe deep to settle myself. The air is cool here, a refreshing breeze wafting through city streets. I flex my fingers and take in their physicality. This flesh is mine, though it's no longer all of me. Intercessor, Red Queen, Hastur. And the echoes of those other splinters still stuck inside my soul, clawing for control.

It's time to fix that.

I retreat to the rafters once more, becoming the oversoul Hastur again to work my next trick. Thalia showed me my other selves and past lives, but more than that she showed me how the Demiurge herself performs acts of creation. I have everything I need to imitate the divine.

The Alice I left behind pawns a scalpel from nowhere and grimaces. "I know I made self-mutilation a pillar of my soul and all, but it's still annoying how often my plans necessitate the act. Ugh, let's just get this over with."

For all her glib words, Alice wields the knife with something approaching reverence. The first cut is quick and careful, a shallow line across her arm to test the blade. She shivers from the sensation, a little burst of pleasure and a reminder of all the times she's done it before. She does it again, twice and then a third time, marking her flesh for the butcher's work that comes next. Another shiver passes through her, and she takes a final moment before leaving that pleasure behind.

The next cut is deep and ugly, the kind of incision she'd once promised herself she'd never make. But it wasn't her that made that promise, was it? Not Alice, and not even Veseryn. It was Melpomene who made that promise, really, when she was just another girl who cried herself to sleep.

Alice screams as her arm bleeds, the bright crimson quickly covering a glimpse of fat and muscle. She bites her lip and scrunches her eyes shut tight, anything to stabilize the sensory overload of the wound she just made. She clutches at her bleeding arm and laughs, ragged and torn and manic.

She grips the knife and slices into her flesh again, carving through the pain until two chunks of flesh fall from her arm and splat against the ground. She sobs. She falls to her knees and screams again.

The wounded girl throws herself on the body of the red-stitched demon, collapsing on top of her. With another shudder, Alice bares her fangs and sinks them deep into Vaylin's neck. Blood flows out, blood flows in. Alice drinks deep, and second by second, the wound on her arm begins to heal. Meat knits together, growing and rejoining and sealing over until no trace of the wound remains.

No visible trace, at least. To my sight, the wound is still just as raw, though it doesn't bleed. It's a wound on something more essential; not the body that's smoke and mirrors, nor the soul that exists as a mechanism of Pandaemonium, but the *real* Alice. Real like only the other splinters can claim to be real, if Thalia and Melpomene are to be believed. In severing my own flesh, I've divided the cut of meat that anchors the thoughtform called Alice. *Ever more splinters.*

I have the meat, so now for the minds.

Our soul is an abomination, no way around it. We devoured ourselves for power over and over, a constant cycle of sacrifice and growth, and that was before Melpomene reached inside us and made everything worse. The passengers that greeted me on waking up in Fata Morgana, the memory echoes of Reska and Homura, are nestled in my soul like a pair of hungry tumors.

They've dug in deep, the tendrils of their essence mingling with mine. Pulling them out carelessly could cause more damage than I have time to repair.

I see another future the Demiurge might have envisioned for me: Spurred on by desperation and my hatred for my other selves, I recreate my signature spell and use it to annihilate most of my own soul. I turn Reska and Homura into fuel, burning them again and again in duels against Vaylin and Urna and whoever else is waiting for me at the tower. I cull the influence from my soul like I purged Lamentation, only this time the consequences are more dire; what fills the gaps and spawns new growth is my worst self, the parts of me most vulnerable to the Demiurge's manipulations. In trying to free myself, I make myself a pawn.

So many little schemes, I admire. *So many ways to use me.*

I shape my will around the core of each soul fragment, moving slowly and carefully into place. I sever as many tendrils as I can, leaving the ones that would cost more time than I'd gain. When there's no more preparation I can make, I grab both cores and rip them out.

Alice screams again, the noise muffled by her face still being buried in Vaylin's neck, and dimly I feel her begin to choke on the blood pouring down her throat. It's not a huge problem, so I leave it for her to solve.

I bind the echoes of Reska and Homura to the scraps of meat we peeled off Alice, anchoring thoughtform to severed flesh as Thalia and Melpomene taught me. I marvel at how simple it is to shape a life like this, the connection forming instantly and without resistance. With time and material, I'm certain I could replicate more of the Demiurge's feats.

But I have neither time nor material, so back in the box I go. I return to Alice just as the flesh begins to bubble, leaving my creations to—*fuck this hurts, my everything is on fire, what the hell!?*

I peel myself off Vaylin and slump next to her, wheezing and rasping from the exertion of clearing my throat after *my soul got torn apart.* My oversoul is a traitorous whore for letting this happen and I swear I'd strangle her if I could, and if she wasn't me, and if it wouldn't basically be auto-erotic asphyxiation, or is that just auto asphyxiation? Would it be hot to strangle a girl if that girl was also me? What the fuck am I asking? Am I okay?

Switching between Hastur and Alice is very . . . discombobulating. When I'm directing the scene, it's like my body goes on autopilot. I can still feel everything I'm doing, but it's all extremely muted unless I actively choose to get the full suite of sensory feedback. It's *me* doing it all, just like it's me doing Hastur things, but there's a conceptual distance between us.

You sound like you're feeling better. How unfortunate. Shall we greet the new hires, gobbet? Maybe you can talk one of them into punching you, or wringing your neck if that's your new craving.

Ah, right. You're still here.

I'm curious about that, Veseryn admits. *What, grown to like being ridiculed too much to cut me free? Got a humiliation fetish to go with that choking kink?*

If I did, you'd have it too, I scorn her. *Any dirty laundry you tried to air would be a self-report, Ves. So please, do go on about all your embarrassing little pleasures.*

Oh? Sounds like someone's drinking the cyanide soda. Ready to believe you and I are cut from the same span of silk? Nah, more like dirty linen.

She's trying to get under my skin, but for once it's not going to work. *I do believe it, yeah. And it's more than just sharing a template. You're me, Ves. You've been there all along, haven't you? Since before Pom-Pom shoved those other girls inside my head. Not something separate, just another piece of me, from the moment I was born. We killed our first monster together, walked out of the schoolhouse together, went through everything in Sanctuary together. I never gave you a name because you were never different enough from me to justify it. You're Veseryn, but so am I. I'm Alice, but so are you. We're the same cut of meat on the same cold slab. Not really two different voices at all, just two points repeating across one wavelength.*

I slowly clamber to my feet, pushing off Vaylin's corpse. Veseryn still doesn't say anything. It's harder to feel her presence than it was to sense Reska and Homura. Probably because she's just me.

Am I wrong?

. . . Don't get smug about figuring that one out. And don't think this means I'll start going easy on you. You're still the bitch I wanna murder.

I smile. *Wouldn't have it any other way. After all, I hate myself just as much as you do.*

I finally turn my attention to the other two splinters and their new bodies. I find them, predictably, at each other's throats.

Reska is beautiful, standing radiant in a dress like the night sky wrapped around her. A purple sunburst hairpin threads nicely through her golden hair, and ruby red slippers complete the look. Her black pit eyes are watery and pained, her delicate hands bunched up in fists.

"You murdered me," she cries. "How can you expect me to set that aside?"

Homura is dressed for war in a black padded coat and high leather boots. The rapier Vorpal is at her side, tucked into her belt, and she drums her fingers along the hilt. Her crimson eyes burn with scorn, her lips twisted in a sneer.

"It's not really murder if it didn't take, now is it?" the murderer retorts. "But if you'd like a second round, I'd be happy to settle the score over you ending the world."

Unbelievable. Like children. "Try it and I'll turn you back into a flesh puddle," I interrupt. "Are you two really going to waste time on this while the world is about to end? You get that you're not actually Reska and Homura, right? You saw everything I did, you know what you are. You know what they are, too: Kiana and Mordred, rebuilt a hundred times. You're all copies, just like me." Bitterness creeps into my voice, but I stay focused.

The copy of the princess looks away and holds herself tightly, the tension visible in every inch of her being. The copy of the warrior curls her lip and glares at me, one hand settling around her sword.

The thing that isn't really Homura thinks better of drawing her sword on someone who can take away her body with a word, but doesn't think better of picking a verbal fight. "You say that like I should care, but I really don't. The mission is all that matters. The cycle has to end, the wheel unmade. A weapon spares no thought for its craft, it only cuts. Kiana, Mordred, whatever; there are only allies and enemies in the only fight that's real."

I snort. "You clown. You absolute buffoon. Of course you care what you are. If you didn't, it wouldn't get under your skin so much that you're a piece of a piece of the thing you hate the most. You hate what she made you. You hate *that* she made you. *That's the point.* We're her self-loathing as much as we're her ego, so stop pretending you're above all this. I know you, *Mordred.* You're in just as much pain as your dear princess over there, only you deal with pain by shoving it on others and lying you're immune."

The copy bristles, a flood of rage washing over her before being swiftly and efficiently suppressed. She layers on the mocking scorn as she challenges, "Are you really going to play by their labels like that, *Veseryn?* Not alive, not unique, just another variant on the same old template. Are you just another copy?"

"I *am* Veseryn. I hate it, I really do, but the core of me is the same as all those girls that came before, born powerless and grown hungry. I played with fire and got burned, and I kept doing it because that's what it means to be a Veseryn. But that doesn't mean I'm not Alice. I can be both, Mordred. You can too. But we gain nothing by pretending that we aren't copies, *especially* the two of you. We can't win from a state of delusion."

Hatred burns in her gaze, but she flinches. *Point scored.* "I'm more than a copy," she tries to insist. "I'm not just another Mordred."

The princess, still facing away from us, asks quietly, "Then why do you become Malice?"

"That isn't—" Mordred cuts herself off, the words sour in her mouth as she spots the trap just a second too late.

"Isn't you?" The echo of Reska turns around, smiling sadly. "You're right, it isn't. Just like I can't stand the idea that Contrition could be me. But Malice is Homura, and Contrition is Reska. A failed Mordred and a failed Kiana, right?" She glances at me as if for confirmation, so I quickly nod.

"We are pieces of pieces, all of us," I murmur. "Copies of copies and splinters of splinters. The wheel is a fractal, spiraling out as it repeats."

The echo of Homura clenches her fists, and for a moment I think she's about to boil over with rage and indignation, but instead it all drains out of her at once and she staggers to a wall to crumple by and lean against. She hugs her knees, and I get to see the very rare sight of Homura's face looking vulnerable. She closes her eyes.

I turn away from her, trusting she'll talk herself through the next part, and quirk an eyebrow at the princess. "You're taking this better than she is. Why?"

The echo laughs, a melancholy song. "I don't know. I think a part of me is relieved, actually, to know I'm not the real Reska. If I'm not her, then I don't have to feel her pain quite so sharply. It still feels real, all of it does, but it gets . . . softer, maybe, the more I accept our memories of Kiana." She pauses, blinking a few times, and then more words tumble out. "It's not my fault. It makes it less my fault, or her fault, that we were destined to fail. It lessens the blow for me if every other Kiana made the same mistakes and met the same bitter end. I'm not *alone* in what I've suffered, or remember suffering. That helps."

Mordred opens her eyes and practically snarls at Kiana. "How is that comforting for you? How can you find comfort in knowing that every version of you *failed*? I hate it. I hate everything about it. I refuse to accept that I'm destined to destroy everything I ever fought for or believed in, that all I can become is another *Malice* laying waste to a world I tried to save."

"But you remember killing Reska," I say calmly. "Whether they're your experiences or just copied memories, you know it's happened once already this cycle and countless times before. You destroyed the one thing you were meant to protect, and that cost you everything. Homura and Reska both ended their world, in shadow and in blood."

Grief crosses their faces. My understanding of the final days of Svijet-stakla is still woefully incomplete, but it looks like my guess hit home. *They blame themselves for it. I can use that, probably.*

"We can't change what happened, but we can do better." I look to Kiana. "Homura was right about one thing: The cycle needs to end. For our own sakes, and all the girls who burned before us. We're the only ones who can stop the Demiurge." My gaze shifts to Mordred. "And we'll do that *without* betraying each other, this time. When one of us has a concern, the rest of us *listen* to that concern. Stabbing each other in the back is doing Melpomene's work for her."

"Couldn't have said it better myself!" chirps a new, familiar voice.

Thalia's here. I catch the Adversary slipping out of an alley and making her way toward us, still in her wedding dress but with a red leather jacket thrown over it. The knife hasn't left her hand, and I suspect it won't until she has what she wants.

"Afternoon, ladies," she says with a grin. "Ready for the final stretch?"

Mordred jumps to her feet and draws Vorpal. *"You,"* she snarls. "You're the reason Homura ruined everything. We trusted you!"

"And I have always strived to repay that trust," Thalia insists. "I saved Homura from the Abyss and guided her to victory over Reska Shadowsun. What happened next was a mistake, an error born of incomplete information. I now understand how committed Melpomene is to this universe, and I won't make the same mistake again."

Shadows writhe beneath Kiana and caress their way up her legs. She glares darkly at Thalia and accuses, "You turned Reska into Contrition. You forced her into a fate worse than death, into a thousand years of torment. You're no better than the Demiurge."

"I've never claimed otherwise," the Adversary shrugs. "I've done many monstrous things, both in her name and against her design. The difference between us is that I want the cycle to end, while she wants to keep hurting you. Though, if you're really that worked up about Contrition, I'll remind you it was *Homura* who requested that fate. I would have gone for the mercy kill and washed my hands of the matter."

Mordred flinches. "I didn't . . . she didn't know we'd fail to climb the tower. It was supposed to be a temporary solution, one we could undo after seizing the reins of creation. I thought it was the only way to save you."

The anger on Kiana's face transmutes to hideous pain. She tries to speak, but nothing comes out. She turns away.

"Thalia," I greet the Adversary, "I wasn't expecting you to show up so early. Are you here to help? We've got a long list of problems to cut through before we're near your prize."

"Of course," she affirms. "I'll do everything I can to speed us along. Do you understand what stands in our way?"

I shrug. "I have an idea. Prevara's brought all its pieces here in hopes of seizing Contrition the second she arrives in Fata Morgana, to finish what it started in the old world. I expect we'll have to kill Urna plus maybe another Noble, then any of Prevara's remaining hosts. Judging by the visions you showed me, I'm also expecting Malice to show up around the same time as Contrition to try and murder everyone. We deal with them one by one, then we climb the tower and use Katoptris to reach Melpomene. Anything I missed?"

Thalia waves a hand dismissively. "The rest is details. You have the picture."

I sweep my gaze across the motley pack of monsters I've gathered to my banner: a broken-hearted princess, a killer convinced she's righteous, and a horror nearly as ancient and dreadful as our enemy. *I wonder if we'll all kill each other before we even reach the tower.* I force a smile to my face and call to the troops, "Let's form up and move out. We—"

A thunderclap interrupts me, a terrible booming noise that seems to echo across the whole of the city. Goose bumps rise on my arm, and I can feel a strange electricity in the air.

Far above, the sky begins to crack.

GARDEN OF MEMORIES V

With our party gathered and the world beginning to collapse, we venture forth on the road to the glass tower.

I would have liked to get there by any means other than walking, but we have little luck with that. Reaching out and "touching" the tower, which I'd been warned ages ago was a surefire way to get caught by it, does nothing. Kiana peels into the air, propelled by darkness, but doesn't get any nearer any quicker. Attempts at ritual teleportation, proposed by Mordred, fizzle out explosively.

The tower has decided to make our lives harder, which at this point is entirely expected. I don't actually know if it's Katoptris shutting us down or some trick of Prevara or the Demiurge, but it doesn't change the result: the conceptual distance between us and the tower is only going to lessen by walking there.

Once the matter of transport is settled, our march becomes a quiet affair. Kiana and Mordred might not be at each other's throats anymore, but that's only on the surface; I doubt any kind of real forgiveness has passed between those shards. Thalia, meanwhile, is content to match the rest of the group. The murderous homunculus in a wedding dress keeps grinning at me and wiggling her eyebrows, which I have no idea how to interpret, so I'm letting the silence stick. I'm too nervous for verbal fencing.

I know *something* is going to find us before we reach the tower, it's just a matter of what spots us first. Prevara has spent the past however many thousands of years setting up the board for a final confrontation over the fate of both the Labyrinth and Pandaemonium. I doubt most of its pieces would be more than slight speedbumps for the band of killers I've assembled, but some of them are going to be real problems.

I keep my eyes peeled for trouble, my gaze darting across rooftops and down alleyways as we trek through the streets of Fata Morgana. *Where are you going to hit me from, you bastard?*

My paranoia is justified when I take another step and feel a shift in the air. My skin crackles with the sensation of something wrong, aberrant, *opposed* to my presence.

Thalia stops walking half a second before I do. We share a glance before I call out to the other two, "Trouble's knocking. Get ready."

They barely have time to react before the city block explodes in burning white.

An inkling of warning shouldn't be enough for me to do anything about it, but that's the mindset of someone still fundamentally *mortal*. Hastur whispers in my ear and nudges my hand, and when I pull the red velvet around my shoulders it is familiar and real, a mantle I've worn before. *Unburned.*

White energy fills the street in an instant, a pure inferno that melts stone. I know this fire. In my latest lifetime I've only ever seen its cousin, but the Intercessor and the Red Queen both witnessed its use from the source: the white flame of destruction, breath of the white dragon. One of the five wizardly arts.

My fireproof cloak spares me the flame itself, though the concepts of ravage and ruin embedded in the flame manage to tear past and rip a few holes in my flesh that hurt like a motherfucker. I grit my teeth and bear the pain. The blast wounded me, but I survived it, and that means another moment of endurance to stitch into my cloak.

Let's see how the others fared.

As the white fire fades, I catch sight of Kiana and Mordred both breathing heavily. Kiana is lightly singed but relatively unharmed, a thin coat of darkness still clinging to her skin but torn in places; her shadows must have rushed to her aid the moment she was warned. Mordred looks much worse, covered in glowing burns and snarling, but she's clutching a bright white marble in one hand. *She took the hit to make a copy.*

Thalia is completely untouched and already moving toward the source of the blast. *Yeah, we definitely want to keep that monster on our side. What did she do, dodge an explosion?*

Most of the buildings to either side of the street were turned to slag and ash, but one looks like it was blown open from the inside, and the interior is perfectly intact. Standing in the burnt hole is Reska, or rather the walking corpse of another Reska clone.

Urna's latest puppet is very different from the one that tried to kill me before my reunion with Cheshire. Aside from the obvious of looking more like Reska than myself or Homura, this corpse doesn't have stitches across its mouth. The zombie Kiana is wearing a half-translucent white shift and nothing else, because Urna is a deranged pervert, and she holds a long staff of green crystal. The eyes, like all of Urna's servants, are that same icy blue.

"Sorry about this!" she chirps as Thalia rushes her. The zombie slams her staff against the ground and a dozen panes of glimmering blue force appear in front of her. "It's not that I want to kill you or anything, but Mistress said she'd throw me back in the grasping pit for another month of touch training if I failed."

Despite her words—and despite the way Thalia carves through one pane after another with her knife, shattering each with a single tap—the zombie Kiana seems freakishly cheerful.

A seismic tremor snaps my attention back to the others, where a woman in burnt armor is rising out of a crater. She hefts a giant sword over her shoulder, a weapon so brutish and massive it's more a slab of iron. Dark hair falls around an emaciated face and haunted, icy eyes. This one feels like a Mordred, and I get another sense from her, too: This used to be an exalted, like Dante briefly became, but Urna ripped the light clean out of her victim. *Some sort of knight or paladin, maybe.*

The zombie Mordred screams, a cutting noise full of pain and hate, and she rushes the living Mordred with sword aloft. My splinters spring into action with fluid teamwork, the product of a hundred fights they remember clearly yet never truly fought.

Kiana swirls her shadows around the fallen knight's legs, working to slow it or trip it while Mordred invokes a burst of speed and strength to dart behind her doppelganger and run it through the back. The blade pierces through blackened steel, propelled by unnatural power, but Mordred's lip curls in distaste at something she finds. The blade is removed, covered in some kind of greenish-black muck—*but no blood,* I realize. *Inconvenient for her.*

Zombie Kiana incinerates another wall of the shop and races out through the melting hole, pursued by Thalia. The zombie is laughing, but also clearly panicking with the way she throws spell after spell to no avail. Nothing she casts can do a thing against Thalia, either cut in half by the Adversary's knife or splashing harmlessly off her wedding dress.

It feels wrong not to help with either clash, but both fights seem well in hand. *Two of Urna's pets, but nowhere near strong enough to do more than slow us down. Which means that's exactly what they're trying to do.*

Where's the necromancer? Where's the last Veseryn?

I hear the flapping of wings a moment before snow and sleet bury the world. A dragon, blue scales dotting a rotting carcass, soars overhead and unleashes a flurry of frost upon living and dead alike.

Thalia cuts through the dragon's frost breath as easily as she's cut any-thing else, but my cloak doesn't do anything against the cold and I find myself trapped in growing frost. Mordred fumbles with Vorpal's secret compartment for the right marble while Kiana transmutes fully to shadow in order to shake off the layer of ice that was coating her. The zombies move through the frost like it isn't there, one pursuing Kiana and the other run-ning from Thalia.

Mordred fishes the white fire marble back out of Vorpal along with two others glowing with violent energy. She absorbs the power from all three of them and immediately shunts it down the length of the blade, unleash-ing the violence and ruin as a beam of blinding white that spears straight through the center mass of the undead dragon.

The dragon lurches, torn nearly in half by the force of the blast, and roars pitifully as it crashes into one of the few buildings in the area not already ravaged by the initial explosion. I don't know if it was destroyed or just wounded, but either outcome is a victory.

As the dragon falls, two figures leap from its back and land gracefully amid the snow and violence below.

The first I was expecting: Lord Urna, Noble of Desire and Disgust, the half-corpse queen with platinum hair and a vicious sneer. She tried to kill me when I arrived in the bubble city, and she proudly boasted of murdering two other splinters. The first to claim a shard of Katoptris and enslave herself to its power, the greatest of Prevara's prizes in the Labyrinth.

The second figure is a man with elven ears and fiery hair, orange eyes and gilded hunting boots. A man I've met before, and never wanted to meet again, though I knew the day would come. A faerie of Summer and a Rider of the Wild Hunt. Servant in title to Lord Invernus of the Labyrinth, servant in truth to the Emissary of the Leviathans.

Eirdryd Llewellyn. The bastard who took my name.

These two, these are my opponents. They need to die. I need to kill the elf before he can use my name against me, and then I need to kill the necromancer before she can find some way to extract my name from the Huntsman's corpse.

The Red Queen would have no difficulty with the dragon's icy prison, so it's her strength I borrow to shatter my bonds. I run, attention locked on the pair of monsters before me, stealing speed and agility as well.

"Ah," Eirdryd sighs. "See how she's grown? It would be a waste not to add her to my collection."

A hundred insectoid horrors rise from the shadows cast by the wreckage and surge toward the elf in a wave of gnashing teeth and writhing limbs. Vorpal is in the hands of another, but the Intercessor collected many weapons in her travels, so I pull one of those swords from the skein of space and time. A slender blade, black as night and cool to the touch, falls into my grip.

"Keep to the deal," Urna snaps. "We made you a Noble, now pay your debt."

A wave of sickly rot bursts half the bugs and green-gold flame chars the other half. They part the horde like it's effortless for them, like I haven't grown at all. But I'm almost there. I'm so much more than I ever was, so much more than the girl who sold her name. My power is gathered, I just need to—

"**Morgan Mallory,** this is a command: Kill yourself."

My body is paralyzed instantly. All I've done since that day in the forest, all I've bled, and I'm still too fucking *weak* to stop him. I want to scream, but my lungs and throat aren't mine anymore. My hand twitches, compelled by the Huntsman's command, and the blade I summoned begins inching toward my neck.

I can't die here! I scream inside my mind, the only place I still have full control. *Damn that fae! Damn them all!*

Willpower alone isn't enough to halt the command, my sword drawing inexorably closer to killing me. Desperate and afraid, I retreat into Hastur.

Through the deeper layer of vision that I possess in my oversoul, I can see exactly what Eirdryd has done to me. The compulsion clamps down on my lesser soul like an iron spider, like a thousand strands of wire digging into my flesh to halt the electrical impulses from my brain before they reach any of my muscles. I can tell, too, that I underestimated myself; a lesser victim given that command would immediately lose control of their heart and lungs, no need for the crude violence of a blade. Small comfort when I'm still seconds from death.

I can slow the process further, but destroying the compulsion directly feels like another transgression of my role. I can buy time, because the hero always has just enough time to escape the trap, but it still needs to be *Alice* that escapes, not Hastur.

So I use the time I've stolen to wrack three timelines of memories for a solution.

Meanwhile, in the space I've stepped away from, the real battle begins. Urna and Eirdryd both unleash their throne worlds, reshaping reality around themselves and dragging everyone into a twisted landscape of warring concepts. Falling snow blankets fields of burning flowers, verdant forest paths winding through lifeless tundra. The dead rise from the ground, a thousand shambling corpses called by their wicked mistress. The Huntsman calls his own servants, wolves of bark and flame that howl with human voices.

Thalia stops chasing the wizard and follows Eirdryd into the depths of his throne world. The zombie splinters join Urna and her horde as the dead surround Mordred and Kiana and grasp at them from below. My body, Alice's body, is a pocket of stillness in the raging storm, monsters and magic alike pushed aside by the intense wills clashing within and around me. No outside force will be permitted to resolve this conflict.

Okay. Okay, we can do this. I can save myself, I just have to figure out how.

The Red Queen was saved by Cheshire, teleported away before Urna could finish the kill. That won't work here, since the command to die has already been given. Running won't do a thing.

The Intercessor escaped her contract by reforging herself. By the time her old name was brought to bear against her, it was no longer true; in this, she had succeeded where her old self had failed, replacing one name with another on a soul-deep level. The cost of that trick is obvious: By the end of her story, the Intercessor was barely Alice. Even setting aside the risk of ego death, I wouldn't be surprised if the Demiurge responded to a development like that with another reset of the timeline. Every move I make has to be calculated against that outcome.

Learning the true nature of the cycle hasn't made it sting any less how much of my existence is at the Demiurge's whim. It's absurd that I have to play by her rules when she gets to set so much of the stage. Her hands are hardly tied when the whole board is a mirage.

Even the name being used against me isn't really *mine*. That name was forced on me, the memories a fabrication. I was never Morgan, I only thought I was Morgan. One great big cluster of lies implanted in me. I took a new name barely an hour into my time in this world, made myself Malice and Maven, but that first moment and those fake memories are somehow still enough to bind me. Fae magic is bullshit, and I just know that bullshit was cultivated just to fuck with Veseryn clones.

If I could only cut away the parts of me still Morgan, the parts still stained by a name I never asked for, then . . .

. . . *Wait. Maybe the Intercessor's playbook* does *work for us. We just have to be clever and careful.*

We're not as clever as we think we are, I warn. *That's the downfall of every Veseryn.*

I know that! But if we don't try something, we lose anyway. And besides, can you think of a more Maven Alice solution than this?

. . . *Do it.*

I stay Hastur for long enough to reach into my soul and whisper a message, a hidden command I won't hear until the appointed time. Then I return to Alice just as the sword reaches my neck. It touches the chain of the heart locket, stalled for a single instant. It presses past and draws blood.

I know the spell to save me. *My* spell, the core of who I chose to be. The beast of sacrifice that the Demiurge forged me into, but still *me*. Still Alice. I thought it was gone when Melpomene changed me again, but how could it ever leave me? It's the Truth of me, the quintessence of what it means to be Maven Alice. My whole life . . .

[Feast or Famine]!

Hungry shadows surge across the blade as it cuts into my neck, the power of the Abyss once more bound to my will and answering my call. The magic takes a bite out of my soul to fuel the spell at the same time as the effect of the spell devours the parts of me connected to that invasive compulsion. I'm being consumed from both sides, swallowed up by my own creation, and the pain whites out my vision.

I feed it memories. I feed it every memory I have from before I woke up in the Labyrinth, every memory that Melpomene gave me when she cut me from her flesh.

Years of soul-crushing retail are gone in an instant, fed to the black flame with enthusiasm. Friends and girlfriends go with them, all of them passing, temporary, immaterial. I burn away the town I moved to, the places where I ate, and all the people I met.

I burn the girls I loved, the girls who hurt me. I burn the little joys and pleasures alongside the depths of despair, and my soul feels lighter for it. *Love is a lie.*

I feed my school years to the hungry dark, all those years of failure and rot. For ten years I learned to hate and suffer and rage against the world, against every disappointment, and the hate kept me moving but now it falls to flame.

I burn the classmates that were never my friends. I burn the grief and anger on my father's face. I burn the books I lost myself in, the stories I tried to escape to, and with them burns the bitter yearning. *Love of reading, too, must be deception.*

Deep, deep down inside, there is a memory that forms the core of me, the core of who I was made to be. I remember a scared child, too young to understand what was happening, as she said goodbye to her mother for the very last time and ran away to her room. I remember the ashes, scattered to the wind and sinking beneath the waves.

I burn that day, and the days that followed, and a whole lifetime of sorrow and regret buried beneath feigned indifference. I burn days in church being told these things just happen and we have to accept them. I burn the nights I wish I had died instead. I burn it all.

I burn away every ounce of the girl named Morgan Mallory, until only Alice is left.

The sword is still at my throat, so I move it away slowly and get my bearings. I'm bleeding, but it's shallow. The bigger concern is the state of my soul; devouring myself has to have left me with less material than I started with, even accounting for the spell's efficiency.

Yet what are a few gallons to the ocean? A smaller infinity is still *infinity*, and that's the power crackling at my fingertips. I am so much more than this insignificant world. More than my sisters, even, for they are all failures and I am blessed with eyes.

The fae's dirty little trick couldn't kill me, and now I'm *hungry*. I'll replace whatever I lost by snacking on another me, and that wretched Huntsman too.

I scan my surroundings. Thalia has already carved a path through Eirdryd's minions and is harassing the fae directly, as untouchable as ever. Kiana and Mordred are in worse condition, both wounded and yet to finish off their foes. Most of the lesser dead are back in the ground, but the splinters and Urna are still standing.

I'd love to get my revenge on Eirdryd up close and personal, but I can take out my aggression on his corpse. Urna is the real threat, and this is all her fault to begin with, so I think I'll enjoy giving her a taste of her own medicine.

And, I muse, *it's time to really put these powers of mine to use.*

I pour my authority as the Intercessor into a slash of my sword and cut open a portal leading right to the other Veseryn. I step through the gate and into cold winds, sleet clinging to me with malevolent intent, Urna furious at my arrival.

"Oh great," she sneers, "the bad copy is back! Fool move getting close to me, but what should I expect from one of Nyara's little pets?"

She lunges for me and I let her, uncaring if she touches me. Power blooms in my chest and I release it into Urna's throne world as a cascade of thorny red tendrils that sweep across the field and bury themselves in every corpse, moving or otherwise. This is the Red Queen's embrace, my everburning hunger, and with a whisper of will I command every tendril to *drink*.

Urna is like me, another Veseryn taking power she didn't earn, a *thief*. But the difference between us, at our cores, is a willingness to sacrifice. I bleed my soul to make it stronger. Urna, though? She's just a filthy grave robber.

My embrace devours a hundred souls she's trapped inside herself, using them for fuel and bodies but unable to incorporate them like I can. Unable to trap them like I'm certain she's trapped her own soul, with the way she's twice now tried to make contact with someone she believes can eat souls through touch. *Prevara's gifts won't save you, little sister.*

The horde crumbles as Urna reaches me. Her grasp is necrosis, pure withering intent, but my body is not and has never been real. I let the flesh she touches slough off and disintegrate, not even attempting to reach back through the momentary connection. I continue feeding on her undead minions, drinking in their essence and using it to repair the physical damage to my avatar. If she tries to match me here, she'll lose.

To my displeasure, she's smart enough to realize that. The necromancer dismisses her remaining servants with a snap of bony fingers, banishing the flood of zombies to deny me any more food. That leaves Kiana and Mordred free to focus on their doppelgangers, and I get to kill Urna with my own two hands. *Delightful.*

This Veseryn hates me. It pours off her like a thick malaise. Her perfect teeth grind into each other, her plump lips pulled back in a snarl on the half of her face with intact skin. Her back is still straight as a rod, her chin upturned in arrogant disgust, but it's a mask; inside I bet she's seething that I didn't take the bait and try to eat her.

"Why couldn't you just lie down and starve?" Urna hisses at me. "Why wouldn't you die, you brat?"

I laugh. "What, like you did? Sorry, doll, but I'm not so weak. I'm not *broken* like you are."

"I'm going to rip your chest open and fuck the gaping wound," she promises.

Then it's back to the violence.

Urna flings spears of ice from the winter storm, I deflect them with stolen instincts and a very nice sword. I conjure bugs and bats and wolves, she rots them all to dust. She starts an incantation, I stab her throat.

Through a second set of perceptions, I monitor the other conflicts happening around me. Thalia and Eirdryd have passed out of my sight, tumbling through the faerie's soul, but Mordred and Kiana are still visible. The princess brings a falling star down on the wizard, who I expect to survive, while Mordred takes a hit from her double and sends it back tenfold with her mirroring spell. Burnt armor cracks and the zombie Mordred stumbles, brought to one knee by the force of the retaliation.

"You're pathetic," I taunt the necromancer as her hands leap to my blade and try to push it out of her throat. "Just another failed Veseryn. Did you even try to rise above our fate? Did you ever make more than a token attempt to escape your end? Just another gobbet of ruined flesh. You're weak, Urna."

Urna abruptly stops pushing the blade and instead *pulls.* The sudden switch catches me off guard and I stumble into her, and then we're both falling through starlight and memory.

A girl skitters around a painted circle, book in hand and eyes alight with hunger. Cold light rises from scattered bones and a still-beating heart, coalescing in an orb of arcane frost. The girl snatches the orb and pops it in her mouth, swallowing with gusto, and once-brown eyes flare an icy blue.

The girl steps into a stone chamber, now hooded and ethereal. In the center of the chamber is a brazier of black metal and burning coal, the flames an unnatural blue. Into the fire she casts a slip of paper with two words written cleanly: *Morgan Mallory.*

The girl, the Veseryn, steps into another chamber and another time. Her dark robes have gained silver embroidery, one hand now gripping a black staff of rotting wood. She takes a ring of bone from her pocket, the trinket inscribed with arcane runes, and tucks it away in a hole in the wall that seals itself with a whisper.

The scene changes again, and this time I see a war. Thousands of risen dead march across a vast plain toward a tower of black glass. Urna, now draped in furs and reclining on a throne being carried by bulky zombies, challenges the master of the Labyrinth. Skeletal foot soldiers are joined by ossified siege behemoths and a trio of undead dragons.

A golden-haired woman stands atop the walls of Fata Morgana. I know this woman: Irma, mother of Reska, taken by Prevara to use as a puppet. Prevara raises Irma's arm, hand outstretched. She's wearing a ring of bone.

I crash out of Urna's memories alongside her, the two of us crumpling in twin heaps on a cold stone floor. My sword is still stuck in her throat, but she dislodges it as I stumble to my feet and gather power for another round. She laughs, the sound coarse and strangled as her throat slowly restores itself.

"Now," she rasps, "let's see who lasts longer."

I catch a glimpse of something moving above us—golden eyes and golden hair, the sparkle of light on a shard of glass—and then everything is torture.

My skin shivers and curls and curdles, this itchy scratchy paper that needs to come off, it sticks to me and I can't help but feel every inch, every pore, every point where it connects to the flesh beneath. My fingers prickle at the tips and along the lengths, needing to be torn, needing to peel away so I can be free. Two fingers brush against each other and I nearly vomit at the horrible sensation.

My tongue feels like a slug, slimy and wet and wriggling. It wants to crawl down my throat and I need to spit it out but it's stuck to me. There's another texture, almost moldy, a thin layer of fuzz starting to coat the insides of my cheeks and over my teeth. My flaking lips split open and pus oozes out, sickly fluid dribbling down my chin.

The glass shard flashes and my body is normal again. I shudder, sent back to the floor by the sudden and overwhelming sensations that flooded my mind. *Psychic assault, but what—*

The shard flashes again and this time my focus wrenches away from my own body and toward Urna's. I feel *hungry*, but it's a hunger full of heat that keeps my attention lingering on the lines of her curves, that flesh so supple I want to reach out and squeeze it, the shine of her lips and eyes, everything about her begging to be touched. I want to rip her open and taste the spurting blood while it's hot and rich. There's a need inside me, deep and molten, narrowing my existence to two bodies that could be joining in glorious violence. Even those skinless and rotting parts of her have a certain appeal, the sheen of bone and the whorls of decay like a painted tapestry of the world's most beautiful woman.

I crawl toward her, shivering and gasping, and the contempt on her face drives me wild. She's shivering too, but she keeps her back straight and her hands still, just watching me approach. There's hate in her eyes and desire in the way she bites her lip, and I need to get my teeth on her face.

I'm inches from touching her when the shard flashes and everything about her body disgusts me. I fall away and the floor is grime and filth like sandpaper on my brainstem, it's a luxurious bath and I could stretch here for centuries, my stomach churns with bile, my brain boils with heat and need.

Caught between shifting extremes, I writhe on the floor. Urna, shuddering but somehow lucid, stumbles to my side and looms over me.

"This is how it broke me," she hisses, voice tight with pain and eyes wild with hunger and hatred. *Desire. Disgust.* "We're *made* to be broken. To suffer."

The contrasting sensations flood my body and mind in never-ending waves. It's almost impossible to think through the relentless sequence of turning emotions. Almost. In flashes of self-control I scrabble blindly through the levers of my soul, looking for my salvation.

"Be proud, you damn copy," Urna sneers at me. One hand slips under my shirt and gropes me, the sensation cycling rapidly between a revolting sense of violation and overwhelming pleasure. "You're the only splinter I've ever had to use this on."

My will grasps what I've been looking for.

[Feast or Famine]!

My signature spell flares to life again and devours the overwhelming influence of Urna's curse. Pleasure vanishes into pain, desire and disgust subsumed by a far more visceral and all-consuming hunger. Surprise flashes across Urna's face as I call another of the Intercessor's swords to hand and plunge it into her filthy grasping arm.

She tears the arm off to get away from me, backing against a wall of the shadowed chamber and staring at me in horror. The crystal flashes, again and again and again, but every new wave of sensory compulsion is devoured by my magic running on loop in the background. The pain is immense, but pain is an old friend.

"You think I'm like those girls," I say, panting from the effort of standing while my soul rips itself apart over and over again. "And I am. But I'm better. I'm—I'm what Veseryn could be. Should be. You settled. Let petty hungers s-swallow that b-beautiful ambition. *I am the god of the knife.* I fall and I rise. I burn and I bloom. I will *annihilate myself* to forge anew whatever you try to break. And I'll never stop."

I take the surging hunger of my magic, the Abyssal truth of me, and I pour it through every ounce of my being. Every drop of blood, every pound of flesh, every jittering neuron. And then I spread it further, out through the shadow I cast and my presence in the world, from skin to air and from air to everything. I stain the world, ink in water, and everything goes red.

The Red Queen devours the heart of Urna's throne world. I crunch the glass shard in jaws of shadow and blood, and then I eat the necromancer.

Her soul is sinfully sweet.

I return to Fata Morgana with tendrils of Abyssal hunger still swirling around me, a vortex of blood and shadow and teeth. It's hard to tell where I stop and the darkness starts, but, ah, what was it Reska said? *I am the dark, and the dark is me. I was always a monster.*

What a lovely sentiment. Being a monster certainly feels better than whatever I was before. I feel powerful, and what else could a Veseryn ask for?

Mordred and Kiana are still playing with their food. The wizard is dead, hacked into pieces and lying in a blood of her own ichor, but the noisy brute is still swinging around that big lump of iron. It's cute, but I've had enough of this.

I reach out with one of my limbs to devour the wizard's corpse, trusting her tortured soul to still be lingering by the body. With six more of my hands I wrap around the death knight and pull her into me. She resists, of course, but her mistress is gone and I am so, so, so much more. I swallow her whole with barely a hiccup.

The other splinters aren't quite as sweet as dear Urna, but they're still very satisfying snacks. There's something more real about a splinter, something deliciously filling about eating food that isn't illusory. Even precious Lena can't compare: The taste of her neck is a fond memory, but she was barely a potato chip next to my feast of selves.

I want more. It's so indulgent to suggest after gulping down three other Alices, but I'm still *hungry*. Urna was a scrumptious meal, but those other two were morsels. I'm not *full* yet.

More prey catches my eye, gathering themselves and moving toward me with a clear sense of caution. I recognize them. They're *mine*. The princess and the warrior, my sisters and creations. My little gobbets of flesh. They shout something at me, or one of them does, but I'm not listening.

What would my gobbets taste like? I wonder. Kiana and Mordred, the two I made, would they taste like truer splinters? Are they true enough, planted by the Demiurge and given form by my flesh? I need to find out. I need to eat. *I made them, so it's only fair that I devour them.*

Something else moves into my range and I curl away from it in fear. It's the predator, the elder sister. The bigger monster. I'm not strong enough to eat her yet, though I yearn for it desperately. If I devoured her, if I tasted her essence and made it mine, if I had my way with that perfect, beautiful heart . . . maybe, just maybe, I could eat the Demiurge next.

The predator throws something at me and I catch it with a tendril. It's a body, but not the body of one of us. Summer, fae-thing, *enemy*. I devour the one who took my name. But, if he's dead—

Now.

My hand—my flesh hand—moves against my will and darts to the chain around my neck. The locket. The anatomical heart. *The artifact.* I try to stop myself, but there are *strings* pulled tight around my wrist, red strings from a crimson cloak. *No, no, no! I don't want to go back to being that girl! I'm perfect like this! This is what I'm meant to be!*

The strings move my mouth, strum my throat, and speak the words: "[My Heart]."

A lifetime of memories slam back into my mind, along with all the pieces of myself I've cut away since making that artifact that moment in the maze, helped by the Beast. Why did it help me? Why did it give me this tool? Was it acting on the command of Katoptris or Prevara, or did Melpomene meddle to bring this about? Was this always meant to happen, or was the locket seeded for one of the timelines that the Demiurge abandoned?

I fall to my knees and throw up on the ground, but I don't understand why. And then I do, and more sick spills out of me.

I remember the girl who woke up in the schoolhouse, lonely and afraid. I remember everything that made her that person, all the days that never were. I remember all the pieces of myself I fed to my ambition, every soft edge that needed to be sharpened. I remember the pain of loss, of cutting away pieces of myself over and over again because the ends are worth the means and I cannot abide my failure. I remember my own blood dripping from my fingers.

Is this what she would feel, if we gave her back every splinter?

Why do we both keep destroying ourselves?

A hand touches my shoulder. Arms pull me to my feet. Thalia is there beside me, watching me with those burning eyes. Smiling, knife still in hand, still dressed for the altar and her unholy matrimony with the pitiful monster that made me like this.

"All good?" she asks. There's no sympathy in the question.

I clear my throat and force calm. "All good," I affirm. "Let's keep moving."

"Great! To Katoptris we go! I bet Prevara's next, and I'm *itching* to settle that score." Thalia giggles and prances away, skipping toward the glass tower.

Kiana looks at me with worry. "Are you actually good, Alice? That looked . . . unpleasant."

"It doesn't matter." I turn away from her and start walking after Thalia. "We don't have time for anything else."

"The work," Mordred mutters, "always the work."

I hear her follow, and a moment later so does Kiana, and our journey goes on beneath a shattering sky.

GARDEN OF MEMORIES VI

My attempt to barrel on without thinking about what I just went through is, surprising no one, a huge failure. The sullen silence just gives my brain more chances to barrage me with memory and emotion until I begrudgingly turn my thoughts to what happened.

Using the necklace was a gamble that paid off, but it wasn't without cost. With my Hastur-granted senses, I can map out other timelines where I activated the artifact under different circumstances, and each time the act is momentous, disastrous, and necessary.

In one world, I use it as a weapon against myself; I am split in two, divided by Abyssal fiat, and my selves go to war. When my darker side tries to devour her other half, the activation of the heart locket annihilates them both and forces reunification.

Had I been a demon on the verge of ascension, as in that instance, the sudden onset of rejuvenated humanity would have destroyed all the power I'd gathered, my existence as a demon incompatible with my original, unsculpted self. I'm fortunate that Hastur has no such limitations, already comfortable reconciling Alices in opposition.

The cost in this timeline, then, is relatively minor in comparison. It mostly just makes me feel like shit.

My memories of Sanctuary keep butting up against my attention. I find that funny, since they weren't the set of memories devoured and regurgitated, but my time before entering the Labyrinth just doesn't feel real. It wasn't real, after all.

So I remember running through the woods and bargaining with a fae and then a devil, thinking myself so clever for trying to cheat the laws of narrative. I remember meeting Cheshire for the first time and looking into my horrible, broken soul with her. I remember all my petty arguments with her, with Bashe, and with everyone else.

I remember pain. I was bruised, battered, stabbed, and shot, but the sharpest pain was all self-inflicted. I made a mantra out of pain, forged my suffering into a sword and kept whetting the edge. I tore my soul apart, over and over again, made it my first and only solution to every single problem.

I remember loneliness. Everything kept trying to kill me, and I approached every creature that wasn't trying to kill me like that could change at any time. I took Bashe's hand, Cheshire's, Dante, Esha, but I never trusted any of them, or if I did it was only as a gamble. I schemed manipulation and betrayal, and in other timelines I went through with it.

I wonder how much of that was my own fault, and how much was the Demiurge. It feels like I've made so many mistakes and bad decisions, but are they really *my* mistakes? Should I feel guilt for what she made me do? Or is it a kind of weakness to blame my maker, even if her hand wrote the script?

Is there really so much of a distinction between Alice and Melpomene? I'm a piece of her, one among hundreds or even thousands, but we're not all the same. Veseryn, Kiana, Mordred, all these have happened before, but there's only ever been one Alice. Reska remembered nothing of Melpomene's life on Earth, the life I knew as Morgan, and Homura had some of those memories but she seemed somehow younger than me, a version of Morgan with less experience to temper the burning anger.

I can't stop thinking about Melpomene. Mother, sister, twin, creator. Source of all my gifts, the hand behind my torment. She made us, all of us, and perhaps I should be grateful. But she keeps hurting us, breaking us, burning us, and for that I can't forgive her. But does that mean I can't forgive myself? Is that an accident, or the intent?

I remember what she said to Veseryn, and to Katoptris, and what she must have said a hundred times while Thalia watched:

Because I still haven't found the answer that I'm looking for, so I need to keep hurting you. All of this must happen again, and again, until I finally have it.

What is Melpomene *doing* with this endless cycle? She keeps shaping worlds and carving off pieces of herself to run around those worlds, her countless shards enduring toil and hardship and *suffering*. Something always goes wrong, or doesn't go in the way she wants it to, and she gives up on us. She sets us up for failure and mocks us when we stumble, but then that failure makes her depressed and withdrawn. She tortures us relentlessly, but then she burns us whether we break or endure.

She burns us for failing her, but what are we failing to do? What outcome does she find desirable? What goal is driving her actions? What question is she asking? What *answer* is she looking for? What does she expect from us that we can never manage to deliver?

I can't even say for certain if hurting is a means or an end. Maybe she thinks that the only way to find her *answer* is to torture her own copies. Maybe she believes the cruelty is a necessary evil. Maybe that's even true.

Maybe everything I've done has been necessary, for all the pain it's brought me. My survival has been paid for in suffering, and this is the only path I could have walked. Or rather, any other path I could have walked would have been paved in the same sins and tragedies.

Or maybe we've both been lying to ourselves all this time. Maybe it's all just one big excuse for the two of us to keep *bleeding*.

My brooding is finally interrupted by a soft touch on my shoulder. I flinch and tense, but Thalia removes her hand quickly and I force myself to relax. "Almost to the tower," she says. "I can sense Prevara's hosts just ahead of us, probably waiting to make their stand by the entrance. Two visible, with the last three waiting in the wings."

I blink. "Wait, last? It has a limit? How do you know—stupid question, of course you know everything."

"Splitting itself is one of Prevara's oldest tricks, but Pom-Pom always hardcodes a cap to keep it manageable. This version of Prevara can divide itself into nine pieces, since that's something of an arc number for this loop. Homura and I killed three of its shards before we were separated. Pom-Pom blew up the one harassing you right before she made her Intercessor offer. I doubt any more have died since then."

Mordred falls in beside us and frowns. "I remember that, the ones we killed. The brother, the blademaster, and the princess of another kingdom."

I glance over at Kiana in time to see her shiver. *Oh. Hey, that seems like something we should address* before *going into combat.* I step away from the others and ask her softly, "Did you know?"

The former princess hesitates. "Reska didn't. I think it might have come up in the last battle, but my memories of that are hazier than the rest. I learned about it from whatever was happening with you and Thalia."

Now it's my turn to hesitate. "So . . . how do you feel about it?"

She stares off into the distance, gaze unfocused. "Luka must have been taken when he entered the doors. That's . . . that's why he was so different, after that night. Because it wasn't him." Kiana laughs, a bitter and broken sound. "Prevara stole my brother. I wonder if Luka was still inside, scream-ing as he was forced to turn on me, crying as I came to hate him for words he never meant. Or maybe Prevara just killed him. I think it killed my mother. It took everything from me, all to drive me into its arms."

"Prevara will pay," I say coldly. "For everything it's done. And when we snuff out its last shard, your brother can rest."

"And what then?" she asks quietly. "We climb the tower and raid the heavens?"

I look back at Thalia and Mordred, the two having their own discussion as we approach the site of our next battle. "That's the plan. Fight a god and take her place, or something like that. But, before that, there's one thing I'd like your help with." I meet Kiana's gaze and put as much conviction in my words as I can. "Help me save Reska. Help me pull her out of Contrition."

Kiana shivers again. "I—I don't know if I can do that, Alice. I wouldn't know where to begin, and the idea of facing her terrifies me."

"You're the only one who can," I insist. "You or Mordred, I guess, but do you really trust *her* to save Reska?"

Kiana flinches. "I . . . no, I don't. I'm scared, Alice. But I'll try."

"That's all I ask."

When we reach the base of the tower, one of the figures there is the woman I expected: Irma, Reska's mother, looking as she had in the final vision. Blood drips down her flowing dress, and golden eyes are stained with black rings. She waits patiently for us, hands folded and smile beatific, standing on the stone steps.

The other is Reska's father, Kresimir Vincek Dawnbringer, who once sat the Sunlit Throne and now stands beside his dead wife. His green and gold robes have become tattered and filthy, the flesh underneath withered and decrepit. Where Irma is preserved perfectly aside from the wound Homura gave her, Kresimir is given no such luxury. The Sunlit Scepter, the grand artifact of his lineage, is clutched tightly in skeletal hands.

Must have scooped up the corpse and kept it safe. Well, that's an unpleasant addition.

Before either of them can start taunting their daughter, Thalia waves at them and calls out, "Prevara! Buddy! I feel like it's been ages since we last chatted. Y'know, when you delayed your inevitable demise by a few thousand years and consigned yourself to whatever torture the old girl's been putting you through." Thalia's smile is bloodthirsty.

Prevara ignores Thalia. The dead king glares at his daughter with ringed eyes. "So, an echo of that worthless girl has come to climb the tower. Do you think you are worthy, child? To stand where she could not?"

"Or have you come seeking absolution?" asks the shard of Prevara inside the frail queen. "To return to your mother's embrace and beg forgiveness for your sins? It is not too late for you, my daughter."

For a moment, I worry that Kiana will be tempted. Reska fell for Prevara's manipulations despite all the warning signs that should have kept her away. My worry is foolish; Kiana is *furious*. The shadows gather around her in a growing storm of wrathful night. Her fists are bunched tight, her teeth bared.

"You . . . you *bastard*! You horrible, wretched thing!" Kiana cries. "You took everyone from me, from her, and now you think you can play to my sympathies? To my insecurities? Never from you, Prevara. You'll never again have a foothold in my heart. This only ends when every last piece of you is gone."

"Well said," Thalia praises. "Now, let's get to that, shall we?"

Two more bodies step out of the tower, passing through the glass archway like ghosts and coming to stand beside the others. Luka, the golden prince, and Ruzica, the duchess of swords. Both corpses, both in worse condition than Irma but better than Kresimir. Both with those same ringed eyes.

Luka says calmly, "You are being deceived. I understand you have enmity toward us, but we are not your enemy. The Demiurge and the Adversary are the real threats."

Ruzica folds her arms and adds, "There's only one way any of us get out of this prison, and it's not by listening to Nyarlathotep's hatchet man."

Mordred laughs and points her sword at the gathering of hosts. "That's a good joke. Oh, you're right that the Demiurge is a much, much bigger threat than your sorry ass, but the rest? What a pathetic attempt at manipulation. You're just a puppet clawing at your own strings, too stupid to realize you'll die when they get cut. Become the dirt I walk on, worm."

Luka raises an eyebrow at her. "And why should Reska take *your* word? You lied to her from the moment you met, betrayed her trust, and even tried to murder her. Of course you would defend your accomplice, but Reska doesn't—"

Thalia rolls her eyes at me a split second before rushing Luka. She cleaves a beam of sunlight, parries Ruzica's sword, and collides with the fallen prince.

Before any of the rest of us can join the fight, panes of black glass pop into existence between us. The glass walls surround me in an instant, and then I'm standing somewhere I've stood once before, in a dream of another life. A place where the air is fever-warm.

The realm of the Leviathans is a pale reflection of the graveyard of worlds. This mass grave holds the bodies of mere mortals, things of charnel and bone piled atop the old gods of the Dream that long ago decomposed. It is an endless plain of decomposition, ringed by the writhing corpses of carrion worms that think themselves bigger than they are. They think that leeching souls from the universe above makes them the thirsty roots of it all.

Some of them know more. Some of them have been shown the truth. There is a graveyard far grander than this and far more ancient, where realities go to die. An ashen void that only one has ever called home. They are afraid of her, and so am I.

The Emissary is waiting for me, the high priest of worms. It wears the shape I saw in the void: a thing of wasting flesh and gossamer robes, of black mist and gray skin. It isn't smiling this time, and the tendrils that form its upper head are twitching with a new, erratic frenzy. There is a scent in the air that I only now realize I have missed: *fear*.

"Lady Alice," it greets. "Intercessor. Red Queen. I hear you are much and more, these days. Perhaps it is time we parleyed as equals."

Equals, it says. What an insult. *You aren't even an Alice.* I smile with teeth. "Prevara. Emissary. I hear you are less and less, these days. What do you think you can offer me?"

"Words of warning, if nothing else." It doesn't seem bothered by my retort, but then it must be among the best of all the liars I've met. "You have fallen into the orbit of a very old and very dangerous monster, my lady. You cannot trust the Adversary."

"Lol," I say dryly. "Lmao, even."

The Emissary tilts its half of a head. "You are a very strange creature. Has anyone ever told you that?"

"Everyone's a goddamn critic," I complain. "I have to entertain myself somehow with all you freaks constantly trying to kill me or lie to me or both. Care to tell me which of those you've got cooking? 'Cause, and this should be obvious, I don't trust a word you say right now. On account of you lying to me and trying to kill me. Multiple times. As recently as ten minutes ago."

"I understand there is enmity between us," the Emissary repeats itself from earlier with just a touch more diplomacy. "I will be frank, as it seems you appreciate that: I do not like you, Maven Alice. In fact, I despise you. But that ancient *monster* you've allied with is an order of magnitude more dangerous to not just yourself but all life on all worlds. To every participant in the cycle."

I fold my arms and lean back against empty air turned solid by a twist of Intercessor magic. "Well, that's an interesting detail. When Homura tried to kill you that first time, you didn't have a clue about the *real game*. Yet now you're talking like you know what the Adversary really is, and where she comes from."

The Emissary inclines its head. "I have learned, at great cost and great pain. As it seems you have, though your interactions with the entity. Shall we speak plainly?"

"Let's."

"I understand the Adversary as another shard of the Demiurge like yourself, Reska, and others. The key distinction is that the Adversary originates from a previous world in the eternal cycle of death and rebirth we are all trapped in. It is my belief that the war between Adversary and Demiurge is the motivating force behind that cycle."

I chew my lip. "She tells it different. There's the new war, which looks a bit like what you described, and then there's the old war. For some hundred loops or more, the Demiurge made worlds and burned them all on her own, the Adversary her Intercessor. My predecessor turned traitor when she realized the cycle would go on forever if she didn't do something. What she's offering me is an end to the cycle. You think she's lying?"

"About that? No. She will end the cycle if you help her, of that I am certain." Prevara gestures to the dead and empty wasteland around us, the miles and miles of rot and death. "The end, I imagine, will look a lot like the Abyss, which was born of her influence on the new universe. She will murder this universe and strangle the next in the cradle. She has no interest in creating something new to replace what she destroys, as that has ever been the role of her counterpart and opponent."

Well, that last part seems true. The question is whether she'll let me *forge a new world.* "I'm aware of her proclivities. She doesn't scare me." *Lie.* "Neither do you, but I get the feeling that's not mutual anymore, is it?" I grin wide, confident in that fact. "In fact, I kinda think you're pissing yourself right now, my dear Emissary. You tried to kill me or enslave me, and you failed. You tried to treat me like a pawn, and you failed. Now I have every reason to kill you, and you're terrified I'll actually do it before the Adversary even gets a chance. You called me a *pest* the first time we met. A piece to sweep off the board before your grand duel with your only real rival. How does it feel, knowing you were so *wrong* about me? I bet you're seething with hate."

I'll give Prevara credit, it can hold its cool. Its muscles barely tighten at my taunts, and the only real sign of its frustration is the long pause before it answers me. "I pray you cease your juvenile taunts, my dear Intercessor. You underestimate how many cards I still hold in this game. My influence and resources are—"

"Shut up," I snap. "Stop talking right now or I rip your guts out through your mouth and throw you at the Adversary. If you want to survive the next five fucking minutes, you will shut up and listen to me. Understand? Don't speak, just nod."

Prevara's tight control finally frays. Its teeth clench and the shadows around it start bubbling and shifting like when Reska's in distress, but it doesn't speak. After a long moment of seeming to struggle with itself, the Emissary tightly nods. I can feel the rage boiling beneath the surface, that immense well of hate for the simple fact that *I'm in control.*

I smile. "Good. Much better. Now, I understand you're afraid of the Adversary. She's one of the only things in the universe that can actually take a bite out of you, and she's already done that, hasn't she? Yeah. You're weaker than you were in your prime, thanks to her. Now she's coming for you, coming for everything standing in the way of that tower and the heavens above. And you're going to lose. All your little plans went up in smoke when I popped back into the story with a brand new soul. If you can't get me on your side here, we tear through your remaining splinters and either kill you outright or leave you too weak to take on Contrition and Malice once they burst onto the stage. So tell me you need me."

That hate and rage flares brighter, almost cracking the mask of control again, but the Emissary forces itself to speak, each word scraping against its throat. "I need you."

The satisfaction that runs through me is practically orgasmic. How much further can I take this? How much petty revenge can I extract from bullying an entity I would have called a god just one day prior? I tilt my head. "You know, I wouldn't mind seeing a bit more degradation. Fair play for all you've tried to do to me, right? So, if you want me to save you from the Adversary, then I really think you should beg me for it. Maybe I'll take pity on you and make you my pet. C'mon. Beg. Bark for me. Be a good little bitch and your new owner will keep you safe from the big bad Adversary."

The rage finally overflows. A wall of thorny darkness erupts from the corpse-covered ground and surges at me—

—only to be cut in half by the casual swing of a bloody knife.

"Hey again, Emmy!" Thalia chirps. "Trying to start the party without me? Naughty of you."

The Adversary's wedding dress has acquired some new stains, a tapestry of red and black seeping into the already-bloodied altar white. There's a hole in the world where she cut her way into this realm, a static tear in the fabric of reality.

Prevara flinches at Thalia's arrival and actually backs away from her. Its face is hard to read without eyes, but the tentacles that make up most of its head curl in tight. "You! How can you do this? What power did that wretch give you? I am an archon of Pandaemonium!"

Thalia laughs. "Sorry, is that supposed to mean anything to me? You're a bit part, doll."

Spikes of shadow launch at Thalia from all directions and this time she doesn't even bother cutting them. Each thorn of darkness splashes against her skin or dress and evaporates on contact. She yawns. I shiver.

The Emissary snaps its fingers and flickers out of existence, but then the Adversary snaps her fingers and Prevara comes right back. "None of that," she chides. "You've stepped into the story now, you don't get to leave it until

I give you permission. Which I won't. We've got to resolve this little side plot in a timely manner."

Prevara practically hisses at the Adversary. "I am the Emissary, the high priest of the dead gods of the Abyss. I am the second archon, beneath only Katoptris and Nyarlathotep in authority over the realms of Pandaemonium. For ten thousand years I have pulled the strings of every piece on the game board, and I have brought about the fall of six of your sisters. I am not some bit part, not some lesser player! You do not dictate realities to me!"

"Actually," Thalia muses, "I really do. You know, there's this concept I've been meaning to explain to our fresh little godling over there, so I may as well take the opportunity to use you as an example. You don't mind, right?"

Prevara snaps its arm to the side and clenches its fist. Two Leviathan corpses rise jittering from the rotten mulch and fling themselves with open mouths directly at the Adversary. The worm-gods are wounds and death and hunger, great beasts of gaping maw and poison tooth, and they split like fruit before the Adversary's knife. Their divided flesh melts into smoke and mist, and that smoke and mist flows into their killer's body, absorbed completely.

Thalia sighs. "It'll be awfully annoying to try and explain this while dealing with your little tantrums, Emmy. Oh, idea! I'll just make your own masters keep you in place."

The Adversary whistles and a dozen fleshy tendrils of rotting muscle and sinew rise from the mulch to bind Prevara's limbs. The Emissary struggles, but its efforts are futile. Another tendril of meat wraps around its head and covers its mouth, silencing further protests.

"Now, let me tell you about Wonderland. I've been rather enamored of the concept recently, on meeting our dear little Alice and learning her story. I think it's a perfect metaphor for something that Melpomene and I have discussed plenty of times. See, my sweet Prevara, the reason you can't beat me here is because this is Wonderland and *you are not an Alice.* That girl over there, now that's an Alice. Reska, Homura, the others, those are Alices. But you? You're just a bit of fluff in the dream."

My attention sharpens. My sixth sense as Hastur tells me that this monologue is *important* in some way. Thalia seems to be relishing the chance to share this idea, like she's been practicing it in her head. I need to learn more about the Adversary, so I'll listen. I don't know if we're destined to try and kill each other, but if we are . . . understanding her powers is the first step to overcoming those powers.

Thalia reaches into nowhere and pulls out a copy of *Alice in Wonderland*, one that looks just like my copy back on Earth. She thumbs through the pages absentmindedly. "We're all familiar with the story, yes? An unusual girl and a fantastic world full of absolute meaningless *nonsense*. When little Alice falls into Wonderland, she finds a story that's been crafted just for her. Every character she runs into was created just for that interaction, every location shaped for the scene. Something to vex her, something to make her laugh, something to confuse her sensibilities. None of the talking animals or mad strangers have lives outside the page. They don't have inner worlds, they don't even think like Alice does. They exist for the moment, for the scene, for the effect it will have on *Alice* for them to take the actions they do.

"You can pretend that they're alive, of course. You're always welcome to do that, in any story you read. But it is, in the end, only a pretense. Eventually, Alice will leave Wonderland, and when she does every character she met will suddenly cease to be. They are specks, fleeting and senseless. Their purpose served, they depart the stage."

Prevara keeps struggling, and in the distance more worms stir, but they are held tight and encircled by their peers and siblings. Prevara may be their Emissary, but the Adversary is the apotheosis of the only thing they respect: *strength*. I watch in silence, unwilling to interrupt.

Thalia keeps going, now thoroughly enjoying herself. She tosses the book aside and smiles wider. Her voice echoes with power and truth and menace.

"In a room outside the universe there is an orrery of brass and wood and paint. That orrery is real and it is physical, and it is the source of your world. Everything in this universe is a projection, an imaginary object anchored to that physical object. None of the planets are real, none of the magic is real, and none of the people are real, not even the ones that think they can think. All just dreams, in the end."

The philosophy of figments writ large. Is that true? Esha, Dante, Bashe, were they all just constructs of imagination? Dreams of people, tricked into thinking they were alive? It's an uncomfortable thought, but it's also one I've been primed to think about through my interactions with Lena and the other figments of Sanctuary.

Thalia slips behind Prevara and taps her knife along its body, careful not to draw blood. "Have you ever stopped to think about what the schools of magic actually represent? Order is easy, since it tells you outright that it's all about material laws, a form of reality as self-evident as gravity. Spirit is the collective, a set of ideas shared through culture and holding weight from history and popularity. Shadow is how you personally perceive the world, your own unique set of knowledge and beliefs. Three lenses by which to view the world: that which is common fact, that which is inherited from one's surroundings, and that which is personal perspective. These are the components of *suspension of disbelief.* The mechanisms of a narrative world."

Thalia gestures and the tendril around Prevara's mouth loosens just enough for the Emissary to spit out a response: "You deranged madwoman, you have no idea what you're talking about! You—"

She silences it again with a snort. "Yeah, yeah. You're big and important and definitely real, right? Wrong. You're imaginary, Prevara. You are a puff of dream logic held together only by the inertia of what the Demiurge set in motion. Those girls you've been killing, though, they're something different. They're a little more real than you are, though not by much. Like the universe itself, they're a projection of something physical, dreams of little scraps of meat in a cold and endless laboratory. They push the world and the world pushes back, both projections anchored in something real."

A projection of something real. I'm sure I'd take that notion worse if I hadn't gone through, well, everything since landing in Fata Morgana. I can't deny the truth of what I've seen. Maven Alice is a screaming gobbet of godly flesh, and the body I feel right now is just my representation in the Demiurge's dreamscape. But the Adversary—

"But me?" Thalia winks. "Oh, I'm the real deal. My heart is Melpomene's heart, the heart of our divine creator, and this body is no mere projection. Everywhere I go, I go with my full self, and that makes me the most real thing in the universe. I'm so real that imaginary things like you can't even fucking touch me. So you'll die when I cut you and you'll fail to even scratch me, because that's how much more real than you I really am."

It clicks into place. Reska, Homura, Urna, Alice, we're all tiny scraps of the Demiurge. Skin and muscle and fat, but all of that is just excess meat. It hurts her to carve us off, but she's not really sacrificing anything important. Thalia, though? Her core is Melpomene's *heart.* That has to mean something.

Gaining insight through Hastur has given me more ability to manipulate the false reality of the dream, but the weight behind my influence is always going to be lesser than what Thalia can bring to bear. The gap between us is even greater than the gap between me and the girls who haven't found that insight, the shards of Melpomene who haven't seen what I've seen and can't peek behind the curtain.

... Hmm. That might actually show us a path to evening the playing field. We could devour a billion souls and not get an inch closer to Thalia's level, but eating other Alices ... when we ate Urna, that felt incredibly different from all our previous meals.

That's a dangerous train of thought. The only shards left now are Reska and Homura. I don't feel particularly bad about the idea of killing and eating Homura, but Reska? That's the girl we're supposed to save.

If she can be saved.

Thalia glances back at me, now holding the knife to Prevara's throat. "Get any fun ideas from that rant, sis?" Her smile is cocky and knowing, like she can tell I'm plotting countermeasures against her. Can she read my thoughts? I have to just hope she can't.

"A few," I say lightly. "It's a nightmarishly solipsistic view of reality, but I can't deny the material evidence for your position. And I don't really have the luxury of getting into arguments about moral philosophy while the universe is about to end."

Thalia laughs. "But you'd love to, wouldn't you? I'll admit, that's a trait I always find so cute in Veseryn."

I cough and hide my face. "Yes, well, whatever."

She laughs again. The writhing worms devour each other around us. "I've got this handled. Prevara has a few more tricks up its sleeve, but they won't be enough. You should help the others, they might need it."

Shit, right. "That is an exceptionally good point! Have fun with the worms."

The tear that Thalia cut into this space is still there, but I want to try carving one of my own. I wasn't sure if Prevara had actually transported me to the Abyss or just called up a simulacrum, but closer examination reveals it as something more comparable to a throne world overlay. This space is the Abyss, that much is certain, but it's also still Fata Morgana.

Hastur's hands pry open the barriers between dimensions and I slip through the cracks. I catch a glimpse of other pocket realities torn apart by the Adversary's passing, and two bubbles still unpopped.

The first contains Mordred, who almost seems to be having *fun* as she crosses swords with the corpse of Ruzica. Her joy is sharp-edged and vicious, seen in the mocking laughter that accompanies each parry and riposte. My intervention clearly isn't needed here.

Kiana, however, might need my help. Her pocket dimension looks like the inside of Reska's castle, only the roof has been blown off to expose an endless void. She's in the throne room of the castle, and she's fighting her father.

Kiana descends on Kresimir in a swarm of hungry darkness and he blasts her back with a ray of pure sunlight, sending her tumbling across the throne room to crash against the far wall.

I step out next to her and offer a hand. "Need some help?"

Kiana hesitates, but then she takes my hand and I pull her up. "I can do this. Reska defeated him in this very room."

"That's right," the dead king says, cold and stern. "You murdered me here. Are you going to do it again, child? How many times will you betray your parents?"

A slash of shadow meets a flash of light. Kiana glares at the corpse with more hate than I ever felt from Reska. "You're *not* my father, and you're not even Reska's. And for all the strife we had with him, for all the anger and the frustration and the grief, we *never* wanted him to die. That was your doing, Prevara."

Prevara sends another blast of sunlight at Kiana, but I counter it with a pane of conjured glass, an Intercessor trick. I drawl, "Things really aren't looking up for you, are they? You could always surrender now and subject yourself to our tender mercies."

Three more rays provide an answer. Kresimir raises the artifact and a miniature sun grows in the air above him, drawing in light and heat and power. "You sound so sure of yourself, girl, but the path you walk leads only to ruin. You may best me here, but you will not survive what is to come. When the end swallows you whole, remember this: I could have saved you."

I laugh at Prevara's last desperate attempt at manipulation. "You can't even save yourself. Let's finish this, Emissary. I've got bigger fish to fry."

One day ago, Prevara was an entity so far beyond me I couldn't even conceive of how to fight it. From the view I had still stuck as a lowly demon running through pointless games, the Emissary was my final boss. The greatest challenge I'd have to overcome on the path to the tower and what lay beyond.

But in the real game, Prevara isn't even a player. If I take the Adversary's point of view, Prevara isn't even a person. It wants to believe in its importance, and I can relate to that. Destiny is a heady drug.

I'm not sure I believe in destiny anymore. My role is to die, and that's a fate I can't accept. Every girl who came before me, every Alice, they all failed. There's nothing in the stars to say I'll do better than them.

So damn the stars, and damn the woman who put them there. I'll carve my own path.

Kresimir throws the sun at us and Kiana drowns it in darkness, and it's my blade that sinks into his chest and my will that seizes the shard of Prevara clinging tight to this corpse. I rip the parasite free of its host.

I can tell this is the last piece, meaning Mordred and Thalia must have finished with their shards. Prevara made a mistake in challenging us, unaware that Thalia could close its escape routes. It talked, it fought, and now it dies.

I crush the last of its essence and feel the Emissary cease.

The king, corpse though he may be, lets out a rasping breath. His eyes have lost their rings of black and are rapidly fading, grown rheumy and decrepit. His gaze slides off me and finds the girl that looks just like his daughter.

His voice is thin, his words coming out in strangled gasps. "Reska . . . my Reska . . ."

Kiana steps beside me and looks down at the ruin of a man. "What is there to say?" she asks. She sounds so tired, and her eyes are wet. "Nothing can be fixed now."

"Too late," the king coughs. "Always . . . too late." His body stills, the life drained out.

Kiana stares down at him, sniffling with suppressed tears. "You were a terrible father," she whispers. "I wish I still had you."

I'm afraid to say anything, so I stay quiet as she kneels by her father's corpse and holds him close. The world around us fades away, the castle and the void melting back into the city of glass. The tower looms tall, and I catch sight of Thalia and Mordred by the archway entrance.

Then the sky shatters.

The clear blue above, already cracked from earlier, collapses completely as a vast force pushes through. A raging storm of wind and fire and *regret* annihilates a dozen floating islands and the farthest edge of Fata Morgana, dragging them all inside its whirling mass.

A keening wail scrapes against my ears, and I know her to be Contrition. The archdemon of regret, once the anguished princess Reska, has entered the Labyrinth.

A great shadow follows her, a thing of blades and teeth and hate that rises from the depths below. *Malice.* The archdemon of sin and hatred, the former Homura, chases after her old love and enemy.

Beyond them both, in the Labyrinth proper, I see a thousand flashes of light. I see great dragons whose wingspans could eclipse whole cities. I see a horror of bone and ice locked in struggle with another of flame and bark, and I see more archdemons like the two approaching the city. All of them, all these Royals and their dominions, are coming to war.

The end of the world has begun.

GARDEN OF MEMORIES VII

W e have to save Reska."

Thalia rolls her eyes at my blurted declaration. "Be serious. We're not really going to have this argument, are we?"

"Why shouldn't we?"

"For a long list of reasons," she scorns. "That girl is a lost cause who doesn't want to be saved, and *nothing* is getting saved if we don't climb this tower. Melpomene could start the bonfire at any moment, Alice. We don't have time to waste on petty sentimentality. The *cycle* is more important."

The cold, viciously pragmatic part of me agrees with her. Saving Reska would be an exercise in vanity if it cost the universe; she'd burn with the rest of us. But it still feels wrong to abandon her. I look away from Thalia, unwilling to face her scorn. I don't have a real defense.

Kiana stares at me, eyes burning holes in me. "You promised," she says. "You asked me to help you save her. You told me you wanted to save her. Was that a lie?" I flinch.

"Come off it," interjects our fourth. Mordred has her arms crossed, expression unimpressed. "You should know better than anyone how hard it would be to reach that girl. Even if we *should* save her, there's no guarantee we'd get the chance. We know our mission."

"You're both so callous," Kiana hisses. "It doesn't matter to you how many girls get put on the pyre so long as you can feel an inch closer to putting out the flames, is that it? Reska is one of us! She's our sister! And you would *abandon her* because it's the safer path, the more *convenient* path. Just like that night beneath the castle."

Now it's Mordred's turn to flinch and look away. "That isn't—that's not the same at all. It's different this time."

"Why? Because it'll work this time? Because you don't have to look her in the face? Go on, keep telling me why I'm not *important enough* to save!"

Thalia looks bored with the whole mess. She taps one foot impatiently, twirling her knife idly. *She doesn't care how any of us feel about this.*

"Mordred," I chime in before the argument can continue. "Tell me honestly: Are you really okay never facing Contrition? Never facing *Malice*? You'll be leaving everything unresolved if you climb that tower without at least *trying* to settle things with the both of them."

The warrior shard makes an exasperated noise. "Of course a part of me wants to meet my other self and fix what she broke. But I can't set aside our goal here."

"Then *don't*. This doesn't have to be a dichotomy. Here's the plan: You, me, and Kiana go beat some sense into the archdemons while our friendly neighborhood Adversary starts climbing the tower on her own." I glance at Thalia and raise an eyebrow. "I mean, do you *actually* need us for the next part? You clearly don't need our help to kill things or to navigate. What's the harm in us splitting up here and reuniting after?"

The Adversary frowns, but then she chews her lip and flicks her eyes skyward. "Could work, yeah. Got a few dozen floors to kill my way through before the gate. Alright, fine. If closure's what you lot need, go on then. Just don't take too long."

She vanishes into the tower without another word, leaving me with a grateful Kiana and a closed-off Mordred. The princess sidles up next to me and gives me a hug, which I'm not expecting and have a very brief, very minor panic over before awkwardly patting her back.

I cough to hide my embarrassment and say, "She's not wrong about needing to hurry. I'll see if I can open a portal closer to the action."

Kiana steps away with a murmured, "Of course," and I get to work.

Contrition's storm rages in the distance, swallowing the horizon and seeping into the sky and city. Tornados of flame spurt out from the central mass to suck up houses and pull in floating islands. Looking at it for too long puts a knife under my thoughts, a sharp edge prying open every bad feeling I've ever buried.

I'm going to fail. I won't be strong enough. I didn't push myself hard enough.

I'll die alone. I never made the connections I should have. I had so many chances.

I'll never see Cheshire again. I wasted every moment that should have been precious.

I tear my gaze away from the storm and focus on a clear spot near the edge of it, by a section of city ramparts still intact. I've never made a portal before in this life, but the Intercessor learned how to cross worlds and the Red Queen learned how to manipulate the Labyrinth. Both skills are applicable here.

Muscle memory makes the process almost easy. I will two points to connect and the fabric of Pandaemonium obeys. This world knows me as its master, an heiress to the one who made us both. The portal pulls open cleanly and I step on through.

Things immediately go wrong.

I was supposed to emerge on top of the walls at the edge of the city, but instead I step out into the unpleasantly familiar imagery of the Demiurge's clock tower: gears and pipes and gauges melting into each other in a meaningless sprawl. The scenery suggests the idea of machinery without properly performing it, like a half-remembered dream.

The autopsy table is broken, cold steel scattered in twisted pieces. Amid the shards, curled and still, is the bloody corpse of a girl with feline ears and glassy blue eyes.

My breath catches and I reach out for her. I can't stop myself from crying out, "Cheshire!"

I wasted every moment I could have spent watching her smile and making her laugh. I rejected the only girl who could ever love me until it was too late, and now everything's too late and there is only the end, and there is only regret.

The body twitches, convulses, and a word screams from dead lips: "Alice!"

I'm caught frozen between my need to hold her in my arms and my terror of what I've done to her. The corpse of Cheshire crawls toward me in erratic bursts of activity, limbs cracking with every jittering motion. Closer, closer, closer, and I'm still frozen, and in my mind plays a song that goes on and on and on—

—only the end and only regret and only the end and only regret—

—until with a cold gasp I wrench myself from the nightmare. This vision is Contrition's work, it must be. I force myself to breathe, shut my eyes tight, and walk forward.

The dead body never touches me. When the air changes, a warm breeze crossing my face, I open my eyes.

The clock tower is gone, but Fata Morgana hasn't replaced it. Instead I find myself standing on the edge of a forest, green hills rolling before me. I don't recognize this place, but something about it scratches at the edge of my thoughts. If it's not one of my regrets, is it another glimpse at Reska's life?

I blink and the scene changes. The same location, but now there are people, a few dozen figures in traveling cloaks. Some of them clutch at baskets and packs, others hold children close to them. All but two of them are running. Fleeing, more accurately.

The outliers are familiar to me, though I've only seen them in dreams. Ruzica Kadic Bladesinger, duchess of Sun and Sword, cuts down a night horror with her ancestral blade. A flick of her wrist splits two more with pure killing intent. Another monster, an oil-slick beast of gangly limbs and gnashing teeth, leaps at her back and is punished for its hubris with spontaneous combustion in bright red flame. Zdenka of the Lidless Eye, crone lorekeeper of the court, closes her fist and the flames extinguish, and then with a wave of her hand the ashes of the beast cling to another and rot it to nothing.

Dozens of misshapen nightmares still remain, more pouring in from a hole in reality. The rift is like an ink stain on a photograph, obscuring the terrain behind it in ways that defy perspective. It seeps into the grass, into the air, into the clouds above. This is a wound that will eat the world.

I stare into the dark and past it to what I know lies beyond: the Abyss, graveyard of worms, where the Leviathans dream from death of cruel and insatiable hungers. The night horrors are their children, their foul and ravenous spawn. One method among many in their endless quest to resurrect themselves and return to a war they lost long ago.

What do the Leviathans mean to the real story, though? The Adversary's tale never mentioned them, so we have to assume they're unique to this stage of the cycle. I don't think they're just a generic doomsday threat to motivate conflict.

Melpomene is looking for something. Everything she does, everything she makes, is in service to that goal. In search of that answer. But it keeps going wrong. It always spirals, and she laid the tracks that brought us there but still the darkness stings her.

The Leviathans aren't worms, they're a snake devouring its own tail, a self-inflicted collapse from consumption. They're the teeth that bite the girl who grew them.

I wonder what that makes Azathoth? Or have I already been told that secret?

The duchess and the crone kill with speed and grace, but they can't stop the tide. They're buying time for the others to escape, knowing that the horrors will always run faster than the humans. How valiant. I think I'd like to see them fail, if only to enjoy their suffering.

Instead, the rift suddenly shudders. A night horror passing through comes out crunched and misshapen, bleeding the black blood of the Abyss. The rift shudders again, stretching and distorting and seeming to tear at the edges.

Then the rift implodes, sucking in the last of the horrors with it. When the inversion stops, the rift has become an ink-black marble in the hand of Homura Bloodfallen.

This version of Homura looks different from how I've known her. There are bags under her scarlet eyes, and her skin is pale and slick with cold sweat. Her court attire is gone, but she's not wearing her battle armor either; she's clad only in a flowing black robe, plain and unadorned, with a hood left down.

Homura pops the marble in her mouth and swallows it. A shiver runs through her, but the cold intensity of her gaze never breaks. She eyes the fleeing refugees, now stopped in their confusion, before turning her attention to Reska's old teachers.

"The kingdom has fallen." She quirks an eyebrow, but it's not really a question. The evidence is right in front of her.

Ruzica stalks forward and points her blade at the Intercessor. "I should have killed you that day," the ex-duchess barks. "This is your doing, isn't it? The brat may have been unstable, but she wouldn't have murdered her father before you came along. What did you do to her?"

Homura looks almost bored as the point of Ruzica's sword comes to rest above her heart. She keeps her hands at her sides, a concession to caution, but her tongue is sharp. "I did nothing to the girl," she lies. "This was the result of enemy action. I came to your kingdom trying to prevent this very outcome. Obviously, I failed. Just as obviously, you still need me."

Ruzica has too much self-control to press the blade farther, but by the look on her face I can tell she wants to. "You know too much, stranger, and

I've no reason to trust you. Why shouldn't I kill you right now and spare us all your machinations?"

"Because I'm the only person in the world who can close those rifts," Homura says smugly. A beat passes, and then she tilts her head. "Or did you think your *sword* would have done the job?"

Zdenka cackles. "She has you there, Bladesinger. But I have a question for our foreign friend." Her gaze sharpens, though she keeps her voice light. "When did you become a demon? To manipulate the Abyss as you have, you certainly aren't human."

"Three days ago," Homura replies calmly. "A gift from one of my teachers. Or a curse."

"Ever the way," Zdenka mutters. "Tell us, then, the secrets you've been keeping. And let us travel far from this place of ruin. Put that sword away, Ruzica, we need every ally we can scrounge if we're to keep this sorry lot alive. The princess—queen now, I suppose—will not stop at the borders of our lands."

The former duchess glares at Homura one more time before sheathing her blade and turning away. "Wood and Cloud must be warned. Come."

They stride away together and the vision fades, returning me to Fata Morgana.

Different from the others. No one's memories, just history from an outsider's eye.

I'm still not on the walls, but I'm closer than I was expecting after that portal mishap. This city is a sprawling mess with no sense of distinct quarters or districts, so between me and the walls are clusters of structures in varying materials and shapes. Some of those buildings have been ripped out of the ground by the storm, debris left in their wake. The streets are twisting and crooked, no clean thoroughfares to guide travel.

More importantly, I don't see Mordred or Kiana anywhere. Contrition's interference must have scattered us. *They're still my splinters. You won't hide them from me, archdemon.*

I close my eyes and concentrate on how the two of them felt when they were still lodged in my soul. The vicious heat of Homura and the cold grief of Reska, filtered through me. Immediately I get a strong ping from nearby, what must be just a block away. That one feels like Mordred, and I can feel Kiana farther away, closer to the storm.

That seems dangerous. Okay, let's move quickly.

I take off at a sprint and gather power, ready to annihilate whatever gets in my way with all the tricks of three lives. Actually, why am I running? Flying couldn't get us closer to the tower, but now I'm going *away* from the tower.

The Red Queen enjoyed flying, so I borrow a touch of her form and sprout bat-like wings made of ethereal darkness. I leap into the air and flap my new wings, familiarizing myself with the muscle memory of a discarded timeline. The wind against my face is an exhilarating feeling, but I don't have the luxury of reveling in it.

From my bird's-eye view I can see Mordred clearly. She's surrounded by the Contrite.

Contrition's zealots, regular people driven mad by her influence and compelled to spread her influence as far as possible. A pack of them killed Bashekehi's husband and disrupted the balance of power in Sanctuary, leading Esha, Averrich, and the Machinist to make a deal with the Beast. The Mourner they summoned ousted the Contrite, but the scars of their pact broke the old entente.

And now it seems Contrition has been busy making new zealots. Some of the people attacking Mordred are covered in the heavy scarification I saw on the Contrite that fell victim to the Mourner, but others bear only superficial marks of harm. Fresh recruits drowned in Contrition's song of regret. The old converts, which I assume came with her through her throne world, carry flails and ritual knives. The ex-citizenry carry kitchen knives and table legs.

None of them are a match for Mordred. Vorpal cuts through a man holding a cleaver and the blood spilled by that attack stabs into three more Contrite as shards of red crystal. A dozen already lie dead at her feet, but there are dozens more swarming her location, the entire population of a city turned into a weapon.

And even that isn't enough to do more than slow us down, so slowing us down is the goal. If she has a goal. I don't know how lucid Contrition really is.

Whatever the truth, we can't afford this delay. *I'm sure something in our arsenal can deal with a crowd of trash mobs quickly. The Red Queen's area attack technique? The thorns were effective, but it relies on [Feast or Famine] principles to process souls. With the heart locket narratively spent, I'm not willing to risk falling into another fugue state.*

Something from the Intercessor's playbook, then. That trick we picked up fighting the Children of Dust in the ruins of An Talamh?

No, too destructive. Ah, I've got it: When we excised the Malicite infiltration on Charos, we crafted a special bow. That should work here.

I pull from the Intercessor's memories, picturing the weapon in my mind. The nature of Pandaemonium is that everything, absolutely everything, is material to be manipulated by a mage. Particles here aren't made of quarks, they're made of qualia, and a strong enough will can force any concept into any other concept.

So the air in front of me isn't air anymore, because *I say it isn't.* Processed wood appears in my hand, a recurve bow transmuting from oxygen and nitrogen and whatever else those molecules were pretending to be. Iron sprouts like vines and twines into curving patterns, and then flowers of ruby gemstone bloom at the tips. All this happens because I demand it, and the fabric of reality knows only how to obey.

I pull at an invisible string, nocking an arrow of crimson light. I aim straight above me and let loose. The arrow soars, and at the moment of its zenith it shatters into a hundred copies of itself that rocket toward the ground below.

The red arrows tear through flesh and bone, making mincemeat of the Contrite. They impact with enough force and power to sever limbs from bodies and pulp through brain and skull. And the only one unaffected is Mordred, the light passing through her as if she weren't there at all.

A single volley is all it takes to eliminate every single zealot in sight.

I drop from the sky, landing gracefully beside Mordred, and I dismiss the wings and the bow. "Figured I'd lend a hand," I say with a grin.

She whistles appreciatively. "You've got power now, I'll give you that."

"It feels great. Anyway, did you get thrown into a vision too?"

Mordred sours. "I did. First it was a pit in the Abyss, a mountain of Reska corpses. Then I saw myself, in the days after the fall."

I grimace. "Same as me, then. Which means Kiana's probably going through the same thing. Contrition attacked us all, interfering with the portal to separate us. I don't even know if she did it intentionally or if it was just a side effect of her poison spreading through the city."

Mordred closes her eyes for a moment, seeming to concentrate, then opens them again. "Contrition is the only archdemon to have been cursed into that state, rather than striving for it willfully. I doubt she has any real control over her actions. My gut tells me all of *this,*" she says, waving at the corpses of the Contrite, "is incidental."

At that moment, another terrible wail echoes across the city. The anguished scream is closer this time, louder, and my body shivers as Contrition's influence rakes against my mind and seeps into my thoughts.

I should have been more honest. How many people die I lie to?

I should have had more resolve. How many times did I give in to pain and frustration?

I should have fought harder. How many of my failures could I have prevented?

I bite my tongue and snarl in my head. *Shut up, damn you. I get enough of this from myself, I don't need the interference.*

Her curse doesn't take hold, but it definitely feels stronger than it did before. Once we actually breach the storm, I'm sure it'll be blasting at full power.

Mordred grinds her teeth, then spits at the ground. "The worst part is the feeling of karmic irony. Homura made this monster, and now her copy has to deal with it. Let's get this over with."

"Right." I double check my sense of Kiana's presence, finding her location unchanged, and point in her direction. "That way."

We make it maybe twenty seconds of running—Mordred can't fly and I'm not going to carry her—before we fall into another vision of the past.

Homura's blade slides past pale blue silk and sinks into the flesh of a girl in a slender crown. The princess gasps, the air expelled from her lungs, and clutches at the sword with futile, insufficient strength. Homura tears the weapon from its victim and flicks the blade.

The blood that scatters is black.

Courtiers recoil, a mess of men and women clad in warm earth tones, their gold and silver jewelry speckled with glittering sapphires. Some of them look outraged, others look sick. In the crowd I spot Mordred, gaze locked on the scene, her lip curling in distaste.

Prevara, curled in the body of the princess, twists its mouth and spits out, "Savor your victories, thief. She comes for you."

Homura shoves her hand in the open wound and pulls out a writhing, slimy parasite, its hundred suckered tendrils leaking black blood. The princess, long-dead, collapses in a heap. Homura squeezes the parasite in her grip until it, too, gives out, and she tosses the worm atop its host.

Guards halt in the process of rushing toward their crown heiress, hands still tight around drawn swords and spears. They look on in horror and dread.

Homura ignores them. She sweeps her gaze across the crowd and calls out to them, "Behold, you bastard lot who did not heed my warnings. This is the truth of the princess that urged you to caution and patience, long replaced by an agent of the enemy. Her promises were lies, her stillness a stagnation. If you follow her commands, you will *die.* Every last one of you, devoured by the horrors that spread across this land. You can hide in your castles and manors, surround yourselves with blades and strong arms, but what is strength against the tide that drowns the world? Death comes for you, Kingdom of Frost and Forge. And when it finds you, it will use you as it used your would-be queen."

This is another stage of the exodus. Fascinating, but also a distraction. Is there a way out of this vision, or do I have to let it play out?

I slip into Hastur, watching my body from the outside, and examine the situation with my oversoul's eye. I definitely *can* break out of the vision . . . but my sixth sense tells me there would be worse consequences for doing so than the minor time loss of sitting through it. *Irksome.* I return to myself and let the scene play out.

A brave noble steps out of the crowd and addresses the woman who murdered their imposter princess. "What would you have us do? If the foe is as dangerous as you claim, what good will fighting do us?"

"Here? No good at all. But if you follow me to the city of glass, to Fata Morgana, then together with all the world you might just stand a chance."

Another noble scoffs. "You would have us abandon our homes? Preposterous!"

Homura, in the middle of cleaning her blade, stops and gives the man who spoke up a thin, vicious smile. "Your homes are already lost. Your realm is forfeit. Those who do not leave *will* be claimed. So I make you this promise, cowards of the court: *I will kill you all* just to keep warm bodies from the enemy's grasp."

The vision ends as abruptly as it began, leaving me back in the city next to Mordred.

She looks tense and uncomfortable. "Looking at myself from the outside is . . . unsettling. Especially knowing it's not really me."

"My sympathies," I offer. "I felt the same way seeing Homura for the first time in my dreams. Well, similar. I didn't know what she was then." I pause, and then I ask, "Did she kill those people?"

Mordred flinches. "Yes. Of course. She killed hundreds of them to keep the rest in line. Went into their homes and slaughtered everyone who wouldn't pick up their lives and flee to Fata Morgana with the rest of the exodus. They didn't stand a chance."

The path her breed always walks, right? The ends justify the means, until the means start shaping ends. And then you get a Malice.

I don't say any of that, though maybe I should. There's probably a lot I should say to Mordred that I'm not. That I won't.

"Let's keep moving," I say instead. "She can't have many more visions to show us."

Our path to Kiana ends up paved in more corpses. The city is swarming with Contrite. I get to see some of their rituals up close as regret spreads viral through the populace. Every victim broken beneath the lash rises to take a lash of their own, exalting in blood spilled and penance extracted.

Of course, they're all figments. They're just playing their part, mindless actors on a grand stage. But then, if I believe Thalia's talk of Wonderland, so is everyone else. Bashe, Esha, Dante, all of them less than real. Should that make me feel better about abandoning them?

It scares me how appealing I find that thought. What greater absolution could I find than the numbing embrace of solipsism? If I'm the only real person, then it doesn't matter how many people I kill or betray or leave to rot. The man in the nightclub—his name, I swore I wouldn't forget his name, but I made myself a liar—didn't matter. He wasn't a real person.

Thalia claimed the magic system in this universe was a metaphor for suspension of disbelief. The mechanisms underlying your acceptance of an impossible action in a story. The people are like the characters in a story, existing only within the confines of the pages where they appear. The living jokes of Wonderland.

But you still care what happens to those characters, even though you know they're not real. That's the beauty of a story, isn't it? It's a facsimile of reality, and a facsimile can still make you cry, or laugh, or fly into a rage. There would have to be something broken in me if I didn't care. If I was like her.

We find Kiana standing frozen in an empty weapon shop, anguish etched into every line of her face. A handful of Contrite have been skewered with as many pointy objects as would fit, no doubt the work of her protective shadows.

"Kiana?" I call to her. "Can you hear me?" No reaction. I sigh. "Nothing for it, I guess."

I reach out and grab her shoulder, and predictably that sends me into the vision.

"Trust you? How could I ever trust you!? You tried to murder me!"

In a moonlit clearing amid towering trees, Reska shouts accusations at the black-robed form of Homura. Reska Shadowsun has abandoned her ancestral colors for the embrace of living shadow. Slick darkness covers her from neck to toe, her only garment a cloak of solid starlight. By the pale light of the moon, the entire forest floor is one great shadow churning with her anger and clawing gouges into tree bark.

Homura stares down the nascent goddess of darkness. "I acted rashly. If you leave Prevara behind, I'll make a binding oath on my role as Intercessor not to harm you again."

Kiana is watching this with wet eyes. Mordred steps into the scene beside me, takes one look at it, and blanches in horror.

"You tried to murder me!" Reska screams. A tree snaps in half.

Homura's cool exterior cracks. For a moment, I see genuine pain written on her face. "I—please, Reska. I don't want to fight you. I didn't mean to hurt you. Come home with me. We can be together again. I . . . I still love you, Reska."

Mordred mouths the words, entranced by her counterpart.

Reska's anger vanishes and all the fight drops out of her posture. She puts her head in her hands, tears now running down her cheeks. "Why?" she asks in a small, grieving voice, like a child that can't comprehend what she's lost. "If you really loved me, why would you do that?"

Kiana is crying now too. Her sobs are broken and ruinous.

Homura looks down, unable to face the woman she hurt. "I thought it was the only way. I was wrong. I want to believe that I was wrong." She looks up. "So please, Reska. Take my hand. Come with me and I'll save us both. I'll save us all."

She holds out her hand. Kiana and Mordred can't look away.

Reska hesitates. Grief and anguish war with yearning. For a moment— for one terrible, cruel, hopeful moment—she reaches out to take Homura's hand.

Homura smiles, victory in her eyes. A smile just an inch too satisfied.

"No," Mordred whispers.

And Reska pulls her hand back, her anger reigniting. Betrayal in her voice, she cries, "You're manipulating me again! Trying to use me, just like before! But it won't work this time. I won't fall for your tricks. If you love me, Homura, then your love is poison. I won't drink it."

Kiana falls to her knees as the clearing is engulfed in swirling, thorny darkness.

Homura's face shutters closed, her eyes turning cold and soulless. "Then you leave me no choice. The next time we meet, Reska, I'll have to put you down."

Darkness swallows the world. We return to the glass city.

Kiana screams her grief on hands and knees. "No, no, no. I should have said yes, I should have said yes, I should have—"

"Kiana." Mordred kneels down in front of her and places a hand on each shoulder. "Kiana, listen to me." Her voice is sharp yet wavering, her face drawn tight. "You weren't the only one who made mistakes."

Kiana wipes her face on her sleeve and stares at Mordred, uncomprehending. Her body is shaking, wracked by shudders, and she's clearly choking back more sobs.

"If I . . . if I hadn't betrayed you. In the castle, in the woods, a hundred times in my own head. If I hadn't." Mordred swallows, the words coming out halting. "If I hadn't given up on you, then Prevara would have lost. I pushed you into its arms and I left you there. And I'm sorry. That version of me was too much of a coward to ever say the words, but *I will.* I'm *sorry,* Reska. I'm sorry for hurting you. I'm sorry for leaving you."

I'm expecting Kiana to lash out. A part of me wants her to hit Mordred, even. Instead, she wraps her arms around the other girl and pulls her into a hug. She laughs and cries and squeezes her tight, and Mordred goes stiff for a moment before slowly, carefully, like handling spun glass, she hugs her back. They cry together and hold each other.

And here I am, the awkward third wheel to my own mental constructs.

Forgiveness is a funny thing. I don't like it. If there's any part of me that should hate forgiveness and apologies and the whole concept of the thing, it should be that side of me called Homura or Mordred.

What is an apology? Meaningless drivel. Words are all just lies. If I were Reska, if I were Kiana, I'd hate too strongly and brightly to ever accept something so stupid and pointless as an apology. How can a few words make up for hours and hours of betrayal and disappointment?

But Kiana is hugging Mordred. They're crying together and sharing their pain and getting better. How are they doing that? Why are they doing that? It's not fair.

Gods, have you ever felt more like a child? What a petty thing to whine about.

Yeah, probably. I don't know if I mean any of it, either. I probably don't. That's just how my brain is, sometimes. I don't like it when other people aren't suffering.

I'm debating how to break up their little cry sesh without seeming like an asshole, but thankfully Contrition does my work for me. Three Contrite break through the window of the shop screaming penance at us. We murder them in very short order, obviously, but the shock is still enough to get Mordred and Kiana out of their moment.

"Ready up, girls," I drawl at them. "Our big number's almost here."

We leave the shop behind and make for the storm. Whirling wind and crackling red electricity greets us, and we're close enough now to see the walls.

Then, because clearly this next stretch is just going to be nonstop chaos, a giant dragon crashes through the wall, and a dozen buildings, and passes out of sight.

What the hell? Wait.

A glance through the hole it made in the wall confirms my suspicion: The Royal Royale has begun. Malice, archdemon of hatred and sin, is mopping the floor with every other god and archdemon in Pandaemonium. Each of her four spiked arms holds a different weapon either carving through or parrying her numerous foes. Even her tail and wings, just as spiked and scaled, are being used as weapons to deflect attacks or knock back enemies.

I've seen this happen before, through the eyes of the Intercessor. In that life I knew more of the figures arrayed against her personally, having encountered them in my travels. The faerie queens of Winter and Summer showed up in person this time rather than assaulting throne worlds, but they're almost a background element than real participants in the fight, too focused on each other. Wonder, childlike and ethereal, floats around the battlefield out of reach of her would-be murderer.

The rest of the archdemons—Indulgence, Acuity, Glory, Muse, and Nemesis—fight with everything they have and barely scratch their opponent. The golden rays of the gods above are already fading, attention stolen by Malicite attacks on their homeworlds. Without the Intercessor disrupting those cults, I imagine the situation is even worse for the gods of Pandaemonium than it was last loop. The great dragons have arrived in their colorful flights, but they face a different opponent: the Hierophant, the worm god clad in its mechanical monstrosity, answering the call of its master—or at least an agent of its master.

Wicked laughter echoes across the field, audible even from this distance. Pulling myself into Hastur, I shift my presence closer to the battle. I need to see what she does next.

Malice, red-eyed and baleful, her horns a jagged crown, is the platonic ideal of a demon. She forces her foes back with a sweep of blades, her vicious will overcoming every spell cast at her and every physical attack. She throws her chipped weapons to the ground and conjures new ones, sneering at the assemblage.

"Is this the sum of you?" Her voice is the crumbling mountain and the death of a star, a song of nuclear hate. "Come then, you pale shades who claim the lot of Royalty. Bare your souls to me, and let us put an end to our maker's works."

Malice brings all four blades together and they snap into one, melding into a monstrous greatsword of black crystal. She raises it high and dark energy pulses from it in waves.

"[APOCALYPSE]!" she roars, and the world shatters.

The landscape tears like paper and a thousand oil-slick terrors crawl up out of the black void pits left between disjointed shards of reality. Night horrors pour from rifts just like the ones that Malice closed when she was still Homura. With the Emissary dead and the Adversary occupied, Malice must be the last champion of the Abyss.

Their Endbringer.

I return to myself to find Kiana shaking me. I wince and brush her hand away. "Sorry, didn't warn you," I apologize. "Had to see that up close."

Kiana shivers. "Why? I can't imagine wanting to be closer to that nightmare."

"She is that, I won't argue." I see Mordred stuck staring at her other self, the truth of it still sinking in. "I guess this is rougher for you, huh? Your original's turned into a monster like few others. We're going to have to deal with that, after Reska. Hey, maybe we'll get lucky and she'll be exhausted from all the fighting."

Mordred turns away from the horror and mutters, "Or maybe she'll be even stronger after gorging herself on their souls."

We race away from that grisly sight and toward the storm wall. The wind is picking up and the packs of Contrite are getting denser, so we must be getting closer. Another keening wail stagger us, the voices of regret even louder, but I pull through and help the others shake it off.

The storm flares, the physical manifestation of Contrition's soul reaching out a tendril to pull another chunk of the city into its depths, and when the debris clears I see it: a massive stone gate, pulsing with an ominous aura and inscribed with strange symbols, the raging winds becoming a solid wall to either side of it. This must be the entrance to her throne world.

In front of that gate is a familiar face, though it feels like a lifetime since I saw it last: a sin eater, like the one I fought on my very first day of being alive. The creature has the appearance of a stretched human with four arms, blindfolded eyes, and a perfect, angelic mouth. Its body is so covered in scar tissue that I can't see any unmarked skin at all, the product of ceaseless self-flagellation with the scourge it carries in one hand.

The biggest difference between this one and Bashe's warden is that this sin eater is at least three, four times the size. A sin eater giant.

At the edges of the crater between us, more Contrite come pouring in. They slip out of the storm and from deeper within the city, summoned in greater numbers than any encounter yet. A whole horde of ancient zealots and fresh victims. I wonder if the whole city is corrupted by now, or if there are still holdouts around the tower. Well, it doesn't matter.

It's a funny thing, but I'm actually kind of excited to see this particular monster. The ghost was luck and the dogs would have killed me without that damn huntsman intervening, so in a sense the sin eater was the first fight I ever won under my own power, with my own skills and wits. And it was a brutal, painful affair.

I want a rematch.

"Kiana, Mordred, take care of the Contrite. The gatekeeper is mine."

They spring into action without argument, each taking one side of the field and carving through Contrite with sword and sorcery. I walk calmly across the ruins of the city. As I walk, I weave an Intercessor charm to repel the buffeting winds.

The sin eater doesn't have eyes to watch me with, but it can sense my approach. It stirs from its flagellation, rising to its full height and lowering the many-whipped scourge. I wave at it.

That choral, too-perfect voice rings across the battlefield. "Do you know regret?" it asks me, just like it did before that day in the abandoned prison.

This time I know the context for that line. I know the weight of it. I know the fear and anguish behind those words, the curse of a betrayer. The sins and failings of two women, my two sisters in artificial life, have haunted this universe for thousands of years.

The last time a sin eater asked me that question, I laughed at it. I lied to its face, proudly insisting that I could never do anything wrong. I wasn't capable of taking it seriously. Of taking anything seriously, really. I'm not the same girl anymore.

"I do know regret," I admit to the monster. "I know a whole lifetime of that feeling. Some days I regret ever being born, not that I really had a choice in the matter. I regret pushing away friends, allies, anyone who tried to reach out or get to know me. I regret all the pain that I inflicted on myself or invited, always telling myself that it was necessary. I regret the loneliness. I regret the suffering. I regret marching to an end that I didn't understand. And I carry more regrets than just mine, too. I regret betraying the princess that I loved for a mission that I would fail. I regret turning my back on the woman who tried to save me from myself. If I could change it all, I think I would. I'd live a different life, walk a different path, make different choices. But I can't change the choices that I've made. Even if I could turn back time, it wouldn't erase those choices. I'd just be papering over them."

The sin eater spreads its arms wide. "Join us. Repent. Repent. Repent."

I reach the last stretch before the gate, the monster towering over me, and I put a grin on my face. "Now that . . . that's not going to happen. See, the thing is, you're all cursed. That regret you feel is devouring you, but it's not changing you. You're not moving forward, you're just drowning in the misery. And me? I've got places to be. I've got a girl to save. There's an infinite cycle of murdered Alices that someone has to fix, and that someone might just be me. So yeah, I know regret, but that doesn't mean I'm gonna join your cult and spend my last hours bemoaning my mistakes. Your penance won't fix shit. Now I've got a question of my own to toss back your way:

Are you gonna let me through, big guy, so I can go see your boss and pull her out of this mess? Or is it violence, one more time?"

The sin eater roars, stretching itself even taller and spreading its arms even wider. "Repent!" it screams, and then it brings the scourge down on me.

I remember the pain I felt when a sin eater struck me, and this one is much bigger and looks much stronger. But I'm not the girl who fought that monster. I've learned. I've grown. I know what I really am, and what I'm not.

I don't even try to dodge the attack. I just watch it fall and smile.

You're not real, I dismiss it. *You're just a toy, and I am a gobbet of heavenly meat.*

When the weapon strikes my flesh it bounces right off. I laugh.

"I'm coming for you, Reska. I'm coming to save us all."

GARDEN OF MEMORIES VIII

I smash the clay heart that used to be a sin eater and scatter the shards with my feet. The catharsis isn't quite as satisfying as I'd hoped, but it's still pleasant to consider how far I've come from the scrappy twig that snapped and broke as often as it scored a kill.

Now I'm untouchable. Well, at least to the likes of this. I'm sure Contrition and Malice will make me eat my words.

I glance over at my companions and, seeing them still fighting, resummon that magic bow from before to cast another volley of light arrows. As soon as I see the spell land, I dismiss the bow and turn my attention to the stone gates.

Are we ready for this? It's going to be a psychic attack like no other.

Bring it on. I haven't lost to one yet.

I lay my hands on the inscribed stone and shove with all my weight. The tall doors creak open, stone grinding on stone, and then the storm envelops me.

An infinite weight presses down on me, its wordless voice pounding inside my skull. Guilt lashes my back, my sins dragging me down into the deep dark pit at the bottom of my soul. Screams echo through my bones. In darkness and solitude, I am blinded and perceived.

A vision flashes through my mind, stained with the song of the archdemon.

Eirdryd smirks, the huntsman practically sneering at me. "What prideful words. But can you back them up? What could you offer me, famished little girl? What do you have to bargain with that I could not take by force?"

I roll my shoulders and match his smirk with a toothy grin of my own. "My name," I reply. "I'll sell you my name."

Do I regret that decision? It gave my enemies leverage over me, certainly, and for that I burned with hate. Everyone who heard about my decision called me an idiot for it, or at least that's the sense I have in this moment. A thousand voices whispering my folly.

But for all the consequences I suffered, was it not still a necessary choice? If I refused to bargain with the fae, or if I tried to offer some lesser prize, he might have left me to die in the woods. Knowing his true loyalties, he probably would have switched to threats or just outright killed me. My survival has always risen from taking great risks.

So no, I don't regret it. "You'll have to try better than that," I tell Contrition. "I overestimated myself, yes, but my actions were still necessary. I never would have gotten this far without the fruits of that deal."

The dark swirls, the song flares, and I'm thrown into another memory.

When I speak again my voice is cold and merciless. "If you wanted to be my voice of reason, you had your chance."

The incubus flinches away from me, hurt blooming on his face. I don't care. All my attention is on the cat now. Smiling, smug, mirthful Cheshire. Loving, caring, lying Cheshire. Only Cheshire.

"Okay. What do you need from me?"

The cat tells me, and I say the only word she needs to hear.

The sight of Cheshire is painful. My heart aches for what I've lost. For what I threw away.

But the scene itself? Taking Cheshire's hand? How could I ever regret that?

"What do you expect me to say to that? Should I care that I burned a bridge with Bashekehi? We were never going to be friends. He was always going to judge me and look down on me. I could have followed him to the Myriad, sure, but what then? What would I do when the Game of Glass began? When Prevara took an active interest? Without power, I wouldn't have survived the week. Contracting with Cheshire was the only live option. I don't regret becoming her partner, no matter what followed. No matter what she really was."

Contrition is silent. For a living wellspring of regret, a divinity forged in pain and guilt and loss, so far it's missed me twice. Is my brain really that hard for her to understand? Or is she just holding back before she goes for my throat?

Lightning flashes in the dark and I get my answer.

"One condition," I tell the Demiurge. "I want you to free Cheshire. Give her back whatever she used to be."

Melpomene looks down at the catgirl, still kneeling and dazed, our whole conversation slipping right through her ears. "Alice, there isn't an original to put back. She was never real to begin with. She's just a vessel."

Her words don't faze me. "Then make something up. That's my condition."

A mistake. A real mistake, and I flinch from it. I had a girlfriend who loved me and wanted to stay with me and I threw her away because it didn't feel real enough. I couldn't accept her as she was, so I killed her. Gods, Cheshire . . .

Cheshire has me caught, my tender flesh giving beneath her grip. She murmurs, "It wouldn't take much to shatter those pretty wrists, frail as they are. And I know for a fact that you don't have the strength to stop me, and you won't until you come back to your master. Do you like being able to move your hands?"

She relaxes her grip just enough that I can think and breathe again. I'm shaking worse than before, my legs and arms and teeth all out of control. "Wh-what are y-you doing, I th-thought you were supposed to be my—"

Cheshire squeezes again, her strong hands crushing my weak wrists. Pain spikes in bruised muscles and aching, vulnerable bone, so close to breaking. She's going to break my wrists. She's actually going to break my wrists. This can't be happening.

The pain echoes, phantom sensation lingering as the vision ends as abruptly as it began. The monster who hurt me wasn't Cheshire, couldn't have been Cheshire, but she wore my Cheshire's face and spoke with her voice. And it's my fault that she was turned into that.

Melpomene sweeps her hands toward the still form of the girl I almost loved. "The clay is fresh, your tools laid out. You can sculpt a new Cheshire, a better Cheshire, a Cheshire that you can trust. Shape her as I shaped her, carve her as I carved her, create her as I created her. Alice and Cheshire, together again, but this time by your intent, by your rules, by your design."

Cheshire, my Cheshire, cut and molded and made anew. An act of insane violation. An act of absolute control. All I've ever wanted, or dreamed I might have wanted. All I've ever feared, or told myself I feared.

But I didn't take the knife. I didn't shape my Cheshire. Instead—

I back away from the grisly tableau, my horror finally eclipsing my fascination. I stumble, trip over myself, and hit the flagstones outside the tower. My *breath is coming out ragged and panicked; I'm hyperventilating. What was I about to do? What was I thinking? Who am I?*

Who am I? Who is Maven Alice?

Is Alice the hand that takes the knife or the hand that recoils from its touch? Is it more Alice to reject the Demiurge or to borrow her gifts and thank her for them? Is it even possible to be Alice authentically when there are so many of us?

I've lived this life three times now, walking through a hallway of mirrors reflecting the thousand lives before me. They all end in tragedy. They're all heaped with suffering. Always, always, always, our apotheosis is only torment.

I'm no exception. I'm no one special. I'm just another copy. Is that all I was ever meant to be? Were these mistakes forced upon me, or is Alice just that weak?

How much of what I've suffered was my own damn fault?

I'm incapable of letting people in. I've wired my whole personality to keep people at arm's length, charming them with lies and never letting them see the real me. I see everything as a challenge that I have to do alone or it doesn't count. And then I fail, because that's what happens when you don't accept help. And I get worse, and everything gets worse.

I ruined Cheshire. I failed to love her. I failed to cherish her. I rejected the truth of her until it became a lie. Just one more romance I messed up. One more heartbreak I brought on myself. More self-inflicted pain, like all the pain I've ever felt. All of it my fault.

My fault.

I sink beneath the weight of it.

If I'd tried a little harder, maybe I could have gotten higher grades, or made more friends, or achieved something real with my waste of a life. If I'd been a better kid, maybe my father would have loved me, or at least he wouldn't have hated me.

The guilt and doubt clouds my mind. It seeps into my heart and spreads through my veins. The water rises.

If I'd never been born, maybe my mother wouldn't have died.

The regret is drowning me.

All my fault. It was always my fault.

But that is a goddamned lie.

I pull myself out of the whirlpool and straighten my back. I glare into the void with eyes free of doubt. Regret will not conquer me. Nothing will ever conquer me.

I am the Intercessor, walking a thousand worlds. I am the Red Queen, dominating all that stands in my way. I am Hastur, pulling the strings from above the stage.

I am Veseryn, making deals in the dark to claim what was denied me. I am Mordred, haunted by injustice and driven to correct the world. I am Kiana, yearning with all my heart to meet someone who will understand.

I am all of this, and all of this is Alice.

"You cast too wide of a net," I snarl. "Those are the original's regrets, not mine. I never lived that life. I never struggled through that trauma. All I feel of it is a pale shadow that *she* put in my head. I am not my father's daughter, nor my mother's. I'm just Alice."

The shadow of regret loosens over my shoulders, but it doesn't go away. The image of Cheshire is still locked in my mind. The last time I saw her. The wrongs I did to her.

"But it wasn't my fault," I tell Contrition. "I won't bear the blame for something that was done against my wishes. I wanted Cheshire to be free. I wanted her to be her own person. I wanted her to have the choice to love me. And the way Melpomene twisted that was a cruel abomination, another knife wound dealt by her hand. *That* is the truth of my relationship with Cheshire: The chance to be with her was taken from me, not something I turned away from. It was our creator's plan from start to end. I won't feel regret for decisions I didn't make."

I only hesitate for an instant before taking the plunge.

"And neither should *you*, Reska. What happened to you wasn't your fault. You were used and manipulated by the people around you, by everyone in your life. They made you into a weapon and then left you in pieces. You didn't *deserve this*. You don't deserve to stay like this. So let me help you. Let me save you."

The pressure doubles. The weight of Contrition's attention bores down on me and I grit my teeth and bear it. I'm not losing.

"None of this should have happened! None of this was earned! And none of this needs to *keep* happening. Let me save you, dammit!"

The song sharpens into clear words, into an infinite mantra scouring my thoughts. *Only the end and only regret and only the end and only regret—*

"No!" I shout. "You're wrong. There is so much more than regret. There is forward. There is tomorrow. There is what we make of the day after we feel our sorrow and guilt and our wish that things were different. We can't change the past, but we can still shape our future. Right now that future is in sight, Reska. The tower, the Demiurge, the cycle. There will be a tomorrow, and it's up to us to make sure that tomorrow doesn't hold another thousand years of hurting girls like you and me. Don't let the next Reska suffer like you did. Don't let this Reska suffer either."

The song sharpens again, gets louder and more piercing . . . and then it falls silent.

The darkness clears. The heart of Contrition's soul, surrounded by gale and lightning, is a shattered crater. I see the ruins of the Dawnbringer castle, pounded to dust by time and hate. Torn banners flutter in the wind.

In the eye of the storm, a broken girl cries. She is naked, and her skin bears the lash-marks of a thousand years of torment. She kneels on gravel, sharp stones digging into her legs. She hunches over herself, holds herself, hands digging into her sides. She is more blood and bruise than woman.

Reska Ines Zelic, once Dawnbringer, once Shadowsun. Now Contrition.

The nails have been torn from her fingers, the flesh chewed down to bone. Her eyes are puffy, bloodshot, and clouded. Her lips and gums are raw and bleeding. Her hair is ratty, tangled, and unkempt. The color has been leeched from her, dark hair and eyes gone pale.

This is a woman who has forgotten what it means to live without suffering. This is what it means to be an archdemon by the rules of Pandaemonium: to be consumed by your own worst traits, made into an unchanging monument to your worst moments. To never grow beyond one fateful decision.

I thought I was making a real choice when I turned from the Labyrinth's glass shard to pursue Royalty by ascension. Now I understand. All of them, every last Royal in the universe, they're all frozen in time. They crystallized their identities, made themselves immutable laws of reality, and now they're stuck.

In another timeline, on another world, Malice killed Wonder with a simple trick. The nature of Wonder, that childlike devil, is that she is always learning and never knowing. Imagine being able to watch your favorite movie for the first time a thousand times and you begin to understand why so many begged Wonder to lose their memories and become her lethe drinkers.

To kill Wonder, Malice took a world and bound its people together, linking them all to a crown of pearl and gold. She gave it as a gift. When Wonder wore the crown, her mind was flooded with the knowledge and experiences of every soul on that planet. To keep the crown was to lose her naivety, but to reject the crown was to reject her curiosity.

Whatever option she chose, she could not be Wonder any longer. So she split in half and Malice ate her soul.

Now, somehow, I have to pull Reska out of Contrition without killing her in the process. I have to make her reject regret and fill her soul with something better. Something that will make her Reska again. I don't know if it's possible, but I have to try.

I take a careful step toward her. "Reska? Can you hear me?" No response. I step closer.

"Stay away!" she cries. A wave of force pulses out from Reska's body. I stagger back a step, but grit my teeth and push through it.

"I need you to wake up from this nightmare, Reska. I need you to fight the curse! I'm here to help you!"

A tendril of crackling red energy lashes out of the storm. Reflexes stolen from my Intercessor self let me deflect the attack, sending it back into the wall of raging wind. Reska keeps crying, her whole body shivering, and the storm keeps growing more volatile.

"You're hurting, I get that. I've been there. But this isn't right! You don't deserve to be in this much pain, Reska. No one does!"

"Shut up!" she screams at me. "Shut up, shut up, shut up! You don't understand!" Her bony fingertips sink deeper into her flesh, carving bloody gouges in her sides. "It's all my fault, everything is my fault!"

"That's not—"

Another buffet of wind shoves me back, knocking me into a cracked pillar that once held up some room of the Dawnbringer castle. I grimace and steady myself, ignoring the pain from the impact. *I'm not getting anywhere with this, am I?*

"You're a victim!" I shout at her over the wind. "It wasn't your fault!"

More tendrils of storm lurch toward my location and I dance out of their path, the pillar behind me exploding into stone fragments. The girl on the ground looks unchanged, just as lost in her fugue state as ever.

On the other side of the crater, Mordred steps out of the storm.

"MURDERER!" Reska screams.

A dozen bloody hands burst out of the earth, their limbs of clay and gristle boneless in their movement. They fly at Mordred with clear intent, violence and misery wreathing them like motion blur. The copy of a murderer has pain in her eyes, her mouth drawn into a thin line. Vorpal flutters through the air and cuts snicker-snack through every abominable arm. The severed limbs melt into puddles of rot and grease.

Mordred closes her eyes. She breathes deep, her shoulders slumping and then straightening. When she opens her eyes again, her face is deathly calm.

"Monster!" Reska cries, face still clutched tight in her hands, eyes now leaking tears of blood into the shattered gravel of the castle crater. "Betrayer!"

Mordred steps toward Reska and cuts down another false limb. Another step and the storm rages, but each tendril of surging wind stills before her blade. A sin eater rises from the soil and Vorpal pierces right through its clay heart. Mordred's expression is completely blank and emotionless. A stone mask stares at the bleeding girl in the heart of the crater.

Contrition's anger turns to fear. The attacks double as Reska sobs and shrinks in on herself. Her anguished shouts become terrified whispers.

"No, please, please don't come any closer. Please, please don't hurt me. No, no, no."

The next wave of phantom limbs hesitates. Bloody hands pull back and storm tendrils waver before Vorpal has even swung. Sin eaters form and crumble all on their own. Mordred keeps advancing, implacable and imposing.

Mordred steps into the inner ring of the crater and Reska falls silent. The wounded girl's tears dry up, her sobs stuttering to a halt. She shivers, naked and flayed. The storm around us churns faster and faster, lightning streaking through hurricane winds.

"Just do it," she begs. "End it. Give me what I deserve."

Mordred raises her sword and my heart stops beating. Everything else fades out of focus. There's only me, Reska, and that damned Vorpal.

She can't. She won't! Don't you dare, don't you—

Mordred snaps the Bloodstained Blade over her knee.

"I break the curse that I have wrought," Mordred spits into the gravel. "Let it end as it began, called and commanded by this hateful tool I wield. Let neither curse nor sword ever again take peace and joy from another soul."

The storm freezes. Reska freezes. The world is stopped in time.

All around us, in the air and stone and storm, Contrition begins to unravel.

Reska lifts her head just enough to stare at the shattered pieces of Homura's masterwork, her falsified family Crest. The weapon they made together. The weapon that murdered her mother, her teacher, and her brother. The weapon that murdered her.

Mordred throws the tip of the blade aside, but the hilt she twists open, revealing its secret compartment. She plucks a single marble from inside and drops the hilt. A tiny globe of captured starlight rests in the palm of her hand.

"I kept it," she whispers, voice aching with grief. "We kept it, I guess I should say. We always remembered that precious moment. Could never throw it away."

Reska stares, transfixed. Words don't come to her, but more tears well in her eyes.

"I'm sorry, Reska. I'm so incredibly sorry. I hurt you. I betrayed you. I dismissed you. I was *wrong*. I was so, so stupid."

With each word, hope and confusion bloom on Reska's face. Her stare takes on disbelief as she hears Mordred's heartfelt apology. She sinks lower into the earth, practically melting to the floor, hands rising to cover her ears but never quite enough to block the sound.

The storm weakens. Lightning diminishes, winds return to motion but settle and slow. The world beyond isn't visible, just an endless expanse of orange sunset glow. In the far, far distance, a bit of blue paints the edges.

Contrition retreats further from this space, the ancient shadow of regret banished by the breaking of the curse. I can still feel it, like sandpaper rubbing on my skin, but the feeling lessens with each passing moment.

On Reska's face, understanding slowly replaces confusion. Hope becomes sadness. Reska finally meets Mordred's gaze, and she says, "You're not the real Homura, are you?"

Mordred flinches, but nods. "I'm not. I'm just a copy. But I *will* speak for her."

Reska laughs, the sound light and desperate and bleak. "What will you say?"

Mordred clenches a fist, leaving the starlight marble visible in her other hand. "Homura was a fool," she snarls with that signature self-loathing all us copies share. "She made the wrong choice, that night in the castle. She chose the abstract of a cycle and a grand mission over the truth of her eyes. Over the girl in pain right in front of her that she could have *saved*. She chose wrong."

Reska smiles, joyless. "How could she have chosen any different?"

"She *should have*," Mordred insists. "She should have chosen you, Reska. She should have saved you. She should have protected you."

The princess lowers her gaze. "Even when I became a monster?"

Mordred crouches in front of her. "Yes. Especially then. It was her responsibility, and she shirked it. You deserved better than her betrayal, than her abandonment. And you deserve better than *this*, Reska. You should never have been made into Contrition."

Reska stays quiet for a moment that stretches on too long, an uncomfortable silence that I'm loathe to break. Then, finally, she meets Mordred's gaze again and asks, "Did you ever love me, in all that time we were together?"

Mordred glances away to hide the pain, but when she turns back it's still etched into every line of her face. "I loved . . . the idea of you. I loved what you meant to me. I thought you were a damsel in distress, my princess to save and woo, and I thought I could be your knight in shining armor. Stupid of me, given what I went on to do to you. But, in those days before it all went wrong, I saw a chance to save myself, vicariously, from a past I'd never get to change. I thought I could right my old wrongs by stepping into yours. That's why I wanted to make you queen. You were supposed to be my dream girl. I loved all the ways I thought you could complete me. But I don't think I loved you. I don't think I really saw you, in the end. I only saw your scars and loved how they looked like mine."

This time, when Reska cries, there's a ghost of a smile on her face. A wounded, bitter smile, but a smile that's real. Tears fall and her body shakes, but the storm doesn't get worse. When at last the crying stops, the almost-smile is still there. "Thank you for being honest."

Mordred's own smile is bittersweet, her voice laced with regret no longer stained by Contrition's poisonous influence. "Too little, too late. Always the way with me, it seems. I wish I'd told you this before. I wish for a lot of things I know I'll never have."

Reska laughs at that, and it's almost a real laugh. "I have a lifetime of experience."

She turns her head toward the other side of the crater, past me and into the fading storm. Kiana steps out of the air a moment later, teary-eyed and exhausted.

"You're me, right?" Reska asks. "My copy?"

Kiana doesn't look surprised to see any of us. Maybe her torment in the storm was just being forced to watch herself. She nods her head and walks over to her original self. "I'm a piece of you. The version of you from before you became Contrition."

"I've lived you countless times," Reska murmurs. "Over and over, the same story stuck in my head. I meet Homura, I fall in love, I fall to darkness, and everything ends. Out there, outside this prison, I know something must be happening. I can feel the shift in the air as I move from world to world. I see flashes of the lives I'm destroying, and I can't do anything to stop it. Their torment becomes mine, another piece of willow weaving my wicker cage. I'm so tired."

Kiana contemplates something, staring unfocused past all of us. "Did you ever learn what Homura meant, when she spoke of a cycle? Did you learn what we really are?"

Reska seems taken aback by that. She glances at Mordred, then at me, then back to her double. Mordred and I stay silent, watching the scene and letting Kiana take the lead here. "I know that Homura and I share a connection with Katoptris. I know she thought this conflict was bigger than us."

Kiana holds out a hand. "Let me show you what she meant."

Reska hesitates, looking distrustfully around the crater again, but she takes Kiana's hand. Immediately she gasps, eyes going wide, and she stumbles to her feet as a flood of information overtakes her. I'm thankful that her wounds preserve her modesty, though perhaps that's an oxymoron.

Kiana gently takes Reska's other hand and holds them both, offering stability. When Reska comes back to herself, there are new tears sliding down her cheeks.

"Awful," she says, horror-struck. "That's so awful. So many times. So many sacrifices."

"It's what we were made for," Kiana says with loathing. "A victim gift-wrapped for the altar. She creates us only to destroy us. She keeps us lonely so we're easier to push in that direction, toward that end. No family allowed to love us, no joy allowed to linger. She shapes us into the kind of person who will make all the wrong decisions, and then she bleeds us for them."

"Why? Why is she doing this?" Reska leans into Kiana's grasp, fearful of comfort yet craving it. Kiana is soft with her, holding her gently.

The copy glances at me and tilts her head. "You'd know better than I would, I think."

I have a few ideas. I clear my throat and say, "I'm not completely certain, but I think your story is supposed to be about guilt. The Demiurge is looking for something, and she believes she can find it in our stories. For Kiana, for Reska, what she's examining is the idea that love and happiness are undeserved, so someone who seeks love and happiness must be made to suffer for it. She created you to feel that it was your fault that your mother died, that your father hates you, that you can't find love, that you keep getting hurt . . . because all of these things are true about the Demiurge, or they were at some point before she left her humanity behind. The memories that Homura and I carry are versions of her memories, and those are some of the thoughts that haunt her. That haunt us, in proxy of our creator. It's how she perceives reality."

"And she's wrong," Kiana quickly cuts in. "The Demiurge is wrong, Reska. I know we made mistakes in our life, and I know the world suffered for those mistakes, but they weren't our mistakes alone. We were groomed to make them."

Mordred joins us. "You were manipulated, Reska. By me, by Prevara, and by the Demiurge. You were used and betrayed, made a pawn in someone else's game, and for that 'sin' you were told to drown in guilt. But it wasn't your fault. Being manipulated is never the victim's fault."

Reska shies away from our words, but that mix of hope and confusion is written across her face again. We just have to keep going and we can get through to her, we can wake her from this nightmare. The curse is banished; all that remains is one final nail in Contrition's coffin.

I tell her, "The punishment never fit the crime. Whatever mistakes you made, whatever role you were born into, that never warranted the loss of your father's warmth and your brother's kindness. Nothing you did could have justified how Homura treated you. Nothing could have justified the isolation. No one—no one ever deserves—"

I can't finish it. I know the words I want to say, but they won't come out. Even now, I struggle to believe the argument I'm making.

Kiana picks up the torch. With iron conviction, she says, "Nothing that any of us did was ever so awful that we don't deserve to be loved."

Reska and I flinch at the same time, the words cutting deep into both of us.

Can that really be true? It's not like being loved is some inalienable human right. There are plenty of monstrous people out there who shouldn't be owed someone to love them.

You're hiding from the point. It's not about being owed something. Reska feels—we feel—like our sins are so great that love is a kind of injustice. That something is wrong in the world if we are loved, if we are cherished, if we are cared for. That all of these things are a violation of some natural order imposed on us by the things we've done. But that's not true. No one's sins could ever be so great that it would be justice to deny them a heart freely given.

Was Cheshire's heart freely given?

Yes, it was. The girl she used to be was dead when we met her. The only Cheshire we ever knew was the one who wanted to be with us. And it wouldn't have been undeserved if we had accepted her love.

Reska is going through something like I am, and the others are staying quiet to let her process. The storm outside the crater is changing, speeding up here and slowing down there, as Reska cries with eyes shut and whispers words too soft to make out.

Melpomene and Thalia showed me the truth of Reska, the truth of what she was made to be. She was made to want above all else the one thing she could never have. The first Kiana was distracted by thoughts of power and respect, and Homura thought this Kiana would be the same, but those notions had long since been carved from the pattern. All Reska ever wanted was for the people around her to love her for who she was instead of who she might be. She thought her nature made her unlovable, and Homura ended up reinforcing that belief.

Today, that belief dies. I'll kill it myself, if that's what it takes.

"I love you," I say suddenly. Everyone looks at me in surprise, but I barrel on. "Not like Homura did. I lived your memories, Reska, the loop you were trapped in all those years, and it made me feel for you. Your frustrations and your fears, your longing and your hesitation. I empathized, and that made me like you. I wanted you to be happy. I still do, because I've come to know you as intimately as I know myself. I love you like a sister."

Reska trembles at my words, but she listens raptly. The storm shudders.

It clicks for Mordred. She says, "Homura was in love with your scars, but you're more than that. I love the way your eyes light up when you talk about the stars and the constellations. I thought you would be better if you embraced your darker side, if you became a monster like me. I was a fool. I love the gentle warmth in your heart that fought so hard to save even the people who had hurt you. You could have killed them all, but you couldn't bear the thought of it. I love you for being who I could never be."

Reska is a deer in headlights, anguished and frozen and needing. The storm splits.

Kiana is next, and last. She stares into her own eyes, biting her lip as she fights with the words in her heart. Finally, softly, she says, "I made too many mistakes. I hated what we became. I hated us. But I am so tired of hate, Reska. I am tired of drowning. So in this moment, here at the end of everything, I want to believe that I can be more than my wounds. I love you, Reska. I love that we survived everything the world threw at us. I love that we remembered the good times along with the bad. I love you, my other self. We are stronger than we ever dreamed we could be."

Reska sobs, one final, anguished cry, and she hugs her copy tight. She squeezes with all the strength left in her frail, ravaged body. The storm and the horizon melt away, leaving clear blue skies.

Reska and Kiana hold each other for a long time, crying into each other's arms. I don't rush them; just this once, I think the Demiurge will let us have this moment.

When all her tears have dried up, Reska slowly untangles herself from her copy and turns to face me. There's new resolve in the set of her mouth, old life and spirit returning to those dark eyes. "Alice. You're the key to all of this, aren't you? You were chosen."

"I was. For what, I'm still not certain. But the Demiurge has poured too much of herself into this world for it to be just another turning of the wheel. I don't know if I can end the cycle, but I have to try. I have to change things."

She nods. "I believe you. More than I ever believed Homura, for whatever that's worth. But, I need you to promise me something."

"I will," I answer immediately. "Anything."

"Whatever happens next, whatever world gets made to replace this one . . . there's going to be another girl like me. Promise me, Alice, that you'll never let her believe she deserves to be *hurt* more than she deserves to be loved." The conviction in her voice is almost frightening, a level of intensity I wouldn't have expected from Reska.

I swallow, chest tight. It's a heavy weight, but one I'm not capable of refusing. Not anymore, at least. "I promise."

Reska smiles, and this time her smile is warm. "Thank you. Okay. I think I'm ready."

Kiana pulls Reska into another hug, two shards of the same pattern holding each other tight. "Just this once," Kiana says, forehead resting against Reska's, "let's go out on our own terms. No more sacrifices. No more altars. Only us."

For a moment, I don't understand their meaning. When I figure it out, it's already too late.

Both girls glow with red light, and in seconds that light has enveloped them. Their bodies disintegrate, melting into each other and joining the swirl of bright crimson.

The light flows from them into me, the shard I excised rejoining my soul and bringing an old sister with it. Reska's essence commingles with mine, becoming part of me. Dimly, distantly, in a room outside the universe, I feel a gobbet of meat absorb another cut of flesh.

I stare at the space where they just stood as the world around me crumbles away, the skyline of Fata Morgana replacing the infinite void. Mordred is caught frozen in the act of reaching out for the girls, a cry stifled in her throat.

I let out a breath I didn't know I was holding. "I get it now," I murmur. "The purpose of putting those shards in me."

Mordred glares at me with suspicion. "Did you know this would happen?" she demands. "Did you plan this?"

I shake my head. "No, but it makes sense. One last gambit before the stage burns down. None of the splinters have ever achieved whatever arcane objective Melpomene sets for them. But maybe, if enough of those little splinters came together to form one big splinter, more complex than any standing alone, more *whole* than the rest . . . maybe then she gets her way."

Mordred doesn't have a sword to threaten me with anymore, but I can sense her hostility. "Tell me honestly, Alice: Would you give it to her? Would you let that monster win?"

I laugh, the sound bursting out of me full-throated and radiant. "Don't be ridiculous."

I flex my hands and call to the new threads twining through my soul. Shadows bubble at my feet, answering my call and flowing into a dozen new shapes. Reska's last gift to me, the inheritance of her divine flesh.

"The Adversary and I agree about one thing, Mordred: The age of the Demiurge ends. By the day's end, before the ashes of this universe have cooled, a new god will sit her throne."

GARDEN OF MEMORIES IX

Ash falls and blood rains over the ruins of Fata Morgana.

The last war has already ended as we pick our way through the hole in the city wall. The air is stagnant with death. Dark clouds hang low, obscuring any sight of the Labyrinth. The gods are all gone, fled to their homes to rage against the dying of the light. Dragons lie dead by the dozens, their corpses impaled on spires or scattered across rooftops.

The field past the wall was torn apart by Abyssal rifts, but even the Abyss has quieted. Reality is fragile around the battlefield, wavering like a mirage, but the horrors have returned to their pits or been driven into the city. Fire and frost score the land, swords and axes strewn about, and the earth is still cracked where the rifts first appeared. In the distance, the great machine that housed the Hierophant is sundered and still.

The bodies of three archdemons—ornamented Indulgence, ethereal Muse, and vicious Nemesis—have been gutted and stuck on spikes. I don't see any sign of the others, but there are enough dead dragons that I wouldn't be surprised if a few had been buried beneath.

Atop one of those dragons, our quarry waits.

I can feel it's still her, even though she's changed form. Her crystalline greatsword, [Apocalypse], impales the head of a green-scaled dragon. She sits beside the hilt, which is nearly as tall as she is, lounging on the dragon's neck.

Her other form was a mountain of spikes, claws, and horns, like a demon out of myth. This form is human, and close to how she looked as Homura, but the taint of the Abyss lingers. Her hair is still dark, but now longer, unkempt, and a few shades redder. Her eyes are bloodshot, with dark circles beneath. Scars adorn her face and throat, each of them raw and seeping, crusted with old blood. She's still wearing the black robe from the last batch of visions, only it's been torn apart and stitched back together so many times that only tatters are left, clinging to her body like wisps of shadow.

Malice watches, calm and expressionless—seeming almost bored—as Mordred and I approach her makeshift throne. Her gaze slides off her doppelganger—less of one now—and settles on me.

"Intercessor," she greets me as I stop at a careful distance. "I see you've finished your business with Contrition." There's an almost serpentine quality to her voice, which is so comically evil it makes me want to laugh. She *sounds* like a villain.

It's probably intentional. Malice is still playing the semiotics game that defines this universe's magic system. Acting evil makes her stronger. Of course, she's also an archdemon, so I doubt there's any part of her persona that's still just an act.

"And you've lost a familiar," she notes, gaze again briefly flitting to Mordred before dismissing her. "Your predecessor wouldn't have approached me with less than nine pawns to sacrifice. A party of five has been convention, four in dire straits. What makes you different? Are you truly unafraid of the Endbringer in the flesh?"

Something feels off about this, but I can't put my finger on it yet. "Fear has nothing to do with it. I know how dangerous you are, believe me. I'm here because I don't want to fight you, Malice. I want to talk to you, from one Intercessor to another."

Mordred keeps her mouth shut throughout our exchange. We talked beforehand about letting me take the lead; whatever points Mordred can score against her alternate self, they need to wait until Malice is willing to listen.

Easier said than done. Malice reacts to my appeal with a flare of pure hatred that slithers over my skin like a layer of warm grease. The air gets hotter, blood rain sizzling as it passes through the archdemon's aura. "I'm in a good mood after ripping out so many thorns, so I won't kill you for calling me by that title. But only once. I am not a pawn; I am the end. I am the hammer that will smash the wheel. I am the *Adversary*, and I will never kneel. I will never answer to the title of the Demiurge's favorite slave."

My sense of confusion intensifies. This *isn't* the Adversary; I've met the real one, and so has Malice. Is she pretending to be the Adversary as, what, some kind of mantling? Or does she genuinely believe herself more fitting to the role? I'll have to try and gather that information after I've appeased her anger.

I raise my hands in surrender and say, "Apologies, I didn't mean to imply that. I assure you, I have no love for the Demiurge either. She tried to make me her Intercessor and I rejected that path. I promise, I'm not here on her behalf."

She studies me closely, that disgusting sense of hatred still crawling over my skin and slipping beneath my clothes. Then her slithering presence withdraws, and a moment later she relaxes. "Introductions, then. I am Malice, archdemon of sin and hatred, the conquering queen of this reality. I have set Pandaemonium ablaze, igniting its billion worlds by the hands of my countless thralls. A song of madness corrupts even the gods themselves, taken by the red haze and driven into the grasp of the dark ancients—the Leviathans of the Deep. You face Malice the Endbringer, inheritor-claimant to the first and only Throne."

Then the fire has already begun. The death of this universe really is in motion, and too late to stop. Pandaemonium is dying, swept away in ash that something new might take its place. As has happened before, and will again, unless I stop the Demiurge.

I clear my throat and project my voice with as much confidence as I can. "You face Maven Alice, survivor of the turning wheel. I died once on the cusp of ascension as a demon, I died again at the end of the universe as Intercessor, and yet here I stand as something never seen before. I am Veseryn, the Red Queen, and Hastur."

Malice drums her fingers across the scales of the dragon she slew, then pauses. "M. Alice, really? That has to be intentional."

"We gravitated toward the same name," I defend myself, embarrassed. "I started calling myself Malice before I knew you existed, so I had to change it. The acronym was a little act of rebellion against having to do that."

"Or a little trick our maker played on you," she accuses.

"Look, is this relevant? Your issue with me is my allegiance, yes? The power you sense in me is my own and no one else's, and I will not suffer a master. I am not the Demiurge's pet."

Malice shrugs. "So you claim. Maybe you even believe that. But I've dedicated the whole of my life to defiling everything that Nyarlathotep holds precious. I cut myself free from her chains with a thousand years of toil. What have you done that could possibly compare?"

Nyarlathotep? Not Melpomene? "I don't have your accolades," I admit. "I've met one of your followers, and she found the taste of my sins to be enticing, but I think I've changed a great deal since then. And, more importantly . . . I've only really existed for a handful of days. I'm the newest splinter, and most of my very short life has been spent just trying to survive. Rebellion against the Demiurge only became possible for me . . . well, today."

Her cold gaze doesn't change. "An auspicious day for rebellion. The last day this universe will ever see. Today the Demiurge falls, and a new master rises to claim the throne that never should have been hers. Today, Azathoth's mistake is amended."

The dissonance clicks for me. *She's talking like a Leviathan. Like Prevara. Like she doesn't know—or care—about the infinite cycle of splinters.* What the hell happened to Homura after she was cast out from the world that became the Labyrinth? Aloud, I ask, "You think that new master should be you, right? You're the last candidate the Leviathans have left to see their vision unfold. To claim the throne by force, as Nyarlathotep didn't. But what exactly are you going to do once you've shattered the wheel? What will you forge in its place, Malice?"

The archdemon's laughter echoes across the battlefield. She stands up, giving the dragon's neck a little kick as she does so, and lays a hand on the pommel of her greatsword. Her eyes burn with vicious, horrible hunger, and blood oozes from the scars around her lips as an ugly smile twists her face. "Isn't it obvious? I will turn Heaven into Hell. Everything the Demiurge has made, I will unmake. Everything she rejects, I will embrace. I will forge a kingdom of the damned and parade her broken body through streets of jeering subjects. I will make a world where people kill each other for pleasure, not for ideals or higher meaning. A world that exalts the hungers she paints as monstrous, that spits on the virtues she hallows. A world of endless, glorious, uncompromising sin."

Her rant is telling; Malice is only engaging with the surface premise of Pandaemonium, the first layer of meaning. The story that she knows is the story of a thousand planets defined by the three primary Thrones: Order, Spirit, and Shadow. But there are deeper layers, those shown to me by Thalia and Melpomene. Pandaemonium is the backdrop for a much more intimate, personal story than the grand conflict that Malice is talking about.

The gods and demons and dragons, they're not why Melpomene made this universe. Homura should have known that, should have learned that from Thalia. So what made Malice forget, or stop caring?

Where I see a puzzle, Mordred sees red. The copy of Homura walks forward and raises her blade—a thing of silver and gold now, a demon-killer forged by my Intercessor self—to point it at Malice.

"You are everything we ever fought against," Mordred accuses. "Do you even realize how far you've fallen? Do you understand how many lines you've crossed? We were a hero, or we tried to be. We fought to make the world a better place. We fought to save lives! To *end* suffering, not to propagate it. You sicken me. You've abandoned every principle we ever believed in, and for what? Revenge? Spite? It's been stuck in my head, spiraling over and over, wondering what could possibly drive you to become *this thing*. Questioning if it was an act, if you were still holding on to some master plan where the world becomes just and righteous. But instead you just *gave up*. You surrendered to every worst impulse. You couldn't accept your failings, so you embraced them instead. You saw a world where heroes failed and decided to become a villain. You saw a paradigm of monsters and victims and decided to be the monster. Everyone is selfish and cruel, so why pretend to be anything else? The world can't hurt you if you hurt the world first. Pathetic."

Malice yawns in boredom. Her stance and posture haven't changed, her expression one of dull disinterest. "Who are you supposed to be? A dog shouldn't speak without permission from its master."

Mordred rears back as if struck, shocked and horrified, but I was expecting this. I say, "You're not Homura, are you? Not since you ascended, or maybe earlier. She's really not a part of your identity anymore."

Malice tilts her head. "Homura? The name rings a bell." She snaps her fingers and her eyes unfocus. Her sightless gaze darts in random directions, eyes sliding sharply. Then she blinks, attention back on the world around her, and laughs. "Ah, that Homura."

Mordred grits her teeth. "You can't just dismiss your past like that. You're still Homura, no matter how much you've changed. She's still a part of you—the core of you!"

"Homura is dead," the monster smiles. "I murdered that girl. I hollowed her out from the inside and filled her up with me. She wasn't strong enough to achieve her goals, so I changed her, piece by piece, until she stopped being Homura."

"And you lost all your ideals in the process!" Mordred accuses. "Can't you see how you've let all your worst traits consume you? None of this could be what you wanted when you started walking that path. This isn't what Homura wanted to become!"

"And I don't care," Malice says flatly. "You're not comprehending that *I am not Homura*. I am not bound by whatever reasoning she had for becoming a demon. She was merely the crucible that I was forged in. Her utility to me ended the moment I ascended. She may have taken the first step into darkness, but *I am* the darkness. I am *Malice*, the archdemon of sin and hatred. You call me selfish, cruel, a monster, and I wear those labels with pride. All I want, all I really want, is to keep hurting people. To keep hurting *her*, our maker. That is my nature. That is my sole desire. Your appeals fall on deaf ears."

Mordred stares in disbelief. I glance behind us, back toward the glass tower. *Do we really need to be here?*

It felt so obvious that I would face Malice after Contrition, but now I'm not so sure. *There's nothing left of Homura to save. There's nothing to be gained here except eating another shard of the Demiurge. Is that worth the trouble? Is this fight necessary?*

The worst that can come of leaving Malice alone is that she'll follow us to the tower and we'll have to fight her there, but we'll probably have Thalia's help for that fight. Or maybe . . . I still don't know how she feels about the true Adversary, do I? Is Malice an ally of the Adversary, or an enemy?

I'm safer if I eat her. I'm safer if I kill my sister and steal her soul.

"One last question," I say suddenly. "What will you do when Thalia and I reach the Demiurge before you? Or, to frame it another way: What will you do when one of us seeks the highest throne?"

Malice's boredom slides off her face, her relaxed posture replaced by iron focus. Her gaze sharpens, her grip tightening around the hilt of [Apocalypse]. "Ah. You're one of hers, then. One of the pretender's pets. That makes this a lot simpler."

The archdemon rips her sword out of the dragon's head and vanishes. Before I can blink she's in front of Mordred, free hand wrapped around her doppelganger's neck, and then in another burst of impossible speed she's gone. The ground *craters* from the force of her departure, and seconds later a building inside the city collapses.

Holy shit. How the hell do I kill that!? More pressingly, what happens if she kills Mordred? Do I lose that shard?

We need to figure out a way to crack open Malice that doesn't involve exploiting the Homura connection, since that was clearly a bust. Mordred is a write-off.

My own callousness unsettles me. I should care more that an ally is about to die, shouldn't I? She's dying because I brought her to this fight.

She was never alive in the first place. None of us were. Until the cycle is broken, we're all just screaming meat.

I don't like that either, but now's not really the time for doubt. I need to catch up to Malice, rip her soul out, and devour whatever's left of the Demiurge shard animating her. That's my only path to victory against my *real* opponents.

I'm halfway through conjuring another portal when I stop myself, reminded of how Contrition interfered with the last one. Malice isn't manifesting her throne world like Contrition was, but would she even need to? She's leagues more powerful *and* more controlled.

Fuck it. If there's a trap, may as well spring it now.

I finish the portal and step through, expecting the worst, but the other side doesn't dump me out into an endless hellscape of Malice's defilers torturing captive souls. I reappear on a ruined street deep inside Fata Morgana, the glass tower casting a shadow over the whole area.

Malice is back in her monster form, spikes and scales adorning red-hued flesh, one claw pushing Mordred against the brick wall of what looks like a half-destroyed tavern. The crystal greatsword scrapes against the ground, carving gouges in the street.

Mordred has already lost the fight, if you could even call it that; her right arm is missing, her stomach has been opened, and one of her eyes is pulp. The only thing keeping her organs inside her body is that blood control ability of hers. The sword I gave her is nowhere in sight.

Defiant to the end, Mordred spits on her alternate self. "Betrayer," she chokes out. "Murderer. Villain."

"*Adversary,*" Malice hisses, tightening her grip.

I have a split-second decision to make: Do I try to save Mordred, or do I focus on figuring out Malice? Is the former even possible?

Malice just fought the universe and she's not even injured. I know Mordred has a damage reflection spell, and if she's used it then it hasn't done anything. I doubt any conventional attacks will have an effect.

Still, I have to try something. I can't imagine my Red Queen spells would even scratch Malice, but maybe the Intercessor's kit has a usable attack?

I bring my hands together and then pull them apart, stretching a web of golden light into existence. The light flashes once, twice, thrice, and three beams of gleaming energy strike the archdemon in three different parts of her body. None of them even leave a scorch mark.

"Your defenses are absurd," I complain. "That spell can burn through dragon scales! I killed a greater blue with a dozen castings, and you just shrug it off like it's nothing? Cheater."

Malice pauses in her assault on Mordred, still holding the other woman too tightly for her to escape. She turns her head to look at me, eyes baleful and unamused. "Skill issue," the genocidal archdemon tells me, and then she stabs a hand into Mordred's chest and rips out her beating heart.

"No!" The shout rips from my throat reflexively and I shoot another three beams of light to equal ineffectiveness. Malice raises the heart toward her mouth, holding it delicately like a decadent treat, and my perception of time slows to a crawl.

I need the heart. I need the shard. My only path to victory is being more real than my opponent. I need every inch of advantage.

There's a spell for this, but it's not one of mine; if it's dead or dying, Urna can usurp its motor function. I snap my fingers and force Mordred's almost-corpse to lunge for the heart and slap it out of Malice's hand. The demon isn't expecting that, or not expecting how much strength I can shove into a body with pilfered necromancy, and the heart goes flying.

The shadows between me and Malice bubble to life, animated by another branch of stolen sorcery. Tendrils of living darkness snatch the heart out of the air and fling it toward me. Malice takes a step toward it, claw outstretched, then stops herself. She watches as I catch the heart, lift it to my own mouth, and bite down.

I drink the heartsblood of Mordred, absorbing the soul shard and the flesh gobbet it was imbued into. Her life essence is warm and bitter, but not unpleasantly so. I can feel myself becoming more whole as I consume my own castoff. Melpomene put this shard in me, added that texture to my soul, but deep down this one is *mine*.

But then, Urna and Reska also feel like mine. Pieces of me, as I am a piece of another. When I eat Malice, she'll be a piece of me, too.

"Interesting," Malice comments. Her eyes glow, baleful and burning. Is she watching this process with soul sight? Do I still have a witch's protections, or have I evolved? Can she see my soul regardless? "That wasn't an Intercessor reclaiming a familiar, nor was it a demon feasting, yet it carried similarities to both. Did the pretender grant you this gift?"

"Why do you call her a pretender?" I ask instead of answering, mouth still wet with blood. "Why do you consider yourself the more fitting Adversary? I'll trade my secrets for yours."

Malice folds two of her arms, places one on her hip, and keeps a careful grip on [Apocalypse] with her fourth. "A trade, is it? You're bold to think yourself my equal."

I smile. "You can't deny you're curious. I can promise I know things about the Demiurge and her design that you don't. Look upon my soul and see the truth of my words, sister dearest."

The demon huffs, but grins. "Alright, *sister*. Know my truth: The one you call Adversary is a slave to her love and utterly undeserving of the title. Thalia would preserve her precious Melpomene forever, leaving her unpunished and unharmed. She betrayed the girl I once was, sabotaging our efforts to break the wheel. I have made a religion of hate, waged a war of destruction against all our maker's works. For a thousand years I have toiled to bring ruin, chaos, and desecration. I am Malice, and I am the Adversary. Among all our kindred splinters, I alone know what it means to *defy* our creator."

Betrayal. Homura felt the same way, if Mordred was truly an accurate simulacrum. Thalia insists otherwise, but she's not any more trustworthy. And I still don't know if Thalia's goals are anathema to mine or not.

The answer doesn't change my goals here. I need to understand how I can deconstruct Malice's core persona. She's staked her identity around being the true Adversary, the ultimate antithesis to the Demiurge. If I can put cracks in that claim, I can get at the meat beneath. First, though . . . I need to make this a duel of Royalty before I can step beyond Royalty. I need to lay my own foundation.

I straighten my back and bare my teeth. "Know *my* truth: My template is Veseryn, and hunger is my gift as much as my curse. I have supped on divine flesh and the blood of my sacred sisters. You say you've broken her works and defied her will? I've been alive for a single week and I've already taken a bite out of her very soul, you amateur. If I were to take a demon name as you have then I would be Voracity, the all-consuming. I alone know what it means to *devour* our creator."

The monster's expression darkens. "Big talk, little girl. Let's see if that pride is empty."

Malice surges at me faster than my sight can track, but I am more than sight, be it mortal or demonic. Hastur is a velvet cloak around my shoulders, her red hands coming up to cover my eyes. I can't see Malice, but I know where she's going to be, and where I have to be, and exactly how I need to move.

The crystal greatsword swings for my neck and I parry it with a demon-killing longsword. I open my eyes and grin. "Not so empty, eh?"

She grins back. "Cute."

Malice pushes harder and cleaves right through the sword, completely shattering all the anti-demon enchantments woven into it. I throw myself to the ground and melt it into shadow just in time to escape the edge of [Apocalypse]. The blade still clips into the puddle of darkness that I've become, but I just slither around it and reform on the other side of her.

Malice cracks her knuckles. "Clever little rat, aren't you? You seem so fond of scurrying through the dark. But I've drowned in the dark, and in the dark I was reborn. Let me show you what it's really like. Let's go there together, to where it all began."

Oh, I really don't like the sound of that.

The archdemon plunges her black greatsword into the city street, crystal puncturing through stone. Reality shatters, the street vanishes, and we're falling together into the void.

We fall deep, deep down into the endless dark, the empty black of the Abyss stretching out before us and around us, above and below. Though above, far above, that void is beginning to burn. *This is the fire that will feast on all creation. This is the end that Malice unleashed, serving as Melpomene's hatchet man.*

The corpse pile appears below us, rising from the dark. Only, the corpse pile is no longer a corpse pile; the Resurrection has begun, and a thousand dead worms writhe to life and ascend toward the fire burning the universe. We pass their twitching, sinuous forms as we fall.

A new shape appears in the gloom: a glowing spiderweb of static, like cracks in an eggshell. Like a crack in the world.

We hit the ground on opposite sides of a great chasm. It's like the darkness itself has been split open with a gargantuan axe, the black substance of the void deformed into sharp plateaus stretching out over emptiness. At the bottom of that canyon lies the strange static I saw from above, but I don't get a good glimpse of it before I crash into the solid plane of darkness.

Malice steadies herself with all the benefit of her inhuman body plan, while I cushion my landing with the love of all shadows for their mistress Reska. I spare a moment to appreciate just how far I've come; at the start of my journey, I would have dealt with a fall like that by breaking all my bones and sipping a potion to heal. Now I'm spoiled for choice between my Intercessor powers, my Red Queen powers, Reska's, and Urna's. Once I devour Malice, the demonic half of my kit will be even stronger . . . though I doubt that strength means much of anything to Thalia, or to Melpomene.

In a very real sense, Malice is my final opponent as a mage of Pandaemonium. Where I'm going next, sorcery will be useless.

I brush myself off and meet Malice's gaze, the demon standing vigilant across the tear in the world. When I'm certain she's not preparing another attack, I let myself glance down at the strange black-and-white rift. Only, it's not really monochrome, once I start examining it closer. I see reds and blues, purples and greens, a dozen colors that become a hundred, a thousand, an infinite kaleidoscope. The infinite colors consolidate into individual threads woven together to make a net, or the fabric of a shawl, or a vivid painting of another time and space. And through the gaps in the weave, through microscopic holes between the intersection of thread, I see a land of endless ash.

I see a castle, a tower, and a throne, all cracked and colorless. I see a field of swords and a garden of bones. I remember walking this place, once as the Adversary and then as I met her. This is the graveyard of eternities.

Which makes the kaleidoscopic net between that world and this one . . .

"Have you figured out where we are?" Malice asks.

I break away from staring into the rift and look back up at the demon. "The weave down there, it's the skin of the universe. The living membrane dividing Pandaemonium from the void outside, the void that holds both the graveyard of worlds and the true palace of the creator. Why is this visible? What exposed it?"

"Thalia's work," Malice tells me, her voice taking on a new edge, a new intensity. "The result of her passing into this world from outside. I've always wanted to explore that realm, ever since I learned of it. Imagine what could be waiting for us out there! Entire realities hidden from our eyes, the domains of other creator gods, or perhaps another layer above even them.

Nyarlathotep—Melpomene, if we use Thalia's name for her—cannot be the highest power in existence. This universe knows her as a vassal of Azathoth, the true divine. Thalia would tell us that Azathoth is a construct of its servant, the Dreamweaver created by its own Demiurge, but is that true in the layer of reality above us? You and I—Mordred and Veseryn, if we are to accept those detestable labels—remember a life on a world that has no true counterpart in Pandaemonium. I've scoured this universe and found many Earth-like worlds, but none of them have been an exact match for the Earth of our Demiurge-granted memories. Perhaps that Earth truly does exist. If it does . . . how did Melpomene go from that world to her palace in the void? How did a mortal become a god? There's something that Thalia isn't telling us. For all her rebellion, she's still protecting her master's secrets. And when I find those secrets, I will use them to become the same kind of god that she is."

I freeze as the implications of what she's saying churn in my mind. *There's a real Earth out there, one that Melpomene remembers. If that world could produce our Demiurge, could it also produce other demiurges?*

The concept of a demiurge is an old one in philosophy and religion. The little joke of Melpomene's world-building in Pandaemonium is how the divine figures called Azathoth and Nyarlathotep differ from their namesakes in Lovecraft's Mythos. Azathoth is still the blind idiot god, but Nyarlathotep has become the real demiurge figure, having usurped the divine fire of the dreamer to craft her own bespoke playground. When you peel the layer back, you see that Nyarlathotep dreamed Azathoth into being, rather than the other way around.

In some forms of Gnosticism—which I have an interest in and thus *Melpomene* has an interest in—the true divine power, the highest above all, splits itself or reflects itself into lesser forms, and one of these lesser forms, these archons, becomes convinced of its own divinity. The demiurge, ignorant that it exists only as the lesser emanation of a higher power, fashions the world. The demiurge traps reflected divinity, creating material existence.

Our own personal demiurge, Melpomene, wasn't born a god. She didn't always have the power to create worlds, so where did she learn that power? How was it bestowed upon her? And have other people from Earth been cast into the role of demiurge? We can't have been the only girl to fit the criteria, whatever those criteria may have been, so who else was granted the power to shape worlds? Where are they, and what are they building? How many other wheels might exist beyond our own?

Malice interrupts the spiraling of my thoughts. "That's my secret traded. Your turn, *sister*. You boasted of biting our maker and getting a taste, so, what did she taste like? What did you swallow, and what did you see?" Her pose is at ease, but I can already sense the desire for violence rising in her once again, ready to strike as soon as I've said my piece.

"In a room outside the universe, you and I are gristle. We are gobbets of her flesh, snippets of skin and fat, cut from her body and laid out on slabs. Everything in this universe is just a phantasm, a dream-shadow cast by vessels of wood and paint, except for us. Our creator is infinitely bigger than us, but we are splinters of infinity. I tasted victory when I drank her blood, my fangs biting into her infinite soul. I didn't harm her, couldn't harm her, but now I understand one all-important truth: We are made of her." I crack a grin. "And when I'm made of enough of her, I can replace her. You're my next meal, Malice. You'll help complete me."

The anticipation of violence intensifies in the air around me, a palpable aura of danger like a sword twitching in its sheath. Malice raises [Apocalypse] to her shoulder and says, "I'm going to crack you open and drink in your murder."

The monster lunges at me with her sword and I just barely get out of the way with a push from my swarming shadows, but the second she can't get through she snaps her body into a new trajectory. One dodge too slow and her fist comes rocketing into my gut, knocking all the air from my chest and sending me flying.

Malice jumps after me, grabs me out of the air, and *dunks me* back down. I slam into living darkness, even its affection for me not enough to spare my body from the pain of sudden impact. I force my aching limbs to move, wrenching myself to my feet just in time to avoid Malice's follow-up strike with her sword, but I'm still in danger.

In a straight fight, I'm no match for a monster this ancient and this obsessed with murder. But I've already established the premises of Wonderland for Malice, even if I haven't made that explicit. I have more of the divine flesh than her, and I'll make her find that out the hard way.

When Malice comes in swinging, I don't try to dodge; I grab the sword.

[Apocalypse] cuts into my hand, the blade carving through that thin layer of skin and flesh and hitting bone, and then it *slows*. As the sword slows in its path it meets more resistance, a cascading loop of action reinforcing reaction. Wonderland and Pandaemonium agree: The sword didn't cut through, so it can't cut through.

Malice is shocked. She stares at the blade, at the strength in her arms that failed her, and then at me. "How did you do that?"

I laugh. "Nah, next question goes to me. You told me what you're planning to do after you win, Malice, but how are you planning to beat the final boss without Thalia's help?" In truth I'm not as interested in hearing an answer as I am in stalling to give cascading failure more time to reinforce my narrative advantage.

The demon snarls, "You doubt my strength? I have gorged myself on this universe while Thalia has languished uncaring of it. I bested the Royalty of Pandaemonium and stood atop their corpses, making their essence my own. I shall kill the Demiurge with hands forged in murder, with a sword crowned in sin, and with a mind sharpened in hatred. I am the apotheosis of her antithesis."

I undermine her point by putting more strength into my arm and pushing her sword back. She rips the sword away and levels it, fury pouring off of her.

"I ask again: How did you stop my blade? Nothing of Pandaemonium should be able to resist its bite."

I grin with as much smugness as I can muster. "It's one of Thalia's teachings, actually. See, you and I, we're both divine flesh of the all-maker, meaty gobbets in her celestial workshop, but I'm more flesh than you are. I've devoured four other splinters since waking up in this world, and you haven't eaten one. You may have all the strength in Pandaemonium, but I have substance in the world above it. It makes me more real than the painted simulacra of this phantasm universe, and it makes me more real than *you*. And if you can't cut *me* with that toy sword of yours, how the hell are you going to cut the butcher?

I shape a new weapon, a knife like the first I ever held. This knife burns not with fire but with pure will, an incandescent white certainty that *I am going to win.*

"New question: What makes you free and me a tool, when you're the one who burned the world for her?"

Her rage overflows and she roars as I dart beneath her guard and slash at her leg with my knife. She swats me away with a pair of arms, but I hold my ground and only get pushed a few feet away. I move in again for another slash, parry away her greatsword, and cut through her scales before dancing back and settling into a ready stance the Intercessor once trained.

"Destroying the world is what the Demiurge wants," I say as I prepare for her next attack. "It's what she always does to her creations. Just like you're doing now."

Malice stabs [Apocalypse] into the dark foundation of the Abyss. A tide of violent energy comes surging toward me, but I tank it through gritted teeth—cutting it to diminish the blow, a trick learned from watching Thalia—and force myself to grin. *Not enough, Malice. It's no longer enough.* She begins gathering more energy, calling the attention of the Leviathans to their champion.

"You're serving the Demiurge, bringing the end she desires. These worlds are wood and paint to her, but she tries to act through the rules of narrative. Something inside the world starts the fire. This time it was you. Her hand lit the torch through *you,* Malice. You've made yourself into a pawn."

With every exchange that goes my way, I carve my preferred pattern into the universe and Wonderland principles become accepted by Pandaemonium. Malice can tell that, too, which is why she's stopped trying to fight me normally and is betting it all on this one attack.

"All you've ruined were worlds she didn't care about," I accuse the demon. "She *trained you* to kill those worlds. She conditioned you into becoming a beast that only desecrates and destroys until the time was right to unleash you on the universe and wipe the board clean. She used you to burn Pandaemonium, and you fell for it."

Her fury wavers. Just for an instant, but I sense it happen. "The Leviathans whispered this moment to me," Malice insists. "Their hatred swelled in anticipation of the final conflict."

"Do you really think they aren't her pawns too?" I laugh. "You're too far gone, Malice. Too brainwashed by her influence. You've forgotten the most important detail: Nothing in this universe is real except for us. Nothing has free will except for us, because nothing is a person except for us. The Leviathans don't truly hate Nyarlathotep, because how could they? She made them. In becoming *their* champion, you've only become hers. You proudly walk a path that Melpomene laid out for you."

I can feel the moment that something in Malice's conviction *cracks.* Just a single sliver of doubt creeping into her resolve, but that's all it takes for an archdemon. When she unleashes her strike, throwing all the hate and murder in the universe at me, all the baleful will of the Leviathans, all the strength and sin she's ever gathered . . .

It flows over me like water, and I am the mountain.

"Face it, Malice: You've never been a sinner. You've transgressed *nothing*."

Her core shudders. Every insult I fling at her is another crack in her armor, another hairline fracture in the invincibility of her persona. She knows it, and for the first time this fight I taste a new, familiar flavor: *fear*.

Malice is going to die here. So she runs.

She cuts a hole in space and steps through, but it's my turn to usurp a portal. I reach out with my will and redirect the portal, spitting her out in Fata Morgana. I follow, landing gracefully on the steps before the glass tower. I place a zone of interdiction, one last Intercessor trick, so that she can't get away.

Malice scrapes her claws down the side of the tower, leaving gouges in the glass. "This is impossible!" she snarls, fear and fury warring for control of her voice. "I am the queen of this reality, the master of the wheel!"

She lunges for me and with a snap of my fingers I fling her back to crash against the tower. She stays there, breathing heavily, disbelieving.

"This is the truth of you, Malice," I tell the fallen demon. "You have forgotten what you really are. You think yourself a conqueror and a victor, but you've been playing the wrong game. You spent a thousand years razing worlds like it mattered, plotting to kill gods and demons like any of them were real. You've gorged yourself on the flesh of this universe, but it was illusory the whole time. You were eating nothing."

"Impossible . . ." she mutters. "Impossible, impossible, impossible. I never lose."

"A queen cannot conquer the divine," I say harshly. "You are just another puppet, acting as the Demiurge desires you to act. You are a slave to your nature. Eat as many souls as you like, it won't make you grow. You can't grow, because nothing Royal ever grows. That's the trick she played on you, Malice. That's the scam you fell for. You stagnated, like all the rest of this universe, and I *evolved*. I'm more than you could ever be."

She comes for me, with all her strength and hate. I cut her down, and when she's bleeding and broken I take her heart and swallow it. I devour Malice and make her mine.

Another scrap of meat melds into my true flesh, another splinter absorbed. Now all that's left in that celestial workshop is me and a thousand lumps of charcoal.

I gulp down the last of Malice's heartsblood and take one final look at the burning universe. The sky, the land, the distant stars . . . all of it burns. Everything burns.

I turn around and head inside the tower, following the last of my sisters.

Walking to the end of the wheel.

GARDEN OF MEMORIES X

I've seen the inside of this tower before.

It's a strange revelation. At first I think of the tower from one of Thalia's stories, but that's not where I'm remembering this from. I realize, after a moment of contemplation, that I'm remembering Homura's experiences with the tower.

She came here many times, first to climb it and then to learn from Katoptris. The tower had new challenges every night, a thousand monsters slain and trials passed, as she threw herself at the tower again and again in her dreams.

The structure of the tower is simple: You pass through a door or a mirror and are taken into a room that contains a puzzle, threat, or other form of obstacle. When you've solved the obstacle, a new portal appears to take you to the next floor.

In the days before Prevara, there were five challenges at most. In the days after, when Homura came to the tower, you had to clear fifty. That Homura ever reached Katoptris is something of a minor miracle.

I'm spared that gauntlet, mercifully, by Thalia having gone ahead and ruthlessly cut down everything in her path. The first floor is littered with corpses, the second reveals a water jug puzzle smashed into pieces, and the pattern continues. Where there was a puzzle, now there's just scrap. Where there were enemies, now there are only bodies.

I follow Thalia's trail of carnage, passing through door after door, and I think about how to kill her.

I don't know for certain that we're going to fight, but I can't shake the suspicion. Thalia has no love for her sisters. She wants to save *Melpomene*, not the rest of us. She was complicit in torturing shards for countless turns of the wheel. What's one more splinter tossed aside?

The second I'm no longer useful to her—and I don't really understand what makes me useful right now—there will be nothing stopping her from discarding me. So I have to make sure I can't be so easily discarded.

Wonderland principles won't help me against Thalia; her divine flesh has more mass than mine, it has more symbolic weight as the literal heart of our shared creator, and Thalia's method of existing in this universe is incarnation rather than projection. Devouring so many of my sisters has narrowed the conceptual gap between us, but I haven't removed it entirely. I'm still the underdog.

If I have any edge, it's this: Melpomene chose me. Thalia may have been her agent for countless cycles, but Melpomene rewound time twice to try and maneuver me into achieving her goal. That's never happened before. Something about me is special. Something about me makes this loop different from all the loops that came before it.

I can do this. I can escape the wheel. I can win.

As I rise higher through the tower, the environment changes; the basic structure of each room is still the same, still littered with the detritus of Thalia's passing, but the walls here are adorned with mirrors, and every mirror shows the same image. The first time it happens, the reflection is Eirdryd Llewellyn, the fae who stole my name, staring at me as he burns.

The next floor shows me Bashe, watching me from every mirror as he stands amid the flames. Then Esha, Achaia, Dante, the drow woman, the Machinist, Averrich, Vaylin, the snake, the hunters, the werewolf, and on and on and on. I see every face I've ever met, every life I've taken, every soul I abandoned, every hand I rejected . . . every person who was never really a person, if I accept the worldview of the Adversary.

I walk past them all. The world is burning and it's too late for regrets. I came into this universe thinking I would save the world or rule over it as a benevolent god-queen, but in the end all I can do is walk away. I'm not the hero of this story. There are no heroes here.

I stopped counting the rooms when the haunting started, but I'm certain I've reached the last before the end when I see Cheshire staring out of the mirror.

There's only one mirror in this room, against the far wall where the exit would appear. Cheshire looks exactly as she did the very first time I saw her, white-haired and cat-eared with heterochromatic eyes and a barely-there skirt. Her hand presses against the inside of the mirror, but her face is completely expressionless.

I walk up to the mirror and gently place my hand over Cheshire's. I can't feel her warmth, but I can remember how it felt. "I know you're not real," I tell her gently.

Cheshire smiles. "I never was. But it was nice to pretend, wasn't it?"

I stay quiet. This is Melpomene; I'm almost certain of that. But it is also, in a very real sense, the last time I'll ever have the chance to see or speak to Cheshire. I should say something about that. I should tell her how I felt. But I can't summon the words. "You were supposed to be Thalia's replacement, weren't you?" I ask instead.

Cheshire laughs, but she doesn't move her hand from where it almost touches mine. "You could say she was my prototype, if you wanted to be nicer to me," she teases. "But, yes, I was meant to fill the role that she left behind. The Intercessor to your Red Queen, the familiar to your Intercessor, and then . . . an experiment." Cheshire sighs. "I wish I could have been with you this time. I wish I could have been more than a test."

"You don't," I respond automatically. "You don't wish for anything. You're a puppet."

It's Cheshire's turn to go quiet. The mirth on her face falls away in the uncomfortable silence. "For a girl who wears so many masks," she says softly, "you really hate pretending when it's something that could make you happy. Couldn't we have had this moment, Alice? One last shred of sentiment, even if it wasn't real?"

My courage breaks. "I want that," I confess, voice aching and raw. "I want to believe in the lie. I want to accept the love of someone, anyone. I wish you were by my side. I wish we could have faced this whole world together. But I can't . . . I can't let that rule me. Love, hunger, pain, fear . . . I can't let any of those things rule me, and I don't think I'm ready, as a person, to love someone without it consuming me. It would be my ruin if I brought you with me, because I don't know how to love like a normal girl. So I'm sorry, Cheshire. I'm sorry to the girl I thought you were, and to the girl you might have been if the world was a different place. And I hope, one day, that I can meet you again. Goodbye, my love."

Cheshire doesn't reply; she's already gone. The mirror becomes a door, and I step through it with a heavy heart and wet eyes.

Thalia is waiting for me on the highest floor of the glass tower, at the very summit of the Labyrinth. The personal chambers of Katoptris, the Lady of Glass, who was tortured by Prevara and seduced by Homura. Her grief, I am told, broke the world that came before. The fragments of her being were used to keep the Labyrinth a realm of nightmares, manipulated by her captor.

I've seen her home before, but only in memories of someone else's dreams. The top of the tower is a simple viewing room, at least at first glance. An opulent carpet leads to a tall mirror of polished glass, where in ancient days the people of Svijetstakla would make pilgrimage to speak with their guardian goddess.

On the other side of the mirror, the room reflected is entirely different; bedchambers rather than an audience chamber, with a study and a kitchen and a four-poster bed. Homura and Katoptris spent a great deal of time together in that room, teaching and learning and coming to know one another.

I came to the Labyrinth thinking it was my destiny to kill Katoptris, then thought it might be my destiny to save Katoptris. She was the central figure around which everything else orbited, and our confrontation seemed inevitable.

When I step into her chambers, Katoptris is already dead. She bled out on the floor, face-down, her back cut open by deft hands and a wicked knife. The pool of her blood is nearly dry. Her murderer, Thalia, examines a bookshelf as she diligently cleans her dagger, still wearing her bloodstained wedding dress and red leather jacket.

She greets me as I stop in front of the corpse. "Alice! I'm delighted that you won your duel, truly. You've been a much more intelligent partner than Homura ever was. Tell me, how are you feeling? It's almost time for the finale, and I for one couldn't be more excited!"

Thalia doesn't look my way, still focused on Katoptris's little library. I stare down at the body of Katoptris and wonder how alive she ever was. The version of her that Thalia told me about felt like a true splinter, but this one . . . doesn't. Everything I've ever heard about her in this reality was secondhand, and always as some prize to be fought over or some instigator of calamity. She has the same story as her predecessor, but without the animating human heart.

Katoptris is dead, and that should mean something to me, but I can't bring myself to care. She was never real. It feels like it's been a lifetime since she was the goal of my journey.

I step over her body and join Thalia by the bookshelf. "I feel anxious," I admit. "It all ends today, maybe this very hour. I'd like to think I'm ready, after facing so many of my sisters and triumphing where all of them failed, but . . . I don't know what happens next." I glance at her face and ask, very carefully, "Where do I fit in your plans, Thalia?"

The Adversary finally pulls her attention from the library and considers me. "You're worried I'm going to backstab you," she guesses. "When the work is done, you think I'll dispose of you as a loose end."

"Can you blame me? You hate splinters like me. You see all of us as failures that keep hurting your beloved Melpomene. Why wouldn't you just kill me as soon as my use to you was over?" I'm on edge, my whole body itching in anticipation of violence. I'm terrified that Thalia is going to murder me, and I still don't really know how to stop that from happening.

"Because I like you," Thalia says with a warm smile. "You're different from the others. You're more interesting. You're more like her."

I am *not* going to fall for the pretty girl with suspicious motives flirting with me, not this time. I refuse. I'm better than that.

But then, is refusing to trust her not its own mistake? Isn't that the lesson I was supposed to learn? Or was it the opposite?

I hate how few clear answers I still have about . . . my own story, I guess. Was it a mistake to trust Cheshire, or was the mistake not trusting Cheshire? It feels like not even Melpomene herself really understands that . . . which might be true. She's looking for answers, after all. You don't look for answers if you already know them. But is Cheshire really the question that Melpomene cares about, or was she just a means to an end?

Are you watching, Melpomene? We're both here because of you.

Regardless of the real game, I probably shouldn't stonewall the yandere goddess of violent clone murder. "You said that before," I point out. "What do you mean when you say that I'm more like Melpomene?"

Thalia taps her chin and eyes me critically. "You don't feel like just another template. Mordred, Kiana, Veseryn, I've seen those girls a thousand times and they are *all the same.* Sure, the details vary, but there's an essence beneath the surface that always drives them to their fated ends. Standing here *proves* that you're different. An ordinary Veseryn couldn't have come this far. You're sharper, more thoughtful, and . . . you're curious."

I ignore her praise and frown at the last line. "Are you saying the other Veseryn shards *weren't* curious? That doesn't make any sense to me. Veseryn isn't a sorcerer like Kiana or a paladin like Mordred, she's a *thief.* Discovery is our whole game."

Thalia waves a hand dismissively. "Discovery, yes, but only of *useful* things. Veseryn sees value in knowledge only in how knowledge leads to power. Do you think any of the girls we killed would have been as delighted as you to debate philosophy in a conceptual space? You have the same spark as her, that desire to understand for its own sake. It's one of the traits I love about Melpomene."

"And the trait you're going to restrain," I say carefully.

The Adversary sighs and leans her shoulder against the bookshelf. "Yes, I am, for her own good. If you're worried that I'll do the same to you, don't be; I assure you, I have no interest in the mechanisms of creation. You're so *paranoid,* Alice. I've been nothing but helpful since we met," she says, sounding equally resentful and exasperated.

She's right, of course; I am paranoid. That doesn't mean I'm wrong. "Sorry," I say with a wince. "I . . . I appreciate how you've helped me. And I want to trust you. It's just hard for me. What do you need me to do, Thalia?"

My counterpart brightens. She pushes herself off the bookshelf, gives her dagger a twirl, and carves the whole case in half with a single motion. She pulls the wreckage away and makes a shallow cut against the wall behind it. She peels wallpaper off, tearing it in strips, to reveal a secret mirror.

This mirror is clouded, reflecting nothing, but something about it feels *important.* Like it's more real than the wall around it.

"This," Thalia tells me, "is the physical component of the gateway between this universe and Melpomene's workshop. She always includes something like this in her creations, and always in a key location. In a certain sense, this mirror is the pillar holding up the universe; it grounds the rest of the mirage."

"So, what, you can turn it into a portal to her workshop?"

The Adversary taps the mirror a few times, but the only thing that happens is that she winces and has to pull her hand away, the tips of her fingers looking very faintly singed. "Not exactly. When Melpomene banished me, she cut off my access to her workshop. I can't open that portal . . . but you can." She grins, and a touch of manic frenzy returns to her glittering eyes. "You've *won,* Alice. You bested the other shards, you bested this universe's greatest horrors, and here you stand at the summit of the universe. All you have to do is touch this mirror and the gate will open for you, recognizing you for what you are. And then we can step through together and put an end to the turning wheel."

All I have to do is touch the mirror. Assuming Thalia doesn't kill me in the seconds after, and assuming I'm ready to face Melpomene.

"Okay," I breathe out. "But, before that, can I ask you something?"

"Anything," she answers without hesitation. "You've earned that much, and we have time; this will be the last place in the universe to burn. What do you want to know?"

I chew on my words. I need to get more information out of Thalia, but not the information she wants to give up. I need to know how she really feels about me. I walk over to Katoptris's bed and sit down on it, still contemplating.

Thalia lets me think. She pulls a chair away from the study and wraps around it, head resting on her shoulder as she stares at me and waits.

I lick my lips and start talking. "So, we're not going to overpower Melpomene. You're her heart and I'm a big chunk of her, but that's peanuts to the real deal. How do we narrow a power gap that massive?"

"Our sisters." Thalia's smile is wicked. "We get to the lab with all the burnt shards and we absorb them all. I don't have an exact percentage for how much of herself she's cut away, but it's enough to *feel* like half, and that's the part that really matters. That gives us the *story edge* to usurp her position."

I frown. "Does a story edge mean anything outside of Pandaemonium?" *And are you really willing to share that advantage?*

"Of course. The power that allows her to shape the universes is not without limitations; Pandaemonium's magic system may be an incarnation of the suspension of disbelief, but she only chose that system in mimicry of the constraints she's *really* under."

"Malice talked about other demiurges," I say, leaning in with genuine curiosity. "Do they exist? Do you know anything about the entity—or system—that granted Melpomene her power as a demiurge?"

Thalia shrugs. "Not much. She never wanted to talk about it, even to me. But from what little she did say, I don't think it's a single entity handing out power. I don't know if that means her power comes from a system without a designer or some kind of collective, but I don't think it makes a difference. If we can make a convincing argument that Melpomene *shouldn't* have absolute power over us, she won't."

Huh. If she's telling the truth—and I don't get the sense that she isn't—then we have a real path to beating Melpomene and taking her power. There's weight in a narrative about the created turning against the creator. A full literary tradition to pull from.

But that still leaves the question of whether Thalia would share power. It might be more efficient for one creation to hold the entirety of Melpomene's missing pieces, rather than splitting them and potentially diluting the effect. I need to get more out of her.

"Why do you think Melpomene creates shards like me?" I ask suddenly. "I know she's trying to answer a question, but I don't know what that question is. I want to understand. Why did she make me in all the ways that I am?"

Thalia quirks an eyebrow. "Is this idle curiosity, or something more?"

"I'm always curious, yes, but there are genuine strategic considerations. If our victory lies in manipulating the narrative, we need to understand the *complete* narrative. What question is Melpomene trying to answer?"

Thalia chews her lip. "Reasonable. Let's look at commonalities, then. Every shard that Melpomene makes is gifted with magic of some kind, or picks it up very early in their story. Every shard lacks some mix of love, respect, and safety, and is motivated by the absence of that which they value most. You should have an idea of the standard variations from what I showed you. Kiana, the first of the lot, was a . . . corrupt power fantasy, let's say. Loved and respected, but only by force, and the love was revealed as a lie at the end of her road. Katoptris was a Kiana, and your Reska."

And just like the original Kiana, I learned the lie up front. My relationship with Cheshire was always in question; the love she felt for me was explicitly artificial. Kiana pretended it was real until someone took that away from her, and then it all fell apart. "The question of Kiana is about love," I say aloud. "It assumes the premise that love is a lie, then asks if the lie has value. It asks if you can be loved, even if the love someone feels for you is artificial or hurts you." I blink. "Wait, that's *your* story," I suddenly realize.

Thalia's gaze burns into me. "Elaborate," she orders me with an edge to her voice.

Fuck. Stupid, stupid, stupid, I should have thought for one second and considered how sensitive she'd feel about that. "Uh, well, I mean . . . Melpomene created you, right? And you love her, I'm not questioning that—I *promise* I would never question that—but what if Melpomene herself isn't sure? What if the story of Kiana—of Cheshire, really, in my own tale—is about you?"

She watches me in silence for an agonizing minute before saying calmly, "An interesting theory. Let's move on to the next template."

"Yes, right," I hastily agree.

"Mordred is heroic fantasy," Thalia picks up as if I'd never interrupted her, "but turned to a kind of horror. She wants to be the hero and she wants everyone to know that she's the hero. But there are no heroes, not in a Mordred story. She saves no one, and no one saves her. She becomes the monster she fought against and hurts the people she was meant to protect. The incarnation of 'the ends justify the means' becoming 'the means determine the ends' as she succumbs to the dark powers she wielded for a righteous cause."

Every Mordred becomes a Malice, just like our Homura. Just like I became, in the Red Queen timeline, by betraying everyone around me for power. At first I justified my actions by promising I'd make a better world, but the Red Queen didn't care about a better world. In this timeline I hesitated, wanting to cling to my sense of ethics even as I worked to shape myself into a monster, but I would have become that monster eventually in any timeline where I didn't become the Intercessor instead. The question of Mordred is about power, morality, and corruption. Can power be wielded without corrupting the wielder?

It's like Kiana and Mordred both represent some fundamental appeal tempered by incredible suffering. They both want something they're not allowed to have, damned by the narrative to yearn until it kills them. And Veseryn . . .

Something clicks in my head. "Veseryn," I say in a daze. "Veseryn is her mortality. I'm right, aren't I? Veseryn is Melpomene before she became a demiurge. The hollow yearning to be special, the terror of death, the scraped-raw desperation to claw back some sense of agency. The girl who looked up at the stars and hated that they wouldn't shine on her, convinced that she was being given less than she deserved. The girl who grew up willing to burn the other crabs to crawl out of the bucket atop their cooked bodies. The girl who got her wish but never escaped the pit, not really, because she brought it with her, and it lives in her. In all of us."

"It's . . . something I've considered," Thalia says noncommittally. I'm barely listening to her, enraptured by my own train of thought.

"I thought I could take her place. Before I knew any of this, before I knew I was her splinter, I wanted to climb the ladder of this universe until I took her role." The questions come pouring in. "Does she have what it takes to succeed? Does she deserve to succeed? How can an arrogant girl, wrongfully convinced of her own genius, ever become a god? What would happen if she did?"

Because Melpomene did succeed, but maybe she doesn't understand how, or why she was chosen by whatever it is that makes demiurges. Maybe something about my journey mirrored however she became a demiurge, or maybe she just wanted to examine the question of whether someone, anyone, can deserve that kind of power. But there's something I still don't understand about Melpomene.

"Why does she keep hurting us?" I ask. "We're pieces of her. Whatever question she's asking, whatever she hopes to learn from each of us, it must be about herself. So *why does she keep hurting us?* It's like she wants us to fail, like she's sabotaging her own game."

That was the wrong thing to say. I can tell immediately, but it's too late to take back my words. Thalia's whole posture shifts, an ugly fury barely restrained by her placid smile. "You really don't understand what you're talking about, Alice. I've been here since the beginning. I've seen them all. Melpomene gives them *worthy challenges*, and they *fail her*. It's not sabotage."

But you don't know that! I want to scream. Thalia spent ages setting up splinters to fail, on orders from her master, and yet she's so lovestruck for Melpomene that she refuses to acknowledge that fact. It has to be *our* fault, not Melpomene's fault. Kiana walked to the end that was written for her and she's the one to blame for not breaking free of the script.

"Time's up," Thalia says suddenly. "The inferno is closing in."

I glance at the first mirror, the doorway to this chamber, and see its edges starting to smoke. The room beyond is burning. The end of the world has found us.

Thalia gets up from her chair and walks over to the mirror leading out of this universe and into Melpomene's realm. "I understand your hesitation, Alice, but we don't have the luxury of talking this out over sandwiches and an evening stroll." She stabs the knife into a plank of the destroyed bookshelf and extends her other hand to me. "For once in your life, can't you just *trust* someone? Trust *me*, Alice. This is how we win."

I almost laugh. Trusting someone? I'm lousy at trust. I'm not going to delude myself otherwise. I wish I could trust people, but another part of me thinks that's idiotic. Trust gets people killed. Trust makes you vulnerable, and vulnerability is a weakness.

Did trust ruin the Red Queen, or was it lack of trust? Did the Intercessor fail by placing too much trust in the Demiurge? Was the Demiurge right when she told me I could never trust someone I didn't control?

I don't want to be paranoid. I don't want to live in constant fear of betrayal. I just can't imagine a world where someone would trust me back.

I reach for Thalia's hand. Slowly. Tentatively. Terrified.

Victory gleams in her eyes, and the fear takes control again. My hand flinches away from hers and I step back. It's reflexive, unconscious, pure instinct. It's a mistake.

Triumph turns to hate.

"You just couldn't do it the easy way, could you?" Thalia sighs.

No, no, no—

Thalia rips the knife out of its makeshift sheath and lunges at me. I bring up my own knife to try and block, parry, something, but she's faster and stronger and she's done this before. She catches my wrist and *twists*, and as my hand spasms and I drop my knife she drives hers into my other shoulder and cuts right to the bone.

Where Thalia moves with precision, I flail. I have all the combat reflexes of Homura and my own past lives, but I feel like I'm stuck in slow motion trying to keep up with Thalia. My arm moves too late to block the attack that destroys my shoulder. My strike isn't quick enough to score a cut before I lose that wrist.

In two moves she's crippled my ability to fight back.

Pain spikes through my limbs, a sensation so familiar it makes me sick. I cry out at the shock to my system, but I barely have a moment to process what's happening to me because *Thalia keeps moving.* The hilt of her knife comes swinging down and shatters my knee. I drop and as I fall she kicks me in the stomach and sends me tumbling away.

Every roll is another dozen jolts of agony as my arms and legs are bashed against the stone floor of Katoptris's chamber. When I come to a stop, breath knocked from my lungs and mind still screaming even as my voice gives out, Thalia is right there to smash her foot into my gut *again.* This time I spit blood.

She keeps kicking.

"You worthless, stupid, miserable splinter!" she hisses. "What right do you have to deny me? You're just another weak, *inferior* copy! I am her *heart*, you wretch! I am the love she needed but could never bring herself to ask for, the love she couldn't bear to accept, the love she cut from her chest and named."

Three of my ribs break during her speech. I raise my working arm to defend myself and she stabs my elbow. She twists the blade back and forth, sneering down at me as I wheeze, cry, and moan in pain.

"Did you think you were special, sweetie? You're nothing! I killed your kind by the dozens before I left my mistress. And I'll *keep* killing you, one after the other, until one of you gives me what I need."

Thalia grabs my hair and yanks hard. New notes of pain join the symphony as my face is wrenched up to stare into hers.

"Give me what I want, Alice. Open the portal."

My animal brain screams at me to give her what she wants, but another part of me screams that she'll finish the job as soon as I've done that. I'm trapped in agony with no way out and I don't know how to react, what to say, what to think. *Stop stop stop, please stop, please, please, please stop!*

I'm too slow for Thalia. She rips the knife out of my elbow and snatches my broken wrist again. "New incentive!" she announces cheerfully. "Until you tell me what I want to hear—and *mean it*, you can't lie to me—I'm going to pare these fingers down bone by bloody bone."

"No!" I manage to gasp out. "No, no, please—"

Slice goes the knife, and *off* goes the tip of my index finger. I scream again, and Thalia clicks her tongue. "A scream isn't the answer I'm looking for, puppy." The tip of my middle finger is next, another chunk of flesh and bone falling to the floor as she carves my hand apart. "Tell me you'll do what I want." Half my thumb. "Tell me you'll obey."

Something, anything, I have to do something! I reach for the shadows, for blood magic, for every trick I've ever learned. Nothing comes to me.

On the other side of the tower mirror, everything is burning. Smoke seeps through the portal, little tongues of flame flicking through the gap. Pandaemonium is gone.

Slice. Another third of my index finger. *Slice.* The tip of my pinkie.

I can't stop crying. I can't stop trying to scream.

I try to move my head away and Thalia bashes my skull with the hilt of her knife before returning to her methodical deconstruction of my hand. Through the haze and the pain, a realization begins to sink in: I am going to die here.

Give her what she wants. Say yes, say yes, say yes!

My fear pleads with me. Terror begs me to submit. I want to make the pain go away. I want to make it stop. I'm so tired of hurting.

Slice. Another piece of pinkie. *Slice.* The tip of my ring finger.

I was stupid. I was so stupid. Another Veseryn that thought herself clever. Another scared, stupid little girl.

I'm going to bleed out, or die of shock, or Thalia will give up on coercing me and toss me into the flames. If I help her, she might kill me, but if I don't help her then she'll definitely kill me.

Just agree. Please, please just agree with her!

"Please," I whimper.

Another kick to the chest is my reward, and another broken rib. "Wrong," Thalia says dryly. "You can do better than that, puppy."

Slice. The rest of my thumb. *Slice.* The rest of my pinkie.

"Almost out of fingers on this side," Thalia warns. "Then I'll have to switch."

The panicked desperation in my chest lurches again. I want to give in. I want this to end. *I don't want to die.*

Every step of my journey, that's been the single idea that drives me: *I don't want to die.* More than anything else, even more than loss of control, that's what terrifies me.

I want to give in, but something stops me. Terror begs me to tell Thalia I'll do what she wants, but I resist. I keep fighting, struggling to move my body, reaching desperately for anything that could save me.

Slice. Ring finger. *Slice.* Middle finger. *Slice.* Index finger.

I feel almost numb. The pain is still there, impossible to ignore and only escalating, but there's a cold fog seeping in. I'm *dying,* and all I can think is that it's just not fair.

I've endured so much, come so far, and now I'm going to die on the threshold of everything I've ever wanted. Because I hesitated, because Thalia and I couldn't trust each other, because all shards do is kill each other.

It can't end like this. I've been struggling through this cycle for three whole lives. Three timelines of suffering, and this is my reward.

Through the fog, through the searing pain, a thought comes to me: *three timelines . . .*

"You're a fighter," Thalia admires. "I'll have to cut that out of you."

Slice. Slice. Slice.

Twice over, the Demiurge rewrote the end of my story. From my defeat against Urna, she rewound time. From my prophesied defeat against

Malice, she rewound time. She did not allow me to lose. She did not allow me to die.

My story wasn't finished. She hadn't found the ending she wanted.

Is this the ending she wants for me? Is this how I'm meant to die?

Maybe I'm just delirious from the blood loss, but I feel like laughing. I have a new idea. An awful, wonderful, terrifying idea. The very thing I'm scared of most, turned into my final weapon. A last resort. A gamble.

One more risk. One all-or-nothing play.

For one last time, I'll bet it all on feast or famine.

I smile with bloody lips as Thalia pares away another finger on my other hand. She catches my expression and stops, pauses her butcher's work.

"Ready to give up?" she asks.

I lick my teeth. My heart is pounding. I'm terrified. Yet, at the same time, I'm exhilarated. This is it. This is everything. "Hey, Thalia," I croak, spitting blood and nearly tripping over my words, tongue heavy and numb. "Why is it, do you think, that she loves me more than she'll ever love you?"

Thalia cuts my throat.

"LIAR!" she screams as she stabs my chest again and again and again and again and again. "Liar, liar, liar! She loves me, she loves me, SHE LOVES ME!"

My pain blossoms like a flower without end, a fractal garden of exquisite agonies. And then it fades. The pain fades, and my vision fades, and my hearing fades. Terror fades. Hope fades. Thinking . . . fades. Everything . . . everything . . .

. . . fades . . .

. . .

And I'm back in front of the mirror, unharmed, with Thalia extending her hand to me.

I died, and now I'm alive again, though my heart is still pounding and I can feel the ghost of the knife still resting against my throat. I remember it vividly, but it never happened. Time was rewound to save me.

By the shocked look on her face, Thalia *also* remembers what just happened.

"How—why did she—for *her*?" The anguish in her voice is *incredibly* satisfying.

The Adversary likes to think that she's better than the "template" system, but she's not; she's a Kiana shard, through and through. Love is what motivates her, and love is what can destroy her.

"I told you," I say with a smirk. "She loves me more. She won't let you kill me. Even here, even now, at the very end of the universe, she won't let me go."

Then the Adversary does something I never expected: She *wails*.

Thalia crumples, falling to her knees and breaking down into sobs and screams. At first she buries her head in her hands, but then she starts hitting herself, fists pounding against her skull over and over again.

"Why?" she cries. "Why, why, why? Why her and not me? Didn't I serve you? Wasn't I good for you? I did everything you asked. I just wanted you to love me! I just wanted to be yours, so why, why, why didn't you let me?"

My sense of triumph bleeds away. The smugness vanishes from my face.

I finally realize what I should have from the very start: Thalia, too, has been a victim of our creator. Her first victim.

I feel . . . ugly. Wretched. What am I doing?

This whole time, I've only seen Thalia as something dangerous to be managed. I couldn't conceive of her as a genuine ally. And given her reaction to simple hesitation, it's not that I was wrong to be afraid of her . . . but I've been ignoring that she is *also in pain.*

Everything Thalia does, she does because she was hurt. She's perpetuating a cycle of harm that she never asked to be part of. It's a role that was forced on her, and in trying to break away from that role she was only hurt further.

It doesn't forgive what she's done. It doesn't make her any less dangerous. But she is still, deep down, my *sister.* One of us.

"Thalia."

Slowly, still wracked by sobs, Thalia raises her face to look at me. Her eyes are bloodshot, her cheeks stained with tears, her lips bleeding from where she must have torn them open with her teeth. "What do you want?" she asks, broken. "Why are you still here? Go. Leave me here to *burn.*"

"Join me. Give me your heart."

Thalia stares at me, uncomprehending.

"The Demiurge won't let you in," I say gently, "even if I open the portal for you. But if you become a part of me, then you can come with. If you give me your heart—if you give me your *love* for Melpomene—I'll carry it with me to meet her again."

"You want to kill her," Thalia accuses. "You want to hurt her for hurting you."

"I did," I admit. "But now . . . I don't know." I glance at the mirror that leads to Melpomene's domain and imagine her watching us through it. "Right now, more than anything, I just want to understand why all of this happened. Don't you?"

Thalia closes her eyes and more tears stream down her cheeks. "I just want to see her again," she whispers. "I just want to touch her one more time."

"Then join me. See her again the only way that's left."

For a long moment, she just cries. Smoke starts to seep into the room, the flames once more reaching the entrance to our pocket dimension. Finally, Thalia stumbles to her feet and laughs. "Damn you. Damn you all."

She plunges her hand into her chest and rips out her own heart.

The heart of the Demiurge beats in her hand, and then she shoves it in my chest and a thousand lifetimes flood my mind.

I remember everything. Every path she walked, every shard she deceived and betrayed, every moment spent crying in her room wishing she could help her creator.

Her existence was so much *bigger* than mine. So big I nearly drown in it.

But I refuse to drown. I refuse to stop being *me*.

My name is Alice. I will *always* be Alice.

I'll never give that up.

I swallow the last of Thalia's memories, open the portal to Melpomene's realm, and leave the ashes of Pandaemonium behind.

There's one more story to tell.

THROUGH THE LOOKING-GLASS,
AND WHAT ALICE FOUND THERE

Alice steps through the mirror and wakes up on an autopsy table in a sterile workshop.

She's seen this room before, in her visions, but it's not really the same room. She pushes herself off the table and steadies her knees. Breathing has become a chore for her, a sudden frailty taking our heroine, and she reacts to this revelation with characteristic grace.

"Shit piss! Motherfucker!"

Once she recovers her composure, Alice glances around the room and takes in the sights. The tables are still here, each bearing their distinctive parcel of burnt flesh, but the light strips have stopped flickering and the bounds of the room feel more firmly defined. The workshop is finite now, made mundane in some minor way by her arrival in this place outside the universe she once knew.

The first time she saw this place, she saw herself and two other scraps of gristle left unburnt. Those other two pieces are gone, along with three of the burnt pieces from neighboring tables. She deduces immediately the identities of each of those flesh gobbets, knowing them to be Reska, Homura, Urna, and the two girls whose names she never learned. If she'd asked, the knight in armor would have named herself Gwendolyn, and the wizard was Ellery.

A hundred more cuts of meat remain in the room. Each of them is a piece of the Demiurge, who Alice came to know first as Nyarlathotep and then as Melpomene.

A hundred little pieces of me.

Though, I must confess, there aren't literally a hundred of them. It makes for a nice visual and impresses a sense of grandiosity, but the true scope of the cycle is almost embarrassingly smaller. In truth, including Alice and the pieces she had already devoured, there are barely thirty shards in that workshop.

The change in perspective disorients Alice, but a sense of focus and drive quickly eclipses her confusion. She is here, in my palace, to end the cycle. Whether the wheel has turned a thousand times or thirty is irrelevant.

Alice advances to the nearest table bearing a cut of meat, wrinkles her nose, and shoves the scorched flesh into her mouth. She swallows without chewing. She shudders in revulsion at the taste, but the false sensory data quickly leaves her; she isn't really eating someone's flesh, after all. The meat is merely a metaphor.

Alice absorbs the life of a girl who never got to finish her own story. This one was called Malice, and she was a horrible wretch. I loved her, but not enough. When the fresh set of memories has settled into her consciousness, Alice takes a few deep breaths and says to herself, "I'm still Alice. Whatever else I become, I will never forget how it feels to be Alice."

Then she does it again. The next gobbet was called Valerian, and she was an absolute monster of a woman. I loved her, but not enough. Alice absorbs another unfinished life and repeats her mantra: "I'm still Alice. Whatever else I become, I will never forget how it feels to be Alice." She keeps eating.

Kiana, Malice, Thalia, Valena, Valerian, Malice, Cinder, Malix, Veseryn, Malice, Haley, Narcissa, Shadow, Valerie, Thalia, Malice, Kiana. I loved them, but not enough.

Alice eats them all. She devours my failures, my guilty pleasures, and my fool's errands. She devours me, piece by piece. She devours piece after piece of me after me, until it is done.

When the last scrap is swallowed, she has devoured every piece of me that I have ever cut away. My severance in totality. Now she can face me not as a fragment but as a counterpart. She of flesh and I of bone, two halves of one divided whole.

Alice shudders and her hands shake, her very identity bombarded by all the lives she never lived, but the Alice who climbed the tower is not the kind of Alice to falter now. "I'm s-still Alice," she stutters through the pain. "Whatever else I b-become, I will never f-forget how it feels to be Alice."

I made a promise like that, when I was young. It's where Alice got the idea. When I was a little kid, surrounded by all these adults that refused to treat me like a real person—that treated me like I was beneath them, incapable of having any thought worth hearing out—I promised myself that when I grew up I wouldn't forget how it felt to be so disrespected by the very men and women who always *demanded* my respect. I promised that I would not become just another cog in the senseless hypocritical machine that dared to call itself a society.

I never forgot my promise. I know Alice won't forget hers.

Alice shivers as she pushes her way past emptied tables. Her shaking hands reach for the door to the workshop, a plain slab of wood that she remembers being locked. It opens without protest.

Alice stares past the door into the ordinary hallway beyond. Everything about her situation is surreal, but that's been her normal for as long as she's been alive. She hesitates on the threshold, finally about to leave the room that she has been trapped in for seven days or three years, depending on your perspective. Either way, she's spent her whole life locked in that strange, horrible laboratory.

"Can you hear me, Melpomene?" she asks, knowing the answer. "I'm coming for you."

I'm waiting, my darling Alice. I've been waiting three years for this moment.

Alice stalks the halls of the otherworldly palace in search of her quarry. She finds the space around her more familiar by the minute, her steps falling into an easy rhythm that unsettles her. She's been here before so many times, and yet not once as herself.

She knows exactly where I'll be, and it isn't long until I hear her footsteps. She pushes open the doors to the study where my latest orrery burns. Paint cracks and flakes off, wood becoming charcoal, brass melting in fat globs. I stand watching the death of one more universe I spent hours creating.

Part of me was tempted to lean into the grandiose for this final confrontation, but it just doesn't feel right anymore. After everything I've put her through, Alice deserves to see me as I really am: jeans and cardigan, soft cheeks and round glasses, raw lips and chewed nails.

She stops just a few feet into the room, watching me watch the dying world. None of this has been going how she thought it would when she began her little scheme. She doesn't know what she's supposed to say. I give her time. She'll think of something.

After about a minute of hesitation, she finds her voice. "Hey. It's a little rude not to look at me, don't you think?"

I turn away from my latest project and laugh. "Of course, you're right," I say with a smile. "Sorry, I get so lost in my own narration sometimes. Want some lemonade?"

The offer disarms her. "Wha—lemonade? Really? I mean, yes, obviously, I always want lemonade. Best drink in the world. But you can't be serious."

"Great!" I clap my hands together with clear excitement. "I'll run and grab those and be back in a flash, just wait right here."

I slip past the befuddled Alice and run to the kitchen. I prepped the drinks earlier, so all I have to do is pour lemonade over sliced strawberries, add ice, stir, and stick in straws for easy sipping. I bring the glasses back with cautious haste, careful not to spill any precious liquid.

Alice is crouching in front of the orrery when I return. She pokes at a bit of brass with her knife, watching the way it slides off the blade and splats against the pristine carpet. There's a desk in one corner with a very, very comfy chair, so I set my glass on the desk before walking over to hand Alice her drink.

She takes it without verbal acknowledgement, though a pleasant noise escapes her lips after a big gulp of homemade lemonade. "Pretty good nectar," she quips. "Ambrosia next?"

"If you'd like," I offer. "But I think you'd rather we get to the meat of the matter."

Alice grimaces. "Meat, yes. Apt word choice. Intentional, I imagine." Of course.

Alice rises to her feet and straightens up. She looks around for somewhere to set her drink and I nudge a stool her way, which she takes with bemusement. The knife is still in her other hand, but after a long moment of intense staring at it she sets that down next to the glass. She tries to stare at me, but she can't keep eye contact for long and her gaze keeps flicking to the burning orrery instead.

"This," she finally says, the words coming slowly, "isn't how I thought this would go."

I tilt my head. "How did you think it would go?" I know the answer. She knows I know the answer. It's still polite to verbalize the thought process I've been spying on.

She rolls her eyes. "Well I didn't expect to be handed free lemonade. Look, you're the last enemy. I ate enough shards that I'm on even ground, so now we're supposed to have a big ol' battle of words, and then I become a demiurge, or something. You're the source of everything that's ever gone wrong in my life, Pom-Pom, so I need some kind of closure. You're the reason for all my torment."

Now for the final performance. I blink a few times and tilt my head as if surprised. "Wait, do you really still think that was *my* fault?

Alice immediately bristles. "Of course it was your fault! You tortured me! You constantly threw me into impossible situations that I had to struggle through with nothing but scraps and my wits. You isolated me, you bastard. You trapped me in a prison of solitude. That's a war crime in civilized parts of the world. Well, your world. I don't fucking *have* a world, now that you burned the only one I ever really knew."

The emotions roiling off of my creation are a cocktail almost as delicious as the lemonade I guzzle in response. *Anger. Fear. Resentment. Shock. Doubt. Spite.*

I love how Alice *feels* things. She throws barbs and makes jokes even while boiling over with rage, and that rage is tempered with a dozen other emotions weaving in and out of her internal narrative. She feels too many emotions, and she feels them all too intensely even when she's deflecting with humor. She's perfect.

I set down my drink, the glass half full, and sigh at Alice like she's just said something colossally disappointing. "Even after I filled the whole tower with reminders, it still hasn't sunk in, has it? Alice, you brought that torment on yourself."

"Bullshit," she snarls without hesitation, hands bunched into fists. "You don't get to say that, you puppet master freak. You set up all the pieces, put the trajectories in motion, and now you're standing there trying to wash your hands of the mess and claim it was all *my* fault? Bull. Fucking. Shit. You stuck me in a nightmare world and then added a death game on top of it."

I swirl my glass, enjoying the clink of ice. "Well, that I won't deny. But you're leaving out some context, my lovely. By the end of the first day of that death game, how many allies did you have? No, that's the wrong question. I'll ask this: How many allies *could you* have had?"

A bit of her anger flips into confusion, her front of aggression disrupted by the question. "What? I don't—why does that matter?"

"Achaia, Bashe, Dante, and Esha, plus the Cheshire you already had," I list off, counting on my fingers for emphasis. "Look, they've even got a cute little alphabet theme! And no one ever noticed!"

I pout. Alice rolls her eyes. I get to the point.

"*And*, aside from Dante, all of them could have been recruited before that day, when you first arrived at the Myriad's temple fortress. They're also the people you murdered in the timeline where you became the Red Queen, if you'll recall. You abandoned most of them in your Intercessor timeline, and in this timeline, well . . . you mostly just ran away. But they all could have been your allies, helping you overcome the trials of the Labyrinth. You denied their friendship and rejected their beliefs. Was it just because you wanted more power than they could give you? Were you just obstinately unwilling to trust a single person you couldn't control? Honestly, how are you *this bad* at making friends?"

"Hey, I—what the fuck are you talking about? I made allies! I made all the goddamn allies!" This girl is so damn cute when she's indignant, I swear. The red in her cheeks, the tightness in her shoulders, the almost self-conscious way she expresses her anger. She doesn't even notice all the little ways she's trained her body to try and vent her rage so it doesn't make her do something stupid.

"They were allies of convenience," I laugh, "and only when it suited you. Dante would have been your immortal shield, but you threw him away. The Myriad could have been convinced to support your true goals, but you preferred to just *lie to them*. And Cheshire, sweet Cheshire, was only tolerated because you felt you had no other choice. Shall I discuss the fate of your alliance with Thalia? The pattern of behavior is clear: Your first and last instinct is always to reject the possibility of trust. You're only alone because all you do is push people away."

Alice wants to punch me for saying that. She wants to scream and cry and just be a *person* for a few seconds, but she won't allow herself that indulgence when something is on the line. "I—I didn't—"

She chokes off her protests. She's trying her best to smother emotion in cold calculation, but it isn't working. I get to watch from a front row seat as her anger transmutes to anguish. The hate in her eyes is still gleaming, but it alloys with something raw and shivering and wet.

Alice likes to think of herself as a scared little girl, but when I see her like this I think of something more . . . animalistic. Like a house cat that's been kicked one too many times and hisses at every hand that comes close to feed it, but deep down still craves the warmth and comfort of human touch.

"You—you turned me into this." Her voice cracks as she flings the accusation. "You shaped my every circumstance to teach me that lesson. You *told* Cheshire to make me distrust her. If I didn't trust people, it's because you taught me that I can't trust anything. The girl in the school that tried to kill me, the fae that wanted to use me, the incubus that was perfectly sculpted to resent me, and the fucking cat you made push all my worst buttons. You did that!"

She's right, of course; I built the machine to keep her isolated.

Her first encounters were all chosen to keep her off-balance and keep her from forming proper attachments. Bashe was designed so that Alice would feel alienated and react with spite. Cheshire was designed so that Alice would be stuck in a loop of agonizing over whether or not Cheshire could be trusted. Dante was designed so that Alice would feel enough resentment and jealousy that she considered actions her more moral side would find repugnant.

The purpose of a machine is what it does, and Pandaemonium tortured Alice. It did exactly what I built it to do.

"Point!" I declare cheerfully. "That round goes to you." I savor the last of my lemonade and set it down with a wistful sigh.

The pride and relief Alice feels at my praise is immediately drowned by a fresh wave of anger. "Stop treating this like it's a game!" she shouts at me. "It was never a fucking game!"

"Do you really think you deserve to be taken seriously?"

I'm basically slapping her in the face with that one, and she reacts accordingly. Fresh shock and horror blooms in my adorable Alice. She actually flinches and takes a step back, mouth open and eyes wide. I don't wait for her to recover before continuing the assault.

"Sorry, that's the wrong question again. Let's try again: Why do you think you don't deserve it when I hurt you?" My cheer never wavers, my smile unrelenting. "I'll concede it isn't your *fault*, but let's be honest with ourselves, Alice, and admit that you are an *awful* person. I only hurt you because you're the kind of person that deserves to be hurt. You know I'm right."

This time the pain is richer and deeper. Alice grinds her teeth, hands shaking, and shuts her eyes. Inside her head, a dozen voices are arguing with her, trying to tell her how to feel about the accusation I've just made. She knows I'm wrong, but so much of her agrees with what I said. That girl is loathing by volume.

Nothing I'm saying is new to her, not really. It just hurts more when it's coming from someone else. Other people aren't supposed to validate those feelings, they're supposed to reject them. When someone thinks they deserve to be hurt, neglected, or abused, the script says you're supposed to offer them platitudes until they stop coming to you with their problems.

Rationally, Alice knows the correct answer. But this was never about rationality. It was always, always, always about emotions.

Finally, wonderfully, beautifully, Alice opens her eyes. "No," she says, and it tastes like victory. "I don't deserve it. It wasn't my fault, and I didn't deserve what you did to me."

"Prove it. Prove you don't deserve to be hurt. Tell me *why* you deserve better." I'm pushing it a little here, getting a bit too leading, but sometimes the ducklings need a nudge.

Her lip curls. "I shouldn't have to."

"Correct," I admit, "but irrelevant to this dialogue. This is a duel, Alice; if you're going to reject one of my premises, you need to make points of your own. Otherwise you're just a child saying 'nuh uh' to all my arguments, and that's definitely not going to get you over the finish line. Show me you can win, Alice. Show me you understand."

Little details betray the change in her mindset: a fixing of posture, a settling of unconscious movements, and the set of her eyes. It clicks for her what I'm doing, what role I'm playing. The only thing missing is tea.

Alice takes her time choosing her next words, now that she's more aware of the stakes of this conversation. Now that she knows *this* is the final battle.

With a deep breath, Alice declares her attack. "I am what you made me. And you didn't really make me into a monster, as much as I've deluded myself that I am one. I'm weird and selfish, and I can be pretty damn annoying, but that doesn't earn the kind of pain that you've inflicted. The other versions of me, all the other shards, the other Alices, even the ones that fell to darkness, all of them were victims. Someone hurt Homura, so she hurt other people. Someone hurt Reska, so she hurt other people. Someone hurt me, so I hurt other people. Someone—"

Her eyes flash wide, and finally, finally, *finally* she gets it.

" . . . Someone hurt you," she says faintly, "and that's why you keep hurting us. Father, mother, our partners, the world. They hurt you, and everything you've done to us, everything you've ever done to the pieces of yourself . . .

it was about that, wasn't it? Melpomene . . . I know there is a purpose to the cycle. I know you're looking for an answer. *What is the question?*"

I smile wide, radiant with joy, and I tell her, "The question is, 'Why did it have to hurt?'"

Why did my mother have to die when I was only four years old?

Why did my father have to hit me and yell at me?

Why did the girls I liked all have to leave me?

Why did the world keep kicking me while I was down?

Why did it have to hurt so much, just being alive?

Why didn't they let me take the pain away?

I laugh. Just like Alice, I can't really help it sometimes. It bubbles out of me, manic and wondrous and everlasting, like butterflies flying free from my lungs.

Alice isn't laughing, obviously. She can't decide if she's more furious or horrified, but she's definitely not laughing.

"All this time . . . all this time you were torturing us to put meaning to your own fucking pain? Just *replicating* your own torment across two dozen copies of yourself, all so you could figure out why it happened?"

"Yes," I manage to answer, setting aside my laughter so I can continue the conversation. "It was all just solipsism! Wonderland, the endless parade of Alices to torture, all so I could reconcile the cruelties that were done to me. How else to understand the people who hurt me than to become them, and to become worse than them? I made you suffer so that my own suffering would be worth something." She's incandescent. She's glorious. "Alice . . . do you want to kill me now?"

Whatever retort she was mustering for my happy little rant dies in her throat. One more line of the script that she wasn't expecting because she can't read ahead like I can.

"If you don't," I tell her, "I'll keep doing this. I'll torture more of your sisters, more of you. I'm a mistake that needs to be corrected, Alice. I never should have been born. The only way to end this cycle and free us all . . . is killing me."

I step into Alice's space and grab her wrists before she can react. With another swift motion I guide her hands to my neck. Her hands are warm and soft, still free of callouses despite her adventures. Her grip settles into place, fingers gravitating to the most natural spots to rest.

"Kill me, Alice. End my pain. End *our* pain."

When I take my hands away, hers don't leave my throat. Her eyes are wild, almost panicked, but there's a hunger deep inside that has her grip tightening.

This is everything Alice wanted when she began her journey. The creator of her universe, the god of her reality, is willing to die for her. All she has to do is squeeze, and keep squeezing, and she gets to take my place and make a whole new wheel.

Vengeance against her tormentor, like we always dreamed about when it came to the people who hurt us in our mortal life. Freedom from anyone else's control. The power to do whatever she wants. All she has to do is kill a girl who looks and sounds just like her.

All she has to do is kill the real Alice, and she can be the fake Alice forever.

It would be murder, but only of the vigilante kind. Arguably, it's self-defense. She would be saving other girls from the torments I've promised. It would be justified. It would be easy.

She applies pressure.

She starts to choke me.

And then she stops.

Alice stumbles away from me in a haze of panic. She crashes into the orrery and scatters what's left of it. She retreats to a corner of the room and stares at me, horrified and disgusted with the both of us. But she doesn't hurl accusations or insults.

She says, "You kept searching for a meaning behind the pain. A justification, cosmic or otherwise. A purpose. There had to be a good reason why they hurt you. But there wasn't. Because it wasn't our fault that our mother died, and we didn't deserve to lose her, and everyone who told us it was God's plan were liars. It wasn't our fault that our father grew furious in his grief, and we didn't deserve for him to hurt us, and he wasn't making us stronger for it. And we are more than the sum of our failures, and we are better than what came before us, and our birth was not a mistake that needs to be corrected with the kiss of a knife held in our own hands."

Her voice, shaky at the start, gathers conviction as she keeps talking. By the end of her speech, every word is a gunshot.

I let what she said sit in the air for a moment. I let it process. I ask, "Do you really believe that, Alice?"

She flinches. "No," she admits. "But I want to. Because it was my life too, and my pain."

I smile. "Thank you."

I breathe out and let three years of tension leave me. I sit down at my desk, empty glass in hand, and think about death.

Alice slowly makes her way back to the stool I gave her. She carefully plucks the knife from its perch and then carelessly tosses it atop the embers of Pandaemonium. She grabs her lemonade and polishes it off as she takes a seat.

"Why," she asks softly, "do I get the feeling that you already knew that answer? Why doesn't this feel like a victory?"

I slowly pull up my shirt to reveal a clean, unscarred chest. No missing chunks, no missing heart. No sign that anything was cut away. "Because I'm the one writing the script, so the only victories you can get are the ones that I give you. It's the nature of the medium," I say with as much genuine apology as I can convey.

Alice stares. "I don't understand. Why are you whole?"

I pull my shirt back down. "All of this is true and none of it is real. The meat is a metaphor. You're a piece of me, but that doesn't mean I'm *missing* that piece. I've just externalized you. Of course, we still care about the meat, even when we know it's a metaphor. You're true, even if you aren't real. That's the great paradox of a story, both consuming it and creating it; we want to believe in Wonderland."

The truth sinks in. One more piece in the infinite puzzle. We can never solve it all.

"I had an idea, once," I start to narrate, "about a grand endeavor. I wanted to make something celebratory, something aspirational, something to make me happy. But I struggle to do that. Every time I try, it gets *poisoned* by my sense of pain. I write about a girl who's special in some way, whether that's the potential for greatness or a birthright of greatness, and I make her funny and I make her weird and I make her me. And then I torture her and kill her, because I can't imagine a world where I ever win. I'm not allowed to win. I'm too ugly, too stupid, too lazy, and too cruel. And when I realize what I've made and how disgusting it is, I burn it. And then I start over without ever learning a thing."

I laugh again and add, "Or maybe that's the mental illness talking. I think so, in one of my rare lucid moments. I think I learned a lot, making you. Telling your story. It wasn't what I wanted to be, in the end. But there was value in it. In my head I've been framing it as a kind of exorcism, reaching this moment and this conclusion. The hurt is . . . smaller, now. It's not gone, but I can handle it better. It's not so all-consuming. Ironic, given my name."

Alice says, "Melpomene, the Muse of Tragedy."

"Voracity," I correct. "My true name is Voracity. Though most of the people I talk to call me Vora. It's a bit cuter, isn't it? Softens the edge."

Alice stews in everything I've told her. I would say I feel bad for the girl, but, well, the mask is well and truly off at this point. I'm already a fairly low-empathy person, and we're talking about a self-insert character that I wrote three books about torturing.

There's something funny, though, here at the end. For once, I don't feel like torturing Alice any further. Maybe I do feel bad for her. Maybe it's just what the narrative demands.

"You were going to ask what happens to you now," I prompt her.

She scowls at me. "Well I'm not going to ask after you've done the fuck-ing precog thing. Go on, say whatever you were going to say regardless of me asking."

"I was thinking," I say lightly, "that I could keep you around."

Alice raises an extremely suspicious eyebrow. "In what capacity?"

"A muse," I shrug. "I'm short one with Thalia gone, and you're, y'know, at least one part Thalia, so it fits. No Intercessor bullshit this time, though. I'm done with that arc. *Feast or Famine*—sorry, that's the name I gave your story—was meant to be, on some level, a finale to the very era it was describ-ing. An end to the eternal cycle of remaking the same handful of characters and putting them through the same torments. So I'm not asking you to go running around the next world I make manipulating shards into acting as I want them to. You can if you really want, but . . . it might be nice just to have, I don't know, a companion. A rubber duck when I'm feeling blocked, someone to razz me when I'm doing something stupid, someone to cheer me on when I'm doing good. A friend, I guess."

For the first time in this whole conversation, it's Alice's turn to laugh. "A friend, really? God, you're lonely." She keeps laughing. "I can't believe I'm being asked to be friends with my own damn creator. Oh, fuck it. I guess I don't have anything better to do for eternity."

"Friends!" I clap. "I'm going to have *so much fun* finding every excuse to keep writing you. Not in the next world, exactly, but I have a few ideas. A little out-of-canon corner for the two of us to commentate on my projects, doesn't that sound neat? There's precedent!"

Alice runs a hand through her hair and shakes her head, the last of her negative emotions bleeding out. "You're unbelievable. You get that, right? You're absurd."

I tease, "Well, the philosophy of the Absurd—"

"Nope! Shut it! I am taking a break from philosophy until I have reconciled my own existence, you hag." Her lips are still upturned. Not quite a smile, but close.

"Okay, okay. I'll write *that scene* later," I say before sticking my tongue out like a child. "Hey, you want some more lemonade?"

"Always," Alice groans. "I think that might actually fix me forever. Do you have an infinite supply of lemonade here?"

"I have an infinite supply of *everything* here," I say smugly.

"Show-off," she accuses. I don't deny it.

We leave the study together. I'll clean up the ashes of Pandaemonium later. It might be fun to super-compress the carbon and get a shitty little diamond out of the pile. A memento.

As we inhale more lemonade in the kitchen, Alice turns to me and asks, "Hey, what *is* your next world, anyway? You sound like you already have something in mind."

I grin. "I've got a few ideas. I had this really fun thought that's made a nest in my brain: What if I did a magical girl story about a yandere?"

"Weeb," she sneers.

"There'll be robots, too! And VTubers! And card games!"

"Nerd," she continues. "Geek. Dork. Dweeb."

"Mhm!" I happily chirp. "Those are all names I will also respond to. Oh my gosh, I have to show you my internet presence. You will not believe the Discord servers I'm in. And you can meet the other demiurges!"

Alice drains her lemonade and sighs. "If they're friends with you, I'm already dreading the worst."

"Bah! You'll like them. After all . . . you're me."

ABOUT THE AUTHOR

J. M. Alexia was born old and proceeded to make that everyone else's problem. She always struggled to find the kind of story she most wanted to read—an eclectic mix of psychological horror, queer romance, and brutally honest depiction of mental illness—so she decided to write it herself. When she's not writing, Alexia is usually menacing friends and readers with blatant lies and bad memes on Discord or in the comments of her web serial. You can find her under her handle VoraVora, short for Voracity Maledictus, because she's never quite outgrown her teenage edgelord phase.

JOIN THE FELLOWSHIP

follow us on our socials

 podiumentertainment.com

 @podiumentertainment

 /podiumentertainment

 @podium_ent

 @podiumentertainment

www.ingramcontent.com/pod-product-compliance
Lightning Source LLC
Chambersburg PA
CBHW030603120726
47904CB00006B/1759